Avenging Angel
A Pilot's Story

"A date which will live in infamy . . ."

Those words, spoken by President Franklin D. Roosevelt on December 7, 1941, spurred young Carl Bridger, the son of a Montana cattle rancher, to answer the call to duty in the Pacific Theater of Operations. Join Carl as he is transformed from a cowboy into a warrior-pilot of the B-25 Mitchell. Go into combat with the 501st "Black Panthers" Squadron of the famous 345th Bombardment Group "Air Apaches" whose assignment was to slam the door on the advance of Japanese forces in the South China Sea and the Indo-Chinese mainland. Fly with Carl in this gripping odyssey that rips him from his family and beloved Annie and takes him through the heroic and often nightmarish air battles of the last few months of WWII in the Pacific. Buckle-in with the crew of *Avenging Angel* on sorties inspired by the true WWII mission logs of the "Air Apaches."

Reader Comments About
Avenging Angel

◆ *Avenging Angel: A Pilot's Story*, rocks every emotion and gives truth to the statement, "The violence of war is an insult to the soul." The author skillfully weaves the business of flying in combat situations with the realism of the human spirit and its vulnerability. Spencer Anderson has captured the heart, soul and spirit of this special breed of individuals and I didn't want it to end.
– *Judy Little Winkler*

◆ A great read – entertaining, fast paced, and filled with emotion, information, and excitement. This book reminded me of those wonderful old classic war movies - there is something for everyone: a great story, engaging characters, excitement, romance, adventure, danger, and tragedy. The air combat sequences are gripping, precise, and feel absolutely authentic. – *Joseph Gordon*

◆ What an incredible story! *Avenging Angel: A Pilot's Story* captivates the reader by tapping into the raw emotion of soldiers going to war. This is a well-written and descriptive story that shows how human stamina can be pushed to the utmost limits while staying focused on the greater good. – *Lori Robbins*

◆ You have a winner here for sure! The story is remarkably compelling, and the characters and missions come alive! You have captured the gritty reality of combat without losing the human touch! As with any good book, you have left me wanting more! – *Brad Root*

◆ Spencer Anderson's representation of WWII, the events, places and people in *Avenging Angel: A Pilot's Story* are magnificent. The feelings he raises in the heart of the reader can't be suppressed as you live with the characters he has created. As with Mr. Anderson's first book, *The Last Raider*, you will not be able to put it down. – *Mike McFarland*

Avenging Angel

A Pilot's Story

A Novel By

Spencer Anderson

Visit the author at

www.spencerandersonauthor.com

Synergy Books Publishing, USA

Text copyright © 2016 by Spencer Anderson
Cover Art © 2016 by Spencer Anderson
All rights reserved. Published in the United States by Synergy Books Publishing, USA.

First Edition —
—First Printing, February, 2016

Visit us on the web at www.synergy-books.com
Visit the author at www.spenceandersonauthor.com

Hard Bound: 978-1-936434-77-0
Soft bound: 978-1-936434-78-7
E-Book: 978-1-936434-80-0
Audio Book: 978-1-936434-79-4

Cover illustration: The Valiant Clan: North American B-25 Mitchell. "Pappy" Gunn Mods hit Simpson Harbor, Rabaul.

Printed in the United States of America

Special Thanks

To Carole, as always, for your inspiration and support which make all things possible, my love … "only forever, if you care to know."

To David W. Smith and Synergy Books Publishing for keeping the work alive.

To my editor Caroll Shreeve whose editing skills have made me a better writer. Thanks for your patience.

To Bob O'Hara for the fine pen and ink renderings used to depict the story of the *Avenging Angel.*

To the Commemorative Air Force whose vision keeps the Warbird legacy alive. I'm proud to be named an honorary CAF Colonel, guys.

To my readers without whom none of this would be possible. Your comments both humble me and inspire me to keep writing. Thank you!

Prologue

January 25, 1945

Central Luzon Valley
–First Command–

"Room, ah-ten-hut!" Col. Coltharp's adjutant yelled. The pilots in the room snapped to attention. Coltharp stepped in front of the microphone. A battle map of the South China Sea filled the wall behind him.

"At ease. Take your seats. Gentlemen, the 345th will be busy over the next few weeks. In two days we need to begin hitting targets farther north in Formosa; mostly shipping targets in the South China Sea and along the Indo-China Coast. In order to do that, we will need to move our base of operations farther north with the goal of setting up some of our planes at the airfield at San Marcelino by March. Between here and there, however, we will continue hitting the enemy in the Central Luzon Valley where the Japanese road and rail networks continues feeding supplies, arms, and troops to the various enemy strongholds throughout northern Luzon Island. Our mission is to attack and destroy as much of that network as possible. Tonight, at 1800 hrs, I will lead seven planes of the 501st Black Panthers, followed by six planes each from the 498th, 499th, and 500th Squadrons. We'll fly from Tacloban northeast about 475 kilometers to the airstrip at San Jose, on Mindoro, where we will refuel. Tomorrow morning at 0700 hrs we'll strike at the heart of the enemy's transportation network from Campanario across to San Miguel and southeast to Laguna de Bay." Col.

Coltharp traced a line with his pointer dissecting the island of Luzon from east to west along the Central Luzon Valley. "Each plane will carry eight 100-pound para-demolition bombs and standard ammo for your guns.

"Flight Leaders for each flight of three bombers are as follows: For the 501st I'll command the group from the Flight Lead position of Alpha Flight. Lt. Bridger will lead Bravo Flight ..."

Carl's heart leapt into his throat ... *Bravo Flight Leader! My first command! Can I do this? Three crews depending on me to get them home safely.* Every self-doubt hit him hard. He was being entrusted with the most overwhelming responsibility he had ever faced. He gulped and swallowed sour tasting bile that threatened to escape like a projectile from his mouth. Alex Chekov glanced at him and grinned. Carl managed to return a tentative smile. *If he only knew how frightened I am, he wouldn't be smiling.* That last thought brought an inward chuckle which calmed him considerably.

For the 498th, your Flight Leaders will be Capt. Stein and Lt. Willis. The 499th will be led by Maj. Reichman and Capt. Daniel. The 500th will be led by Capt. Ruiz and Lt. Gauche."

"Air Apaches! Ah-ten-hut!" Capt. Carl Strauss, Assistant Intelligence Officer for the mission, called out. Everyone stood, and Col. Coltharp dismissed all but the Flight Leaders.

When Capt. Strauss closed the door after the last man left, Coltharp addressed the remaining officers.

"Gentlemen, it's going to get crowded up there. This is a low-level strafing and bombing mission. Your targets will mostly be moving ... truck convoys, trains, perhaps a few armored personnel carriers. The tendency will be to pick a target of opportunity and concentrate only on that target. The problem with that is you may lose your situational awareness. There will be a lot of planes up there. It is essential to know where your aircraft is located relative to the overall battle picture. I do not want to write letters home for any of you knuckleheads who get rammed by another '25. Am I understood?"

"Yes sir!" came the unanimous reply.

"Good. To minimize the risk of collision, all attacks will be made in three-plane staggered-line formation. Questions?"

"Yes, sir." Carl cleared his throat. "Can we expect any enemy resistance from the air? If so, will we have air cover?"

"Possibly, and no ... in that order. Watch for bogeys. If you spot any you will need to assess the threat. I know there are four of you who have never led a flight into combat until now. I have reviewed each of your mission performance evaluations since being with the 345th. You were chosen because you possess the skill and judgment to lead your flights on this mission. It's time to raise the bar on your own expectations as both pilots and commanding officers. You are officers and pilots in the most powerful air force in the world. Get it done!"

The pilots in the room snapped to attention, and Coltharp exited the briefing room with his pointer tucked securely under his right arm.

At 1500 hrs, Carl sat on the edge of his bunk. His hands were trembling from the anticipation of his first command mission. On the other side of the narrow walk way between the two rows of bunks Lt. Jackson Hayes closed his locker, glanced across at Carl and walked over to him.

"Mind if I sit, Bridger?"

"No. Sit down, Hayes." Carl scooted over and made room for the affable son of a Kansas farmer.

"You okay, Bridger?"

"Yeah ... just a bit spooked by my first time as Flight Leader." Carl realized that he may have given voice to something better left unsaid.

"Good. If you weren't scared, I'd worry about flying with you. A little fear keeps you sharp." Jack slapped Carl on the shoulder.

"Just don't say it out loud in a crowd."

"I suppose you're right. When the fight starts, I hope I can keep everybody in the right place on the game board." Carl managed a chuckle. His hands had settled down.

"Your job is to make sure your flight is vectored in for the attack and that they're in proper attack formation. They're all experienced crews, so, you trust them to do their jobs. After the battle, you assess any damage to your flight, report your flight's status to the Group Leader, and get your flight back in formation for the return trip. The rest is pretty much seat-of-your-pants stuff: assigning secondary targets, not letting any of your planes take any undue chances ... just common sense."

"Sounds easy enough. Thanks, Hayes."

"One more thing, Carl, you can't personally control every possible outcome. If you try, you'll burn out. Constant stress and guilt causes battle fatigue. Mourn those who die, celebrate with the living and *get over it*. Keeping yourself and your own crew alive is enough for any man to worry about. Providence will have its way, my friend."

Lt. Hayes stood, began to walk away, and then turned back to Carl. "My first time as Flight Leader, another plane in my flight clipped a palm tree while he was turning for another run on a target. He nosed in with two armed 100-pounders aboard. Both bombs detonated on impact. Call it pilot error, bad luck ... whatever. I wrote the letter to his wife and parents. I got crap-faced drunk and took off two days later on another mission. It happens, man, so learn to forgive yourself ... and get back in the cockpit. Like I said ... providence."

Two hours later, Carl snapped the buckles closed on his harness. He and Alex Chekov went through the engine start sequence for both engines. Soon, the Wright-Cyclone 2600 engines were idling smoothly at 1200 rpm. Carl glanced to his right taking note of the other eighteen B-25s down the line in various stages of readiness. *Please, Lord, let my decisions be guided by thy holy hand. Watch over and protect us from our enemies. Amen.* The short silent prayer calmed his nerves.

Col. Coltharp's plane was positioned for takeoff, and the other three planes of Alpha Flight stood in line behind him awaiting their turn.

When the Group Leader began to accelerate down the runway, Carl applied just enough throttle to start *Avenging Angel* rolling into position behind the last of the Alpha Flight planes. The two '25s of Bravo Flight taxied out in line behind him.

"Comm check, boys. Call in." Carl ordered over the intercom.

"Navigator, ready, Skipper." Phil Ortiz announced.

"Engineer, ready to go. Instruments are all green." Zed Carthage called in from his position.

"Radio. Tuned and ready, Lieutenant.," Sgt. Price reported.

"All cozy in the tail. We're locked and loaded, sir," Harry said.

"We're good to go, Alex. Take us up, and form up with Group Leader at 2,000 feet."

"Roger that. Flaps set at one-half ... adding power." Alex moved the throttles forward in a firm and smooth motion.

A/P173 rotated into the air. When she reached 200 feet altitude, Alex called for the flaps and wheels to be raised.

"Flaps up ... wheels up and locked," Carl confirmed as the bomber climbed out, turning to join up with the rest of the Black Panthers of the 501st Bomb Squadron.

Twenty minutes after the Group Leader took off, the 25 Mitchells of the 345th Air Apaches were formed up and turned on a heading northeast toward Mindoro.

There were two functioning airstrips on San Jose. Built by Australians and local natives, they were designed to receive single-engine fighters as opposed to the heavy B-24 and B-29 bombers. The medium bombers of the 345th Bombardment Group, however, found the airstrips adequate for use as a staging base for

5

sorties into the Manila and Central Luzon Valleys. U.S. Navy fuel tankers had brought in aviation fuel which was held in storage facilities built by the 33rd Naval Construction Battalion (Seabees). Since the December 15th invasion of Mindoro, the building of airstrips became a major priority as part of Gen. McArthur's "Musketeer III" operation leading to the scheduled January invasion of Luzon Island.

The sun hung low in the western sky, and dusk was settling in. In the eastern twilight the drone of 25 Mitchells of the Air Apaches caused the eyes of several hundred Army, Navy, Australian and Filipino civilians and guerilla fighters to look skyward. The formation began to orbit above San Jose Air Base as, one by one, they descended and landed.

The B-25s parked in a line, front to rear along the full length of the shorter of two runways. Fuel trucks immediately set to the task of refueling the bombers with 115-octane aviation fuel.

In anticipation of their arrival, the pilots and crew were housed overnight in a dozen 16-man tents hastily erected atop corrugated steel slabs of the type used for building temporary airstrips and covered over with slabs of plywood. Though not made for walking on in bare feet, they provided a moisture free surface. Cots were stacked in each tent. Each man had the responsibility of claiming a cot and rolling out a thin mattress to sleep on. The mess tent provided some kind of soup/stew concoction consisting of what barely passed for meat (whose source was a matter of conjecture) floating in a brown broth. Water and crackers rounded out the spartan meal.

Carl, Alex, and Phil bunked in with the rest of the crew of *Avenging Angel*. It was Carl's idea. He felt he felt he wanted to get to know the men with whom he shared the sky, and he saw this as an opportunity to become better acquainted.

As he settled in, he thought about his crew ... his friends. He thought back to his years on the Double-B when he first took on full ranch duties at the age of 12. He was told to call the ranch hands by their first names, but only after getting to know them and gaining their respect. *"Mister" is a word only to be used for strangers and folks outside the family,* his father had taught him. Carl was an equal to the hired ranch hands as far as his skills were concerned, and deserved to be treated as such. How Carl was to earn that respect as a man was up to him. He thought of the stock trough and one particularly feisty breeding-stud quarter horse that served to earn him that respect.

–Double-B Ranch, 1936–

"Ride him Chad!" Raz Ortiz laughed as he slapped his dusty jeans with his sweat-stained Justin hat. Carl watched from astride the corral fence.

Chad Plunkett lasted about four seconds on old Bristlecone before he got thrown head-over-spurs onto the dirt throwing up a cloud of dust upon impact. Chad's older brother, Clete, Raymond Ruiz, and three other hands roared with laughter as Chad climbed to his feet and dusted himself off.

"Ain't been but one man ever rode Bristlecone and that was Ed Bozeman here. Ed doffed his hat and performed an exaggerated bow worthy of the Broadway stage.

"Just got lucky is all. He makes a fine breeder, but he's too darned crazy for cuttin' cattle."

"I'd like to try!" Carl hollered.

"Hell no, boy. Your pa would nail my hide to the barn if he knew I let you up on that animal." Ed shook his head. "I like my job too much to risk you breakin' your scrawny neck."

"Mister Bozema ... Ed, it's my neck. If I live through it, I'll be sure to let Pop know it was my decision. Bring him over here, Raz." Carl squeezed between two of the log fence slats and walked up to Bristlecone. "He seems peaceful enough." He stroked Bristlecone's muzzle, and the horse snickered quietly. He appeared relaxed ... ears up and breathing slowly.

Carl knew the horse's reputation for being temperamental. His father bought the horse for a song at auction because he was useless as a cutting horse. He could be ridden, but couldn't be trusted. The animal didn't like to be used as a cutting horse. He liked to run. However, after assessing the stallion's excellent overall conformation and record as a show horse, Gifford Bridger decided to buy him as a stud breeder. He had already produced four promising offspring for the Double-B.

Carl eased himself into the saddle and took the reins. Raz backed away and scurried over the fence to enjoy the show.

Bristlecone just stood there. Carl tapped him lightly on the flanks, and the horse snorted and tossed his head. Still, the horse just stood where he was. Carl tapped harder, and Bristlecone tossed his head and started into a loping canter around the perimeter of the corral.

"See, nothing to it!" Carl announced jubilantly. Bristlecone stopped, lowered his head, pulling Carl forward and off balance. The horse flattened his ears and bucked one time, throwing Carl forward, cartwheeling into the large stock trough with about two feet of water in it.

Carl sat up, waist deep in the water and sputtered, "Okay! Okay! The joke's on me. Ha ha!"

Bristlecone added insult to injury by lowering his head and drinking thirstily from the trough.

"I'm not done with you yet, big boy." Before anyone could say anything, Carl had swung himself into the saddle. This time, when Bristlecone tried to lower his head, Carl pulled back on the reins. The snaffle bit dug into the animal's mouth, and his head shot up. Bristlecone spun around and tried to run, but Carl pulled back harder forcing the recalcitrant beast to rear up. Carl squeezed

8

his thighs tight into the horse's side and gripped the saddle horn with one hand while holding the animal's head up with the other. Bristlecone crow-hopped a couple of times and settled down.

"Open the gate, Ed!" Carl called out. Ed Bozeman lifted the latch and swung the gate wide. Carl spurred Bristlecone, who reared up again, then took off like a shot. Carl let him get through the gate and then hauled back on the reins. The horse didn't like being told what to do and dug his rear hooves into the dirt, spun first to the left and then to the right and started bucking. He tried to pull Carl forward again, but Carl let him have his reins. The big stud quarter horse arched his back and started bucking ... leaping into the air ... twisting and turning every which way. Carl got into rhythm with the horse, anticipating every leap and twisting turn. After 20 seconds or so, Bristlecone came to an abrupt stop. He was heaving for air and frothing at the mouth. Carl saw his chance.

"Ha ya!" He yelled and dug his heels into the animal's flanks. The big roan quarter horse took off like a thoroughbred out of the starting gate. Carl turned him toward the road leading from the ranch to Highway 89. He gave Bristlecone his rein and leaned low into the wind. At about 50 yards short of the highway, Carl reined in the horse. Heaving heavily and frothing from his withers to his flanks, Bristlecone was too spent to fight back and allowed himself to be turned back to the corral.

Carl climbed down and let Bristlecone drink from the trough. "Raz, will you take him into the barn, please? I'll brush him down and feed him in a minute."

"Hoo-wee! Now that was some fine ridin' young Master Bridger," Chad Plunkett said with unabashed admiration.

"Thanks, Chad. But, call me Carl. My name is Carl to all of you!" Carl grinned and turned to walk toward the main house when he caught sight of his father and older brother, George, standing with the rest of the hands.

"Okay, boys, fun time is over. Let's get back to work," Gifford ordered.

As soon as the other hands were out of earshot, Giff Bridger clapped a gloved hand on Carl's shoulder. "Your mother has lunch ready. Go inside and get yourself cleaned up. And Carl ..."

"Yes, sir?"

"Well done, son."

Carl had a new family now, at least for the foreseeable future; a family melded together by the fires of war, a brotherhood whose bond was welded steel-hard by the common purpose of survival and dependence upon those around you for another day of life. In a time when humanity has taken a vacation, the only connection to sanity comes from one's brothers, and the hope burning inside that a happier and safer world beckons.

Carl rolled out the thin mattress and laid it over the cot. He folded an army-green woolen blanket and made a pillow out of it. He checked his chronometer, 2100 hrs. Harry Osborne huddled in conversation with Zed Carthage and Wendell Price. Carl nodded at Alex Chekov and Phil Ortiz to follow him over to the non-coms.

"How's it going boys?" Carl asked, sitting down in a steel folding chair.

Harry Osborne smiled at Carl. "Hi ya, Lieutenant. We're just chattin' about our families back home and the mission tomorrow." Alex and Phil sat nearby.

"You know, we never had much of a real chance to talk. I'd like to know more about what makes you guys tick." Carl's eyes moved from man to man, engaging the eyes of each crew member in turn. "Where are you from, Harry?"

"Me? Oshkosh, Wisconsin."

"What did you do before the war?"

"Grocery store produce manager. I lived at home, so I had plenty of dough for a car and taking the ladies out. Got my eye on a sweet young thing ... Lynette Chapman. Want to see a picture?" Harry removed a dog-eared black and white photo of himself and a gorgeous young woman. Carl guessed the slightly out of focus photo had been taken at some carnival five-cent picture booth. "She's waiting for me to get home, then we're getting hitched."

"What about your family? ... Brothers and sisters?" Carl liked how Harry's eyes lit up at the opportunity to talk about his family. It was as though time had suspended the war for a brief moment, and he was home again.

"My Pop is an accountant for General Electric. Mom was a teacher until I was born, then she quit her job and became a full-time mother. My three younger sisters are all at home." Harry paused and dropped his eyes. "I miss them, Skipper. Sometimes, like now, it's as though I'm there with them, but most of the time it's as if I'm living a whole different life ... one that's too far away to get back to."

"You'll get back home, Harry. If I have anything to say about it, you and I will see a lot of each other after the war." Carl grinned. Of all the crew, he felt a special fondness for the ever-jubilant punster of a gunner.

It was like that for everyone. Alex Chekov from Queens, New York, spoke of his new wife and of his longing to get back to her. A recent letter revealed she was four months pregnant with their first child and was due in late June. Phil Ortiz, from Albuquerque, New Mexico, looked forward to building up his father's new car franchise after the war. At the present, Fernando Ortiz was making ends meet by being the owner and only mechanic of Ortiz Motors. New cars wouldn't be built again until after the war, so keeping the older cars running kept the business alive. Zed Carthage, son of a Baptist minister from Texas and oldest of three children, wanted to preach the word of God; but he worried that the war would harden him and turn off the light of the gospel. Finally, the newest member of the crew, the bright Wendell Price, wanted only to serve in the memory of his brother. There was no girlfriend or wife to worry about, and after the war he planned on finishing his Engineering degree in Madison. He and Harry had formed a friendship as fellow Wisconsinites, and Wendell was feeling very much a part of *Avenging Angel*'s family. *After the war ... after the war,* Carl thought. It's as though their humanity had been checked at the door to Armageddon. Much of the time going home seemed a surreal and distant dream.

Carl's eyes snapped open at 0430 to the sound of Reveille being blown over the camp PA system. He saw the other men were rising as well and decided to head for the showers located directly behind his tent and about 40 feet down the line. He put his boots on and picked up a helmet and a zippered bag containing his shaving kit which he carried with him. The showers were already occupied, and a few men stood in line awaiting their turn to step onto the wooden-floored, draped shower stalls. The drapes consisted of parachute material hung over bamboo poles to provide some modicum of privacy. The six shower heads and plumbing of galvanized-steel half-inch pipe were fed by an elevated water tank. Two hand-operated hydrants stood outside the showers. Wooden benches were lined up nearby. Forgoing the shower, Carl filled his helmet with water and sat down on one of the benches. He removed his straight razor, mug, and a bar of Williams Mug Shaving Soap, mixed up thick foam in the mug and lathered up. After shaving, he refilled the helmet and used it as a sink to wash up. *It will have to do,* he thought and walked back to the tent where he dressed for the mission.

"It's 0530, guys. I'm heading over to the mess tent for some chow. You guys want to grab a bite? This is our last chance to eat before we land back at Tacloban." He didn't have to ask twice. Everyone except Phil Ortiz and Zed Carthage were dressed and hungry.

"Zed and I will be right there, Skipper." Phil finished lacing his boots.

Breakfast consisted of re-hydrated eggs, shredded canned

beef, gravy over toast, and as much coffee as one could drink. The "S.O.S" wasn't half-bad, and the dehydrated eggs were made palatable after drowning everything in catsup, salt and pepper.

"What do you think, Skipper? Does the shredded beef taste like your Double-B Angus?" Harry Osborne quipped.

Carl laughed at the reference to his family business. "Don't remind me, Harry. What I wouldn't give for a juicy, thick T-bone grilled outdoors over Mesquite wood ... and a cold American beer. Man, I'd die for an ice-cold Schlitz."

"Copy that, Lieutenant. Back in Wisconsin the beer of choice was Stroh's. Hey, maybe we should smuggle in some of the popular beers from the states and have a real old fashioned beer bust," Wendell Price chimed in. Everyone laughed and cheered his suggestion knowing full well that such a thing was impossible to bring about.

"I'll tell you what, after the war, you're all invited to the Double-B for the wedding, and we'll have that beer bust ... the steak fry, too." Carl raised his tin cup of coffee. "A toast! To better days ahead!"

–0700 hrs–

Col. Coltharp lifted off the runway in A/P190, followed by the rest of the Black Panthers of Alpha and Bravo Flights. The two flights each from the 500th Rough Raiders, the 499th Bats Outta Hell, and the 498th Falcons joined the formation, and the 345th Bomb Group headed up the west coast of Luzon Island toward their first target ... the rail lines at Campanario.

Jack Hayes flew off Carl's right wing in A/P178, and Lt. Lamar flew left wing in A/P002. Both maintained excellent formation off the port and starboard wings of Carl's *Avenging Angel*, A/P173.

The 501st Black Panthers' assignment was to seek out and destroy road and rail transportation from Campanario to San

Miguel in the Central Luzon Valley and then proceed southeast to Laguna de Bay and take out any targets of opportunity there. The first target appeared 10 miles north of Diliman at about 150.2 degrees north and 120.57 degrees east.

> *Bravo Flight Leader to wings, there at 1 o'clock low! I see a train. Lamar, you follow me in. Hayes, you're behind Lamar. Staggered-line formation, boys. Starting my run now.*

Carl nosed *Avenging Angel* down while banking toward the Japanese train. The train had one locomotive pulling six boxcars and was blowing thick black smoke indicating it was carrying a heavy load up an incline. Carl descended in line with the tracks and put his gun-sight on the rear boxcar. At 280 mph and playing his rudders to keep the bomber lined up on the target, he pressed the red "Guns" button on his control yoke. All eight fixed .50 caliber guns erupted, raking the boxcars from caboose to engine. Several rounds penetrated the boiler of the steam locomotive, and three spouts of steam shot out. Lt. Lamar followed Carl and the third boxcar exploded. The blast brought the train to a stop. There were no signs of Japanese troops aboard the train.

> *Bravo Flight, follow me. Banking left to come in for another run.*

Carl banked left in a shallow turn in order to allow the other two planes to remain in a tight formation.

> *Here we go. Let's make it count.*

Carl came in low and opened fire again. The barrage of explosive .50 caliber rounds from *Avenging Angel*'s eight forward facing AN/M2 guns tore into boxcars and the locomotive. Twice more the train and its cargo of supplies and arms were torn apart by 1st Lt. Eddy Lamar in A/P002 and again by Jack Hays in A/P178 until there was nothing left but a line of smoking rubble.

> *Flight Leader to flight, changing course to zero-six-zero degrees for Diliman. Watch for other aircraft. We're*

going to take out any rail or motorized transportation we see. Remain in line-abreast formation until targets are sighted.

Flying at 1,000 feet above the tree-tops, Bravo Flight spotted another locomotive with two flat-beds and two boxcars. Col. Coltharp and Alpha Flight had the train zeroed in, and Carl directed Bravo Flight toward the main road leading from Diliman to San Ildefonso. A convoy of armored personnel carriers and six-ton trucks was moving rapidly to escape the barrage on Diliman.

There! Below us! Same as before boys ... staggered line formation. Making my run now.

Carl nosed down toward the enemy convoy and accelerated to attack speed of 300 mph. He raked the lead trucks stopping the line of vehicles in its tracks. At least 50 armed Japanese soldiers bailed from the trucks and made for the tree line where they opened fire on the three Mitchells with small arms. Lamar and Hayes made their runs, and the three B-25s of Bravo FFlight banked around for a second attack. Before they could get into position, ack-ack erupted around them.

Stay in formation! Continue the attack! Hayes, go right and strafe the tree-line. Lamar, do the same on the left. I'll hit the convoy.

The planes separated slightly and laid down a blanket of machine gun fire. The small arms fire stopped.

Climbing to 1,000 feet. Did anyone see where the ack-ack is coming from?

An exploding anti-aircraft round hit close enough to rock A/P173.

Alpha Papa One Seven Eight to Flight Leader, I spotted a bunker about 3,000 meters at my 9 o'clock. Request permission to hit him with my hundred-pounders.

Carl gave the order:

Take lead, Hayes. We'll follow. One sleeve of

hundred-pounders each ... line-abreast formation. Bombardiers, arm your bombs!

Phil Ortiz armed four 100-pound high explosive bombs with four-second time-delayed fuses. Carl took up position to the right and behind Jack Hayes. Eddy Lamar positioned himself off Jack's left wing.

As the three B-25s drew within 1,500 meters, the concentration of anti-aircraft fire intensified. Puffs of black smoke burst all around them, each time rocking the planes with their blast concussion. Shrapnel tore at the fuselages, sounding like hammers banging on the aluminum skin.

Two concrete bunkers, each holding Type-96 twin-barreled 25 mm anti-aircraft cannons, maintained their barrage as the three American bombers opened fire with a combined 24 barrels of .50 caliber armor-piercing rounds. When the bombardiers had them pinpointed with their Norden bombsights, the command "Bombs away!" was heard over the inter-plane radio simultaneously by all three bombardiers. Twelve bombs tore into the bunkers and adjacent sand-bagged ammunition storage bunkers. Red-orange balls of fire billowed skyward as the three B-25s of Bravo Flight climbed out and re-formed. They had been fighting for over an hour.

Lt. Col. Chester Coltharp called over the Command Radio system which allows for plane-to-plane communication and air-to-ground communications over short distances,

Air Apaches, form-up! Course one-niner-five degrees. Report damage.

"Skipper. Group Lead is calling for us to re-form. Heading one-niner-five degrees. He wants a damage report." Sgt. Wendell Price advised. "I have you on the comm now, sir."

Bravo Flight to Group Lead. Forming up.

Carl toggled over to the frequency assigned to his flight and called out to the other two planes in his flight.

Flight Leader to Bravo Flight. Damage report.

Alpha Papa Zero Zero Two. A few holes, but we are combat ready.

Alpha Papa One Seven Eight. A-Okay, Flight Leader. A few dents are all, Jack Hayes reported.

Carl called in Bravo Flight's status report to the Group Leader.

Bravo Flight was still below and about two miles behind Coltharp's Alpha Flight when Harry Osborne's voice filled everyone's headphones.

"Bogies, 6 o'clock high. I see four of them!"

"Gunners charge your weapons," Carl ordered.

Bravo Flight, tuck in close and maintain formation. Applying military power now. Turret and tail gunners, you are cleared to fire when ready!

Four Nakajima Ki-43 fighter-bombers bearing the red rising sun roundel of the Japanese Empire, winged-over and descended in attack formation. They dived on the formation of Mitchells with the sun behind them, partially obscuring the vision of the B-25 gunners. The "Oscars," as they were named by the Americans, opened up with their twin 7.7 mm cannons. Tracers raked the American formation cutting through the aluminum hulls of the American bombers. Carl felt a *thump!* at his back, but paid no attention. The Japanese fighters sped ahead and below them pulling up to get in position for another run. The American gunners returned fire, but to no effect. Carl needed to make a decision before the Japs blew them all out of the sky. He keyed his plane-to-plane mic:

Bank left. Let's force them out of the sun!"

Carl banked *Avenging Angel* left and the rest of the flight followed on his wing.

Hold your bank angle until I tell you to level out.

"Here they come again, Skipper!" Harry called out.

Follow my lead boys. On my command, drop your

nose and throttle all the way back. Lay in full flaps. Put those fighters into your tail gunner's sights ... Now!

Carl pulled his throttles back and ordered Alex to apply full flaps. The other planes did the same and held formation.

The "Oscars" didn't anticipate the maneuver and found themselves in the sights of the B-25 turret and tail gunners. They opened fire as well, but were not able to get a sight-picture as quickly as the Americans. Harry Osborne's .50 caliber gunfire plowed into one of the fighters. The Ki-43s propeller was shot off, and the engine burst into flames. Another Jap fighter pilot found himself fighting an out-of-control spin after losing most of his empennage courtesy of Carl's right wingman Jack Hays in A/P178. The enemy plane disappeared into the jungle below exploding on impact.

Not anticipating the sudden slowing of the three Mitchells, the remaining two fighters sped in front of the bombers. This time, when the Japanese pilots pulled out of their attack dive, the '25s matched their flight path and waited for the enemy to rise up into their forward sights.

Full throttle, now! Line em' up, boys!

The business end of the B-25Js, a total of 24 machine guns, each firing 800 rounds per minute, breathed fire at the Emperor's best. They nosed up as the fighters tried to climb to safety. One of the two remaining "Oscars" waggled his wings as if saying hello. Instead, he was saying "good-bye" as black smoke streamed from the enemy's engine cowling. The sudden loss of power forced the plane to stall, roll over and drop vertically into the water off the coast of Luzon Island.

"Damage report! Call it in!"

"Osborne. Locked and loaded!"

"Navigator is good, Skipper."

"Radio is undamaged, sir. Myself as well." Wendell was not without a subtle sense of humor, Carl noted with a grin.

"Engineer is good. Hydraulics ... engines ... all good." Zed Carthage reported as his eyes scanned his instruments.

Flight Leader to flight, how are you doing, Hayes ... Lamar?

Alpha Papa One Seven Eight is good. No injuries, Flight Leader.

Alpha Papa Zero Zero Two. Left wing damaged ... losing fuel. I may need to feather the port engine to prevent a fire. We can make it home, though.

Copy, Zero Zero Two. We're over the water. Dump all of your ordinance. That should help. We'll hang back with you. Carl responded.

Bravo Flight Leader to Red Group Leader, sir, we've been hit by four Oscars. Two planes are undamaged. Alpha Papa Zero Zero Two is damaged but airworthy. Bravo Flight Leader is hanging back to provide air cover.

Roger that, Bravo Flight Leader. We caught the skirmish over the radio. Nice work Lieutenant. I'll be interested in reading your report. Should be clear sailing from here. We're only 20 minutes out from Tacloban.

Roger, sir. Bravo ... uh! A sudden stab of pain shot through Carl's left side. *Bravo Flight Leader ..., out.*

"Skipper, are you alright? You don't look so good," Alex asked.

"I don't know, I ..." Carl reached down to his left side and pulled back a bloody hand. "I ... must have taken a piece of shrapnel when those Oscars hit us." His vision blurred and cleared again. He felt as though all of his strength was draining from him.

"Take the controls, Alex. I'm going ... to ..." Carl's head slumped forward.

"Price, get me Tacloban ... now!" Alex ordered.

Sgt. Price dialed in the frequency for Tacloban Operations. "You're on the air, Lieutenant."

Tacloban tower, Alpha Papa One Seven Three declaring a medical emergency ... one wounded man aboard. We are 10 minutes out. Request ambulance. Over.

Alpha Papa One Seven Three, fly straight in approach runway two-seven. All other traffic, maintain position, we have an in-bound medical emergency, the controller announced.

Ten minutes later Alex Chekov landed and taxied *Avenging Angel* to the waiting ambulance. Phil Ortiz lowered the crew ladder, and he and Alex lowered Carl's unconscious body to the waiting medics. When the ambulance started for the Army Surgical Hospital compound, Alex ordered the crew ladder brought back up and throttled up the idling engines. He taxied the plane over to the parking ramp and shut down the engines.

Carl woke up on a bright sunny morning looking up at the sun. The bed was familiar, but instead of being in his bedroom, he was lying beneath the old cottonwood tree whose shade cooled him and Annie so many times.

Annie sat up beside him and rubbed the sleep from her eyes. "Good morning, my love." She lowered her head down to his lips and kissed him warmly. "How about some breakfast before you leave for work?"

"Sounds good." He threw off the covers and stood up. He noticed the clothes he had on. His first thought was that it was strange he would sleep in his uniform. The second was ... *Why am I dressed in my uniform at all? Where are my ranch clothes?*

"Breakfast is on the table, son. Come and sit down." The kitchen was ebullient with the laughter of family. George, in his Navy uniform, was laughing at something his father had said, and Penny was seated awaiting the blessing on the food.

Carl sat and was hit by a sudden flare of pain. He reached down to the source of the pain and brought up a blood soaked hand

and looked at Annie. Her hands flew up to her face to stifle a cry of despair.

"I'm sorry, Annie." The kitchen blurred and the members of his family faded.

"Lieutenant, wake up ... wake up," a voice called from the fog of anesthesia.

Chapter I

June, 1938

–Cascade, Montana–

Students streamed out of the three-story school building at the conclusion of the final day of the school year. Fourteen-year-old Carl Bridger headed down Central Avenue toward the bottom of the hill. The mile-and-a-half walk to the Rocking Double-B ranch, affectionately known as just the "Double-B", didn't bother him. He could almost taste his mother's fresh home-made potato bread with freshly churned butter and honey awaiting him as it did at the end of every school day.

"Hey, Bridger, wait up!"

Carl stopped and turned as Annie Petersen trotted up to him, and the two continued down the hill together. The afternoon sun transformed Annie's straw-blond hair into fine strands of gold. Her pale blue eyes twinkled with the unabashed joy of youth. A broad smile graced her countenance with a happy glow showing perfect rows of gleaming white teeth. At 14, she was already a leggy five-foot-three.

"Hi, Annie. What's up? I figured you and the gang would be headed downtown for a soda after school."

"Oh, we are. But I wanted to walk with you a ways. I'll cut through the block and meet them at the drug store. Hey, my dad said yesterday an airplane is going to land near town tomorrow to deliver mail." Annie's father was the editor of *The Cascade Courier* and made it a point to know of any newsworthy event in Cascade County.

"Really? When? Where is it going to land?" Carl was excited by the news and grateful to be in the know thanks to Annie's father.

"Daddy said they've built a landing strip west of town across the river. He's going to take lots of pictures and write a feature for the *Courier*. We're all going over at noon. Why don't you come? I think it will be fun." Annie smiled over at him and wrapped her fingers around his free hand. A thrill of electricity shot up his spine as they walked toward the highway. He met her smile with one of his own. *Gosh! I wish I could kiss her.* The thought brought a flush to his face, and he squeezed her hand a tiny bit harder.

More than 30 cars, trucks, and a few horse-drawn wagons lined the length of the 1,200-foot grass strip. An air of celebration filled the day for the townspeople. Families milled about chatting and laughing. Blankets, dotting the grassy area adjacent to the runway, were spread out in multi-colored squares as though waiting to be joined into a single gigantic quilt. Many of the locals were opening picnic baskets. Children ran about playing tag, and their laughter completed the atmosphere of gaiety. The festive gathering punctuated the purpose of the event: the arrival of the first airmail delivery to Cascade.

Carl sat on the end of the bed of his father's 1937 Chevrolet stake-bed truck and scanned the blue cloudless sky for a sign of the airplane. His mother spread two blankets on the cool grass, and she and Carl's father Gifford laid out picnic goodies. Penny Bridger, Carl's sister, was off playing with friends among the crowd. The Bridger's eldest son, George, had chosen to stay back at the ranch to oversee the bringing-in of 500 head of the Double-B's beef cattle to the corrals in preparation for the next day's drive to the stockyards.

The volunteer fire department's 10-piece band played on

such events as the 4th of July, Decoration Day, the annual Founders Day celebration in August and the welcoming of dignitaries to the town. On this particular occasion, the dignitary of the hour was the current Postmaster of the state of Montana, Harry Hendricks, whose tireless efforts to bring airmail service to Cascade and other rural communities scattered around the region resulted in the celebration.

"Don't get a crick in your neck, boy. You've been starin' at the sky for quite a while." Gifford sat next to his son and put an arm around Carl's shoulder, pulling him close

"Hi, Pop. I won't. Do you think he'll get here soon?

"He'll get here when he gets here, I reckon. He'd better be quick about it, though. There's work to get to, and we need to head back before too long. Don't you worry none ... shouldn't be long now." Carl squinted his eyes as his father tousled his hair.

"Aw, c'mon, Pop." Carl felt too old for hair tousling.

The unmistakable drone of an airplane engine announced the arrival of the de Havilland DH-82C Tiger Moth bi-plane. Everyone's eyes turned as one toward the sound. The plane came in low, flying downwind to the right of the runway. Carl had a good view of the pilot whose head sported a thin leather helmet. Aviator goggles covered his eyes, and a white silk scarf trailed out behind him. He waved down from the open cockpit which brought a chorus of cheers from the spectators. The plane banked left, lined up with the center of the grass strip and descended for a perfect three-point landing.

I wish that was me. Man, how I wish I could fly! Carl decided then and there he was going to learn everything he needed to know to become a pilot!

–Three Days Later–

"Millie, these rolls are delicious. Dinner is wonderful as usual." Gifford winked at Carl's mother. She reached over and patted her husband's weathered hand.

"Eat up, everyone. We have a big day tomorrow. George, I need for you to oversee the cutting of the first crop of sorghum. I'll see to the branding of the new calves myself. Carl, I want you to ride the fence after you take care of the morning milking. Check for breaks, and keep an eye out for wolves. Kurt Plunkett told me yesterday he lost one of his best breeders last week; her throat was ripped out. Dammed critters oughta be rounded up and shipped off to Yellowstone. Anyhow, take the 30-30 in case you run into trouble."

"Yes, sir ... Carl fidgeted in his chair. "... uh, Pop, can I ask you something?"

"Always. What is it?"

"Well ... um." He hunted for the right words.

"For Pete's sake, boy, we all need to go to bed sometime tonight. Spit it out. Say what you need to say, son."

"Okay. I've been talking to Mister Temple, er, Charles Temple, the pilot who flies the airmail route between Helena and Great Falls. He lives over in Castner Falls. Anyway, I asked him if I could help around the hangar ... you know, sweeping the floors, washing his plane and stuff. Can I, Pop? PLEASE!

"I'll think on it, Carl. What hours would you be working for him?"

"In the afternoons from two until five at first. When school starts up, I'd work from after school until 6 p.m." *He's actually thinking about it!* Carl's excitement grew.

"Absolutely not. It's out of the question. Summer is our busiest time of the year at the ranch, son, you know that. I need you here. You won't have time to work for Mister Temple and keep up with your chores, and I sure don't have the money to pay out for airplane rides."

"Well, what if I could earn my own money and do my chores, too?"

"When did you come up with this crazy idea, boy? You've

been talking about nothing else but airplanes and flying since the airmail plane flew in the other day."

"I know, Pop, but I haven't been able to think of anything else since then. Please, can I do this?"

"Well, you come up with how you can pull it off, and I'll think on it, son. Right now it's time for Bob Hope. What d'ya say we adjourn to the living room?"

Gifford turned on the radio: a furniture-sized, polished walnut cabinet which displayed the brand name PHILCO in gold letters above a single round glass-enclosed dial and three knobs. The dial glowed brightly, and he adjusted the tuning knob until the needle settled on the correct frequency. The announcer introduced:

"The Pepsodent Bob Hope Comedy Hour starring Bob Hope and Jerry Colonna."

Later, lying awake, Carl stared out his open bedroom window at a full moon. Thousands of stars dotted the clear night sky, and he imagined himself up there ... flying between them like an angel cavorting in the heavens. His eyes tracked an occasional cloud as it passed in front of the moon. A plan began to form in his mind, one that might make his dream a reality. Finally, with a smile on his face and with heavy eyes, he slept.

The next morning, He arose early. With his plan firmly set in his mind, he descended the stairs, dressed and ready for the day. He sat down at the table. His mind raced with thoughts of how he could talk to his father. His mother stood at the stove humming a tune. He wanted to ask her for advice.

"Mom, I ... "

The aroma of bacon and eggs wafted through the house, an olfactory alarm clock which brought the rest of the family downstairs to breakfast. Carl was on his own. Mildred Bridger smiled at him and placed a pitcher of cold milk on the table.

"Were you going to say something, sweetie?"

"No, Mom, that's okay."

Millie served up platters of eggs, fried potatoes, bacon, and toast with home-made raspberry preserves.

"Mornin', everybody." Gifford greeted as he took his seat at the head of the table.

Carl's heart raced. He swallowed hard and summoned up the courage to move forward with his plan. *Well, here goes.* "Pop, I know how I can earn the money for flying lessons and keep up with my chores."

"Ya don't say. Let's offer a prayer on the food, and you can tell us all about it. Maybe you should do the prayin', son." Gifford chuckled.

Carl understood his father's message: *Don't get your hopes up, boy.* Everyone joined hands and Carl prayed. "Oh, Lord, we thank you for the bounty we are about to receive and for all other blessings you see fit to grace us with this day. Amen."

"Okay, son, what's your plan?" Gifford stuffed a fork full of potatoes and egg into his mouth.

"Mister Petersen down at the *Courier* told Annie he's looking for someone to deliver papers and clean the office. I figure if I can deliver the papers early I'll be back here by six-thirty in time for the morning milking and chores. Afterwards, if you agree, I can go down to the *Courier* at around five in the afternoon and clean for a couple of hours. I'd be home by 7 o'clock." He fell silent, waiting for his father's reaction.

"Two things, son: first, you'd have to be up by 4:00 a.m. in order to do what you want with the paper route; second, you'd be taking on a huge responsibility. You wouldn't be able to quit because you're too tired or think you've bitten off more than you can chew. The *Courier* is Mister Petersen's life, Carl. You need to talk to him before you get your hopes up."

"Thanks Pop. I'll call him after breakfast if it's okay with you." Carl watched his father, trying to measure his reaction by his expression.

"You go ahead and call him. If he agrees, I reckon I'm fine with it." A smile spread over his weathered face. "There's one other thing, though. You mentioned flying lessons. I don't believe a 14-year-old boy can get a license to fly a plane. Aren't you supposed to be a little older?"

"I know. I can't start until I'm 16. By then, I figure I will have enough saved to pay for lessons myself. Can I please do this, Pop?"

Gifford looked at Mille who gave a barely perceptible nod. "Alright, but don't forget you'll be taking on a two-year commitment, and a lot of people will be looking at you to see how you handle yourself. You're a Bridger, son. You know what that means. I know you won't let us ... or yourself, down." Gifford nodded and stood up from the table. Carl welcomed his father's reassuring pat on the shoulder. "Now, let's get to work."

A flood of relief replaced Carl's earlier anxiety. He finished his breakfast and joined his father and George in the morning chores.

Summer, 1940
–The First Lesson–

Charles Temple walked into the hangar where he found Carl hard at work. At present, the 16-year-old would-be pilot was finishing up with changing the oil in the Tiger Moth.

His 18 months working for Annie's father had come to an end when the paper cut back from a daily to a weekly publication. The depression forced a number of local businesses to close their doors, and the *Courier* was not immune to the economic downturn. For the aspiring pilot, the paper's plight turned out to be a blessing in disguise. Charlie Temple took him under his wing and put him to work in the hangar. Carl grew to admire and respect the airmail pilot and spent the next six months learning everything about the mechanics and principles of flying from him. In return for the instruction, he agreed to maintain both the plane and the hangar in shipshape order. Even Gifford Bridger relented and allowed his son to work for Charlie Temple, calling it, "A reward for your hard work and responsibility toward mister Petersen over the past year-and-a-half."

Carl tightened down the oil filler cap and wiped his hands on a shop rag when Charlie approached him. "How ' bout you take a break, kiddo?"

"I need to finish this, first. My folks expect me home by 8 o'clock."

"Good. We have another hour. Help me push her out. You're going to have your first lesson."

"Wha ...?" Carl couldn't believe his ears.

"Well, don't stand there with your mouth opened. Grab hold and start pushing." Charlie laughed.

"Yes, sir. YES, SIR!" Carl tossed the rag on the work bench and put both hands on the wing root. Together, he and Charlie pushed the olive green and yellow bi-plane out into the fading light. His heart pounded a staccato beat in his chest. Filled with excitement, he couldn't suppress a nervous giggle.

"You say something over there, Carl?"

"No sir. Clearing my throat is all." Carl stifled another giggle of elation.

"Alright, I want you to climb into the front seat and put your helmet on. I rigged it with a tube and ran it back behind your seat to mine so I can talk to you when we're airborne. You can't talk back, so when I tell you to do something, give me a thumbs-up, okay?" Charlie cocked his thumb and raised it high. "Like this. I'm going to show you how to set the switches and throttle to start the engine, so pay attention. I'll be on the ground to pull the prop through. Go ahead, climb on up."

Carl climbed onto the lower wing and lifted himself into the forward seat. Charlie stood on the wing and began to teach him what to do, pointing out and explaining the functions of all the gauges and switches.

"First, make sure the switches are in the 'OFF' position. Now, open the throttle wide ... good. You've filled the lines with fuel. I'm going down to pull the prop through to blow any air out of the lines." Charlie climbed down, pulled the propeller through and stood clear of the blades. "Turn the switch on and call it out!"

"Contact!" Carl yelled out in the same manner Charlie had demonstrated on countless occasions.

Carl watched from the open cockpit as Charlie grabbed the two-bladed wooden propeller with his left hand and pulled down hard while taking a step to the side and away from the prop. The engine caught immediately, and Carl eased the throttle back to a smooth idle.

Charlie removed the chocks from in front of the tires and climbed into the rear seat. He put his helmet on, picked up the mask with a tube attached to it, and drew the straps tight so it pulled snuggly against his cheeks.

Putting the tube to his mouth, he spoke in a loud resonant voice, "Can you hear me, Carl?"

Carl raised his hand in a thumbs-up gesture. Charlie's voice was muffled but readable.

"Good. Now, you've learned everything you can on the ground about the Tiger Moth's flight characteristics and the controls. Do everything I tell you to, and you'll be fine. I've got the controls for now."

Carl repeated the thumbs-up sign, and Charlie taxied the bi-plane to the end of the grass runway.

With the "Tiggy's" nose lined up and ready for takeoff, Charlie added power with a firm steady motion. Carl watched the rpm needle rise, and he felt the engine vibration through the seat of his pants. As the plane gained speed the tail skid lifted off the grass. A moment later, the smooth rubber tires lifted off, and they were airborne.

The ground dropped away beneath the wings, and Carl's

excitement jumped skyward as well. Looking forward through the blur of the spinning prop he saw only sky and the distant hills rising above the quilt work of farmland below.

The "Tiggy" grabbed more altitude and climbed to 1,000 feet.

Charlie yelled into the tube, "Take the controls, Carl. Keep us level. Don't gain or lose more than 100 feet. Got it?"

"Got it," he said to himself while he gave the affirmative thumbs-up to his instructor. Carl took the stick and placed his feet on the rudder bars. Anxiety pressed on his mind, and he was momentarily struck by a stupor of thought. Everything he had been taught fled from his mind in the world's worst case of stage fright. The plane's nose dropped below the horizon.

"Charlie to Carl. Did you go to sleep up there? Bring the nose up."

Carl snapped out of his brief fugue and brought them back to level flight. He began to relax against the urge to over-control the tiny plane. His racing heart slowed.

"I want you to bank right toward your father's ranch. Be sure to add a little power and a little bit of right rudder. Apply a little back pressure on the stick to maintain altitude. She'll lose speed in a turn, so keep it at 60 knots. After the turn, bring your speed up to 70 knots. You ready?"

Carl started into the turn, but held the control stick to the right, instead of centering it, to hold the bank angle steady. When the wings tilted past the desired bank angle, Charlie made the correction from the back seat with a gentle movement of the stick.

C'mon, Carl, you learned all this in ground school, he admonished himself.

"Remember, Carl, the ailerons need to be neutral to keep a constant bank angle. Now let's try it again. This time give me a 30-degree turn to the left."

Carl repeated the procedure. This time he held the angle of the wings steady until the ranch came into view about two miles in front of and below them. He performed the maneuver perfectly, losing only 50 feet of altitude. As he leveled off he allowed his airspeed to climb and throttled back when the needle read 70 knots. *Yes! I got it right that time!* Charlie had him repeat the process in the opposite direction. They practiced a few more "S" turns until Carl got comfortable with turning the aircraft.

"Good job, kid. You're a natural at this. Okay, this is what we're going to do. I want you to do a slow decent of 500-feet-per-minute until you reach 3,900 feet. Maintain 60 knots until you reach 3,900 and level off while bringing your speed back up to 70 knots. We're going to give your family a thrill. You can even waggle your wings if you want to," Charlie offered.

Gifford was walking back toward the main house from the barn when George joined him after securing the gate to the corral.

"I can't wait to dig into mom's roast and spuds. We got a lot done today." The words had no sooner left George's mouth when the drone of an airplane's engine caught their ears. Turning, they both craned their necks skyward in time to see the Tiger Moth fly overhead. The wings waggled a wave and banked toward town.

"Wow! That was a surprise. You don't suppose ... nah, couldn't be." Gifford followed the plane with his eyes as it descended to the airport.

Carl chocked the tires, and he and Charlie walked toward the hangar.

"So, what do you think, kid? Ya still want to be a flyer?"

"More than ever! That was a killer-diller! You had me cookin' with gas on those 'S' turns."

Carl's chain of slang brought a chuckle from Charlie.

"Well gee, Carl; I thought you might be a little more excited," he quipped.

"Okay, okay. I get it. Whew! That was a gas to the max,

though! Hey, Charlie, can I ask you a question that's been on my mind?"

"Sure ... what?"

"Well, you've never talked much about when you were a kid or what your plans are for the future. So ... I'm curious. Why didn't you ever get married; you know, start a family?" Charlie had become something of an enigma to Carl, and he wanted to know more about his new friend.

"Ah, I see. I'm pushing 22 and not dating. I get it. First, I'll tell you ... I really like girls, okay? I had a girl up in Helena for a while. I was gone too much with my flying, and we sort of drifted apart. The short answer is, I never settled in one place long enough to start a long-term relationship. Maybe I will, someday. I'd like to have a family, but I honestly never had a clear picture of myself raising kids and growing old. The thought of being a father and a grandfather just doesn't fit the scheme of things for me, I guess."

They walked into the hangar and put their flight gear in the locker behind Charlie's desk.

Carl wanted to press the discussion further. "But, why can't you picture getting married and having a family? It's all that matters, isn't it? I mean, I can see me and Annie together forever, having a family ... the works."

"Carl, I'll tell you the same thing I told my mother when I was your age. I've never told anyone about this, and you have to keep it between us, okay?"

Carl looked at Charlie, wondering what kind of secret prevented him from a happy future. He thought it a sad thing. "Sure, Charlie, I won't breathe a word. I promise."

"When I was 16, I came home from school one day, and I found my mother crying. I asked her what was wrong. The police had been there about an hour earlier. My grandparents were killed in a car accident. Well, the tragedy started a long discussion about life and death and all the religious stuff that's supposed to explain everything. I only felt emptiness and sadness at the loss of two of the most loving, kindest people in the world. Their death hit me hard; but worse, it taught me something that shook me to the core."

"What, Charlie? What did it teach you?"

"I realized I couldn't see myself ever having a family. The feeling was always there I suppose, hiding in the back of my mind, waiting to come to the surface. You can picture marriage with Annie; family ... grandkids, right? But, I can't. In fact, after thinking about it for a few days, I told my mom that I had no vision of my life at all past the age of 26. I had a clear sense that something was going to happen by then ... still do. My life will either end or forever change, and I don't mean in a good way. So, there you have it, pal. How could I bring a wife and children into my life only to be taken from them? It wouldn't be fair to them. Call it what you want, a premonition ... nonsense ... whatever. All I know is, until and UNLESS something or someone comes along to change my mind, I'll continue to be happy just being at the controls of an airplane."

Speechless, Carl searched for the right words. He felt sad for Charlie. He couldn't imagine such a dark thing could haunt a person into denying one's self the joy and fulfillment of love, marriage, and family. Those were the things he saw as the source of his parents' happiness, and he desired no less for Annie and himself.

"I'm so sorry for your loss, Charlie." He said goodbye and headed for home, pondering Charlie's words. A shiver cascaded down his spine, and he shook his head in sadness for the man.

Carl walked into the kitchen as the family was finishing dinner.

"Hi, everybody. Sorry I'm late. Can I still help myself to some roast, Mom?" He slid into the chair next to Penny.

"Where 'ya been, son? It's not like you to miss dinner. George had to finish up your chores, by the way." Carl saw neither anger nor joy in his father's matter-of-fact expression.

"I'm sorry, Pop ... you too, George. It won't happen again.

Charlie needed me for an extra hour, and I lost track of time."

"He probably couldn't drop you out of his plane in time to get you home for dinner, I figure." George chimed in with a grin and a chuckle.

"Yep. Before long, I'm going to need to build you a landing strip of your own so you can sit down at the table with your family on time." Gifford's remark brought a nervous laugh from Carl. He sensed the other shoe about to fall.

"Son, I'm happy you got to go up in the plane. I'll admit I was excited when Charlie waved the wings at us. But, Carl, if you want there to be second time, you will not be late getting home, and you will not … and I emphasize NOT, ever again pass your responsibilities to this ranch and to your family off on someone else. Are we clear?" Gifford spoke in a calm, but determined voice. Carl understood very well the meaning behind his father's words.

"Yes, sir. It will never happen again. I'm sorry, everybody." He dropped his head down. "By the way, Pop, Charlie wasn't doing the flying, it was me." He lifted his head and grinned.

"You got to fly a real airplane? Wow! That's the cat's pajamas for sure!" Penny blurted.

–April, 1941–

Carl waited for Annie Petersen in front of her English classroom on the third floor of the school. He had a question to ask her … one that produced a warm rush of anticipation. After the dismissal bell rang, he practically ran down the hall to catch her.

"Hi, Carl." She handed her books to him and took his arm with her left hand. The two walked downstairs and out the double doors. Annie pulled up the collar of her jacket against the slight chill. Snow dusted the peaks of the distant mountains … winter was not ready to let go quite yet.

"Hey, Annie, the prom is in two weeks. *Poydesh' na tantsy*

so mnoy?" He asked in his most sophisticated Russian (he practiced *will you go to the dance with me* for four days). He was surprised at his own nervousness. He and Annie had been dating regularly, as much as time would allow, since the previous summer. The new school year produced the happy consequence of allowing the two to spend a lot more time together. They worked out their class schedules to take four of the same classes. Both signed up for a second year of Russian and found themselves enjoying practicing their use of the language in conversation. Walking home from school together every day and attending Saturday matinees at the Rialto every other week, provided opportunities to learn much more about each other. A distinct bond … one greater than friendship, drew them increasingly closer.

"Aw, golly, Carl, … um … *Ya zhelayu vam poprosil raney.* Harold Finch already asked me to be his date, and …"

"Harold Finch?" … he interrupted ... "I didn't think you even knew him; let alone wanted to go to the prom with him. Criminetly, Annie. I don't want to go to the prom with anybody else." Carl felt truly hurt.

"I thanked him but told him I already had a date." She said with an impish smile and took hold of his free hand.

"What? Oh, you're a mean one, Annie Petersen. Man, you had me flippin' my wig." He released a nervous laugh. The two walked on, basking in the shear presence of each other.

Annie's expression changed inexplicitly, and she became somber.

"Something's bothering you, Annie. What's going on?"

At first she said nothing. Her eyes began to glisten with tears, and her cheeks flushed. "Last night I overheard my parents talking about moving to Great Falls."

Taken aback by this sudden revelation, Carl stopped and stared straight ahead with a stoic expression. Fearing the worst, he turned to meet her eyes.

"Why, Annie?" *Something terrible must have happened to bring this on*, he thought. "What's happened?"

"Daddy's shutting down the paper. It's breaking his heart, but he says the cost of keeping the paper running is more than he's bringing in. He's going to take a job with the Tribune." A tear welled up and ran down Annie's face.

"Ah, jeepers, Annie. I'm really sorry." The news came as a blow to him. "I ... I don't know what to say."

"I guess we won't be at school together our senior year. What are we going to do, Carl?"

"I don't know. We need to decide something. I don't want to be away from ... I want us to be in the same school." A rising sense of despair and hopelessness Carl had never experienced rendered him speechless as he absorbed all of the ramifications of this new development. *Different schools ... no more Saturday dates ... Annie will find some other guy ... oh, no!* Neither of them had mentioned the "L" word in all their time together, but Carl was feeling it beneath the turmoil of his thoughts.

Annie looked into his eyes and completed his first sentence. "I don't want to be away from you either, Carl." Trembling with emotion, the words they both wanted to say came to Annie's lips, "... I love you."

"I ... I love you too, Annie." He began to bend to kiss her, but decided better of it. Holding hands, the two walked on together.

–Solo–

A perfect spring day greeted the town of Cascade. In time for the prom, Carl bought his first car; a black 1932 Ford Model-B coupe. He had saved $292.00 since going to work for Charlie Temple. He no longer accepted allowance from his father and took it upon himself to begin paying his own way a bit to lessen the burden on his family. The car, owned by the Plunkett family, had been a second car for them; one which they were unable to keep because of the Depression. Nearly everyone, including the Bridger family, was feeling the economic crunch of the times, mostly due to the falling price of beef at auction. The Plunketts offered the car to Carl for $200.00 cash. After discussing the matter with his parents, he took delivery.

On Saturday, the 14th of May, he drove to the airport to put in his usual four hours of work. Charlie stood by the plane waiting for him.

"Carl, c'mon over here, pal. I need to talk to you."

Carl correctly read Charlie's troubled expression. "What is it, boss? Something wrong?"

"Maybe … could be something right, I hope. The U.S. Airmail service is going through some purse-tightening. They're dropping some of the routes and concentrating on the more remote areas. Cascade is going to be the hub for the entire region including Teton and Lewis and Clark Counties."

"Cripes, Charlie. What does that mean for you?"

"Not sure, yet. The mail service is cutting back to two planes to cover the same area that four used to. I'm pretty sure I'll be staying here in Cascade. More than likely there'll be less time for flying lessons, though. They're thinking of bringing in one of the other planes to our hangar, but I haven't been told who the other pilot will be."

"How about my job, Charlie? Am I going to be laid off? I'm only in high school. Do you think they'll let me stay on?"

"Carl, you know the Tiger Moth inside and out. You've logged almost 18 hours in the front seat, and you've turned yourself into a pretty darned good mechanic. I'm going to push to keep you on. We're good at least through the first of the year, so we don't need to worry about it for now. How about let's get down to the fun stuff. Are you ready?"

"Yep!" Carl loved his lessons and couldn't wait to get into the "Tiggy."

"Climb on up, then," Charlie directed.

Carl climbed onto the wing and worked his way toward the front cockpit.

"Where do you think you're going, partner? You're flying in the back seat today." Charlie grinned.

"What? Do you mean …?"

"Yep. It's solo time for you. Now listen up. I want you to stay in the pattern. Show me four touch-and-go landings and a full-stop landing. If you haven't broken anything, taxi back to the hangar. Clear?"

"Yes sir!" Heart pounding adrenalin flooded his veins as he buckled his shoulder harness. Carl checked the magneto switches to confirm they were in the "off" position and opened the throttle. Charlie pulled the propeller through three times to draw fuel into the cylinders. "Switch on?" He called up to Carl.

"Switch on. Contact!" Carl called back. He toggled up the magneto switches and cracked the throttle open with his right hand.

Charlie gave the prop a firm pull, and the engine caught hold. Carl throttled back to a smooth idle while his instructor re-moved the chalks. When Charlie stepped clear of the plane and threw a sharp salute, Carl grinned down at him and returned the salute. The excitement was palpable …as though his heart was about to leap out of his chest.

"Okay, you can do this." He said aloud to himself. "Taxi out to the runway. Now full right rudder and kick her tail around." He added power, and the prop wash struck the vertical stabilizer swinging the nose to the right until it pointed down the center of the closely-mowed grass strip.

Carl pushed the throttle forward in a steady firm motion. The little plane wanted to yaw to the left, and he added a little right rudder. The airspeed indicator reached 15 knots … 20. The tail lifted off the runway. At 40 knots the plane's wheels lost their grip on the ground, and he was in the air.

"Yay! I'm flying! I'm flying!" Being in the cockpit alone was exhilarating and frightening at the same time. The thought crossed his mind that there was no Charlie to get him out of trouble if he made a mistake.

Carl concentrated on the three "As" of piloting a plane: Airspeed, Altitude, and Attitude. "Nose on the horizon. Wings level. Speed at 70 knots. Turns at 60 knots," he recited to himself.

At 500 feet above the surface, he banked left on his crosswind leg. When he flew away from the field at a 90-degree angle, he leveled his wings, counted to 10 and turned left again onto his downwind leg. He flew parallel to the runway until the end of the grass strip lay slightly to the left and below him. He reduced power and began his descent for landing. He remembered Charlie's words: *The best landings are made on the downwind leg.* Carl kept an eye on his rate of descent and turned the Tiger Moth onto its base leg. When he was in position, he turned again, lining up the plane with the landing strip. *Point the nose to the middle of the runway ... throttle back to 50 mph*, he recited in his mind. He held his airspeed steady on final until he was over the edge of the mowed portion of the field and about 50 feet off the ground. He pulled the throttle all the way back and let the "Tiggy" settle into ground effect ...seeming to float above the grass momentarily. The plane slowed and touched down. After bouncing twice, the main wheels settled into the grass. He immediately applied full power and repeated the process.

The final touchdown was a perfect three-point landing. The wheels and tail skid touched down a fraction of a second apart. Carl taxied over to the hangar and closed the throttle. He turned off the magneto switches and climbed down from the de Havilland DH-82.

"Take your shirt off, Carl," Charlie commanded in a firm, serious voice.

"Wha ... why?" Charlie, what are you going to do with my shirt? He didn't quite know what to think about the strange request.

"Only your T-shirt. We're going to paint it and hang it on the wall of my office. Take it off, Pal. It's tradition."

Carl handed his T-shirt to Charlie who promptly ripped it up the side and inscribed it in red paint, *Solo - May 14th, 1941 - Carl Bridger*. Charlie nailed the shirt to a peg-board behind an old desk in the small storage room he called his "office."

"Congratulations, Carl. You're going to make a fine pilot."

"Wow, Charlie, that was keen! I can't wait to tell everyone!"

Later that same evening, at 6 o'clock, dressed in his Sunday suit and his only white shirt with one of Gifford's ties, Carl climbed into his car and headed to Annie's house. It was prom night, and he was flying high from the adrenaline rush of the day, and from the excited anticipation of picking up the prettiest girl in Cascade for a night of dancing. Annie's father met him at the front door and invited him in. Annie walked into the living room dressed in a silky blue floor length gown tied at the waist with a blue sash and bow. Her shoulders were covered by drop sleeves. Her hair was done up in the *victory roll* style popular at the time. She wore ruby red low-heeled shoes. Carl's breath caught in his throat.

"Wow, Annie. You're the bee's knees! … I mean, um … you're beautiful!"

"Why, thank you, kind sir." Annie fluttered her eyes at Carl in a coquettish manner. They both laughed, and Carl offered her his arm which she took with a gloved hand.

"Be back home by 10, Annie." Abe Petersen called out as the couple walked to Carl's Model-B parked in front of the house.

As they drove to the school, Annie snuggled close to Carl.

"Guess what, Annie. I soloed today."

"You did? Oh, Carl I'm so proud of you. I know it's what you've been working toward all this time. I wish I could have been there to see you. Was it the greatest thrill ever?"

"It sure was. I would have asked you to come with me, but I didn't even know myself until Charlie told me to climb into the pilot's seat." He related to Annie all of the details until they pulled into the school parking lot.

They entered the decorated gymnasium beneath a balloon arch welcoming the Junior class to their last dance of the year.

"Oh, Carl, look! It's beautiful!" Annie's eyes were wide with excitement. Three floor lights behind red, blue and green revolving color wheels cast the room in a collage of changing colors. On the wall above the bleachers was a large tinseled sign announcing:

Prom Night, 1941
"Swinging to the Big Bands"

Al Dublin's "Anniversary Waltz" played over the loud speakers from a 78-rpm phonograph positioned on a table on a raised dais. The young biology teacher, Ed Nievaard, was spinning the platters.

Carl took Annie's hand, and they walked onto the dance floor. He placed his right hand around Annie's waist. She moved closer to him and caressed the back of his neck. The soft warmth of her gentle touch sent a tingle down his spine. His breathing quickened with excitement. Annie pulled his head down to her lips, and she kissed his ear. "I love you," she whispered.

"Everything is going to be swell, Annie, I promise. I love you, too." Carl drew her closer to him, and their bodies moved in unison to the music of Glen Miller, Tommy Dorsey, Johnny Mercer and others. Vocal performances by Billy Holiday, Bing Crosby, and the young crooner sensation, Frank Sinatra, added variety to the evening. Finally, after three hours of dancing and talking to old friends, Mister Nievaard announced the closing number, Bing Crosby's *Only Forever.*

When Bing sang the lyrics: Do I want to be with you as the years come and go? Annie's body shuddered in his arms with the splendor of the moment. Carl whispered the next phrase into Annie's ear as Crosby's voice filled the room: *Only forever, if you care to know.*

Carl rose early the next morning and completed his chores by 10:00 a.m. He and Annie had a date to see *Here Comes Mr. Jordan* at the Rialto. He put on a clean shirt and drove to the Petersen house. Annie greeted him at the door.

"Mom! Carl's here. I'll be back in time for dinner!" Annie didn't wait for a reply, and she and Carl walked down the steps to the car. Twenty minutes later they were settled into their seats in time for the Movietone Newsreel featuring U.S. Army Air Corp cadets training to become pilots and navigators.

The actor, Jimmy Stewart, stood in front of a B-17 and encouraged young men to join the Air Corps. The film also showed aircraft manufacturing plants hard at work building warplanes for Britain and the U.S. One segment of the story showed a medium bomber. The B-25 Mitchell caught Carl's attention. He thought of what it might feel like to command such a powerful weapon of war. *A whole different experience from the Tiggy,* he mused.

"Gosh, I hope America isn't drawn into the war in Europe. It scares me when I think about you being drafted," Annie said and snuggled closer to Carl. She helped herself to some popcorn from the bag he held.

"The Brits took a beating last year, but they ended up pushing the Krauts out of the air. I think it's only a matter of time before America gets involved. Maybe the war will end before then. We can only hope. Shhh! The feature is starting."

Here Comes Mr. Jordan, starring Claude Raines and Edward Everett Horton entertained them for the next two hours. The improbable story of a saxophone player who dies in a plane crash and is brought back to life was a comedy-drama fantasy about choices and consequences both temporal and spiritual.

Carl and Annie's thoughts were more about each other and her move to Great Falls in two days than about the movie. They watched on in silence and bore the burden of their pending separation without a word.

Monday morning came, and Carl drove to the Petersen house to lend a hand with the rest of the packing. A truck, carrying the furniture and other large items too big to fit into their car, pulled away from the house. An hour later the Petersen's car, loaded with a few remaining belongings, stood ready to leave for their new home on Albemarle Street in Great Falls.

"Good bye, Carl, it's been a pleasure to work with you, young man." Mister Petersen offered a hand, which Carl shook appreciatively.

"Thank you, sir. Thanks for everything. Good luck, Mister Petersen."

Annie's parents waited in the car for her to say her good-byes. She made sure her parents weren't watching, and she stood on her tip-toes. Carl bent to kiss her. It was a sweet and bitter embrace. She touched his face gently with the palm of her hand. Smiling sadly, she turned toward her father's car.

"Annie?"

She stopped and looked back at him.

"Only forever, if you care to know." He forced a smile.

"Me, too." She mouthed back before climbing into the back seat.

The rest of the summer was spent working on the ranch and helping Charlie at the hangar. Carl completed his cross-country and night flying requirements and passed his Civil Aeronautics Board pilot license written exam. He was licensed to fly on his own and with a passenger. He logged as many hours as he could cram into the time before the first snow fall and as many as his skimpy wallet would allow. He saw Annie every other weekend. Their times together cemented the bond which began over six years earlier when they were shooting marbles in the dirt in 5th grade.

Pearl Harbor – Dec 7, 1941

Chapter II

–War–

The back door to the main house slammed shut behind Gifford, George and Carl as they stepped into the mudroom off the kitchen. After stomping the snow off their boots, they hung their coats and hats on hooks on the wall next to the door.

Carl pulled off his wet boots and placed them side-by-side on the floor in front of the heat vent. "I'm frozen to the bone!" he remarked.

"We all are, son. Judging from the weather the past few days, the Alaska Express is moving down from the north. We need to make sure there's plenty of food and water for the cattle and get as many as we can under shelter."

"The hay situation is good, Pop. There's enough stored to tide us over for quite a while. We'll need to ship more up from down south, but probably not until March." George shuffled into the kitchen in stocking feet where Millie stood at the stove stirring a five-gallon sized pot of chili. What they didn't eat would be stored, frozen, in the ice shed.

"Sit down, boys, dinner is ready. There are fresh muffins, coffee, and milk; and peach cobbler for dessert."

Carl couldn't wait to dig into his mother's chili and cornbread muffins. "If we get snow tonight, I think we should all hunker down here at home. What do you think, Pop?"

"I reckon Bishop Pierce will have to do without the

Bridgers on Sunday. It's nasty outside." Gifford slid a chair out from the table and sat down.

George nodded his agreement. "Sounds right. I'm for catching up on some reading and some radio shows in front of the fireplace."

"Mom, can we decorate the Christmas tree tonight?" Penny had been begging to get out the decorations ever since Carl and George brought the seven-foot spruce into the house the previous day.

"Why, that's a wonderful idea, sweetie. How about it, boys? Are the Bridger men up to some hot cider and Christmas decorations after dinner?"

"Heck yes, Mom. We'll bring down the lights and stuff! Hurry up and eat, Penny." Carl and his sister cleaned their bowls and raced upstairs. Minutes later four large boxes of tree ornaments lay on the living room floor.

For the next hour, the Bridger clan enjoyed the traditional tree decorating. Penny claimed the honor of placing the golden angel atop the colorful tree while the radio played the half-hour "Abbot and Costello Show" followed by the crime drama "Ellery Queen."

–December 7, 1941–

The aroma of coffee, bacon and toast lingered in the house long after breakfast the following morning. Millie and Penny were baking bread and oatmeal-raisin cookies. Penny handled the cookies having spent many hours over the last couple of years helping and learning from her mother.

Carl and George sat across from each other in the living room doing battle at the chess board, while Gifford relaxed in his easy chair reading the previous day's issue of the *Tribune*. The paper was delivered daily by truck from Great Falls and dropped off at Barkley's Grocery Store in Cascade. Local residents had to travel to the small market to buy their copy. The syndicated paper drew from national and state sources and provided vital business updates on the cattle market which was of interest to Gifford.

The radio, tuned to the Great Falls Network affiliate KPFA and a program of Big Band music, opened the festive evening. A Glen Miller number was currently filling the Bridger house with "Fools Rush In."

At 12:15 p.m. the music stopped abruptly, and for a few seconds nothing came from the radio speaker but faint static. Then:

We interrupt our regular program with this news bulletin from the WOR studios in New York:

At 7:45 a.m. Honolulu time, about one-half hour ago, the United States Naval Base at Pearl Harbor was attacked by an estimated 300 or more fighter planes and torpedo bombers bearing the red sun markings of the empire of Japan. The attack is on-going as of this announcement. Many fires are reported, most of which are in the harbor area where U.S. warships are docked. Stay tuned to this station for updates on the attack as details come to us. Once again ...

"Millie, Penny, come in here now!" Gifford called out.

"What does it mean, Pop? Is Japan starting a war with us?" George was the first to try and put the surprise attack in perspective.

"It's stupid. Japan is a small island no bigger than Montana. Why would they want to start a war with us?" Carl added.

"Like all wars, son, they either want something they can't have without killing to get it, or they have something they're afraid of losing."

"If we're at war, Pop, what does that mean for us ... for the Double-B?" An overwhelming flood of possible ramifications filled Carl's mind.

"Dear God, Giff! Our boys! ... the draft!" Millie's eyes misted.

"Calm down, everyone." Gifford held his wife close to him. "We can't decide anything right now. Let's stay by the radio and listen to the reports. We're going to be fine if we just keep our heads." Gifford engaged each member of his family with a steady confident gaze. Carl was only slightly calmed by Gifford's outward resolve. At 16, he was safe from the draft for now, but George was 22. Carl feared for his brother.

Reports throughout the day gave more details, none of which were encouraging. Some 385 fighters, fighter-bombers, and torpedo bombers of the Imperial Japanese Navy attacked not only Pearl Harbor, but bases on Ford Island and the Army Air Corp base at Wheeler Field on the island of Oahu. In a period of four hours, the Japanese forces had sunk four U.S. battleships, including the Arizona, California, West Virginia, and Oklahoma. Four more sustained severe damage. The aging auxiliary battleship Utah was also sunk. Three heavy cruisers and three destroyers went to the bottom as well. One hundred and eighty-eight American aircraft were destroyed on the ground. The death toll reached 2,402 with 1,282 wounded. The American Seventh Fleet was decimated except for the four U.S. aircraft carriers and one battleship which were at sea when the attack took place.

The following morning, at 10:30 a.m. Mountain Time, every radio station in the country aired President Roosevelt's speech to the nation. The Bridger family gathered around the radio in the living room of the main house. A light snow fell outside, and the snowflakes glistened like specks of gold as they tumbled to earth through the sun's rays.

Mr. Vice President, Mr. Speaker, Members of the Senate, and of the House of Representatives:

Yesterday, December 7th, 1941 – a date which will live in infamy – the United States of America was suddenly and deliberately attacked by naval and air forces of the Empire of Japan.

The United States was at peace with that nation, and, at the solicitation of Japan, was still in conversation with its government and its Emperor looking toward the maintenance of peace in the Pacific.

Indeed, one hour after Japanese air squadrons had commenced bombing in the American island of Oahu, the Japanese ambassador to the United States and his colleague delivered to our Secretary of State a formal reply to a recent American message. And, while this reply stated that it seemed useless to continue the existing diplomatic negotiations, it contained no threat or hint of war or of armed attack.

It will be recorded that the distance of Hawaii from Japan makes it obvious that the attack was deliberately planned many days or even weeks ago. During the intervening time the Japanese Government has deliberately sought to deceive the United States by false statements and expressions of hope for continued peace.

The attack yesterday on the Hawaiian Islands has caused severe damage to American naval and military forces. I regret to tell you that very many American lives have been lost. In addition, American ships have been reported torpedoed on the high seas between San Francisco and Honolulu.

Yesterday, the Japanese government also launched an attack against Malaya.

Last night, Japanese forces attacked Hong Kong.

Last night, Japanese forces attacked Guam.

Last night, Japanese forces attacked the Philippine Islands.

Last night, the Japanese attacked Wake Island.

And this morning, the Japanese attacked Midway Island.

Japan has therefore undertaken a surprise offensive extending throughout the Pacific area. The facts of yesterday and today speak for themselves. The people of the

United States have already formed their opinions and well understand the implications to the very life and safety of our nation.

As commander in chief of the Army and Navy, I have directed that all measures be taken for our defense, that always will our whole nation remember the character of the onslaught against us.

No matter how long it may take us to overcome this premeditated invasion, the American people, in their righteous might, will win through to absolute victory.

I believe that I interpret the will of the Congress and of the people when I assert that we will not only defend ourselves to the uttermost but will make it very certain that this form of treachery shall never again endanger us.

Hostilities exist. There is no blinking at the fact that our people, our territory, and our interests are in grave danger.

With confidence in our armed forces, with the unbounding determination of our people, we will gain the inevitable triumph. So help us God.

I ask that the Congress declare that since the unprovoked and dastardly attack by Japan on Sunday, December 7th, 1941, a state of war has existed between the United States and the Japanese Empire.

George stood up and eyed his father and mother. "That pretty much makes my decision. Pop, Mom, I'm driving in to the 'Falls' tomorrow to enlist in the Navy. I'm 22 and prime draft age. I need to beat it while I still have a choice."

Millie leapt up from the sofa. "No, Georgie! No!"

George took his mother in his arms. "I know, Mom ... I know. But I need to do this. I see no other choice."

Gifford gave his oldest son his endorsement as he gathered

his family into a private and intimate circle. They all knelt on the oval woven rug in front of the fireplace. He cleared his throat and began:

"I've always believed a patriot never knows he's a patriot until he fights for his country. I never fought in Europe in the Great War. I served in the army for 13 months in the states in a non-combat unit of the quartermaster corps. The government figured my cattle experience on the Double-B could best be used managing food shipments and handling beef contracts here in the states. That duty, as inglorious as it was, taught me that we all served where we were needed the most. The important thing is we answered the call. If you feel you need to go, then … Georgie … you go, son," Gifford choked out the words. "For now, I think we need to pray."

The Bridger family joined hands and prayed thanking the Lord for their bounty and for their good health. Through Gifford's gentle supplications, they asked a blessing to be upon all of the young men about to give their all … even their lives, in the defense of their country, their liberty, their families, and their God.

Millie stood, turned away with a sob and ran upstairs. Penny was right behind her.

George turned to his father. "I'm sorry, Pop. Am I being selfish?"

"Son, I reckon there are thousands of families having this same discussion with their boys. We'll be fine. Carl and I can run the ranch until you get back. I'll drive you into Great Falls myself. Carl, we need to get back to business as usual for now. I'm afraid there won't be time for flying or working for Mister Temple. You'll be needed at the Double-B more than ever."

Carl, who had sat quietly by watching his family being torn apart, simply nodded in agreement. He wanted to run upstairs to his bedroom and shut the world out, but decided to remain in the room.

On Saturday the 13th of December, Carl stood with his family at the Greyhound Bus terminal in Great Falls as George hugged each of them before boarding the bus for San Diego with nothing but the clothes on his back.

When it was Carl's turn to embrace his brother, the hug came as an act of desperation for him. "I'm afraid for you, George. Promise me you'll come home. ... Please?"

"I promise. So long, little brother. Take care of the family while I'm gone, will you?"

"I will. G'bye George."

Thirty-nine other young prospective sailors and soldiers climbed aboard with George. Carl's heart was heavy as he watched the folding door close and saw George sit in a window seat. He waved to his older brother as the bus pulled away and disappeared from view into the lightly falling snow.

"Mom, Dad, I'm going to drive over to Annie's. I'll be home in time for dinner." Gifford, Millie, and Penny drove back toward Cascade, and Carl left for the Petersen's on Albemarle Drive.

Carl parked his '32 Model-B at the curb in front of the Petersen house. Annie had been waiting for him and came running out of the house and down the walk. An expression of worry etched her face which caused Carl concern.

"Can we go down to the matinee at the Mansfield Theatre, Carl? I need to be alone with you for a little while."

"Sure. I'm ready for something to boost my spirits. Are you alright?" He put the car in gear and pulled away from the curb.

Annie put her hand on his thigh and squeezed ... ignoring his question. "I can't imagine how hard saying good-bye to George was for you. How's your family doing?"

"They're handling things okay, I guess. Look, Annie, I don't know if we can keep seeing each other every Saturday. With gas rationing and food shortages coming, I may not be able to get here except on ranch business."

"I know, Carl. My parents are struggling, too. Money is scarce. They pretend everything is fine, but I can see the look in their faces. They're scared; not just because of the war, either. They're scared of losing the house. I overheard Daddy telling Mom the landlord may need to move back in. I guess he's going to sell the house he's in now."

"Oh, no, Annie. What're your parents going to do?"

"They won't tell me until their decision is made. It's all speculation right now. They'd need to find another house somewhere, of course. Oh, Carl, I'm worried sick." She rested her head on Carl's shoulder.

"The Lady Eve," starring Barbara Stanwyck, Henry Fonda, and Charles Coburn filled the screen at the Mansfield. Only a handful of people were in attendance, and Carl and Annie were alone in the back row. The romantic comedy was lost on them as they sat together, absorbed in their own thoughts. For two hours they gripped each other's hands as if that link between them was the only thing that could keep the demons of an uncertain and fearful future at bay.

After the movie, they walked to the car. A thin layer of snow covered the windshield, and Carl brushed it away with his gloved hand. He climbed in beside Annie and started the engine.

"I have no idea what the movie was about, but it was nice to just sit and turn my brain off for a couple of hours." Carl smiled over at Annie, who smiled back at him and squeezed his hand.

"I know what you mean. Sometimes I think things will never get better. But when I'm with you, I can pretend there's no war, and all of the sadness and worry are pushed away for a little while."

As they pulled up in front of Annie's house, Abe Petersen came out onto the porch and walked over to Carl's car. A scowl line furrowed his brow.

Carl rolled down the window. "Hi, Mister Petersen. I'm glad

to see you again, sir." Carl extended his hand and offered a tentative smile, curious about the cause of Abe's apparent consternation.

"It's always a pleasure to see you, my boy." Petersen shook Carl's hand warmly. "Annie, sweetheart, go in the house while I talk to Carl here for a minute, will you?"

"Sure, Daddy." Annie cast a quizzical glance at Carl and got out of the car. When she disappeared into the house, Abe Petersen climbed into the seat next to Carl.

"Carl, ..." he began. His face grew flushed, and he paused to choke back the well of emotion which threatened to embarrass him.

"Carl, we are about to lose our house. Mrs. Petersen and I will be moving into a one-bedroom apartment within walking distance of the paper. By doing that, I can sell our car and perhaps save some money to find a larger place later ... possibly after the war."

"Sir, I ... "

Abe Petersen cut him off with a raised hand. "Please, let me finish. We're looking for a family to take Annie in. Our first thought was your parents. If we could get Annie a place in Cascade, she might not take the separation so hard. We haven't talked about this with her, yet, of course. So, Carl, will you discuss this with your mother and father tonight? I'll call your father tomorrow. Tell him I can pay him a small sum each month. It won't be much, but it should help."

"Yes, sir. If I know my father, he'll make his decision and will want to call you himself. I'm sorry for your troubles, sir."

Carl's heart ached for the forlorn Abe Petersen as the former *Courier* owner stepped out of the car and lumbered back up the walk to his house; shoulders slumped in defeat. Carl shook his head sorrowfully. *What's this war going to do to us all?* He shivered at the possibilities flooding his mind. He stepped on the starter and pulled away from the curb.

A somber silence blanketed the kitchen when the family sat down to dinner. George's empty chair was reason enough for the thick gloom filling the room as Gifford, Millie, Penny, and Carl prayed over the food.

"... and, Lord, please bless our George. Watch over him and keep him safe, and, if it is thy will, return him safely to us." Millie concluded the prayer with a whispered "... Amen."

They ate without saying a word. After several minutes, Carl broke the silence.

"I spoke to Annie's father earlier."

Gifford put his fork on his plate. "Oh? What about?"

"It was the oddest thing. Before I could walk Annie to the door, Mister Petersen came over to the car and asked Annie to go into the house, and he got in beside me."

"What did he have to say to you, Carl?" Millie asked.

"Mom, Pop, it involves all of us. He asked me to tell you they are losing their house. Their landlord is moving back in. Mister Petersen can only find a one-bedroom apartment near the newspaper where he works. They've fallen on hard times, Mom. So hard, in fact, they need to find a place for Annie. They're selling their car, and Mister Petersen will have to walk to work."

"Oh, those dear, *dear* people." Millie clutched her hands to her breast. "Gifford, we must move Annie in with us. She can take George's room until he comes home."

"What? Now, I don't know, Millie ..."

"No buts about it! It'll be wonderful to move Annie into the house. She can pick up a lot of the slack from George's absence," Millie pressed on. "I happen to know she's a good horseback rider. Why, she took third place in the barrel race the year Carl won the team-roping championship."

"Alright, alright. I know she can ride. How about it son? Can you teach her to milk a cow and feed the chickens?" Gifford managed a smile at Carl.

"Sure, Pop. I can show her the ropes. She'll be paying her own way in no time at all," he said as casually as if talking about hiring another hand. It was all he could do to control his excitement as he thought of the two of them graduating from Cascade High School together. The reality of seeing her every day was more than he could hope for and sparked his fantasies to run amuck in his mind.

"Well, now, let's think about this, son. I thought you'd maybe be a little more excited," Gifford teased and cast a knowing grin toward his youngest boy.

Carl brightened. "Then ... we can do this, Pop?"

His father nodded affirmatively.

"Thanks, Pop! Thanks, Mom!" He stood up from his chair and gave both of his parents a hug.

"On one condition, Carl. If Annie is going to live here, there needs to be some ground rules between the two of you. She's going to be a member of this family. That includes doing her share of the chores, and it most *certainly* means that the two of you will be on your best behavior ... understood?"

"Yes, sir. I promise, Pop."

"I can't wait!" Penny added to the gaiety. "I get to have a sister! Yay!"

For the moment, the earlier gloom lifted from the kitchen and was replaced by an air of joyous anticipation in the hearts of the Bridger clan.

Gifford rose from the dinner table and walked over to the telephone on the side table next to his easy chair. He removed the friends and family list of phone numbers from the drawer and dialed the operator as Carl sat close by.

The next morning, Carl pulled up in front of Annie's house and walked up to the door. He knocked and a moment later, Abe Petersen answered.

"Hello, Mister Petersen."

"Hello, Carl. Please, come in."

Carl followed Annie's father into the living room and sat in the chair that was offered him.

"Carl, I need to convey my deepest gratitude to you and to your parents. This is not easy for us, you understand. As much as our Annabeth cares about you, my boy, this move is a sad occasion for her as well. I need to ask a favor of you."

"Of course, sir, anything," Carl replied.

"I need you to bring her to visit us as often as you can. I need you all to love our Annabeth and care for her as you do your own family. Do you understand?"

"Yes, sir. We will, I promise."

"I believe you will." Abe Petersen patted Carl's shoulder, stood, and walked toward the stairs leading to the bedrooms. "Annie! Come down here, please."

Annie appeared at the top of the stairs with a suitcase in each hand. "Hi, Carl," she said in a whisper.

Carl stood up and approached her. He could see she had been crying. "Hi, Annie." He approached her and took the suitcases from her. "I'll take these out to the car. Do you want me to wait outside?" Carl figured Annie might want a moment to say her good-byes.

"Yes, please."

Five minutes later, Carl watched Annie step out onto the porch. Her parents looked on as their daughter descended the three steps to the sidewalk and passed through the picket gate to Carl's car. She turned and blew a kiss to them, which they returned.

As Carl pulled away from the curb, Annie turned for one more look before the car rounded the corner and passed from view of her home.

Annie sat with her hands in her lap. "This is so hard. At first, all I could think about was being with you, and going to school together. It seemed as if the last few weeks never happened, and all of the sadness was no more than a bad dream."

"I can't imagine. I know how much I love my own family. When George left, I felt like I was losing him … that I would never see him again. But I promise you, Annie, you will see your parents as often as you want. Heck, I'll bet they'll even be invited to the ranch for Thanksgiving, and Christmas and stuff. It'll be okay, Annie."

"I'm sure you're right. I guess I need time to adjust to things, that's all." She slid closer to Carl and rested her head on his right shoulder.

Monday morning came and Carl, Annie, and Penny climbed in Carl's car and drove the mile-and-a-half to the school.

A few of Annie's friends from last year spotted her and swarmed around her with a barrage of questions. She renewed old friendships until the bell rang for first period to begin.

"Take my class schedule, Annie. Do you want to match some of my classes?" he asked.

"Of course … like we did last year." She smiled. The business of getting into school took some of the sting out of her new living situation.

As it turned out, the school counselor assigned her Chemistry and English Literature with Carl, but that was all. Chemistry was the last period of the day, which suited the two just fine.

After school, Carl, Annie, and Penny met at his car.

"I need to drive over to the airport to see Charlie Temple. The last time I saw him was the Friday before the Japs attacked Pearl Harbor and changed everything. Do you mind?"

Penny's eyes grew wide with excitement. "Do you think Mister Temple will let me sit in the airplane, Carl? I think it would be keen."

"Sure, Pen, I think he'll be jake with that." Carl put the car in gear, and they headed toward the airport.

Charlie was at work sweeping the floor of the hangar. The Tiger Moth stood nearby, shiny and looking pretty as ever.

"Hiya, Carl. Long time no see. Hi, Penny." Charlie smiled at Annie. "Say, you're Annie Petersen. Am I right?" Charlie walked up to the three.

Annie nodded and smiled. "I'm glad to finally meet you, Mister Temple." They shook hands.

"I'm Charlie. *Mister* Temple is my father." He smiled warmly.

"I'm sorry I haven't had time to talk to you, Charlie. I just dropped by to tell you I won't be coming to work anymore. My Pop needs me more at the ranch now with George being gone."

"Gone? Did that big brother of yours go and enlist?" Charlie asked, shaking his head.

"Yeah, well, he figured to beat the draft and enlisted in the Navy."

"I understand. Your family needs you at the ranch. As a matter of fact, it looks like I'll be shipping off in a couple of days myself for advanced pilot training at Randolph Field in Texas for fighter pilot training. A new Airmail pilot will be coming in tomorrow, some old guy that's been around a while."

Charlie extended his hand. "Well, Carl, it's been grand working with you. Maybe you'll get your chance in the Army Air Corps one day."

Carl and the girls turned toward the door when Charlie stopped them.

"Hang on just a minute. Carl, can I talk to you alone for a sec?"

Carl asked Annie and Penny to wait in the car and walked over to his friend.

"What's up, Charlie?"

"Say, pal, do remember the long talk we had a while ago about why I never got married?"

"Yes, I remember. How are you feeling about your future now? Has anything changed?"

"Sort of. I just want you to know, whatever destiny is in store for me is going to be fulfilled in the Air Corps. Maybe I only need to get through this war and things will work out later. I hope that's the case. For now, up there is where I belong."

Carl wrapped his arms around Charlie in a hug. "They'll be getting the best darned pilot ever. So long, Charlie. Thanks for everything. Good luck."

–May, 1942–

Winter passed and the wild grasses turned the rolling hills green. Gifford, Carl, Annie, and the three remaining Double-B hands began the drive of the 28,000 head of cattle to summer pasture. Kurt Plunkett and his two younger boys helped. The ranchers in the area had joined together in a co-op to share the work load caused by the absence of available young men due to the draft.

June 3rd greeted the graduating class of 1942 with clear skies and a warm spring day. The school was unable to acquire fabric for the parents to make caps and gowns, so the graduating students wore their Sunday best. The Petersen's had managed bus tickets so they could be in Cascade for their daughter's graduation. They sat next to Gifford and Millie Bridger in folding chairs. The ceremony was held outside on the football/track field. When Annie walked up on the dais to receive her diploma, she waved at her parents and smiled. Carl had already received his diploma and sat with his classmates watching the remaining students take their turn. When Annie waved, he blew a loud whistle and waved back.

The family enjoyed a festive dinner that same evening in honor of the two graduates. The Petersen's stayed the night in Annie's room while Annie shared Penny's room. The next day Annie's parents caught the bus back to Great Falls, and life on the Double-B settled into its normal routine.

That evening, the family gathered around the radio to listen to their favorite radio programs and catch up with the latest news of the war.

"Before we begin, I have a little surprise for everyone." Millie removed an envelope from her apron pocket.

Carl recognized the envelope from the tell-tale "V" mail stamp. "It's about time George wrote. We haven't heard from him in a month."

"It's from George? Yay!" Penny clapped her hands. "Read it, Mom!"

Mille removed the single sheet from the envelope as Gifford sat beside her and snuggled close.

Dear family, she began ...

My ship is being reassigned. Our brief stay in England gave us a much needed rest, but it's back to work for the crew. Of course, I can't tell you where we're headed, security and all that, but I'm doing fine. We're kicking Kraut butts over here.

I miss all of you. I'm glad Annie Petersen is staying with you. I'll bet she's a big help. Carl must be living his favorite dream. How are things at the Double-B? Are you all managing with the rationing?

Oh, guess what? I ran into Nate Plunkett. He's Army Air Corp stationed here. Again, I can't tell you exactly where or what unit he's with. We had some beers together and talked about the good days back in Cascade before the war.

I'll write more later. I love all of you ... you too, little sister "wink".

—George—

The government offered Gifford a contract for 80 percent of the Double-B's cattle at a price that, although slightly more than half of pre-war prices, provided enough for the family to get by. Of even greater benefit, when gas rationing began early in 1942, the Bridgers were given a red "C" sticker which assured them ample gas for operating the business and travel expenses. Carl's little Model-B was issued a "B" sticker which allowed only eight gallons of fuel per week. If he used his ration sparingly, he could drive Annie to Great Falls once each month to visit her parents.

Millie, Penny, and Annie expanded the vegetable garden into a full-fledged "Victory Garden." They were able to take their produce to town and sell it at the new Farmers Market set up in the parking lot of Barkley's grocery store and operated from May through October. As far as food went, the family was self-sufficient. Annie and Penny became excellent "scratch" cooks under the loving tutelage of Millie. Canning of fruits and vegetables became an art form for Annie. She learned to add a variety of spices to her pickles, beans, tomatoes, and other garden vegetables. Her chutney became a staple at the dinner table.

As the nation's industrial complex became fully converted to the war effort, demand for iron, steel, tin, brass, copper, rubber, and nylon stressed available resources. Even butter became a high-demand item for the military. Americans everywhere tightened their belts as war production reached a fever pitch.

While 1942 passed, the war continued, and by the spring of '43, American wartime production was at its peak as was the demand for American workers. The high unemployment and long soup lines of the '30's gave way to the demand for workers. Women, by the tens of thousands, went to work in the factories and steel plants, doing the work of men. They became riveters, electricians, sheet metal mechanics and painters. Women worked in every area of manufacturing previously occupied by men.

Families moved out of rural communities into the cities to

find work. Urban sprawl evolved to provide housing and infrastructure for the unprecedented influx of people. The most productive rural businesses, the farms and ranches, remained stable. Such was the case with the Rocking Double-B.

June, 1944
−Tragedy−

The morning of June 10, 1944 greeted another summer workday on the ranch. At 6:00 a.m. the sun peeked over the hills to the east ... nature's reveille pulling everyone from beneath their comfortable blankets. The day held the promise of hard work. Carl was always up to the task, if less than overjoyed by the prospect.

"Good morning, son. Ready for pancakes and eggs?" Millie had been cooking for 20 minutes. Pancakes, eggs, thick slices of ham, oatmeal, toast and jam were placed on the table.

"Sure am, Mom." He turned around toward the sound of voices. "Mornin', Pop. Hi, Annie."

"Good morning. Can I help with anything, Mother Bridger?"

"No, thank you, Annie. Just sit yourself down to breakfast."

Penny was the last to join the family. She dropped into the chair next to Annie. The two had formed a "sisterly" bond over the last two years.

"Why don't you and Annie go up to the north pasture? Check the fences and see that the cattle are doing okay," Gifford directed.

"Sure thing, Pop."

"Penny, I need you to handle the milking and gather the eggs, then come back and help your mother. Okay?"

"Okay, Daddy." Penny had stepped up to performing more adult tasks since George's absence had left a sizeable gap in the available workforce at the ranch.

At 12:30 p.m. Carl and Annie climbed down from their

horses and let the animals graze nearby while they sat in the shade beneath a 70-year-old cottonwood tree. They finished their work in the north pasture and decided to take a break before returning to the ranch. Annie had packed a simple picnic and spread it out in front of them.

"It's peaceful out here, isn't it, Annie?" Carl leaned back against the tree, plucked a blade of prairie grass and stuck it between his teeth. "I love the Double-B. I love you, Annie." He turned toward her and met her gaze. "I've loved you all my life."

Annie cuddled up close to Carl, and he wrapped his arm around her. She turned her head up to meet his eyes. "I love it here. I love you, too, Bridger."

As they were about to eat their sandwiches, a subtle change in the sound of the nearest group of cattle, about 60 yards away, perked up Carl's ears. The normal lowing had changed pitch; higher and more excited. The herd began to walk in circles, as if looking for an exit … a path of flight.

"Trouble, Annie. Mount up, fast!"

The pair turned their horses toward the herd. They didn't want to spook the cattle by galloping full bore into them. Instead, they cantered along the fence line in the opposite direction of the cattle's movement.

Carl held his hand up and they reined in their horses. He removed the Winchester 30-30 lever-action rifle from its scabbard and stood tall in the saddle.

"There!" He said pointing. "Wolves! Three of them. Dammit!" He leveled the rifle, held his breath and squeezed off a round at the lead wolf. Butch, Carl's roan quarter horse, flinched beneath him at the sound of the rifle report, but stood fast. The alpha-wolf went down. The others stopped. However, two more came through the fence from the tree line. Carl fired twice more and another wolf lay dead.

"Let's ride, Annie. Hiyah!" Butch shot forward. At a full

gallop, Carl charged the remaining wolves. Annie veered off in the direction of the cattle.

The wolves saw him coming and turned toward the fence. Carl reined in his horse and took aim. The bullet struck the trailing wolf behind its left shoulder, and the animal dropped with a yelp, but the wound was not fatal. Carl climbed off Butch and walked over to the fence. The mortally wounded wolf lay 40 feet on the other side of the barbed wire, its tongue lolling out and chest heaving painfully. Carl levered in another round and mercifully put the animal down. He turned to check on Annie.

Annie had aimed her appaloosa toward the cattle and expertly turned them away from the fence on the far side of the pasture about 200 yards away. The cattle were near to the point of stampeding, but she got them under control and managed to slow them down.

Carl whistled and waved for her to join him at the fence line.

"Look here, Annie. They dug underneath the fence. Pop isn't going to like this."

"That was amazing, Carl … and scary. You went after those wolves without any hesitation. I've never seen anything like it."

"Let's go home. We need to tell Pop."

They turned the horses out into the corral and hung up their tack. The two entered the house through the back door and walked from the kitchen toward the living room.

"Hey, Pop, are you ho …" His voice fell silent … the word home stuck in his throat. Annie grabbed his hand and gripped it tightly.

Gifford and Millie Bridger were sitting on the sofa. Millie laid her head on Gifford's shoulder … weeping quietly as her husband held her. Two men, a Navy Lt. Commander and another sailor, stood in front of the couple.

"We're very sorry for your loss Mr. and Mrs. Bridger," the officer spoke softly.

"Thank you, gentlemen. And, thank you for your service." Gifford choked out. With that, the two men departed.

Carl and Annie sat down across from Gifford and Millie.

"It's George, isn't it?" Carl said. Gifford nodded.

Carl stood and walked out the door onto the front porch. Annie followed him.

"Carl ..." Annie started to speak.

He turned toward her and buried his face on her shoulder and released a shuddering sob. His legs started to buckle, and Annie helped him to the swinging love seat. He wept freely in the arms of his Annie as she held him tightly.

Later in the afternoon the family gathered in the living room before dinner. Gifford opened the official report issued by the Navy, of the events surrounding George's death.

"On June 3rd, the U.S.S. Fiske was part of a group of ships patrolling the North Sea. They were engaged by a pack of three German U-boats. The Fiske began laying mines to protect the larger ships: two destroyers, and a cruiser. Two German torpedoes struck the U.S.S. Fiske causing her to sink with all hands. Two U-boats were destroyed by the Fiske's mines and the third escaped."

Penny had been crying steadily since she got home from the grocery, carrying a few items her mother needed, and heard the tragic news. "Daddy, wh ... when will George come home? His body, I mean?"

Gifford dropped the report on the coffee table and lowered his head into his hands, unable to speak.

Millie spoke softly, "Honey, sweetheart, George is with his friends aboard his ship. He won't be coming home,"

The day ended without any mention of Carl and Annie's run-in with the wolves.

A graveside service for George was held by the family at the Cascade City Cemetery. They filled an empty casket with many of George's mementos: his high school letter jacket; ribbons from county and state rodeo events; his favorite boots; and many photographs of George, his family and friends. A headstone read simply:

George Franklin Bridger, USN
Beloved son and brother – still at sea
1920-1944

Carl withdrew into himself over the next few weeks. Even Annie couldn't pull him out of his melancholy. One day in early July, he changed. He went about his ranch work with renewed energy … even fervor.

"Carl, honey, I'm so glad to see you acting like your old self … What's changed?" Annie asked. They sat alone on the swinging love-seat, out of ear shot of the rest of the family.

"I'm enlisting in the Army Air Corp, Annie." He spoke quietly, but firmly.

"Wh … what did you say?"

"Annie, I can't sit here all safe and cozy and pretend the war isn't still going on. George didn't hesitate when he made his decision. I have to do my share. If I don't go, someone else will go in my place. I'm not going to let one more man die for my comfort and safety … I can't!"

Annie fixed her gaze on him. Carl remained silent and stared at the floor. She stood and ran into the house, the screen door banging shut behind her.

An emotional conflict raged inside Carl. *I need help. I love Annie … and my family. What will this do to Mom? Yet, I can't NOT go. Oh, God, help me!* Carl ran to the corral and saddled up Butch. He rode out to the big cottonwood tree where he and Annie had picnicked the day the wolves came.

The meadow grass smelled earthy and fresh as he knelt in the shade beneath the branches. Butch grazed nearby. Carl removed his sweat-stained Stetson and interlaced his fingers. The feelings in his heart were tearing him apart. It was all about loyalties. His father's words about what defines a patriot came to him ... *a man never knows he's a patriot until he fights for his country.* He needed to ask his God what to do. He poured out his supplications, yet not a word was spoken. His was a prayer of the heart. Suddenly, an inexplicable warmth and peace enveloped him, and he knew what he needed to do. The only words he uttered beneath the old tree were ... "Thank you, Lord." What had seemed like minutes had in fact been over three hours. Carl's knees were stiff as he stood. Butch had wandered off, but Carl's whistle brought him running from across the pasture.

When he broke the news to the rest of the family, Millie and Penny begged him to change his mind. Annie sat beside him ... silent, and held his hand while they all went through the painful process of reconciling themselves to the fact that Carl was leaving.

–July 6, 1944–

At the bus terminal, Carl hugged his mom and dad, and they said their good-byes. Penny fought back tears and forced a smile.

"You come back home, big brother. You have to promise."

"I promise. I'll be back before you know it. Take care of Mom and Dad for me?"

"I will." Penny kissed Carl's cheek and joined her parents on a bench.

Carl took Annie aside and removed a small box from his pants pocket.

"Annie, this is for you." He smiled and opened the box. Inside lay a ration token which had been bored out and smoothed to the approximate size of her ring finger.

"Will you wait for me, Annie? Will you, please?" he asked humbly.

"Yes, of course I'll wait for you. I'll be here at the Double-B until you come home. Remember our song, Bridger? ... *Only forever ... if you care to know.*"

"I love you, Annie, only forever." Their bodies shook and tears were shed as the two embraced. Finally, Carl pulled away and held Annie at arm's length. "I WILL come home to you, Annie. The fires of hell can't keep us apart."

Carl boarded the Greyhound bus for Texas. He couldn't help remembering George's departure from this same bus station nearly three years earlier.

Chapter III

September 17, 1944

–Avenger Field AAF Base; Sweetwater, Texas–

Carl completed Primary Flight Training at the 31st Flying Training Wing at the top of his class. The PT-17 he trained in reminded him of the old Tiger Moth. The Kaydet was larger and more powerful, but it had the characteristics and familiarity of the tail-dragger bi-plane he soloed in under the instruction of Charlie Temple.

He felt himself ready to move into twin-engine advanced pilot school, and was not looking forward to nine more weeks of single-engine instruction. Admittedly, during Basic Flight Training, he would be flying larger and more complex aircraft, but that didn't lessen his desire to move on. He was too tall for fighters and found himself channeled into the group of men slated for medium and heavy bomber training.

If I can't train for fighters, it doesn't make sense to spin my wheels another 10 weeks in single-engines, he thought as he lay back on his bunk.

He hadn't written to Annie and the family in a week, and he wanted to take advantage of the opportunity while he had the chance. He opened the drawer in the small nightstand next to his bunk and withdrew his pad and pencil.

> *Annie, my love – I miss you terribly. As busy as we are here, it doesn't lessen the loneliness in my heart. I can't even call you ... security reasons. We finished Primary*

Flight School today. We'll be shipping out tomorrow for Basic FS and another 10 weeks of the same, followed by another 10 weeks of Advance Flight School before I get leave time to come home for a few days. So, it looks like I'll see you all around the end of January next year. Well ... it is what it is, I guess. The Allies are gaining more ground every day in Europe. The war in the Pacific seems to be improving, especially since the Marines secured the islands of Midway.

My Air Corps education so far reads like a textbook, informative but mostly boring and uneventful except for the flying part which I truly love. We're short a few cadets; two because of crashes. No loss of life, but one fellow buried the nose of his plane in the ground during landing, and the aircraft flipped upside down. Another cadet attempted to abort his landing and turned his Stearman into a hanger. The plane was a total loss, but the candidate and instructor made it out with some broken bones and hospital time. Anyway, I ended this phase of my training at the top of my class.

I may not get a chance to fly combat, after all. For now, we continue to train and let the future take care of itself. Give everybody a big hug, will you? I love you, Annie ... only forever – Carl

The answer to his frustration at the snail's pace of his training came the morning of his departure for Maxwell Field. He was ordered in front of his commanding officer, Maj. Bryan Clark.

Carl couldn't imagine what he had done wrong to be called before his CO. His stomach was leap-frogging with worry, and he felt nauseated. He swallowed hard and rapped on the door.

"Enter!" Came the yelled voice on the other side of the door.

Carl stepped into the room and closed the door behind him.

"Sir! Cadet Bridger reporting as ordered, sir!" he announced firmly and held a salute.

"At ease, Bridger. Sit down." The Major opened a manila folder and laid it out on his desk.

"Bridger, your instructor reports that you seem to be wasting your time here. In fact, he feels that it would be in the Army's best interest if you did not move on with your class to Basic Flight School at Maxwell."

Carl was stunned. I'm at the top of my class. This shouldn't be happening. What did I do wrong?

"But ... sir, I ..." he started to protest.

"Settle down, Cadet. You're being promoted to the rank of Sergeant. You will report directly to Blackland Field in San Antonio for Advanced Flight Training in preparation for transition to the B-25 medium bomber. Your performance here is outstanding, Bridger, and I'm not only talking about your demonstrated flying skills. Your personal conduct and military bearing are exemplary on all counts. Your commitment to helping your fellow cadets shows a level of maturity and judgment exhibited by older commissioned officers. Keep up the good work, Bridger. At Blackland you will be challenged to your maximum potential. You will call on every ounce of your resourcefulness and determination to pass this final stage of your training." Smiling, Maj. Clark stood up and extended his hand and smiled. "Now get out of here and pack your bags."

"Yes, sir. Thank you, sir!" Carl wanted to hug the man, but wisely chose to salute his CO instead.

He sat on the side of his bunk next to his packed duffel bag. The bus wouldn't arrive to pick him up for another hour, so he rushed back to the barracks to write a post script to his letter to Annie and his family.

P.S. Annie, I just got some wonderful news! I'm being advanced to Medium Bomber Training and will be

75

leaving in about an hour. I miss you, my love. I never realized how alone and lonely I'd feel being away from you and Mom and Dad and Penny. I miss all of you more than I can find words to describe.

Oh, yes! I'll be seeing you sooner than I thought; in time for Christmas, I hope. The good news is, they promoted me to Sergeant. The three stripes will add to the money I am able to send home. The extra money should ease some of the burden at the ranch.

Only forever (I seem to be saying that a lot ... but I mean it),

— Carl

–Blackland Field, Texas, 73rd Pilot Training Group–

Carl stepped off the olive-green U.S. Army bus after it passed through the main gate at Blackland AAF Base in San Antonio. In mid-October the temperature was a pleasant 74 degrees.

He lowered his duffel bag to the ground and waited for the rest of the men to join him.

The drone of multiple aircraft overhead caught his ear, and Carl turned his eyes skyward, shading them with the palm of his hand. A group of six B-25 Mitchell bombers were stretched out in a line. Descending on their downwind leg prior to landing, the lead '25 banked onto its base leg and turned again until the pilot had the plane's nose lined up with the runway. The remaining five twin-engine Mitchells followed suit until the last plane lined up on final approach as the first to land exited the runway.

"In 10 weeks, that'll be you, Sergeant, if you're lucky."

Carl turned to see a uniformed young man in his late 20s wearing Army Air Force aviator wings over his left shirt pocket and Captain's bars on his collar. Carl immediately snapped to attention and saluted the Captain. The men standing with him did the same.

"I'm Capt. Alan Miller. I am one of the instructors here at the 73rd Pilot Training Group. Behind me is your home for the next 10 weeks. Each floor houses 16 men. 'A' Flight will take the bottom floor. 'B' Flight is on top. As I call your name, pick up your duffels and run, I repeat RUN for the barracks. Inspection is in 30 minutes."

"The following are assigned to 'B' Flight. Sound off as I call your name: Anderson, Barkley, Bidwell, Cannon, Carlson, Calvert, Delshire, Everett, Hogan, Rawlins, Sheldon, Willis, Zoolander." Each man responded with: "Here, Captain."

"Move out, Bravo Flight!" The men ran for the barracks as directed.

"Listen up, Alpha Flight. Sound off when you hear your name."

"Bridger."

"Here, Captain."

"Crabtree."

"Here, Captain."

Fourteen other names were called out, and the men headed for the barracks at a run.

Carl knelt by his footlocker organizing his belongings. The other members of Alpha Flight were also busy settling in when a non-com and an officer entered the barracks.

"Atten-hut!" The First Sergeant called out from the front end of the open-bay barracks.

Immediately, the men stood at the foot of their bunks at rigid attention.

"At ease, gentlemen." Capt. Miller strode to the middle of the room.

"You men are about to enter the last phase of training before being commissioned officers in the United States Army Air Force and receiving your pilot wings. If you are among the fortunate few to meet the requirements, you will be assigned to combat units as pilots certified in the B-25 Medium Bomber. There are 16 of you men. You are to be congratulated for completing Primary and Basic Flight Training. However, you are about to begin the final and most arduous weeks of your education. Many of your fellow cadets failed to make the mark and were moved on to non-pilot training as navigators, flight engineers, bombardiers, and gunners. Others are re-assigned to the regular Army in non-aircraft related roles. Whether you join them is up to you. I will tell you that only the top 20 percent will become B-25 pilots. If you wish to resign as Flight Officer Candidates now, then you may do so without prejudice. You will then be transferred to other Army Air Force units for training in the aforementioned career categories. Questions?"

"Yes, sir. When will we actually get to fly the '25?" Candidate Del Finney asked.

"As soon as you've convinced us you won't accidentally land the plane on top of the Alamo, candidate. Classes begin at 1100 hrs … in 20 minutes. Take charge, First Sergeant."

"Atten-hut!" The senior NCO called as Capt. Miller turned and exited the barracks for the outside stairs leading up to the second floor where he would repeat his instructions to "Bravo" Flight.

All 30 newly arrived candidates filled their seats inside the hot classroom. The windows were opened, and fans had been placed around the room for air circulation. Their training regimen included the completion of 62 hours in communications signal training including voice and Morse code; navigation; aerial photography and identification of enemy aircraft; Navy vessels and troop identification. Basic aircraft maintenance and learning the flight characteristics of the B-25 held more interest than the rest of the class work, but not by far. Mostly their work was hot, boring and repetitive. Each candidate's schedule included 10 hours in the Link trainer which had to be completed before he could see the inside of a real airplane. In all, ground school consisted of a total of

150 hours. At six hours per day, ground school lasted 25 days. The rest of the day, beginning the second week and after simulator training in the Link, the candidates finally took to the air.

On the sixth day of Advanced Flight Training, Carl and the rest of Alpha Flight walked out to the flight line to meet their training aircraft, the Cessna AT-17 Bobcat. The small twin-engine trainer was a tail dragger, with a tail wheel instead of a skid. The tail assembly consisted of a single vertical stabilizer mounted on the horizontal stabilizer. The plane held six passengers.

The candidates trained in two-man teams throughout their instruction. Carl partnered with Del Finney. Del, a year older than Carl, was raised on a dairy farm in western Ohio. He had an easy, relaxed style about him that appealed to Carl. Del enlisted following the death of his best friend the previous June on Utah Beach at Normandy. while his new wife remained in Ohio.

Their Squadron Commander, Maj. Ralph Burrows, a veteran B-25 pilot with 17 missions to his credit, was Carl and Del's instructor.

"Gentlemen, the AT-17 is powered by two Jacobs R-755-9 7-cylinder air-cooled engines producing 245 horsepower each. Cruising speed is 175 mph. Her service ceiling is 22,000 feet. As you know from the classroom, the flight instruments, engine and propeller controls are in a similar position to those in the B-25. This little lady is both light and maneuverable as all get out. Let's get started."

"You're in the left seat, Bridger. Finney, you are in the rumble seat behind us. You'll each get 30 minutes at the controls during which you'll practice basic maneuvers over the training range. You'll each perform one take-off and landing.

"Bridger, I'm just going along for the ride. After 10 hours in the Link you should be familiar with the controls in the AT-17. Talk me through each step just like you're the instructor and I'm the student. Got it?"

"Yes, sir."

"Throttles and mixture full open." Carl began.

"Prime fuel lines." He reached down to the right, grabbed the red fuel-pump lever and pulled it up-and down several times until the fuel lines were primed and pressurized.

"Throttles closed. Mixture at engine shut-off."

"Magnetos on."

"Port ignition switch on."

"Prop rpm at full."

"Throttle advanced one-quarter inch."

"Clear one!" Carl yelled out the open Plexiglas side-screen.

He held the energizer and starter switches down, advancing the mixture simultaneously. The two-bladed propeller started turning to the whine of the starter. The right engine coughed once and started with a blast of white smoke.

He repeated the sequence with the left engine and soon had both engines idling smoothly at 1100 rpm. He waited until the temperature and the oil pressure gauge needles settled into the green normal operating range.

Maj. Burrows radioed the tower.

Blackland tower, Army One Seven Three Seven is ready to taxi to runway three-one for departure to the training area.

Roger, Army One Seven Three Seven. You are number three behind two other aircraft on the taxi way.

Carl advanced the throttles a little, adding slightly more power to the starboard engine to help him turn the plane toward the yellow taxi line. With the nose pointing up, the pilot could not see the ground directly in front of him. He started a weaving path down the taxi way so he could see the tarmac out the wind screen.

While he waited for the planes ahead of him to leave, Carl performed a run-up test on both engines: at various rpm settings, he checked all of the engine instruments to assure himself that all was in order. Then, it was his turn.

Carl lined the AT-17's nose with the center line of the runway. Adding power, the sound of the engines rose in pitch, and the Bobcat began its takeoff roll. The aircraft, with its bamboo-ribbed fabric fuselage, vibrated with the power of the engines and lifted off the ground.

Carl held the plane in a steady climb.

"Sergeant, did you forget your after-take-off checklist?" his instructor asked.

"Huh? Oh, yes sir." Carl brought up the flaps followed by the gear. "Sorry, sir."

"Relax, Bridger, you're doing just fine. They were right about you back at Avenger Field. You seem to have a knack for this. Just keep doing what you're doing."

"Yes, sir." Carl possessed an eidetic memory and could visualize the flight manual in his mind with detailed clarity. He performed a series of turns and maneuvers at various throttle settings before heading back to runway three-one.

On his downwind leg, 1,000 feet above the ground, Carl slowed the plane to 100 knots and lay in one-quarter flaps followed by the landing gear.

He turned onto final approach, lowered the flaps the rest of the way, and reduced his speed to 80 knots, about 92 mph. When the apron of the runway passed beneath the nose, Carl pulled the throttles back to idle. The Bobcat slowed to 50 knots, and the main wheels touched down without a single bounce followed by the tail wheel.

"Taxi to the ramp, Bridger. Well done for a man who skipped 10 weeks of single engines. Sgt. Finney, you're up."

Carl traded places with Del. He felt proud of himself and more confident about his abilities after Maj. Burrow's comment.

Two weeks later, the 19 remaining pilot candidates in Carl's group, gathered in the classroom to be briefed on the next phase of their training: the B-25 Mitchell.

Carl and Del had been paired up again with Maj. Burrows.

The three men approached a B-25B. She was heart-pounding to look at; powerful, deadly, and beautiful as a princess. Carl released a whistle of admiration.

"She's the B-25B model. There is no dorsal gunner's turret … nose gunner and tail gunner positions only. How is she powered, Bridger?"

"Sir, the B-25 is powered by two air-cooled Wright 2600 Double-Cyclone radial engines capable of producing 1,600 horsepower each," Carl replied confidently.

"Finney … armament?

"Sir, when configured for bombing missions, the B-25 carries a payload of 3,600 pounds of bombs. There are three .30-caliber guns located in the nose and waist positions, and one .50-caliber gun in the tail gunner's position." Del Finney concluded.

They performed a pre-flight walk-around of the bomber checking for proper strut height and tire inflation; rudder, aileron, and elevator movement; fuel tank levels which required them to climb on top of the wings; and a dozen or so other items.

"Climb aboard, gentlemen. Bridger, take the left seat. Finney, you're in the right seat. You will switch places when we're back on the ground. The right seat man will handle the radios. Check?"

"Yes, sir. I get the radio." Del confirmed.

Maj. Burrows followed the two pilot candidates up the crew ladder.

"Okay, Bridger. I want you to call out the start-up sequence."

"Yes sir." Carl began:

"Starboard ignition switch on." He turned the paddle switch to the ON position.

"Booster pump on."

"Energizer on for 10 seconds."

"Primer … two seconds." Fuel filled the primer lines.

"Engage!" Carl held down three toggles: energizer, primer, and engager switch with his left hand while his right hand held the mixture knob. The engine caught hold, and he eased the mixture lever forward to the full-rich position."

"Oil pressure at 40 pounds," he called after 30 seconds. Candidate Bridger repeated the sequence for the left engine.

"Well done. Finney, what are the settings for idle power, suction, hydraulic pressure, and brake pressure before taxiing the B-25?"

"Sir, rpm is at 1200, hydraulic pressure is 800 to 1100 psi, brakes at 1000 to 1200 psi, and suction reading is 3.75 to 4.25 inches Hg."

Carl began to taxi the bomber, turning in front of the row of six B-25Cs following him to the end of the runway. He performed an engine run-up, checking the instruments for the correct temperature and pressure readings. Then he pulled the throttles back to idle and set the flaps to 25 percent.

"Finney keyed his mic:

Blackland tower, Army 38-3304 requests permission to depart straight out runway two-four.

Roger, Army 38-3304. You are cleared for departure. Please expedite. There is traffic on downwind.

Carl lined up the B-25's nose wheel on the center line and eased the throttles forward, using the rudders to stay centered on the runway. He increased power to take-off rpm and, when the aircraft reached 50 mph, he eased back on the yoke. The nosed tilted upward slightly. When the speed increased to 100 mph, the bomber lifted off the ground. He raised the landing gear and flaps and held his climb speed at 160 mph before leveling off at 5,000 feet above the surface.

Carl performed brilliantly at the controls of the bomber. Maj. Burrows took him through a series of steep climbs; evasive maneuvers; and in-flight emergencies from engine fires, to engine-out emergency, and precision flying. After a full two hours in the air, it was time to return to the field and switch seats with Del Finney.

December 4, 1944
–Graduation–

"Squadron! Atten-hut!" The First Sergeant bellowed. The 63 cadets of the original 124 candidates, who started Advanced Flight Training with Carl, snapped to attention.

Carl watched the flight instructors including Maj. Ralph Burrows, and the Commanding Officer of the 73rd Pilot Training Group, Col. Marcus Philbright, step onto the raised dais behind the podium and sit down. Philbright stood and addressed the group.

"Be seated, gentlemen"

Carl sat down and nudged Del Finney. "This is the best day ever!"

Del smiled and nodded. "Shhh! He's starting."

Col. Philbright cleared his throat and tapped the microphone to make sure it was "hot".

"It is with pride that I stand before you today. You young officers represent the best that the United States Army Air Force offers in the defense of our nation. Soon, you will enter Transition Training where you will be introduced to your crews. With them, you will complete your final nine weeks of training before being assigned to combat units in Europe and the Pacific Theatres of Operation. As officers, you will command the crews of B-25s, B-26s, B-17s, and B-29s. You must lead your crews. You must be both an instructor and disciplinarian at times. You must possess a clear, uncompromising vision of your mission and be able to communicate it to your crews with clarity and confidence. It is to you whom they will turn for leadership, and you must stand ready … ever prepared to do your job. Now, as we call your name, please step up on the dais to receive your commission as 2nd Lieutenants and your pilot wings."

Carl and the other graduates understood that they would have their new brass bars pinned to their collars, so they all removed their stripes prior to the ceremony. One by one, the candidates stood before their instructors who pinned on their gold 2nd Lieutenant bars and silver pilot wings. Carl's excitement was palpable. He was 12 years-old again and standing in the center of the arena with his 1st place trophy before a cheering crowd. How proud and happy he was that day. His turn came, and he stepped in front of Maj. Burrows. Carl trembled as his instructor pinned on the bars and wings of a new Army Air Force pilot. He remembered the James Stewart news clip on Movietone News when he and Annie attended a matinee movie, and he grinned with joy. Following a salute, the new officer returned to his seat. There was no time for further fanfare. The latest class of pilots was dismissed.

The newly commissioned officers sat on folding steel chairs in a hangar on the flight line awaiting their briefing and written orders. The Training Group's 1st Sergeant entered, stood at attention and belted out, "Atten-hut!" All of the men rose to their feet as Maj. Burrows entered the hangar, followed by another non-com carrying a large box. The man placed the box on a table in front of the senior officer and stepped back.

"I'm sure you men are anxious to learn about your next assignment, so I'll make this short. Your instructors, including myself, attend briefings every two to three days with the Group Commander, Col. Philbright. During those briefings, we review each candidate's performance including a complete assessment of your individual strengths and weaknesses. Your decision-making ability, performance at the controls, military bearing, and self-discipline as well as your studies in the classroom are all scrutinized and become part of your performance evaluation. Your interactions with each other help us identify stand-out qualities of leadership. Finally, we assign you accordingly to the best possible transition training based on the aforementioned items. As Col. Philbright mentioned, some of you will be transitioning into heavy bomber training, the B-24s, '17s, and '29s. Others will train with your crews in the B-25s and '26s. A few of you will transition into transport aircraft such as the C-54, and C-47, while others will be assigned as co-pilots to sharpen your skills for eventual aircraft command. Whatever your orders are, gentlemen, you are expected to comport yourselves in the best traditions of the United States Army Air Corp. As I call out your names, please step forward to receive your orders."

Carl sat on his empty footlocker with his packed duffel bag at his feet. His mattress was rolled up at the head of his bunk. The manila envelope containing his orders lay on his lap. He took a deep breath to calm his racing heart and broke the seal on the envelope.

"Second Lt. Carl G. Bridger is directed to report to the 311th Bombardment Group at Columbia Army Air Base, North Carolina on or before December 17, 1944 for B-25 transition and crew-replacement training for the 345th Bombardment Group, Philippine Islands." Carl read through the rest of the documents and returned them to the envelope.

"B-25s. YES!" he shouted.

"Wow! Early Christmas present, Bridger?" Del Finney sat down on the foot locker across from Carl.

"Yep! Just what I hoped for. What about you, Del?"

"The heavies. B-17 transition with the 385th Bomb Group, 2nd Air Force at Great Falls."

"Did you say Great Falls?" Carl's ears perked up with a sudden compelling interest in Del's plans.

"Yeah. Say, that's near your ranch isn't it?"

"Yes it is. When do you fly out, Del?"

"If I want to turn down leave time with my family, I can leave on a C-54 in two-and-a-half hours, but I'm going to see if there's something leaving for Ohio. Hey, Bridger, are you thinking …?

"I sure am, partner. Let's get down to base ops and see what we can work out." The two men picked up their duffels and caught a jeep to the Base Operations Center.

"Yes sir, I can get you on a C-54 at 1700 hrs for Lockbourne. That's near Columbus, Ohio" the corporal said from behind his desk.

"That's fine, Corporal. Put me on the manifest." Del Finney winked at Carl. "I think this is going to work, buddy."

"I'll just need to see your orders, sir. I have to confirm routing to your next base before I can change the manifest. I'll need your orders as well, Lt. Bridger."

Carl handed the man his orders.

"Give me a moment while I look these over, please sirs." The corporal carried both sets of orders into another room where all of the Air Transport Service Departures, arrivals and scheduling took place. A couple of phone calls later he returned to the two anxious officers.

"Sirs, the transportation itinerary of your orders is being re-typed as we speak. They should be ready in a few minutes. You just need to get your CO to sign off, and you're both good to go."

Carl smiled at the man. "Thank you, corporal."

A little more than an hour after leaving the Base Operations Center, Carl stood at the flight line waiting to board the C-54 for the 1,600-mile flight to Great Falls.

At 2400 hrs, Montana time, the Army Air Transport Command C-54 touched down at Great Falls Army Air Base.

Carl descended the stairs of the plane to the tarmac and immediately pulled the collar of his coat up to cover his ears. It was snowing and cold.

Stamping the snow from his shoes, he entered the door to the Base Operations reception office. A pudgy NCO in his forties sat at a gray steel desk. His uniform shirt with the six stripes of a Master Sergeant was clearly tailored for a much thinner man. The buttons on his too-small shirt strained to the point of popping off. His tie hung askew under his collar, and he appeared to have slept in his uniform. His name tag bore the word "Blysdale." A cigarette smoldered in a much-used tobacco-stained ash tray. He held a report of some kind which hid his face from view. Carl noted that the non-com seemed more than a little engaged in the document.

The sergeant put the paper down, and a photo of a shapely woman's leg slid from beneath it. Carl simply smiled.

"What can I do ya for, Lieutenant?" The man took a final drag on his Lucky Strike and ground it out in the ash tray. Proper military protocol did not make the top of Blysdale's list of priorities. A simple "sir" and an attempt to sit more erect would have improved his image, as would a fresh shirt and neatly knotted tie.

Carl raised his eyebrow in a chagrinned expression, but decided not to school the senior NCO in military etiquette.

"I'm just in from Waco, Texas, on a short leave to visit my family in Cascade. Is there any way I could check out a vehicle from the motor pool? I 'm sure you can understand how anxious I am to get home."

The burley non-com's face turned red, and he released an uproariously full-bodied chain of "hardy-har-hars."

"Lieutenant, it's darned near 2430 hrs. There ain't nobody at the motor pool with the authority to give you a car. We don't exactly run a taxi service here ... sir."

"Okay, okay. I get it, Sergeant. Can I at least use your telephone?"

"Help yourself." The man turned back to his literature.

Carl needed a ride to the ranch and remembered that

Annie's parents lived on Albemarle Street in Great Falls. *Maybe Annie's dad will pick me up,* he thought. He dialed information, but before the operator could answer, he placed the receiver back on the hook. *They don't own a car,* he remembered.

"Sergeant, is there any transportation at all … a bus … something that can get me to Cascade tonight?"

"I'll tell you what, Lieutenant. After my shift I usually like to hit the chow hall for some 'shit-on-a-shingle' with eggs and coffee before I hit the sack. I believe I might just need to run an errand to Cascade before I eat. So, when my tardy replacement gets here, I'll play taxi driver. There's a sweet little Chevy outside … motor pool issue. They let me and the graveyard crew use it to run around in; official business, you understand."

A door slammed shut, and a gust of cold air blew into the room. "Hey, Bo, sorry I'm late. Darned shuttle bus is runnin' late tonight." T/Sgt. Tad Bell was the opposite of his senior NCO counterpart. He was fit looking to the point of looking like Atlas holding the world on his shoulder. Ramrod straight, his uniform neatly creased, and his shoes polished to a sheen, he could be the model in the Army dress code manual. Small wonder that he wore rubbers, which he removed and placed side-by-side against the desk. When he saw Carl, he snapped to attention. "I beg your pardon sir. I didn't see you standing there." Carl respected the man's attention to his appearance and decorum.

"As you were, Sergeant. Ready to go, Sgt. Blysdale?" Carl led the way out into the snow. The car, a military 1939 Chevy 4-door Deluxe sedan painted green with white stars on both of the front doors, stood at the side of the fenced-in building.

"Get in and start her up, Sergeant, while I brush off some of this snow." Three minutes later they were headed toward the main gate.

An MP at the gate waved them to a stop.

"Morning, Sergeant, Lieutenant. A little late to be out, isn't it?"

"Yep, the Lieutenant and I are headed to Cascade to pick up a man who got himself stranded. Thought I'd do him a favor and get him back to the base. Cascade is no place to try to find a room at this hour." Blysdale lied with a smile.

"Roger that, Sergeant. Keep an eye out for icy roads. It's treacherous out there." The sentry waved them through.

Ten minutes later, the snow stopped, and a bright, full moon lit up the road ahead in a fluorescent glow. Stars popped out of the sky like diamonds on black velvet.

Carl needed to break the silence. He cleared his throat. "Where do you call home, sergeant?"

"Little Rock, Arkansas."

"Married?" ... silence. "Kids?"

"Nope. Figured anyone dumb enough to marry me would be better off if she didn't."

"I see. Well ... you been in the Army a while?"

"Fourteen years."

"Since '30, eh? How is it that you decided on the army as a career?"

"Depression. I was a mechanic back in Little Rock ... all set up to buy my own shop when the economy went belly up. I lost my job, and, well, the rest is history. Sir, if it's all the same to you, I don't feel much like chattin'."

"Okay, ... sorry." Carl sat back and listened to the crunch of the tires on the hard snow-pack. The heater warmed the Chevy's interior, and his eyes grew heavy.

"We're here, Lieutenant. Where do you want to go?"

Carl's eyes snapped open to the red glow of the Bailey Hotel sign flashing brightly against the night sky. A lone incandescent street lamp illuminated the corner of the building.

"There's a white fence with a log cross-bar entrance to the Double-B Ranch just ahead on the right. You can drop me off there. I'll walk the rest of the way.

Sgt. Blysdale pulled over to the side of the road, and Carl climbed out into the cold, crisp night. His breath sent forth a cloud of vapor as he thanked the sergeant. Blysdale and his Chevy turned around and headed back up the two-lane highway toward the air base.

Carl slung the strap of the duffel bag over his shoulder and started up the drive toward the main house; each footfall crunched in the fresh snow. With every step he took his heart pounded with anticipation. His mind flooded with a thousand memories of walking up this same dirt road with school books in his hand. He recalled all of the bone-tiring chores that he often grudgingly performed and which seemed now as sweet as honey on his mom's oven-hot bread. He knew that Annie would be there, and his pace quickened.

He checked his wristwatch; *1:30 a.m., I don't want to wake them.* He ran his fingers along the eve above the front porch roof and found the spare key tucked beneath an overhanging shingle. He eased open the screen door and winced as it squeaked on its hinges. He inserted the key in the front door. It turned with a *click*, and he slowly opened it. The creaking of the solid pine door was barely audible.

Carl held his breath as he gently closed the door behind him. He removed his shoes and tip-toed to the sofa in the living room. He stripped off his uniform, draped his jacket and pants neatly over his father's easy chair, and sat on the sofa. Embers from the fire, which earlier warmed the house, still glowed behind the grate. Carl decided to bring up the fire with a few sticks of kindling. He replaced the screen in front of the fire and lay down on the sofa. He pulled over him the sofa throw his mother had knitted and lay for a few moments gazing at the rhythmic dance of orange flames until his eyes grew heavy. He drifted into a peaceful sleep.

At 6:00 a.m. Millie came downstairs to warm up the kitchen and start breakfast. First on the agenda … stoke up the fire in the fireplace.

When she entered the living room from the kitchen her eye caught the pile of clothes draped over Gifford's easy chair. It took a moment to register on her mind, and then she turned around to see Carl sound asleep on the sofa. Her hand went to her mouth to stifle the squeal of delight which threatened to leap from her throat. Turning, she hurried stealthily up the stairs to the bedrooms and awakened the family. Five minutes later, they all crept down the stairs: first Millie, followed by Gifford, Annie, and Penny.

Carl remained asleep as Millie knelt beside him and brushed his hair out of his eyes with one hand. Carl's eyes opened to the smiling countenance of his mother.

"Welcome home, Carl!" Everyone cheered in unison. Annie stood back while Penny embraced her brother.

"Oh, Carl, I'm so happy. Welcome home!"

"Hi ya, kiddo. It's good to be home. Hi, everybody. Wow! Little sister, you're growing into a beautiful young woman."

Carl's eyes fell on Annie standing at the foot of the stairs. He practically ran to her ... his blanket falling to the floor. He neither noticed nor cared that he was in his skivvies.

"Annie. Oh, my love. My Annie ... my Annie!"

"Carl, my darling. You're home. Hold me closer. I've missed you so!" Annie sobbed with joy.

Gifford's turn came to welcome his son home. He walked over to Carl and placed a hand on his back.

"Welcome home, son. We've missed you around here." His voice trembled, and his eyes glistened with love for his youngest son. "Nice underwear, by the way, but why don't you get yourself upstairs and put on your working duds. Cows need milking and eggs need gathering." He winked and smiled.

"Yes, sir!" Carl had never thought of every day ranch chores with such unbridled joy as he did that morning.

"I'll help you, Carl." Annie picked up Carl's uniform and headed upstairs.

He wrapped the quilt around himself and followed Annie.

Annie sat on the bed while Carl washed up and shaved. He changed into jeans, a wool Pendleton shirt, and boots. "These feel good, Annie … really good."

Annie stood, walked over to him and threw her arms around him. "I've missed you so much. How long before you leave again?"

"I catch a train out of the Falls in 10 days. But, I don't even want to think about that. I just want to be home with you and the family. I need to not think about the Air Corp. I want to milk cows, gather eggs, and pitch manure … and be with you." They both laughed.

The family sat at the breakfast table. Millie cooked up a stack of pancakes, eggs, bacon, and toast with homemade raspberry preserves, milk and coffee.

"I'd like to say grace." Gifford said as he extended his hands. Everyone joined hands and bowed their heads.

"Father in heaven, we thank thee for returning our boy, Carl, to us, and we ask a special blessing from thee to protect him as he fights for our freedoms. Watch over him in the sky with thine angels until he returns to us. We thank thee now for thy bounty this day. Bless this food that it may nourish us and strengthen us … in the name of our Savior, Jesus Christ. Amen."

"Dig in, everyone. There's work to do."

His father's traditional morning greeting warmed Carl's heart, and he smiled inwardly. I'm home at last, he thought, as he stuffed a forkful of pancakes dripping with butter and syrup into his mouth.

"Son, we need a tree for Christmas. Why don't you kids hitch up the sleigh and go do that. I'd be much obliged." Gifford winked at Millie who understood that her husband was trying to provide some alone time for Carl and Annie.

"Sure, Pop. You up for a little sleigh ride, Annie?"

"Yes. I'd like that. Let me finish the breakfast cleanup, first."

"Penny can help with that, Annie. Now, you two just run along." Millie laughed and scooted them out of the kitchen with a sweep of her broom.

"Hold it steady, Annie. A couple more cuts with the saw, and it'll come down." Carl knelt in the snow and applied the bow-saw to the cut he had started. In a few seconds, the tree started to lean and then gave-way. He cut the base of the tree so it would rest in the two-by-four wooden stand that was waiting at home. "Let's load it on the sleigh and head back."

"Let's not go back just yet, Carl. Can we just cuddle in the sleigh and enjoy the quiet for a few minutes?" Annie said in a sub-dued tone of voice.

Carl sensed that something was troubling her. "Sure, Annie. Is everything alright?"

"Yes, everything is fine. It's just that ...well ..."

"Something's troubling you, Annie. What is it?" His heart sank with worry. Oh no ... here it comes. He worried himself into a near panic, and could hardly breathe. *Has she found someone else?*

"It's my dad. He's sick, Carl; some kind of lung disease. They called it emphysema. Sometimes he can hardly breathe." Annie dropped her face into the palms of her hand. "I don't know what to do. Should I go home and try to help my mother with him? I've thought about it, but I just don't know."

"Oh, Annie, I ... I don't know what to say. What a relief!"

Annie cast a perplexed expression at him. "What did you say?"

"... I ... I mean, it could be worse, you know, like cancer or something, right? What are the doctors doing for him?"

She seemed only somewhat placated by his quick-thinking recovery. "There's nothing they can do. It's progressive. He stopped smoking cigarettes because they seem to make it worse.

He's still working at the paper, but I don't know for how much longer. What should I do, Carl?"

"Do Mom and Pop know about this? They may be able to help."

"No, not yet. My father is a proud man. If he thought anyone was trying to give him any charity, it …"

Carl interrupted. "Nothing my folks might do would be charity, Annie. You know that. But, when the time comes that your father can't work to support his family, it should fall upon those who love you and your parents to ease the burden. My family would insist on it."

Annie nodded. "You're right, Carl. There's time, yet. We'll tell your parents, but maybe not until it gets to the point where my folks need the help."

Then, Annie's countenance changed back to that of her usual effervescent and upbeat self. "Before we go home, there's one question I need for you to answer … honestly." She turned Carl's face toward hers with the palm of her hand and engaged his eyes with a stern penetrating gaze, betrayed only slightly by a whimsical upturn of the corners of her mouth.

"Okay, what is it you want to know?" Carl asked. His earlier worry was replaced by curiosity.

"A minute ago, when you said *what a relief*, what did you really mean?"

"Okay, I'll tell you. Since I've been gone, I've gotten to know quite a few fellows. Some of them are married, and a lot of them have girls back home … like me. I know a few of the guys who got 'Dear John' letters from them. Almost every time it's because their girlfriends found someone else, or fell out of love. They all say they're sorry and want to remain friends. I don't know, maybe they're afraid their guy will get killed or something. I … well, I was afraid I might be losing you." Carl released a pent-up breath and waited.

Annie giggled and immediately raised her hand to stifle an outright laugh.

This time, it was Carl's turn to be perplexed "Well, I certainly didn't expect that."

"I'm not laughing at you, my darling. If you only knew how committed I am to you … to us. Oh, Carl, if you understood my heart, and my love for you, you would know that I would never write a 'Dear John' letter. Hold me, Carl. Hold me and promise me you'll come back home when the war is over."

That evening, everyone joined in for the annual Christmas tree decorating. Penny no longer had to be held by her father to place the angel atop the tree. This time she used a ladder. With the tree all decorated, Gifford plugged in the lights.

"Merry Christmas, everyone!" He stood before his family. "I know Christmas won't be here for 20 more days, but I'll tell you what I think we should do: I want us to celebrate Christmas with Carl before he leaves. Son, you said you're scheduled to leave on the 15th. I propose we move up our Christmas Eve dinner to Sunday the 10th, exactly two weeks earlier this year. Annie, we'll have your parents here, too. It'll be swell! What do you think?"

"Oh I think that's a keen idea, Daddy. Let's!" Penny said jubilantly.

"It'll be wonderful, Gifford! We can find a nice turkey down at Barkley's. Annie, you need to call your parents. The pantry and root cellar are stocked with plenty of food to make for a fine Christmas dinner." Millie was in her family-event-planning state of mind. "Penny, you and I need to press the good table linens. This will be such fun!"

The following Saturday, the day before the Christmas dinner, Carl found himself alone in the kitchen drinking a steaming cup of coffee laced with cinnamon, cream and a spoonful of sugar … the brew was a rare treat. Penny was upstairs reading, and Gifford and Annie were driving to the "Falls" to pick up the Petersens. It had been decided to invite Annie's parents to spend the weekend at the ranch.

"Carl, honey, I want to show you something. Stay right where you are. I'll be right back."

A couple of minutes later Millie returned to the kitchen. She carried a small box and handed it to Carl. "Open it."

He lifted the hinged top exposing the black velvet lining. Resting in a slot sat a yellow gold band with a single round diamond of approximately one-third carat. The band itself was of a delicate, finely crafted filigree pattern of interwoven strands of gold.

"This is beautiful, Mom. Where did it come from?

"This ring was given to me by my mother, Fiona. You never met her, but you remember your grandfather, Neil Gilbride, don't you?"

"Yes. You said that Grandma Fiona passed when you were about Penny's age. Grandpa never remarried. He brought you and Uncle Garrett to Montana so he could work on the railroad."

"That's right. Well, Papa gave me Mama's ring before he passed when you were barely 10 years old. He said I should pass it on to one of my children when I felt the time was right. Honey, nobody but your father knows about this ring. I want to pass it on to you, but only if you intend to use it for the right reason. It's been sitting in that box for far too many years. It belongs on the finger of a special young woman." Millie closed her hands over Carl's. "Would I be presumptuous if I were to say that I wish with all my heart for Annie to be that person?"

Carl's eyes brimmed with tears of love for his mother. He wiped his eyes on the sleeve of his shirt. "Grandma Fiona's ring … gosh, Mom!" He pulled his mother into a warm embrace.

Two hours later, Gifford's car pulled up to the main house of the Double-B. He climbed out and opened the rear passenger door for Minifred Petersen. Abe climbed out of the passenger side front seat.

"Darned kind of you to make the drive all the way into the Falls, Giff."

"Happy to do it, Abe. With Carl home, we decided to have an early Christmas before he has to leave again. It wouldn't be complete without Annie's parents to share in the joy." Gifford slapped his hand on Abe Petersen's shoulder. "C'mon inside out of the cold."

Gifford entered the house first, through the back door into the kitchen. "Hey, everybody, look who's here," Gifford announced as if it were a surprise to all including him.

Annie and her parents entered the living room. "Daddy, why don't you sit by the fire? Can I get you and Mom some hot wassail?"

"That would be lovely, Annie, and you stop worrying about me now. I'm fine"

Annie took their coats and hung them on a coat rack by the front door.

Sunday night saw the table set with Millie's fine pressed linens and best china. Annie, her mother, and Penny joined Millie in the preparation of the food while Gifford, Abe Petersen, and Carl sat in the living room talking about the war, the economy, and politics.

Carl rose from his chair and walked into the kitchen. "Hi, Annie, can I talk to you for a minute?"

"Sure, Carl." She removed her apron and wiped her hands on a dish towel. "What is it, Carl?"

"Let's go out on the porch. We'd better grab our coats." Carl helped Annie into her woolen winter coat, and the two of them removed the canvas tarp from the porch swing.

"How's your father doing?" His voice had a slight nervous

tremor to it.

"Daddy? Oh, he's having one of his good days. But, somehow I think there might be something else on your mind other than Daddy's health." Annie smiled nervously.

"You're right." Carl slid from the swing and knelt in front of Annie. He was practically overcome by his love for her. For a moment fear threatened to render him speechless. He met her eyes and took her hands in his.

"Oh, Carl ..." She squeaked out, and her left hand flew up to silence a gasp of delight.

"Uh, Annie. I'll be needing that hand." He removed the box from his coat pocket and opened it in front of her. "Annabeth Petersen. With all of the love that any man has ever felt for any woman since this world was created, I ask you before God and his angels ... will you marry me?"

"Yes, Carl. YES, I'LL MARRY YOU!" She dropped to her knees and threw her arms around his neck. "Yes! Yes! Yes! I love you. I think I have always loved you. Oh, my darling."

They embraced with a warm, lingering kiss.

"Give me your hand, Annie." Carl removed the bored-out ration token from her left hand and slid his Grandma Fiona's ring onto her finger. It fit as though it was made for Annie.

"Oh, Carl it's gorgeous!"

They both stood, and Annie fell into his arms. He held her as tightly as he dared and whispered. "Only forever ... if you care to know. I love you, Annie."

"I know you do, and that makes me the luckiest girl in Montana. I love you, Carl Bridger." She stood on her toes and kissed him again in time for the screen door to open. Millie stepped onto the porch.

Upon seeing the ring on Annie's finger, Millie clutched both hands to her breast. "Oh, please let me make the announcement! Don't let anyone see the ring. Dinner's ready, and we're all ready to sit down."

Millie tapped her empty water glass and stood from her seat next to Gifford. "Everybody, your attention, please! Fill your glasses from the pitcher for a grand announcement! It's only grape juice, but it will do." Millie giggled at her own humor.

Everyone complied. Carl held Annie's hand under the table cloth.

"Alright, then. Abe and Minnie, I first want to thank you for letting Annie stay with us. She blesses us all in countless ways, and we love her as a member of our own family." She cleared her throat and continued. "It is my complete joy to announce that, 20 minutes ago, Carl and Annie became engaged to be married!" Millie clapped her hands and smiled broadly. Applause broke out all around the table. Annie waved her left hand with a flourish to show off her ring.

"Oh, it's beautiful, darling! Where did you come by such an elegant ring, Carl?" Minnie Petersen asked.

"Mom gave it to us. It was my grandmother's"

"Well it's truly beautiful, isn't it, Abe?"

"It certainly is. This calls for a toast, doesn't it?" Abe deferred to Millie who remained standing.

"So, then, a toast. Raise your glasses to Carl and Annie! We wish you a long, happy, and fruitful marriage," Millie concluded.

"Here, here!" Gifford exclaimed. They all drank to the happy couple.

Abe stood and spoke in a soft voice. "I don't wish to delay this sumptuous dinner, but I should like to add Minnie's and my endorsement of Annie and Carl's engagement. You all have been a true blessing to our family during this time of need. Carl, we consider you the son we never had. Gifford … Millie, we are honored to be counted as your friends. Carl, Annie … congratulations to you both, and God bless everyone." Abe coughed twice and sat down.

"Speech!" Gifford called out. "Make it short, though, the food won't wait forever."

Carl cleared his throat and spoke from his seat. "Everyone here has played a significant role in shaping the content of my heart. This ranch is … well, it's where my roots are. Mom, Dad, Little Sis, you all … and George … are my family, but now, my family includes three more wonderful people: Abe and Minnie, and the love of my life who is the keeper of my heart … Annie. I am a very lucky man to be blessed with a new, second, family. I love you all."

Annie wiped the tears from her eyes. "I could never imagine being happier than I am at this moment. Now let's eat before I start to cry again." Everyone enjoyed a good laugh, and Christmas dinner of 1944 began.

The morning of Saturday, December 16th, Carl descended the stairs from his bedroom and entered the kitchen. He dropped his duffel bag to the floor and walked over to Millie.

"Mom, it seems as though most of our conversations happened in this room. I'll always remember you just this way … wearing your apron and cooking or baking. The smells of bacon and coffee, eggs and toast …" Carl breathed in deeply. "This is what I want to come back to."

Millie smiled up at Carl and placed her hand on the silver wings on his chest. "This is your dream, isn't it, son? This is what you've wanted ever since the airmail plane flew into town." She turned away from him and dabbed at her face with her apron. "Sit down. Let's have one more Double-B breakfast together before you run off to … *work*."

"Mom, I know what you're thinking." Carl knew her as well as he knew any of his family. "I will come back to you and the Double-B, I promise. I won't let you go through what you went through with George."

"Can I join in the hug fest?" Annie entered the kitchen. "Mmm … smells good. Can I help, Mother Bridger?"

"No. You sit by your fiancé, and let me cook for you. Go on, now, sit yourself down, young lady."

Annie sat next to Carl and reached beneath the table for his hand. Their eyes met and Carl mouthed a silent *I love you*.

Twenty minutes later, Annie pulled the flatbed truck with the Double-B logo emblazoned on the doors onto the main highway and turned toward Great Falls.

"Annie, Pop could have driven me to the Falls. You didn't need to." It pained him to watch Annie fight back the sadness in her heart.

"I'd rather drive. It'll give me something to do on the way back to the ranch." Annie choked back an involuntary sob. "I'm sorry. I don't want to make leaving any harder on you than I know it already is."

"It's alright, Annie. I'm glad to have these last few minutes alone with you. I love you. I feel as though we're already married. We're a family, my love. Tell me that you feel the same?"

"Oh yes, Carl. Only, promise that you will come home to me and make it official, okay? Can I tell you something else?" An unexpected blush flushed her cheeks. "I can't wait for you to make love to me, Carl. I want to start our own family."

"Yes, me, too."

Chapter IV

–December 16, 1944–

The sun shone clear and in the blue sky dotted with only a few scattered clouds as Carl climbed out of the truck. His breath instantly froze in the air glistening from the sunlight on the frozen crystals suspended in front of his face. With loneliness weighing heavily on his heart, he pulled up the collar of his coat and waited until Annie's tail lights disappeared. He headed off toward the two-story brick building that served as the passenger terminal for the Great Northern Railroad.

He entered the terminal, and a thin 50ish looking man in a bow tie lifted his eyes from behind the barred window. "May I help you, Lieutenant?"

"Yes, I have a ticket waiting for me for the 10 p.m. Pullman to Chicago. Here are my orders." Carl slid the papers under the bars. The ticket agent looked them over and passed them, with the ticket, back to Carl.

"There you go. The train will board in about 10 minutes ... track one."

Carl placed his duffel bag on the floor next to him and sat on one of the wooden benches in the passenger terminal.

A 2nd Class Petty Officer, wearing the crossed hammers of a machinist mate above his chevrons, sat next to Carl on the end of the bench and opened a newspaper.

"Where you headed, Petty Officer?" Carl asked.

"Norfolk, sir." the young seaman replied in a near whisper. "You?"

"Columbia, North Carolina. I'm picking up my crew, then flying back to San Francisco."

"Um … well, good luck, sir." The Petty Officer went back to his newspaper. *Well, so much for passing time with idle conversation.* Carl thought. He slouched back on the bench and pulled the bill of his cap over his eyes.

A voice echoed through the terminal announcing Carl's train:

> *Attention, please. Great Northern announces the boarding of the Zephyr for Bismarck, St. Paul, Chicago, with connections to Cincinnati, Raleigh, Columbia and Charleston. Now boarding at Track One. All aboard!*

Carl picked up his bag and walked to the boarding gate. He showed the conductor his ticket and stepped up into one of the coaches. He was able to reserve an opened-section birth, so he could enjoy some privacy and an opportunity to get some sleep. He sat facing forward across from the currently empty rear-facing padded bench. He decided to lift the seat-back up and suspended it above him. The result formed two narrow sleeping births. He found a couple of pillows beneath the lower birth, placed them against the wall and removed his shoes. He stretched out and settled in for the long trip to Chicago.

The train pulled into Chicago 20 hours later, and Carl transferred to the Atlantic Coast Line Railroad for the trip to Columbia. The ACL departure forced a two-hour layover in Chicago. Carl spent the time reading up on the war news in *The Chicago Sun Times* and drinking coffee at a diner a half-block from the train terminal.

He settled into a coach aboard the ACL train and decided to write a letter to Annie and the family. He pulled his duffel bag down from the overhead rack and unfastened the heavy canvas flaps. He touched something unfamiliar as he reached inside and withdrew an envelope with a single word, "Carl", in Annie's handwriting. His heart jumped. With joyful anticipation he returned the bag to the overhead storage space and opened the envelope.

> *My beloved Carl,*
>
> *You will be leaving in the morning. I can't sleep, so I'm sitting in the kitchen writing to you.*
>
> *Oh, my love, my heart is so full! At times I feel it must burst with joy! These past few days with you, Christmas, my family ... our engagement! ... all of it, has been a dream come true.*
>
> *I wondered if you would ever get around to asking me to marry you. I thought I might end up having to do the proposing. When you finally did, on the porch that day, it was all I could do to not run into the house and shout out my happiness.*
>
> *Carl, I know you will come home to me, and I need for you to believe that I will be right here waiting for you to walk through the door. My love for you is more than a fleeting thing; it is truly for only forever. As a matter of fact, and I think I can tell you this now, I was in love with you even before our junior prom.*
>
> *The hardest part will be the waiting. Will the war end next week, next year ... maybe longer? The only thing I know for sure is that you and I are bound together by something that is meant to last for time and eternity.*
>
> *I'll need to find a way to sneak this into your bag without you knowing it. Hee ... hee.*
>
> *With all my love,   Annie*

The void in his heart was gone; in its place was joy. Carl felt certain that his joy, and the memory of the past 10 days, would sustain him. He recalled the advice his instructor at Advanced Pilot Training gave him and thought ... *Maj. Burrows was wrong. Compartmentalizing by forcing out the world lying beyond the horrors of war is not the means of survival for me. That very world is my imperative for survival.* "That's why I'm going to fight ... for my family, for our peace, and for our future," he said aloud, as if Annie could hear him.

–Columbia Army Air Force Base–

Carl entered the passenger terminal at Columbia, South Carolina and spotted an Army corporal. Hoping that the soldier could point the way to some sort of transportation to the Air Base, he approached the man.

Upon seeing Carl, the corporal snapped a brisk salute. "Sir, are you headed for the Base?"

"Yes I am, Corporal. Are you my transportation?"

"A bus is waiting right outside, Lieutenant. If you don't mind waiting, I'm supposed to pick up a couple more guys scheduled to arrive from Philly on the next train. We'll shove off in about 15 minutes."

"Fine by me, Corporal, I'll just make myself comfortable on the bus." Carl walked outside and saw the bus parked in a military-reserved space across the street.

Only four men already occupied the padded bench seats in the bus, and Carl spotted an empty one. He dropped his duffel bag on the seat and sat down next to it.

"Hi ya, Lieutenant ... Alex Chekov." The voice came from a black-haired, blue-eyed, handsome young man wearing gold second lieutenant bars on his shoulders and pilot wings over his left jacket pocket. He reached back from the seat in front of Carl and offered a hand, which Carl shook vigorously.

"Nice to meet you. Do you mind if I join you?" asked Alex.

"Not at all." Carl moved his duffel bag to an empty seat

across the aisle and scooted over to make room. "Carl Bridger. You here for replacement crew training?"

"Yep. I trained for a left-seat slot in the heavies, '17s and '24s. When it came time to move on to a Replacement Training Unit, all of the left-seat slots were filled. I had the choice of right-seat in the heavies, or to apply for the '25s. The only spot available on the Mitchells was for a co-pilot as well. I wanted fighters, but I guess the '25 is as close as I'll get. So, here I am. How about you, Carl? What's your assignment?"

"B-25s ... left-seat. I'm looking to pick up a crew, and then we'll see what happens from there. It's too bad you didn't get a crew of your own."

Alex chuckled. "True that. Timing and the needs of the Army, I guess. I could have stayed on as an instructor, but the idea of training other guys only to stay back and watch them get the combat assignments didn't appeal to me, so I opted for co-pilot. I figure there's a pretty good chance of getting my own aircraft eventually, so I'm willing to wait it out."

Carl liked the affable Alex Chekov. He wanted to know more about the man who traded a comfy stateside pilot instructor position for a second-seat slot on a combat crew.

"I think I'd have done the same thing in your situation, Alex. Hey, maybe we'll be assigned to the same outfit."

They talked while the bus took on four more men and drove them to their destination.

Fifteen minutes later, the bus stopped at the sentry station at the main entry to Columbia AAF Combat Training Depot. The MP waved the bus through and they drove to a building marked Headquarters, 311th Bomber Command.

"This is where you get off, fellas. Inside, you will be processed and assigned billeting. Officers go to room 2A, and enlisted men go to room 12A."

Carl and a half-dozen other officers processed in and climbed aboard a six-ton truck which drove them to their billets in a compound of a dozen Quonset huts housing 16 men each.

That afternoon, Maj. Ralph Schneck, Operations Officer of the 329th Bomb Squadron, 311th Bombardment Group, stood before the assembled officers and enlisted men of the Replacement Training Unit at 1400 hrs.

"Good afternoon, gentlemen. Welcome to the 329th Bombardment Squadron. You men are all graduates of specialized training as pilots, navigators, gunners, bombardiers, engineers and radio operators. Your successful completion of hundreds of hours of training in each specialized field has brought you here for the final phase of your training before being assigned to combat units in the European, Mediterranean, and Pacific Theatres of Operation. The mission of the 329th over the next few weeks is to train you as individual aircraft crew members to become finely tuned combat crews in the B-25 Mitchell. You will be exposed to and trained for every conceivable in-flight emergency that may ... no, *will* ... occur in combat. You will come to know your crew mates as well as you know your own name. You will learn to trust each other's skill as if your life depends on it, because your lives *will* depend on it. You will become as one in the skies, a tour de force to be feared by the enemy.

"The following men will report to classroom 2B in Building G at 1600 hrs to meet your crews and for briefing for the week's activities: Andrews, Archer, Baldwin, Belkin, Belknap, Bishop, Bridger, Butcher, Chekov, Collins, Dinkleman, Ellsworth, Frisby, Hall, Mallard, McMurphy, O'Brian, Pallin, Radley, Roswell, Salinger, Smyth, Tyson, Zabriskie."

At 1600 hrs, Carl and his classmates assembled in room 2B. A Major and four Captains sat at the head of the room facing the men. The Major stood.

"Good afternoon, gentlemen. I'm Maj. Rick Wilkins. You men will be meeting your crew members at 0600 hrs tomorrow. For now, pilots and co-pilots will be assigned to your individual aircraft. Following this meeting you and your instructor ... myself or one of the officers seated to my left, will adjourn to the flight line where you will be introduced to your aircraft. The 329th consists of 12 crews to train and only 13 operational aircraft to do the job. Two other '25s are undergoing repairs caused by inattention and mistakes made by previous aircrews. Don't let those kinds of things happen to you, gentlemen. If you don't end up killing yourself, you may find yourself ferrying supplies for the Air Transport Command behind the controls of a C-47."

There are 24 of you ... 12 right-seat and 12 left-seat. I will read the Pilots in Command first and your assigned aircraft, followed by your co-pilots."

Maj. Wilkins opened a manila folder and began. As he read the names, Carl hoped his would be called as a pilot instead of a co-pilot. One name after another was called, alphabetically, and Carl's name was third in line. He didn't realize he had been holding his breath until his name was called. He exhaled the pent-up air in his lungs. *Yes! I'm the pilot of my own B-25!* The realization sent a thrill up his spine. He sat a little taller in his seat as he listened for the name of his co-pilot.

"And now, pilots, here are your assigned co-pilots. As your names are called, please find a seat next to your pilot in command. Tyson you're with Andrews in 329-04. Roswell, you're with Radley in 329-02. Chekov, you're with Bridger in 329-06."

Yes! Carl was delighted when he heard Alex' named called as his second in command.

Tail number 329-06 was a "C" model of the B-25. Built in Kansas City in 1941, she had seen action over Europe. In 1943, after 51 missions, the Army sent her back to the states as a training aircraft assigned to the 111th Bomber Command at Columbia AAFB.

Carl climbed up the crew-access ladder into the belly of the

'25. She had been patched up and returned to operational condition. Signs of damage from shrapnel and bullets were apparent in spite of the repairs and a fresh coat of paint. A spot of rust colored paint on the dorsal turret frame caught Carl's attention. He scraped a finger nail over it and spread the powdery substance between his thumb and forefinger. A chill ran through him ...*blood!* He moved into the left seat of 329-06. Alex Chekov sat next to him. Their instructor, Capt. Sid Shapiro, sat in the navigator's seat behind them. His job would be to evaluate the performance of each member of the crew in a variety of exercises designed to test knowledge, reaction under pressure, performance, decision making, and adaptation under unique circumstances. Additionally, officer/pilots would be evaluated on their command and leadership skills.

"Gentlemen you're sitting in a B-25 C. Get to know her. Tomorrow you will meet your crew and learn every flight characteristic of this aircraft, its armament, power plant, avionics ... everything. You will need to know enough about every crew member's job to evaluate each man's performance over the next couple of weeks. While you are evaluating them, I will be evaluating you. Understood?"

"Understood, sir." Carl's excitement was palpable. A flood of thoughts passed through his mind: *Can I do this? ... Will I be able to lead my crew? ... Will they trust me?* Learning to fly the '25 was easy. He felt himself capable as a pilot. Commanding a group of men ... bringing them and himself together as a team of brothers? That was the real challenge.

–First Flight–

After a week of ground school studying the specific characteristics of the Mitchell B-25 as they applied to each crew member, crews were chosen and assigned to their aircraft.

Late in the afternoon on the eve of their first training mission, Carl and Alex Chekov sat with their crew in the mess hall to discuss the next day's activity, their first flight in 329-06.

Carl's nerves were stretched as tight as a drum. He hadn't been this anxious since the day he asked Annie to marry him. He began his first briefing with a crew that had never been together on a flight until that day. He swallowed, cleared his throat, and was about to begin when Alex bent close and whispered:

"We're all as nervous as you are, Carl." Alex lightly patted Carl's shoulder.

Carl nodded, smiled gratefully, and began:

"Men, this is our first mission as a crew. We've been studying and working together for a week now. We have sat side-by-side on many occasions in those classrooms. We all passed our qualifying examinations and demonstrated a high level of skill in our individual Military Operational Specialties. As your commanding officers, Lt. Chekov and I know that you men are the cream of the crop. We are fortunate that you were assigned as our crew. You will prove us right starting today. Our mission tomorrow consists of formation flying with 11 other planes in flights of three. We will go through several heading, speed, and altitude changes before flying out over Lake Murray for the second phase of the mission ... low-level bombing using low-yield 100-pound bombs armed with spotter charges. Our target is located on one of the islands in Lake Murray. Lt. Ortiz, you will guide us to the intercept point where I will turn the aircraft over to you for the bomb run. The bombing will be from 500 feet elevation at 240 mph. I'll leave it to you to get updates on visibility and winds. We will make two runs at the target dropping one sleeve of eight bombs on each pass. We will adhere to strict radio protocol during the mission. Don't be surprised if our observer, Capt. Janus, throws us a curve-ball or two. Do your jobs, and we'll be fine. Any questions?"

The tail gunner, Sgt. Harold Osborne, raised his hand. "Lt. Bridger, since you didn't mention anything about a live-fire exercise, I assume we will not be loading live ammo?"

"That's a good question, Sergeant. You will supervise the loading of live ammo by the ground crew just as if this were the real thing. The same goes for the rest of you: Carthage, Rushton, you will make sure your gunnery positions are loaded and ready. Understood?"

"Yes sir!" The other two men answered in unison.

The crew was driven to the flight line and disembarked in front of their aircraft. The crew ladder was extended, and three ground crew members stood by to remove the chocks.

A technical sergeant in overalls walked over to Carl and saluted. "Sir, I'm your Crew Chief, T/Sgt. Cal Danvers, at your service. She's ready to go, Lieutenant. Have a nice flight."

"Thank you, Sergeant. We'll take good care of her." Carl climbed up the crew ladder and worked his way forward to the flight deck. The rest of the crew followed, and Sgt. Rushton brought up the ladder and secured the hatch.

"Okay, Alex, let's go through the engine-start sequence."

As Carl called out each step, Alex toggled the appropriate switches. When the right engine was primed and ready, Carl slid back the Plexiglas side wind screen.

"Turning one!" Carl called out.

Alex held down the ignition switch, energizer, and primer. The three-bladed propeller on the starboard engine started to turn to the whine of the servos. With a loud cough of white smoke, the engine took hold, and Carl adjusted the mixture and throttle. With the right engine idling smoothly at 1200 rpm, they repeated the process with the left engine.

"Turning two!" The starboard Wright 2600-13 fired up and settled into idle.

Three ground crew men removed the chocks and stood clear. Sgt. Danvers saluted. Carl returned the salute and slid closed the side wind screen.

"Crew check. Call in." Carl announced over the intercom.

"Navigator. Check."

"Comm. Check."

"Engineer. Check."

"Tail gunner. Check."

Carl and Alex allowed the engines to warm up and then performed an engine run-up test. A check of the engine instruments: oil temperature and pressure, manifold temperature, rpm, and carburetor temperature revealed that both engines were operating within normal parameters. Satisfied, Carl began his taxi roll toward the end of the runway behind four other '25s. He had to hold short until it was his turn. "Let's do this just like we were taught, Alex … no sweat." Carl's racing heart belied his outward calm.

"Give me 25 percent flaps, Alex."

"Flaps at one-quarter, Carl." Alex confirmed. The whine of the servos told him the flaps were lowered.

Carl advanced the throttles gradually until the aircraft began its takeoff roll. With the nose wheel firmly tracking the white painted center line of the runway, he eased the throttles to the full forward position in a single, smooth motion. He pulled back on the yoke to lessen the strain on the nose wheel and, when his airspeed reached 100 mph, the nose lifted off followed by the main gear. At 300 feet above ground level, Carl ordered the gear and flaps up. He leveled the nose and allowed his airspeed to climb to 140 mph before beginning his climb-out.

Maj. Schneck commanded the 12-plane group. The four flights of three flew in diamond formation. Carl was chosen as "Bravo" Flight Leader. His responsibility was to get the three planes in his flight lined up behind and to the left of the Group Leader.

"Comm, give me the inter-plane frequency." Carl wanted to be able to hear the other pilots and receive instructions from the Group Leader. Alex tapped Carl's shoulder and pointed outside. His wing man in 329-04 was too far away from his right wing.

Bravo Flight Leader to Three Two Niner Zero Four, you're too far off my right wing. Bring it in a little closer. No more than 10 feet.

Carl waited for Lt. Duane Andrews to ease his Mitchell closer.

Good formation position. Hold it steady.

Carl's affirmation of the other pilot's skill demonstrated good, natural leadership ability. His observer jotted in his log. Carl hoped he was adding another positive note to his record.

The formation flew for 20 minutes at 10,000 feet and then climbed to 18,000 feet.

"Pilot to crew. Put on your O-2 masks, boys, we're climbing to one-eight-thousand." Carl put on his A-8B oxygen mask and tightened the straps.

After two hours of flying in a variety of formation patterns at various altitudes, the Group Leader ordered each flight to proceed to its pre-determined rendezvous with the targets for bombing practice.

Six islands on Lake Murray were used for low and medium-altitude bombing practice. Carl's flight of three planes turned toward Bomb Island along the west coast of the 41-mile-long manmade lake. Carl turned onto the heading given him by Phil Ortiz and dropped to 500 feet above the surface.

Carl keyed his mic on the inter-plane frequency.

Flight Leader to flight, move into line-abreast formation. Watch for three buildings atop a hill at the south end of the island. Andrews and Bishop, you take the two outer buildings. I'll take the middle one. We'll make two passes dropping one sleeve of bombs on each run. Drop on my command. Over.

Left wing. Roger. Duane Andrews replied.

Right wing. Roger. Lt. Ed Bishop confirmed.

"Ortiz, arm your bombs and open the doors."

"Bomb-bay doors are opened and ready, Skipper." the bombardier/navigator confirmed.

"Copy that. Holding speed at 240 mph. Altitude 500 feet. Coming up on the IP now. It's all yours, Phil." Carl held the bomber steady.

"I have the aircraft, Skipper." Phil had his eye glued to the telescope of the Norden bombsight which was tied to the autopilot. He was able to make minute adjustments to vector the bomber to the target.

When he acquired a good target picture, Ortiz gave the command, "Bombs away!"

Eight M38A2 100-pound bombs dropped from each of the three '25s flying side-by-side in line-abreast formation. As each practice bomb struck the ground, a 28-gauge shotgun shell fired igniting a charge of black powder producing a visible puff of white smoke allowing the pilot to observe the accuracy of the drop.

"We were a little short on the first drop, Phil. Turning now for our second pass. I think we caught a little head wind just before we dropped." Carl banked the plane left and flew downwind for his second pass.

"I'm reading wind at zero-six knots from three-one-two degrees, Skipper. I'm adjusting the Norden." The bombardier turned a couple of knobs on the Norden bombsight. "Okay, Skipper, set your in-bound course for three-one-two degrees. I'm all set."

"Roger. Turning to three-one-two degrees. Speed at 240. Altitude at 500 feet. Auto-pilot is on. Coming up on the IP. The plane is yours, Phil."

The other two planes of "Bravo" flight maintained tight formation. They had been listening to Carl all the while, so they were in good position without their auto-pilots, relying on visually maintaining position within 10 feet of Carl's lead position.

"Bombs away!" came the order, and all three planes released their second sleeve of eight bombs.

This time all bombs struck well inside the target radius, and the three structures received a number of direct hits. Carl climbed and banked left in time to look down on a blanket of white smoke covering the target zone.

Capt. Janus keyed his mic and announced to all three planes, "Excellent, Bravo Flight! You managed to take out the three primary targets. Now, listen up. There is an enemy gun emplacement with anti-aircraft batteries on Spence Misty Island. Lt. Bridger is in command." Janus silenced his mic and handed Carl the aerial recon photos showing the gun positions.

"Bridger, this is a live fire exercise. You must take them out in one pass. It's up to you to decide the attack strategy, but make it fast."

"Roger that, sir."

Carl felt like he did the first time he explained a science project in front of his teacher and 5th grade class. He was scared he might embarrass himself. He knew the material, yet he felt put on the spot. Get used to it Bridger, it's make it or break it time.

"Alex, take the controls. Turn to one-one-five degrees and maintain 500 feet." Carl released the controls to his co-pilot and spread the recon photos out on his lap. A plan formed in his mind, and he passed the recon photos back to his navigator.

Flight Leader to flight, fall into line-abreast formation. When we reach the target, I'll lead the attack. We'll hit the target in staggered-line formation. Andrews, you follow me in on my starboard side, Bishop, you follow Andrews off my port side. The emplacements are close together, so we need to keep a tight line. Acknowledge?

Andrews. Roger.

Bishop. Roger.

Stay with me now. Gunners, charge your weapons.

Bursts of machine gun fire tracers spewed forth from the turrets, nose, and tail of all three aircraft.

Flight Leader to all planes, we're climbing to one thousand five hundred to get a better view."

Carl added power and started a climb. He leveled off at 1500 ft and approached Spence Misty Island. The gun emplacements sat on top of a hill at one end of the island. It wasn't long before they popped into view.

"I see them." Alex Chekov pointed down at the targets.

Flight Leader to flight, target sighted. There are three vehicles parked near the emplacements. Bishop, take them out. Andrews, you're with me. Hit those bunkers! Starting my run now, Carl announced over the inter-plane frequency.

He nosed the '25 down and entered a 45-degree descending bank until the nose of the bomber was lined up with the center of the target. Andrews and Bishop descended behind Carl in staggered-line formation.

Holding his speed at 280 mph, Carl lined up on the center of the gun emplacement and put it in the cross-hairs of his N3-B optical gun-sight mounted on the instrument panel. Dropping his nose, he pushed the red "Guns" button on his control yoke. At the same time, Ortiz squeezed the firing lever of the flexible nose gun. Both AN/M2 machine guns sprayed the target with .50 caliber BMG rounds at a combined rate of 2,400 rounds per minute. Bishop concentrated his fire on the trucks. The three B-25s roared over the target, leaving behind them total devastation.

"Let's head for the base, gentlemen. No need for a second pass. Well done." Capt. Janus slapped Carl and Alex's shoulders.

Flight Leader to flight, nice work. Form up. We're heading back.

The other two planes fell into position off Carl's left and right wings, and Bravo Flight returned to base.

Twenty minutes later, Carl stood with his crew on the tarmac by the nose of their Mitchell. He waited for Capt. Janus to move out of ear-shot.

"Fellas, I have to tell you something. You were all great up there. You made my job a heck of a lot easier. Every time Janus wrote something on that clipboard of his, I was dying to know if it was good or bad. Thanks to you men, I think we impressed the hell out of him."

January 9, 1945
–Combat Assignment–

The next three weeks of intensive training included over 100 hours in the air practicing everything from night-formation flying, high-altitude and low-altitude bombing, strafing, skip bombing, aerial gunnery, a variety of in-flight emergency response protocols and countless other scenarios experienced by combat crews in every theater of operation. Lt. Carl Bridger and his crew were honed to a fine edge. The time had come to put their skills to the test in combat in the Pacific Theater of Operations.

Carl sat with his crew at a table in the mess hall. He placed a manila envelope in front of himself.

"Well, fellas, this is it. Tomorrow, we leave for our first combat assignment. We're a crew now ... a real crew. I feel like we're brothers, in a way. We've spent hundreds of hours in the sky and sometimes in boring classrooms learning strategies and protocols for every conceivable situation we might find ourselves in except one ... the real thing. Now, it's time to step into the breach."

"Hey, Skipper!" S/Sgt. Harold Osborne interrupted. "Are you going to be making a lot of speeches like this? I may want to request another crew." Everyone, including Carl, cracked up over Osborne's quick-witted retort. Carl approved of Harry's assumed role as team cheerleader with his humor and natural affability.

"Okay ... okay. Point taken. To the orders then." Carl unfastened the tabs and withdrew the orders. He scanned the pertinent details. "Our assignment is the 345th Bombardment Group, 5th Air

Force, Tacloban, Leyte, Philippines."

The men at the table smiled and congratulated each other with back slaps and handshakes aplenty.

"Okay, settle down, fellas. We leave tomorrow for Inglewood to pick up a brand new Mitchell. We'll ferry her to Wheeler for refueling. From there, we're off to Queensland, Australia, for refitting of our aircraft into a strafing and low-level bomber using "Pappy" Gunn's modifications. We'll have much more fire power. It should be one heck of a ride. Your individual orders are in these envelopes. Pack for the tropics. Leave all your winter gear behind. We go by rail to Oklahoma, and by C-54 from there to California. Questions?"

"Can we tell our families, Skipper?" The question came from Sgt. Don Rushton.

"You can only tell them that you're being reassigned ... not where or any unit information. Once we're in theater, we will be able to write home from the Philippines. Secrecy and censorship are alive and well, gentlemen. The bus leaves for the train station at 0600 hrs tomorrow morning." He passed an envelope to each man. "Until tomorrow morning then, you're dismissed."

Later, in the Officers' Club, Carl and Alex sat nursing mugs of beer.

"Alex, I need to ask you a question."

"Sure, Carl. What's on your mind?

"I'm afraid I might let you and the guys down when we get into a fight. I need the men to trust us ... you and me. Do you think I have the right stuff to lead?"

"In a word ... yes. You're our Skipper. The guys trust you. I see it in their eyes, and I hear them say as much when they think no one's listening. Now, let me ask you a question. Am I the man you want in the right seat?"

Carl grinned broadly and nodded his head. "Without a doubt, Alex. I can't think of a better man to have next to me. You're very good at what you do. The guys like you and so do I."

–The Double B Ranch–

Penny stomped the snow from her boots and entered the kitchen through the back door. She had stopped at the mail box on her way home from school and thumbed through the envelopes until she found one addressed in Carl's handwriting. She sprinted to the main house. "I'm home, Mom. I've got mail. We got a letter from Carl!"

"Go get Annie. She's out in the barn."

Less than two minutes later, Annie and Penny ran into the kitchen. Millie handed her the letter.

It had been two weeks since Carl's last letter. He said then that they would be finishing up their training in a couple of weeks.

Annie's cheeks were flushed from the hard work and cold, January air. Her eyes fell on the letter.

Gifford Bridger and family
Double-B Ranch, RR 22
Cascade, Montana

"Can I read it now?" She asked.

"Yes, Annie. Go ahead ... open it." Millie smiled. "Gifford can read it later."

"Okay." Annie ran a knife along the sealed flap of the envelope and withdrew the letter.

Inside she found two folded sheets of paper. One had "Annie" written on it. She put that one in the pocket of her wool-lined denim jacket. She unfolded the other one and began reading:

Dear Family,

Well, training is over, and it looks like we'll be moving out tomorrow. Of course, we're not allowed to say to where. It will be a couple of weeks before I can write again because things will be getting pretty busy.

Mom, Dad, I love you. You have raised me well, and

I promise you that I will do everything in my power to honor the name of Bridger in all that I do.

Mom, when I come home, I want a thick slice of your homemade bread with butter and honey. I miss sitting in the kitchen and talking to you with all of the wonderful baking smells filling the room.

Little sister, I miss your laughter, your energy and even your stubborn bull-headed determination. I miss your loving heart ... I miss you, Penny. Take care of Mom and Dad.

Thank you, Dad, for being my anchor. Thank you for teaching me about honor and courage, hard work and gratitude.

I am so thankful for you all, and I love you. I'll write when I can.

– Love, Carl

Annie folded the letter and placed it back in the envelope. She handed it to Millie.

"Excuse me. I think I'll go to my room for a minute or two." Annie climbed upstairs as she rubbed away a tear with the palm of her hand. She loved hearing from Carl, but each letter made her want him there, with her, even more. The loneliness she felt for the want of him was almost more than she could bear.

She sat on the bed and opened her letter.

Annie, my love,

I miss you. I love you more than words can say. I hope you are doing well. I worry about your parents. How is your Dad? Is he getting any worse? I know that you miss them and would like to be with them. Is he still working at the paper?

Hey, I'll bet ranch work has built a lot of muscle

and turned you into a real cowgirl, eh? Annie, I dream of the day we can ride the Double-B together. Remember the day we chased those wolves that almost stampeded the cattle? You were amazing!

I will come home to you, my love. We will have our own life together and our own family, just as soon as this war is over.

I love you ... only forever,   – Carl

Annie folded the letter and opened the top drawer of the dresser. She removed a shoe box, and placed the letter on top of a stack of a dozen others Carl had written since he left almost four months ago. His 10 days at home in December marked a highlight of that time. She closed her eyes and pictured Carl kneeling in front of her on the porch ... and the proposal.

"Yes, my darling ... only forever," she said.

Chapter V

January 10, 1945

–Inglewood, California–

The Sunshine Plant in Inglewood, California, located at the intersection of Imperial Highway and Aviation Way, used to be the Los Angeles Municipal Airport. It became the west coast North American Aviation assembly plant for the B-25 Mitchell and the P-51 Mustang during the war.

Carl Bridger and his crew sat in a small room facing a wall full of schematics and other engineering visual aids of the B-25. A suited man entered the room, removed his jacket and hung it over a chair.

"Gentlemen, my name is George Welch. I'm an engineer and test pilot here at North American. I'm here to get you acquainted with your brand new Mitchell B-25J. She is tail number 44-3021. She was built at North American's Fairfax plant in August last year. She is one of the last 'J' models to be built. The Js slated for shipment to the Pacific Operations Area are sent here for fuel tank modification. We've added an extra fuel tank for the long flight. I'll go over the specs with you now."

Welch described, in detail, the bomb-bay-mounted 350-gallon fuel tank, the routing of the fuel lines and the location of the fuel transfer switches.

"For weight considerations, her armament is not installed.

The guns will be installed on your arrival in Townsville, near Sydney. She is powered by the two Wright 2600-13 engines. Additional armament will include two to four nose guns operated by the pilot and one flexible .50 cal operated by the navigator/bombardier. He will charge all of them. Other changes include two forward-facing fixed .50 cals in blisters on both sides as well as two flexible .50 caliber AN/M2 machine guns mounted in the tail. Other than the additional fuel tank and armament additions, the 25J is identical to the 'C' model you're used to. Unless you have any questions, transportation is waiting to take you out to the flight line. You will be in a flight of two Js headed for Townsville, so you won't be alone."

Carl, Alex Chekov, Phil Ortiz, Zed Carthage, Don Rushton, and Harry Osborne stood before their olive-drab B-25 Mitchell. The Army Air Force white chevron with a white star on a blue background and a red circle in the center of the star, shone bright and proud. Carl whistled appreciatively. "She's as beautiful as a bride on her wedding day."

"Hey, Lieutenant, we need a picture of all of us. Hold on a second." Zed Carthage opened his duffel bag, reached in and withdrew a Kodak Brownie camera. "Hey, you!" He called to a noncom who stood on a ladder working on the plane next to theirs. "Can you come over here, Sergeant?"

The mechanic climbed down from his ladder and approached the crew. "Yeah, what can I for you, sir?"

"I'd appreciate it very much if you would take a snapshot of us in front of our new '25."

Zed's winning smile sealed the deal, and the mechanic took the Brownie, stepped back a few paces and called out, "Say cheese!"

Twenty minutes later, 44-3021 stood with engines idling waiting for clearance to enter the active runway.

Army Four Four Three Zero Two One, you are cleared to depart runway two-five.

Roger, tower.

Carl had logged hundreds of hours in training for this moment. The B-25 Mitchell was as much a part of him as the old Tiger Moth had become back home. *Charlie, who would have thought I'd be here flying a bomber with my own crew? I'd give anything to know where you are right now.*

"Give me one-quarter flaps, Alex."

Alex pushed the flap lever down to the first indent. "Flaps at one-quarter, Skipper."

Carl taxied the bomber onto the runway and eased the throttles forward. He never tired of the drone and rising pitch of the powerful engines as they accelerated the plane down the runway. At 60 mph he pushed the levers all the way forward to maximum takeoff power, and the needle on the rpm indicator shot up to 2,400. The '25 roared down the runway with the dawn of a new morning rising behind her. A light drizzle spattered the tarmac, and the wheels threw up sprays of water. Carl lifted her nose off the runway, and the main gear lifted off the ground five seconds later.

"Sgt. Rushton, put me on the comm to the other aircraft." Other than a few exchanged words over the radio back at Inglewood before takeoff, he knew nothing about the pilot in the 2nd plane except his name which was written in his mission orders. The lead '25 flew slightly above and ahead off his right wing. Carl had a good view of Capt. Tracy McMahon sitting in the cockpit.

Three Zero Two One to Three Zero One Three, do you copy? Over.

Three Zero One Three. Good formation position, Lt. Bridger. How're you men doing over there?

Top of the world, Captain. We never got to meet you and your crew back at Inglewood ... thought I might put you on the radio to my crew and get to know you fellas. Over.

What crew? There's only three of us: me, a rookie

replacement pilot and a Flight Engineer. I'm headed back in-theater after leave and rehab from a bit of shrapnel. Lt. Clegg here is going to the 345th Bomb Group. T/Sgt. Ramsey, too. I'm going back to the 42nd Bomb Group. Over.

"Rushton, put us all on the com." Carl's communications specialist flipped a switch, and everyone could hear the conversation.

Captain I've patched my crew into the comm so they can hear us. I guess you, being the senior officer in our little flight, will be the Flight Leader. Do you have any orders for us, sir?

Yes, but stop 'sir'-ing me, Carl. We're all in the same boat here ... so to speak. Name's Tracy. Call me T-bird or just "T" will be fine. We have 2,000 miles and about seven hours of staring at the sky and the ocean.

Roger, Cap ... er, T-bird. Where do you call home?

Oshkosh, Wisconsin. You?

Cascade, Montana. The rest of these guys are from all over the place. Rather than jam up the radio with everyone trying to talk over the top of each other, I'd like to give each of my crew a chance to say "howdy".

"Alex, you're up."

Alex Chekov, sir. I'm from Queens, New York. My parents came over from Russia in 1918.

"Ortiz, you're next, then Sgt. Rushton, Sgt. Carthage, and Sgt. Osborne." Carl let each man take his turn and listened carefully as, one by one, his crew talked about their families, home town ... whatever was important to them.

Twenty minutes later, Capt. McMahon ended the "getting-to-know-you" conversation.

Let's give the radio a rest guys. We'll talk again soon. I suggest you two fellas in the cockpit switch-off flying and sleeping. McMahon, out.

"Pilot to crew ... status check. Tail turret?"

"Snug as a bug back here, sir."

"Engineer?"

"All systems in the green, sir."

"Radio?"

"Everything's quiet, sir... nothing but routine chatter on the main frequencies and ship-to-ship channels."

"Ortiz?"

"We're on course, sir. No weather ahead. Clear sailing for now, Skipper."

"Roger. Rushton, pass out the box lunches. Stow your trash when you're done, fellas. No smoking, either. You're sitting next to 350 gallons of high octane aviation gas."

The mess hall at Inglewood always put together boxed meals for the ferry pilots: sandwiches, cookies, and an apple. Don Rushton handed a couple to Carl and Alex and passed around one each to the rest of the crew. Carl thought the in-flight meals tasted a heck of a lot better than field rations.

"Alex, take the controls. I'm going to get some shut-eye. Wake me in two hours."

"Roger that, Skipper. Sweet dreams." Alex checked the course and heading, engine instruments and fuel levels. Since they were flying in formation, they couldn't engage the autopilot. Capt. McMahon, being the lead pilot, set the autopilot on 44-3013, but Carl and Alex had to fly hands-on to maintain formation.

Twenty minutes later Carl's head lay back snoozing with the bill of his service cap shading his eyes from the glare of the sun. Alex piloted 44-3021 through calm skies.

"Tail turret to pilot. I see something below, sir ... a small ship or sub." Sgt. Harry Osborne called over the crew frequency.

"Chekov to tail gunner. Probably nothing at all, Osborne. Rushton, tune your radio to the ship-to ship frequencies and check for chatter."

Thirty seconds later, the radio operator reported back.

"Negative, sir. Everything is quiet."

"Okay, open a hailing frequency."

Sgt. Rushton dialed in the radio. "You're on the air, sir."

Army B-25 to unidentified ship at coordinates north two-six degrees one-eight minutes, west one-three-five degrees five-eight minutes. Do you copy? Over.

Alex waited for a few seconds and repeated the call. Still, he got no response.

"What's going on, Alex?" Carl sat up straight and rubbed the sleep from his eyes.

"Possible vessel in distress, Skipper, or maybe a bogey. She doesn't answer our hail."

"Alright, you handle the controls. Rushton, hail the vessel again." Carl switched his radio to the inter-plane frequency.

Wing to Flight Leader. Do you copy?

Right here, Lieutenant. Over.

We've spotted a vessel, sir. She doesn't respond to our call on standard frequencies. I think she may be in trouble, or worse ... possible bogey. Request permission to go in closer.

Okay, Lieutenant. Make one pass only. We don't have a lot of fuel reserve to play with. I'll orbit up here. Radio in when you confirm the ID of the ship. McMahon, out.

"Pilot to crew, we're dropping down to make a pass at the ship Osborne spotted. Secure everything and buckle-in. Bridger, out."

Carl banked hard right and arrowed down in an attack dive, letting his airspeed climb to 280 mph. The bow wake of the ship appeared in front of the wind screen, and he went to mast height to buzz the ship. As he approached, the target took on shape.

"It's a sub. We need to identify her. Ortiz, check the vessel identification manual. I don't think it's one of ours. She's not flying her colors."

"Copy that. I've got the manual out for Japanese ships."

Carl approached abeam the ship to get a good broadside view of the bogey.

"She's a Jap sub, Skipper. A-2 class according to the silhouette in the manual," Phil Ortiz reported.

Carl glanced down at the ship below the tip of his right wing. "Yep. I think you're right." He keyed his mic.

Three Zero Two One to Flight Leader. We have a positive sighting of an A-2 class Jap submarine running on the surface at high speed on a course of roughly one-one-zero degrees.

Get back up here and re-form. Call in the bogey. McMahon, out.

Roger. Turning back now.

Carl decided to fly one more pass over the sub on the way back to the formation. He banked around and came in at mast height.

The first pass of the American B-25 took the crew of Imperial Submarine I-19 by surprise. Capt. Tatsuki Matsuda stood next to the periscope with his binoculars on the plane and ordered the gunners on deck to man the 144 mm anti-aircraft (A-A) gun. When the bomber returned, the Japanese crewmen were ready.

"Wait for my order!" Matsuda commanded.

A moment later, the enemy bomber was in firing range.

"Fire! Fire! Fire!" he yelled.

Alex Chekov sat upright suddenly. "Skipper, they've manned the deck gun!"

Carl pulled up sharply, banking hard right as the enemy A-A gun opened fire.

A loud metallic *rat-a-tat-tat* sounded inside the cabin of 44-3021 as several rounds struck the fuselage.

"Holy crap! The fools are shooting at us!" Zed Carthage yelled as a bullet passed through inches from his head.

Carl took the plane up and away from harm's way. "Pilot to crew! Damage report!" he called out. His ringing ears and vision closing in at the sides told him he was on the verge of fainting. *No, no, no, no, Bridger! You can't pass out* ... Breathe! He closed his eyes and breathed deeply, emptying his lungs with each breath. His pounding heart began to slow, and his senses clicked back into focus.

"Ortiz. No damage. I may need a change of skivvies, though." He laughed nervously.

"Engineering is undamaged, Skipper. Cripes, I can't stop shaking!"

"Radio. No damage, Skipper. That was scary."

"Tail gunner. Sure as hell wish I had my guns back here. No damage, sir."

"Listen up, men. We're unharmed. We all got quite a scare, but we're fine. Just get back to work. Pilot, out."

"Take the controls, Alex. I'm going back there to check on the crew." Carl needed to calm his shaking hands and frayed nerves before taking the controls again.

"How're you guys doing ... Phil, Zed?"

"Fine now, Skipper. You?" Phil Ortiz answered.

Carl managed a smile. "That was quite an introduction to the war, eh, fellas? Rushton, good work with the radios."

"Thank you, sir."

"You all did a good job ... kept your heads and stuck to business. Well done." Carl worked his way back to the flight deck.

The two B-25s were closer to Honolulu than they were to Los Angeles, so Carl called in the sighting to 7th Bombardment Group, 7th Air Force on Oahu.

When Capt. McMahon saw Carl forming up on his left wing, he keyed his mic.

Welcome back, Carl. Quite a fun little diversion, wasn't it?

It turned out to be more than a diversion, sir. The Jap sub opened up on us with their deck gun.

What? Is everybody okay? How's the aircraft?

We're all fine, Captain. We took a few holes on our 2nd pass, but we're operational. I don't mind telling you that was scary, though. I really didn't think we would get into combat this soon. My chest is still pounding like a trip-hammer.

Did you say second pass? I told you to make one pass only.

Roger, sir. The sub was in a direct line with our heading back to formation. I figured another pass on our way back wouldn't use any more fuel.

Bridger, need I remind you that you are unarmed? You put yourself and your men in harm's way. If you pulled that stunt on a real mission, your Flight Leader would write you up and you'd likely be severely dressed down by your Group CO.

Yes, sir. I understand. It won't happen again.

It had better not, Carl. The fight you're heading into will be tough enough without the grandstanding. Understood?

Understood, sir.

One good thing... you boys just learned the reality of war. It hits you hard the first time you get shot at by real people with real guns, doesn't it?

Yes, sir ... it sure does.

Carl's trembling hands were finally beginning to settle down.

Four hours later, McMahon called Wheeler AAF Base tower for landing instructions. Carl would follow him in on the approach

"Set flaps one-quarter, Alex, and lower the gear."

Alex executed the command. "Gear down ... flaps at one-quarter."

Carl reduced his airspeed to 130 mph and began his final approach. 44-3013 had turned off onto the taxi way toward the hangar for refueling.

"Check gear down and flaps full."

"Gear down and locked and flaps full, Skipper," Alex responded.

At 120 mph the nose of 44-3021 passed over the apron of the runway, and Carl pulled the throttles all of the way back allowing the aircraft to settle into ground effect. The main wheels squeaked onto the runway followed by the nose wheel.

Army Three Zero Two One, exit the runway as soon as possible. Taxi to parking via Bravo 2 to Alpha 1. Park next to the other B-25 in front of the hangar.

Bravo 2 to Alpha 1, Roger, Carl acknowledged.

Carl and Alex ran through the after-landing checklist, and the crew of 44-3021 climbed down the crew ladder.

"It's good to be back on terra-firma after all of the drama, eh, Skipper?" Harry Osborne quipped.

"That it is, Sergeant ... that it is. Let's find some chow, men. We need to refuel and get out of here. Rushton, find a chow hall for us will you?"

"Yes, sir."

Before Sgt. Rushton left, a six-striped Master Sergeant dressed in oil-stained olive-green fatigues with the name "STARK" stamped above his breast pocket, and puffing clouds of smoke from a well-chewed stogie, sauntered up to them.

"Lieutenant, there's a chow hall behind the hangar. They're

mighty good at makin' chow on demand for flight crews. They'll take good care of your boys. May I have a word with you, sir?"

"Certainly, Sergeant, um … Stark." You guys go ahead and grab some chow. I'll be right along." Carl turned back to the Chief Mechanic of the 321st Depot Repair Squadron. "What did you need to talk to me about, Sergeant?"

The grizzled veteran pulled a stub of smoldering cigar from his mouth. "Your '25 got shot up a bit. How did that happen over friendly waters? … If you don't mind me asking."

"Long story. As it turns out the waters aren't so friendly after all. We spotted a Jap sub. I decided to go in closer to I.D. her, and we got fired on."

The mechanic puffed a cloud of smoke, and moved the stogie to the corner of his mouth. "You need to let me check her for damage before I can sign off on letting her fly. Where are you boys headed?"

"Townsville for refitting ... then on to the 345th at Tacloban. We're with another Mitchell ... that one parked on the ramp." Carl nodded to T-Bird McMahon's plane. "Both aircraft are scheduled to be in Sydney by this time tomorrow."

"I'll need four hours to make sure your hydraulics and fuel systems are operational and didn't get nicked by a round ... same for all the cables. I'll put a crew to work patching the holes." The sergeant puffed on the stub of his cigar, dropped it on the ground and mulched the butt to shreds under his boot. Carl knew the man wasn't asking permission to check out the plane, only for his cooperation. The Sergeant ended the conversation with a surprisingly snappy salute, which Carl returned. He thought of M/Sgt. Blysdale back in Great Falls. *The Army must grow these guys from the same garden,* he mused.

He nodded. "Get to it then, Sergeant. I don't want her to bleed out at 10,000 feet ... wouldn't be fun." Carl stuck out his hand, which the mechanic shook hard with his vice-grip of a hand.

Carl joined his crew, Capt. McMahon and his two men, in the mess hall. He passed through the chow line, and the mess guys filled his tray with a sort of bean and noodle casserole resembling something he might have scraped off his boot back at the Double-B.

"I reckon you'll be getting a head start on us, Captain. Maintenance guys need to go over our bird to make sure that Jap sub didn't damage anything. They figure wheels up in four hours."

"Too bad, but we're not going on without you. It's safer with two planes. We'll all leave together. Our flight plan will take us from Oahu to Canton Island ... just short of 2,000 miles. From Canton we fly straight to Fiji ... about five-and-a-half hours. Fiji to Townsville is another 1900 miles which puts us in the air for another 21 hours. I suggest we head over to the crew lounge on the flight line, find us some place to sack out and catch some Zs."

Four hours later, Carl felt a hand on his shoulder. "Wake up, Lieutenant. Time to go. She's good as new."

Carl sat up and rubbed his eyes. Sgt. Stark towered over him.

"We patched the holes ... only four that we could see. One almost hit your reserve fuel tank. You were lucky. No other damage. She's fueled and ready."

"Thank you, Sergeant. You fellas do good work. I'm much obliged." Carl grabbed his leather flight jacket and lowered his feet to the floor from the three chairs that had served as his bed. Everyone gathered together and walked out onto the tarmac.

Twenty minutes later, both B-25 Mitchells took off and turned toward Fiji.

At 1:30 p.m. the following day, both planes and nine weary men landed at Headquarters, 380th Bombardment Group, 5th Air Force, at RAAF Townsville near Sydney, Australia. There, at the huge repair and maintenance depot, 44-3021 underwent a remarkable transformation. She received four AN/M2 .50 caliber guns in the nose, two more in the pair of "blisters" on either side below and behind the cockpit, and two more in the tail turret. The long-range reserve fuel tank was removed and replaced with bomb racks capable of holding two sleeves of four 500-pound bombs. Four rocket pods were mounted beneath the '25s wings, each capable of holding a single five-inch 130 mm HVAR rocket when fully armed. The guns were loaded with belt-fed .50 caliber armor-piercing rounds.

Three days after landing at RAAF Townsville, the crew of 44-3021 boarded their newly transformed gun-ship.

"Finally, I've got my babies!" Harry yelled from his tail-gunner position. I don't feel so much like a passenger, anymore."

"Yep, we're a rootn'-tootn' Zero-shootn' fighting machine!" Zed Carthage chimed in.

"Alright, guys. Cut the chatter, and let's get this sweet lady airborne." Carl announced over the inter-com.

Ten minutes later, the bomber rotated into the air and headed northwest toward Tacloban on Leyte Island, Philippines and Carl's first combat assignment: the 345th Bombardment Group, "Air Apaches."

Chapter VI

January 18, 1945

–Tacloban Airfield, Leyte Island–

The artillery-pocked runway and infrastructure of Tacloban Air Field following the October 21, 1944, American landing and battle against the dug-in Japanese forces, underwent a concentrated reconstruction. Two months later, the 345th Bombardment Group transferred there from Dulag Field, 38 kilometers to the south, enabling the Air Apaches to strike targets farther north on Luzon Island.

Carl and his crew entered the Operations Center on the bottom floor of the four-story HQ building.

An Army Air Corps T/Sgt. smiled up from his gray steel desk. "You must be the replacement crew. Let's see ..." The NCO flipped open a folder in front of him. "Oh yes. Here we are ... you would be Lt. Bridger?"

"That I am, Sergeant. My crew and I are anxious to settle in and meet the other men in our unit."

"Of course, sir. Col. Coltharp is expecting you in his office. Through that door, please, sir." He nodded toward a door to his right. On it hung a placard with the painted design of an Indian warrior wearing a full war bonnet festooned with eagle feathers. Above the rendering the words "345th Bombardment Group – Air Apaches" printed in gold letters told him he was in the right place. Below the unit logo the words "Lt. Col. Chester Coltharp – Commanding Officer" marked the office of Carl's new CO.

Carl gave three firm raps on the door.

"Enter!" came the command from inside.

Carl entered, followed by Alex Chekov and the rest of his crew. They all stood at attention and held a salute which Col. Coltharp returned.

"Stand at ease, gentlemen. I like to welcome every new crew on their arrival to the 345th. It may be the only time I get a chance to thank you personally for your service and to shake your hands." He approached each man, asked his name and shook his hand with a smile of sincere gratitude. Coltharp's larger-than-life persona impressed Carl. He felt instantly moved to trust the man and to serve him as a junior officer. He found himself wanting to prove himself to this man who reminded him of his father in his self-assured, confident style of speaking.

"Sgt. Stroski in the outer office will issue your billets. You are assigned to the 501st Bomb Squadron under acting Squadron Commander Capt. Tad Bingham who is also our Operations Officer. Good hunting, gentlemen. Dismissed."

The men left the building with directions to their respective quarters. Carl located his Quonset hut reserved for the 501st Black Panthers in the officers' housing compound. Chekov and Ortiz bunked-in at a neighboring hut. The enlisted members of Carl's crew were assigned to 16-man tents adjacent to the officers' compound. Each tent had raised netted sides mounted over a wooden frame atop wood-planked floors. All in all, the accommodations provided serviceable quarters but, more importantly, were mobile. The battle for Luzon Island, the East China Sea, and Formosa demanded the 345th to fly sorties ever further north. The Group would need to move their base of operations accordingly.

Carl had learned the singular tradition of bomber and fighter groups to identify themselves apart from other similar organizations by adopting a mascot. The tradition held true for subordinate organizations as well, as in the case of squadron designations. Each of the four squadrons of the 345th Bombardment Group possessed their unique unit badge. The Group badge of the 345th was the aforementioned Apache warrior, and the unit emblem of the 501st Bombardment Squadron took the form of a black panther leaping in front of a crescent moon on a blue background. He spotted the emblem with the "501st Bombardment Squadron" spelled out in arched letters and the words "Black Panthers" beneath, over the door to his Quonset hut.

Turning toward the building, Carl entered and stood inside the door, taking a moment to scan the room. Every bunk had linens on it in various degrees of array. Several officers were lounging about ... some playing card games or writing letters. A steel locker stood next to each bunk. Additionally, each man was provided a foot locker. An empty bed at the end of the open-bay caught Carl's eye. He walked toward it and un-shouldered his duffel bag, thinking to drop it onto the bare mattress when a sudden, powerful impression moved him to stop. He turned around, surprised by the fixed gaze of every man in the barracks. Not one of them moved. In fact, the only animation in the room came from the curls of smoke rising from four cigarettes ... two in ashtrays and two in the mouths of a pair of frozen onlookers.

"Gentlemen, my name is Bridger ... Carl Bridger. I would be much obliged if the previous occupant of this bunk would allow me the use of it. What would he say if he was here to speak for himself?" Carl's eyes drifted from first one man to another.

Finally, one man, Lt. Jay Moore, spoke up in a thick Tennessee drawl. "Lt. Phillip Hardeman has returned home to his creator, Bridger. It's kind of you to honor him, and us, with your sensitive understanding. I'm Jay Moore. Go ahead and stow your gear."

"Thanks." Carl dropped his bag on the bunk and opened the locker. It was completely empty. A strip of adhesive tape was stuck to the door. The word "Hardeman" was neatly printed on it in fading black letters. Carl sat on the end of his bunk, struck by the poignant realization that a man who could have been his friend and *was* a friend to the other men in that room ... was no longer alive. His thoughts flashed to George. The heartache returned with the memory of that summer day when the news of George's death invaded the peace of the Double-B and forever changed his life.

Another man, Henry Lamar, tore the tape off the locker. "Welcome to the Black Panthers, Carl." He offered his hand which Carl shook. "You never get used to losing a brother, but it will happen again before this war is over. It's almost chow time. C'mon, I'll show you the way to the mess hall."

The door in the front of the arched Quonset hut swung open, and a man wearing the bars of a captain entered. Capt. Tad Bingham, acting Squadron Commander of the Black Panthers removed his cap. "Listen up, fellas. Briefing at 0530 sharp. Bridger, meet me in the briefing room in 10 minutes."

Ten minutes later, Carl sat before Capt. Bingham, who leaned in, facing Carl with a firm, steady gaze.

"Lieutenant you will be accompanying the Black Panthers on this mission. We're going after rail traffic near Panique, north of here near Lingayen Gulf. This is your first mission, so I want you on my right wing. If you do exactly what I tell you to do, this should be fast and clean. We're not expecting much resistance from Jap planes, so there won't be any fighter cover. Are you and your men ready?"

"Yes, sir. Ready and anxious to get to work."

"I heard about your run-in with the enemy sub. That took some chutzpah to go in unarmed. You got holed I hear."

"Yes, sir, but we remained undamaged, otherwise."

"Okay, fine ..." his expression turned grim, "but try any of that cowboy crap around me, and I'll ground your ass. This isn't some radio play or Buck Rogers serial, Bridger. We survive because we act with discipline, with clarity of purpose, and as a team. We depend on each other to do our job and *only* our job. Are we clear?"

140

Carl's mouth went dry as sand. He swallowed hard. "We're clear, sir."

Good. Now listen up. Your aircraft identification is Alpha Papa One Seven Three. If I tell you to do something, I won't call you by name. I'll use your identifier. Got it?"

"Yes, sir, Alpha Papa One Seven Three." Carl's heart was running wild. *This is it. I'm going to war! ... God help me to protect my crew. Help me to not screw something up!*

Harry, Don Rushton, and Zed Carthage found three empty bunks in one of the tents reserved for enlisted crew members.

Harry Osborne emptied his duffel bag onto an unoccupied bunk. "Good, we're roomies, guys. I need to find a john."

Four men sat at a makeshift card table ... a piece of plywood sitting atop an empty steel cable spool. Harry approached them.

"Harry Osborne, fellas. Can you point me in the direction of the ... well, *can*?" Harry chuckled. S/Sgt. Paul Loomis glanced up from his cards at Harry. "New guy, eh? Out back behind the tent about 30 yards. Take your own paper."

Harry found the latrine, a 20-foot long trench about six feet deep. Two flat, sanded boards, rounded on the edges ran parallel to the trenches. The boards were elevated to sitting height with a 10-inch gap between them to facilitate access. It was a community latrine, and being outdoors it was not closed off from view by one's seat-mates. Harry did what he needed to do and returned to his quarters.

Half an hour later M/Sgt. Pete Quinley, First Sergeant in the 501st, entered the tent. "Listen up! Crew briefings at 0600. For you new people, briefing is at the Operations building by the tower."

B-25 missions in the Pacific Theatre of Operations had shifted from mostly ineffective high-altitude bombing to low-level bombing and strafing. The Japanese were a highly mobile army and skilled jungle fighters. Unlike Europe where many targets consisted of large industrial complexes that were highly visible in and around large cities and towns, the Japanese forces here used the jungle to hide their movements; the fighting had to be done close-in.

The low-level bombing and strafing capability of the B-25J, coupled with the "Pappy" Gunn modifications on the bombers in Townsville, Australia, that Carl and his crew witnessed, drastically improved the effectiveness of the Mitchells. The heavy bombers, B-24s and B-17s, as well as the B-29s toward the end of the war, continued to strike the larger more visible targets. The '25s of the 345th Bombardment Group were left to attack the less visible, more mobile targets and enemy shipping moving in and out of the many small bays dotting the coastline of Luzon Island. As American bases on Luzon were secured, the 345th would be in position to attack enemy strongholds in Formosa, the South China Sea, and the east coast of Southeast Asia. Carl was smart enough to know that sterile lectures and classroom study only scratched the surface of the complexities of battle. His excitement was laced with fearful anticipation.

January 20, 1945
–Mission #1–

Pointing to the areas of concern on the battle map, Capt. Bingham addressed the crews of the dozen B-25s of the 501st Bomb Squadron:

"Men, our target is here, the railroad along the Whitehead Line to Manila. We need to stop the enemy from resupplying and strengthening their forces against the Allied push inland from the Lingayen Gulf. Eleven days ago, on January 9th, elements of the 6th Army landed on the beach at Lingayen and established a 20-mile-long beachhead as part of the first assault beginning the invasion of Luzon Island. As they moved approximately five miles inland, they encountered heavier resistance. The enemy forces are well armed and are slowing down the progress of the Fourteenth Corp to the north and the I-Corps farther south in this area.

"Five days ago, a second front was established here, along the West coast of the island. Gen. McArthur wants to bring the two fronts together. What stands in their way are the Central Luzon and Manila valleys with their complex rail and road systems ... conduits for the supply and reinforcement of Japanese air and land forces. We're going to start hitting those lines until we force the enemy's retreat from Luzon Island. All four squadrons will participate in this operation. We will strike in four waves. The 499th will go in first followed by the 500th, the 501st, and the 498th. We need to cut off the enemy's fuel, ammunitions and reinforcements. Gentlemen, man your planes." The crews of the Black Panthers boarded six-ton troop trucks and rolled out for the flight line.

"This is it, isn't it Skipper?" Don Rushton said. "We're really going to war."

Harry Osborne laughed nervously. "My Mamma told me I should never leave home without clean underwear. I wonder how clean they'll be after today."

A non-com from another crew, sitting across from Rushton, finished a cigarette and tossed the butt out the back of the truck.

"Rookies, eh? Let me give you some advice, fellas. Shoot them before they shoot you. It's all about who's fastest and has the best eye. If they get you first, just drop your drawers and kiss your butts good bye." He finished the sage remarks with a loud roar of laughter; everyone joined in.

"Hey, Sarge, how many missions you been on?" Zed Carthage asked the jokester.

"Don't count em' and neither should you."

Carl's crew chief, T/Sgt. Ralph Espersen, had prepped A/P173, and the crew access ladder was down and waiting for them as they climbed out the back of the truck.

"She's ready to go, Lieutenant." Sgt. Espersen followed

Carl around the plane as he performed his outside pre-flight check, examining the control surfaces for free movement, tire inflation, wheel-strut height, any visible oil or hydraulic leaks, and examined the propellers for nicks. Satisfied, Lt. Bridger climbed aboard. Sgt. Zed Carthage pulled the crew ladder up, and secured it. Carl eased himself into the left seat beside Alex Chekov.

"This is it, Alex. Let's get us all back here in one piece." Carl forced a half-smile.

"Roger that, my friend. My gut wants a barf bag. I have my mother's nervous stomach." He smiled back. "Let's get the show on the road."

Carl referred to the engine-start checklist and read them off as Alex performed each step.

"Battery.

"Battery ... voltage nominal."

"Inverters."

"Inverters ... all at 26 volts."

"Starboard ignition on."

"Ignition on." Chekov repeated back.

"Booster pump on."

"Booster on, Skipper."

"Energizer and primer."

"Energizer on ... priming for two seconds. Release energizer."

"Turning one!" Carl yelled out the opened wind screen.

"Engage."

Alex held the toggles down for the energizer, primer, and engaging switches. The whine of the servos announced the turning of the three-bladed Hamilton Hydromatic propeller. Almost immediately a loud cough and a blast of white smoke from the engine nacelles announced the engine had caught hold. Carl advanced the mixture to full rich and adjusted the throttle. The rpm needle settled on 1200.

144

"Check oil pressure, Alex."

"Oil pressure at 40 pounds."

"Booster off."

"Booster pump is off."

They repeated the start sequence for the left engine and within three minutes of buckling himself in, Carl had both engines idling smoothly.

He checked the hydraulic pressure. The needle was in the green at between 800 and 900 psi. Brakes and suction were holding in the normal range as well.

"Radio on."

"Radio is on."

A/P173 taxied into position behind Lt. Marshall in A/P172. The 499th and 500th were already airborne and en route to the target. The '25s of the 498th Bomb Squadron sat idling waiting their turn. Carl turned onto the runway. As the wheels of the plane ahead rotated into the air, he firmly applied takeoff power, and the pitch of the Wright 2600-13 engines rose to a deafening roar. On her maiden flight into combat, A/P173 carried Carl, Alex, Phil Ortiz, Don Rushton, Zed Carthage, and Harry Osborne into battle.

AP/173 joined up off Capt. Tad Bingham's right wing.

Tuck her in, Bridger. Fifteen feet, no more, Bingham instructed the new pilot.

Roger, sir.

Carl applied a hint of left rudder and added just enough throttle to bring himself closer to the wing of Bingham's A/P096.

The dozen B-25s of the 501st Black Panthers flew in three flights of four planes. Their distance to target was 950 km or about 550 miles on a heading of 310 degrees. Each plane carried a reserve fuel tank in one of the bomb-bay racks which could be jettisoned prior to entering a combat zone. The extra fuel would allow the bombers to remain in the target area as long as needed and return to Tacloban safely.

The 501st entered the Luzon Valley. The small railhead city of Panique lay dead ahead. Black puffs of ack-ack speckled the sky ahead. The '25s of the 499th and 500th Squadrons were finishing up the first two waves of the attack and forming-up to return to base.

Capt. Bingham's voice came over the plane-to-plane radio frequency:

All planes, target at 7 o'clock low, dead ahead. I see several boxcars and at least two locomotives undamaged. Attack in staggered-line formation. Starting my run now.

The lead plane arrowed down at the rail yard. Carl trailed close behind with A/P189 and A/P080 following on his tail. From the rear turret Harry got a good look at Lt. Hatcher's grim expression behind the controls of A/P189.

Carl's thumb hovered over the firing button of his eight AN/M2 .50 caliber guns. He centered his sights on a pair of boxcars on one track and a group of four large trucks parked next to them. He caught a glimpse of men scattering around trying to find cover. A few of the enemy soldiers stopped to take aim at the line of bombers about to breath fire and damnation down on them.

Carl pressed the "Guns" button on his yoke and held it for three seconds, raking the boxcars and trucks. He pulled up and put the Mitchell into a steep climb. Banking sharply, he decided to target a large building ... *supply depot*, he thought.

"Ortiz, arm the 500s ... one sleeve. I'll line you up. He took A/P173 to 300 feet and turned toward the target.

"She's all yours, Phil." Carl relaxed his hands and took the pressure off the control yoke.

"On target ... bombs away!" Phil Ortiz called out. Four 500-pound bombs dropped from the bomb bay. Each bomb had a four-second time-delay fuse which allowed the bomber time to get clear of the blast zone. Two of the bombs struck the building. The roof blew off, and a roiling ball of black smoke and fire rose into the air. Three secondary explosions sent darts of white arrows from the center of the conflagration skyward, an indication that he had hit an ammunition storage facility.

A close anti-aircraft burst rocked the plane.

"Where the hell is that A-A coming from?" he yelled, to no one in particular.

"There, Skipper! I see the bunker. Six o'clock!" Alex pointed.

Carl banked sharply around and saw the emplacements. He throttled up and went to tree-top level.

"Harry, I'm going to hit them with my 50s. When I pull up, get a sight picture and finish them off with your twin 50s."

The sand-bagged bunkers were not designed to handle an onslaught of the fire-breathing dragon the enemy faced as A/P173 strafed them. When the bomber passed over them, the tail turret opened up. One gun emplacement was destroyed. However, the damage was not enough to deter one brave Japanese soldier from turning the one remaining undamaged Type 98 A-A gun on Carl. The enemy soldier waited until the B-25 banked around exposing the full length of the plane to Jap gunner. His guns spewed fire as tracers sped toward the invading American bomber.

Carl felt the plane buck as eight A-A rounds struck home, tearing away the flap from his right wing. A section of the flap struck the right vertical stabilizer and tore off the top twelve inches and most of the rudder. With the sudden loss of lift and reduced rudder control, the bomber pitched sharply, threatening to put the Mitchell into an involuntary roll. At no more than 300 feet above the surface, Carl and his crew would surely crash into the jungle.

Carl turned the yoke hard left and kicked in hard left rudder. Alex instinctively added full power to the right engine. The bomber righted itself but was crabbing badly to the left in order to maintain directional control.

One Seven Three to Flight Leader, we've been hit.

147

Starboard flap and right rudder damaged. Maintaining control. Over. Carl radioed.

Your call, One Seven Three. Stay in the fight, or head for home. I'll send One Eight Niner with you for cover. Over.

We're still carrying bombs on board, Flight Leader. We're good. His confidence lacked the conviction of his words.

Roger.

Flight Lead to all planes, turning to follow the rail line. Line-abreast formation in four flights of three. Follow me. Pick your targets.

The 501st left the rail yards as the 498th arrived over the target.

Two locomotives, one pusher and one puller, moving toward Baliug popped into view snaking their way through the jungle. Between them, 20 boxcars and two fuel-tankers, spelled major resupply shipment to the enemy.

One Seven Three, take lead. Do you think you can dump your bombs on the lead locomotive?

We can sure scare the hell out of them, sir.

Carl throttled up and positioned the plane dead center over the line of boxcars.

"You got them in your sights, Phil? Drop on your command."

The navigator/bombardier held his eye over the Norden bombsight as the boxcars passed into his target picture. It was a perfect set-up.

"Bombs away!" Phil Ortiz called, and the last four 500-pound high-explosive bombs dropped from the belly of the Mitchell.

Two of the bombs struck the train, one hit the first car ... a fuel tanker, and the other struck the lead locomotive. The other two hit the ground ahead of the train and blew out the tracks. The fuel tanker and locomotive disintegrated as if hit by a 2,000-pound bomb. The explosion sent a mushroom cloud a thousand feet into the air.

"Great flying, Skipper! We blew 'em to smithereens!" Harry announced from the back of the plane.

The other '25s of the 501st Bomb Squadron strafed every boxcar on and off the tracks producing a number of secondary explosions from ruptured fuel tanks and ammunition ... vehicles and weapons that would never again be used against American soldiers.

Flight Leader to all aircraft, form up! Form up! Let's head for home.

"Navigator to pilot. Skipper, Rushton is down ... just now collapsed."

"Damn!" Carl blurted. "Check him out, Ortiz, and report back."

"Engineer. Skipper, we're losing oil pressure on number one. A-A probably nicked a line."

"Copy that, I'm getting the same reading in the cockpit. Is it going to get us back home?"

"Maybe, if the leak doesn't get any worse. Recommend you back off on the rpm and lean the mixture as much as you can."

From the tail gunner's position, Harry Osborne had a good view of the empennage. "Tail turret is good, Skipper. What's left of the right rudder is vibrating like crazy. I hope it holds up."

Missions were planned around the limitations of the B-25s. Distance to target, anticipated enemy resistance, the nature of the targets, ordinance load, and on-board fuel ... all calculated to fit within the performance envelope of the Mitchells. When an aircraft was damaged, or stayed too long over a target, or encountered any number of unforeseen events that stretched that envelope, the pilot had to weigh the ever-narrowing options left to him. Carl knew his crew needed him to make the right decision ... the one that would give them the best chance of making it home.

One Seven Three to Flight Lead, I'm losing oil on number one engine. I have a wounded man on board, and the damaged vertical stabilizer is vibrating badly. Reducing power and dropping out of formation now.

Flight Leader to One Seven Three, roger. Zero Two Niner, take over as Flight Leader. I'll stay with One Seven Three.

Roger, Captain. Moving into lead position now, Lt. Tom Blessing confirmed.

Capt. Bingham climbed up and fell back alongside Carl, while the remaining 10 planes of the 501st Bomb Squadron continued on course to Tacloban.

How's she handling, Bridger? Capt. Bingham asked.

Rough, sir. Airspeed's down to 130. With no flaps and reduced rudder control, she's all over the place!

We're almost home ... about 80 more klicks to go. I see some oil spray coming off your starboard nacelle.

Copy that. Manifold temp is high normal. Opening cowl flaps to full.

"Skipper, Rushton took some shrapnel in his left thigh. I stopped the bleeding, but I think it broke his femur," Phil Ortiz reported.

"Roger. Hit him with some morphine and keep him still. He's your main job now, Phil. If he moves around much he may do more damage. Bridger, out."

Carl understood that whenever an aircraft falls out of formation, it becomes a prime target for any enemy guns ... either from planes or from the ground. He had to weigh that risk against the best chance to get his crew back to safety. Since no enemy resistance was anticipated for the mission, he felt it was the best choice.

A flight of three Kawanishi *Kyofu* seaplane-fighters bearing the rising sun roundel of the Imperial Japanese Navy were returning to their base on Calayan Island north of Luzon when they spotted two American B-25s below them. Two planes alone were an unusual occurrence. They seemed to be flying slowly.

Sub-Lt. Akihiko Iwahashi was the first to spot the American bombers.

"Lieutenant Ota! Two American bombers are below us. They are flying low and slow. Request permission to attack immediately!"

"I see them. We are almost out of fuel. Maintain position." Lt. Kunio Ota ordered.

"Sir, we must attack the American. I will ram them! We must honor the Emperor!" Lt. Isamu Hosokaya responded.

"Very well. We shall attack! To be a part of *The Divine Wind* will bring honor to our families for many generations. Kunio Ota, farmer and father of three, led the suicide attack.

"Bogies, 10 o'clock high!" Phil Ortiz exclaimed from his position behind Carl.

Flight Leader! Bogies at 10 o'clock high! Carl radioed.

The enemy planes came at them in a straight line and then separated into a staggered-line formation.

Break left! Bingham yelled.

Carl banked sharp left as much as he could and throttled up both engines. "Osborne, Carthage: I'm going to try to put them behind us. Fire when you're ready!"

"Hold together, baby ... a little longer!" he coaxed the crippled bomber.

Anger replaced fear; survival replaced desperation. His instincts kindled a blaze of wrath toward the enemy, and the battle

151

scene became crystal clear to Carl. He maneuvered the Mitchell into position.

Zed Carthage manned the dorsal turret. He spotted the enemy diving on them and opened up with his twin .50 caliber guns. The enemy's attack was relentless. The lead *Rex*, as the Americans referred to the N1K Kyofu, opened up with both 7.7 mm nose-mounted guns. Carthage had him in his sights and squeezed another burst. The bogey flashed by them trailing smoke.

"Gotcha!" Zed yelled over the intercom.

Meanwhile, Carl's eyes caught Bingham's plane banking hard left and going on the offensive. One of the enemy planes made the mistake of coming at Bingham head-on. Carl banked toward his Flight Leader to draw away a second bogey. He watched Bingham and the Jap fighter open fire at the same time. The small plane was no match for the eight AN/M2 .50 caliber guns of Bingham's *Daisy Mae*. The Kyofu disintegrated.

"Bogey on our tail!" Harry Osborne called out. "Hold steady, Skipper. I've got this guy."

As the bogey dropped out of the sky, Osborne needed to raise his angle of attack. "Dive, Skipper!"

Without hesitating, Carl dropped the nose 10 degrees, raising Harry's gun sights enough to line up the bogey.

Sgt. Osborne opened up on the inbound fighter. The Jap pilot arrowed toward the rear of the '25's fuselage. At the last moment, Harry's .50 cals found their mark. The Jap plane wobbled oddly and then inverted as it dropped out of sight and crashed into the jungle.

Carl pulled up the nose of A/P173 and roared over the tree tops. He took the crippled plane back up to 1,000 feet and reduced power. The third bogey turned tail and ran.

Hey, Bridger, thanks for drawing off that other bogey. That was a close call. How's your aircraft handling? the Flight Leader radioed from A/P096.

Shaky, Captain. The vertical stabilizer is vibrating badly, and we're yawing all over the place.

We're five minutes out. Let's get you back to base. Capt. Bingham keyed his mic for the tower at Tacloban.

Tacloban Tower, Alpha Papa Zero Niner Six, inbound. Alpha Papa One Seven Three is first to land. Request emergency crew and medics. One wounded aboard."

Carl dropped his landing gear. Without any flaps, he had to come in hot. *Please let me get us on the ground safely.* The thought was more of a prayer.

"Pilot to crew, secure for crash landing. We're going in hot!" He ordered. "Alex, the second we touchdown, cut the throttles. I'll handle the brakes."

"Roger that, Skipper."

They came in low at 120 mph, brushing the top of a palm tree. As soon as he cleared the trees, he dropped the nose and leveled off just yards before reaching the edge of the strip. Because of the damage to the control surfaces, Carl had a difficult time keeping the nose over the center of the runway. Alex pulled the throttles back, and Carl raised the nose. The main landing gear touched down, bounced and touched down again followed by the nose wheel. At 120 mph, the runway was getting noticeably shorter by the second. Carl began braking the plane as hard as he dared. The brakes squealed in protest, but it couldn't be helped. The bomber slowed to 50 mph with only 600 feet left before they would end up in thick jungle grasses and boggy soil. She slowed to 40 ... 30 ... 20 mph. Carl kicked in hard left rudder as Alex played the left brake, and A/P173 made the turn onto the taxiway at the end of the 2,200-foot strip.

"A good landing, all things considered, Skipper!" Alex nudged Carl and released a pent-up sigh of relief.

The army-green Dodge WC54 ambulance sporting a red cross on a white background braked to a stop. Sgt. Carthage dropped the crew ladder down and lowered Don Rushton into the arms of the waiting medics. Rushton was loaded onto a stretcher and then into the ambulance.

After taxiing to the maintenance hangar, Carl and Alex shut down the engines. The crew climbed down to the ground and onto a pair of waiting Jeeps which took them back to their quarters. Carl remained behind and turned toward the hangar. Several maintenance people were already busy moving A/P173 into the hangar. Though his thoughts were on his Radioman, he needed to check with the maintenance crew before heading over to the medical compound.

"Lt. Bridger?" T/Sgt. Rafael "Rafe" Berardino approached Carl. He saluted and continued, "It's a heck of a way to introduce myself, but I'm your crew chief. It's my job to keep your plane flying. I'll be working with S/Sgt. Carthage while we get her ready for her next mission ... or not."

"What do you mean or *not*, Sergeant?" Carl was put off by Berardino's ambiguous remark.

"Depends on if we can find the parts to put her back together, sir. The biggest problem I see is scrounging up an extra vertical stabilizer and flap. I'll keep your engineer briefed, and he'll keep you informed. Nice to meet you, sir." Berardino turned to walk toward the hangar, but stopped short.

"By the way, Lieutenant. Have you named her yet? Every lady needs a name."

"The plane? ... Nope. Haven't had time. I suppose we should come up with something."

"When you do, I know a guy that's done the nose art on a few of the new '25s in the last year. He's pretty good."

"Thanks, Sergeant. I'll keep that in mind." Carl climbed into the waiting jeep and tapped the driver on the shoulder. "Corporal, I need to get to the base hospital."

Medical surgical hospitals and personnel of the 603rd Medical Clearing Company were attached to various Army divisions and followed them, setting up medical facilities along beaches and inland wherever secure areas were established.

At Tacloban Airfield, the 19th and 27th Portable Surgical Hospitals, under command of the 1st Cavalry Division, had their facilities in tents. A total of 100 patient beds were available in two "wards" (tents). Carl was directed to the tent where Sgt. Don Rushton would be taken.

He entered the door of the patient ward and spotted a nurse standing at the foot of one of the patients whose head was heavily wrapped. The man's nose, one eye, and mouth were the only visible parts of his face. There was an antiseptic odor of bleach and alcohol in the tent.

"Excuse me, nurse," Carl spoke quietly. The nurse turned toward him. Facing Carl stood a strikingly attractive twenty-something blonde with sparkling pale blue eyes. She seemed more like a model for Vogue magazine than a U.S. Army nurse. She held a clipboard to her chest like a school girl holding her books, and her hair was tied back with a red polka dot bandana. She wore a long-sleeved khaki shirt with rolled-up sleeves and long khaki trousers. A 2nd Lieutenant bar shone on her right collar, and a medical caduceus emblem with the "N" was pinned on her left collar. He was momentarily thrown off-balance by her delicate beauty in the midst of the harsh world around them.

He could feel the heat of a blush rush over his face as he caught himself staring. He cleared his throat. "I'm looking for my Radioman, Sgt. Donald Rushton?"

"He's not here, Lieutenant. When was he brought in?"

"About a half hour ago. He took some shrapnel in his thigh ... broke his femur, I believe."

"I see. Well, he's probably in surgery. If you want to check back in a couple of hours, I'll have an update on your man's status." She smiled at Carl and waited for his reply.

155

"Thanks. I'll do that." Carl left the patient ward and headed back to the 345th compound. His thoughts drifted to the nurse and of how much she resembled Annie. He was hit with a pang of loneliness that brought a tear to his eye. *God, how I miss you, Annie!*

He opened the door and stepped into the open-bay officer's quarters of the 501st Bomb Squadron. Two things happened: first, he found it odd that several of the men were gathered together in the middle of the room watching him ... grinning; second, before he could react, a bucket of water fell from over his head drenching him from head to toe.

Carl gasped and sputtered, standing there like a half-drowned puppy. Lt. Wilkinson tossed him a towel.

"Welcome back, rookie. We've been waiting for ya," Wilkinson laughed.

The rest of the men in the room walked over to him. Back slaps and handshakes aplenty followed, and then his fellow officers returned to letter writing and card playing while they awaited the mission debriefing.

"I thought you bought the farm when that Jap A-A hit you. That was some fine flying you did to keep her in the air." The compliment came from "Hos" Chisholm, a big, sandy-haired son of a cattleman, to whom Carl took an instant liking.

"Thanks, Hos ... thanks a bunch." Carl wiped his face on the towel. He was accepted as a brother now that his feet ... and the rest of him ... were wet. His heart felt full.

Carl walked over to his bunk and sat. He had been on the move ever since he climbed out of A/P173. His thoughts since landing had been about Don Rushton. *Lord, I hope he's going to be okay. Please, Father, let him be okay.* He hadn't had time to think about everything that happened on the mission ... the Jap A-A, the bomb run on the train, the attack by the two N1K Rex's. His body began to shiver. He was reacting to the release of pent-up stress and the flood of adrenaline that was finally subsiding.

Avenging Angel

Lt. Al Marshall sat down next to Carl on the side of the bunk, put his arm over his shoulder, smiled, and patted his back. Carl's hands trembled, and he interlaced his fingers to hold them steady.

"I gotta tell you, rook' when you dove on that train with half your tail blown off, I thought you were going kamikaze there. No way in hell were you going to be able to line up and drop your load on it. You did, though. It's like watching an eagle dive on its prey, snatching it off the ground, before plowing his beak into the dirt. Cripes! You were like some sort of avenging angel up there."

"Avenging angel, eh, Al? All I could think of was ... Lord, don't let me crash and kill my crew. I didn't think we were heroes avenging anything up there. That was the scariest thing I have ever done. I'm still shaking." He laughed nervously.

"I've got just the thing for that, pal." Al walked over to his locker and withdrew a half full bottle of *Old Hawthorn* and two urine sample bottles that he managed to spirit off a truck of medical supplies over at the hospital tent.

"No more than a shot, Carl. We have'ta stay sharp." Al filled both tiny bottles with two ounces each of the blended whiskey and screwed the lid back on. "I got this from home a month ago. Been nursing it along until I get another one, whenever that'll be. Cheers."

They clinked the "glasses", and Carl tossed back the warm liquid. It burned his throat going down, and he coughed once. "That's pretty good stuff," he choked. The whiskey settled into his stomach and produced a warm glow. He felt himself relaxing a little.

An hour later, Carl took a Jeep back to the hospital. He spotted Don Rushton and walked over to his bed. The young Iowa farm boy was out cold from the sedation. His injured leg was in a cast from his foot up to his hip and was suspended above the mattress.

Carl pulled up a chair and sat by the head of the bed. In less than a minute, his head lolled onto his shoulder, and he began to snore softly.

A hand on his shoulder shaking him gently made him jerk awake.

"Lieutenant? ... Lieutenant?" A soft female voice said.

Carl opened his eyes to the face of the same blond nurse he had met earlier.

"Oh ... uh, hi. I guess I fell asleep. How is he doing, Nurse ..." Carl read the name sown over the right pocket of her shirt. "uh, Franklin."

"The doctors were able to stabilize his leg, but more surgery is needed. He'll be sent to Hawaii on a hospital ship tomorrow. I suspect he'll be gone for at least three months. There's a good chance he may even be sent home. It depends on how much damage was done and how well he heals."

"That's not good. He'll hate leaving his crew back here while he goes home."

"I wish I had better news." She smiled at Carl. Again, he was taken by how much she reminded him of Annie. Their hair and eyes were nearly identical in color. Annie was shorter by about two inches, but they could be sisters. He was hit by another punch of loneliness.

The day after the mission the 345th had a stand-down day. Usually, missions came quickly in sequence requiring crews to fly seven or eight days in a row before having a rest. The reason for the respite this time wasn't for lack of targets but because of weather. A typhoon was approaching up the east coast of the Philippine chain. Everybody was hunkering down for the blow.

On the flight line, ground personnel ran about tying down the airplanes and securing ground vehicles inside the hangars. Tents, which numbered in the hundreds on Tacloban, were anchored firmly and sandbagged around the base.

The unexpected break in the routine of combat allowed Carl, Alex and Phil Ortiz to join up at the Officers' Club for drinks.

The "O" Club was nothing more than two tents placed end-to-end. A bar made from scavenged wood had been built. The planks forming the surface of the bar were sanded and painted. Behind the bar, shelves held glasses, mugs, and a variety of alcohol. Men occupied the 20 or so tables and were engaged in chatter or card games. A few were throwing darts. Cigarette smoke formed a gray fog which hovered two feet above their heads. A radio blared some band tune that Carl couldn't identify.

Phil Ortiz spotted an empty table on the far side of the room. They pulled the chairs out and sat down.

"Good evening, sirs." A smiling corporal, wearing an apron, stood before them. "Can I get you something?

"What ... table waiting is an Army career choice now?" Alex Chekov laughed.

"Oh, no sir. We work all over the base. I'm a clerk over at base HQ. Some of the guys are in the motor pool, flight crews, cooks ... whatever. We do this for tips and to break up the routine."

"Well, Corporal, I'd be obliged if you'd bring us some glasses and three beers," Carl asked.

"Local brew's all there is. No American beer left."

"That'll be fine."

Tacloban Air Base, being the headquarters of the 5th Air Force, as well as playing occasional host to Gen. McArthur, enjoyed a few amenities not afforded other, smaller outposts. Among those amenities was a fair stock of beer and whiskey. However, on this day, the "O" Club was serving up the only beer available, *San Miguel*. The quartermaster for the 345th worked a small miracle when he heard through some Filipino guerillas that a store of 20,000 cases of the beer had been discovered in a cave about three km from the old brewery in Manila. It had been shut down prior to the Japanese invasion. He figured the owners of the brewery wanted to stash the beer so they could seed the market following the American liberation. The quartermaster acquired 600 cases in return for food and two Jeeps which had mysteriously gone missing from the motor pool.

"Phil, Alex, I've come up with a name for A/P173. What do you think of *Avenging Angel*? Al Marshall said we looked like one when we dove on that train at Baliug."

Phil stood up. "Sounds right, Skipper. A toast, then, to *Avenging Angel*."

"Hey-hey, rookie! Welcome to the canvas Copacabana!" Three guys from the 499th Bats Outta Hell greeted the new crew members of the 501st. An intoxicated Lance Anders clapped a hand on Carl's shoulder. "Say, Bridger, you kicked some Jap butt for your first mission. That was one hell of an initiation up there."

"Thanks, Lance, but it wasn't all me. We all had a piece of the action, especially Phil here. He's my bombardier. He laid those 500s down like he was putting a baby to bed."

Just then a group of guys at the end of the bar started singing a version of "Bless 'Em All". Lance and the others joined in and pretty soon the Officers' Club was reverberating with the raucous lyrics:

Bless them all! Bless them all! The long the short and the tall! Bless all the blondies and every brunette. Some we'll remember and some we'll forget! But we're keeping our eye on them all, the long the short and the tall ...

Phil and Alex remained at the club, but Carl opted to walk back to his quarters. He stepped into a downpour of rain, the precursor of the anticipated typhoon. He ran across the muddy road to the row of Quonset huts and stepped inside, removed his boots and left them by the door. It was expected that on rainy days one never tracked in mud.

Carl decided to use the down time to write to his family, so he retrieved the composition notebook from his locker and sharpened a pencil with his pocket knife, the one his father gave him for his 10th birthday ... a bone-handled J.A. Henckels with two blades and a punch. He turned the knife over in his hand. The bone had yellowed somewhat from the oils in his hand, but Carl always kept a sharp edge on the fine German steel blade.

He stripped down to his skivvies and put his pillow behind his head.

Dearest family,

I just returned from my first combat mission. Although I can't talk about any particulars, I will say that our entire unit returned safely. My Radioman took some shrapnel, but he is recovering nicely. "Avenging Angel," which we named our B-25, took some damage, but will hopefully be ready for our next mission. Some good news: The enemy's sphere of influence is shrinking. Since McArthur's return to Leyte, the Philippines are ever increasingly coming under our control. I expect we will be moving farther north one step at a time. I think we are in the last year of the war. I also suspect that some of this letter might not make it past the censors (insert chuckle). Let me just say that things are looking optimistic. Wouldn't it be wonderful if we could celebrate this Christmas together as we did the last one? Ah ... I wish for that so badly! Anyway, I'm doing well, and the spirits of my crew are high. I'm making many friends. This is a terrific group of men ... brothers all.

Annie, at the risk of understating my love for Mom, Dad, and Penny, I need to say that I miss you most of all. It seems I carry thoughts of you in my mind every moment of every day. My every heartbeat is fueled by my love for you. You are with me everywhere, even up there in the clouds. I hear your voice in the steady, reassuring drone of Angel's engines. You're love for me is in her wings, lifting me and carrying me home. More and more each day, I am reassured in my heart by a sense that I cannot explain ... I will return home to you. You and I are one.

Only forever – Carl

Carl sealed the envelope. He would walk it over to the mail-room the next day. His watch read 11:15 p.m., and he decided to get some sleep.

He awoke at 3:15 a.m. to the thunderous sound of 80-mph winds. The typhoon had arrived striking the southeast coast of Luzon Island with a fury. The sirens wailed, warning everyone to stay indoors. Hundreds of men braved the hurricane-force storm to add more rein-forcement to the many tents that housed personnel, supplies, and med-ical facilities. Carl and several of the officers in his hut dressed and headed for the hospital thinking that would be where their assistance was needed the most. Indeed, on arrival at the patient wards every available medical corpsman, nurse, and even doctor fought to keep the canvas walls and roofs from blowing away from their framed skele-tons. The rain was a stinging barrage of needles against their faces, driven by the now 100-mph winds.

A slightly built corpsman, struggling to regain control of a tie-down rope that had been uprooted and was flailing about wildly, was losing the battle. Carl charged in and grabbed the stake-end of the rope. The corpsman had a mallet hanging from his belt.

"Give me that!" He yelled over the howling of the storm. "Hold the rope while I drive it back into the ground!"

The corpsman's utility cap blew off revealing the blonde hair of Nurse Franklin.

"Pull down as hard as you can! Now!" Carl screamed over the howling wind.

The nurse reached up as high on the rope as she could and put all of her weight into pulling it down. The canvas billowed against the rope threatening to pull her off her feet.

"Hurry! I can't hold on much longer!" she cried.

Carl scooped away as much mud as he could until he got down to what seemed to be stable soil and then hammered the stake in until it was submerged in the rain. "There, I think that's got it. You can let go now!"

Nurse Franklin released her grip, and the rope held. They worked their way around the tent, securing the stakes and piling sand bags on them to add weight and to channel the water away to keep it from undercutting the soil. They moved to the next patient ward and repeated the process. Thankfully, the main surgery and critical care units were under solid Quonset huts built over concrete floors. They had been shuttered in anticipation of the storm and required no additional fortification.

"Let's go inside. I need to check on my patients!" Lt. Franklin led the way and Carl followed. He could think of no better way to wait out a typhoon than to help make the wounded more comfortable. His eyes fell on a heavily bandaged man trying to get out of his bed. He was hooked up to two intravenous lines that would pull out if he moved more than four or five feet. Carl approached the man and gently, but firmly, forced him back down onto his bed.

"Let me go! Let me go! ... I'm coming, Johnny!" he yelled. His eyes were glazed by fever.

"Johnny's okay. Keep your head down, pal. Johnny's fine. I've got you ... I've got you." It wasn't until Carl lowered the man back down to his bed and lifted his leg back to the mattress that he noticed the soldier had only one leg. If he hadn't reached him in time the man would have tried standing, not only tearing out the I.V. lines but further injuring himself in the process.

Carl worked through the next four hours going from one patient to another talking to them and learning their stories. An 18-year-old Army PFC ... struck in the neck by a sniper bullet. The boy would be going home. He would never be able to tell his mother or his girlfriend how much he loved them because his larynx had been destroyed. A West Point 2nd Lieutenant from Oregon whose wife, he told Carl, had given birth to their first son two weeks before he shipped out to the Pacific with the X Corps, 24th Infantry Division. He told Carl about participating in the landings in October and had been in-country ever since. He was third in line behind his point man in the platoon he was leading during a routine patrol. He saw the trip wire, but before he could shout a warning, the man on point tripped it. The model 91 fragmentation grenade is equipped with a seven-second time-delay fuse, so the Lieutenant was able to tackle the man ahead of him before the explosion tore into his back. He survived, but a grenade fragment severed his spinal cord between L-3 and L-4. If it had been a more powerful American grenade, he would be dead. The man he tackled was un-injured. *These guys are all heroes*, he thought. He felt honored to talk to them.

"You must be exhausted, Lieutenant. Why don't you get some rest? The worst of the storm is over." The corpsman stood at Carl's side. I've been watching you working with these guys. You have a real knack for patient care."

"Thanks, Sergeant, but I'm more comfortable in my '25 than I am in here. Are you a Medical Corpsman?"

"Yes, sir, but I've been studying up for my Flight Engineer exams. I finished the book work, and I've been in the hangar during any spare time I've got ... which isn't as much as I'd like. I really want to be on a B-25 crew. Every time I hear you guys talking about your missions, it makes me want to be up there with you. Being a medic, I only see the aftermath of what you guys do up there. Just once, I'd like to make a contribution where it really pays off." He lowered his eyes to the paralyzed young officer. "I'm too protected here. You guys put it all on the line ... every day."

"I hear you. What's your name, Sergeant? Maybe I can put in a good word for you when you pass those exams."

"Henreid. People call me 'Doc.'" He smiled and offered his hand, which Carl took. "I'm scheduled to take the test next week, sir. I'd be grateful for any kind word."

The typhoon passed, and Carl found himself exhausted from the rigors of fighting the relentless storm. He ended the day with a deep sense of humility. *So many have given so much.* The thought renewed his own commitment to give his all.

Chapter VII

–January 24, 1945–

The day following the typhoon, four B-25s from the 501st and four each from the 500th, 499th, and 498th squadrons were ordered to strike the Japanese Air Base at Aparri on the northwest tip of Luzon Island. Mostly used as a base for Japanese seaplanes and reconnaissance aircraft, local villagers reported an increase of fighters and torpedo aircraft at the base. Directed by the 5th Air Force, the 345th was tasked to destroy the enemy aircraft on the base, while at the same time, preserving the airstrip. Sixteen aircraft were more than enough to do the job. Carl and his crew were ordered to fly Al Marshall's A/P172 on the mission. Lt. Marshall's crew drew the lucky straw to stand down for the relatively low-priority mission, giving Carl and his crew an opportunity to get another sortie under their belts. Col. Coltharp would lead the attack.

Col. Coltharp stepped in front of the map showing the location of the target, the latest photo recon pics, and the attack route.

"Gentlemen, our target is the airbase at Aparri. Intel shows an increase in the number of enemy aircraft including at least four A6M2 "Rufe" fighter-bombers, several Shiden interceptors, and a mix of approximately 10 A6M Zeroes and Ki-61 Tonys (fighters). We are to destroy or disable as many of the aircraft as possible while leaving the runway intact. The load-out will be standard armor-piercing .50 cals and 70 parafrag bombs each. We expect an enemy presence, so the 348th Fighter Group will provide air cover. Lt. Wilkinson will lead the 501st, Capt. VanPelt will command the

499th, Lt. Steiner the 498th, and I will fly lead for the 500th Bomb Squadron. Wheels up at 0700. The group will rendezvous at 2,000 feet at 0715 hrs. We will fly a wide arc north and turn toward Aparri at a point 10 miles off the northeast coast of Luzon Island. At minimum altitude, our '25s will hit the airfield in two waves of eight bombers each, attacking in shallow "V" formation. Time to target will be approximately three-and-a-half hours. Pilots and crews, man your planes!"

Carl taxied A/P172 behind Ed Wilkinson in A/P041. The 501st contingent was the final flight of four Mitchells to take off. Carl's crew was the greenest of them all, but two of the other crews were relatively new as well. Lt. Lester Hammer in A/P191 had an even dozen missions to his credit, and Lt. Tom Blessing had completed eight missions. Flight Leader Capt. Terry Hatcher's 37 missions and one Distinguished Flying Cross added to his file, made him the most experienced pilot in Carl's flight.

"Gauges are in the green, Skipper. We are good to go."

"Roger that, Alex. It's our turn." Carl turned onto the runway and lined up for takeoff.

Twenty seconds later A/P172 lifted off. At 0715 hrs the four bombers of the 501st joined the rest of the formation orbiting at 2,000 feet, and Col. Coltharp led the group north toward Aparri.

The four Mitchells of the 501st flew on the right outer edge of the second of two shallow "V" formations. The group reached the target and began its attack at 1041 hrs.

Squadron Leader to all planes, drop to tree top level boys. Increasing speed to two-seven-zero mph. Stay close, we don't want to lose anyone in the trees. We'll follow on Group Leader's tail.

The 501st was forced to fly a straight path along the carved-out dense jungle to the right of the runway. All of the enemy aircraft were parked to the left of the runway. Dropping to 100 feet above the surface, the 25s roared over the target. Seventy 23-pound-parafrags dropped from the bomb bay of each plane. The 501st obliterated over 2,000 feet of cut-back jungle growth and one small thatched-roofed structure from which light, sporadic small arms fire was observed before it disintegrated. The left side of the formation, the planes that actually flew over the target, experienced greater success. The airfield was decimated. The mission report would show that at least 14 enemy planes were destroyed along with several buildings and a fuel dump.

At 1044 hrs the 16 B-25s formed up and turned toward Tacloban.

"Hey, Skipper. What was that all about? There ought to be an easier and much more cost effective way of clearing jungle." Sgt. Harold Osborne said from the tail.

"It's a milk run, Harry. Just look at it as one more mission to be checked off. Don't worry, there'll be plenty of times you'll wish they were all this easy."

"She's as good as new, Lieutenant. We replaced the vertical stabilizer and rudder with one we scavenged off a Marine PBJ that buried her nose during a forced landing here back in November. She cartwheeled and ripped off most of a wing. The crew made it out, though, God bless 'em. We were able to hammer out the flap and replaced one aluminum panel." Sgt. Berardino folded his meaty arms and looked at A/P173 with pride.

"She looks great, Sergeant. Oh, by the way, I've been thinking about what you said the other day ... we have a name for her. I drew a sketch for you." Carl handed over the sketch, drawn with pencil on a page from his composition book. "I'm afraid I'm not much of an artist. Can you make it work?"

The crew chief looked at the sketch and smiled. A beautiful blonde woman dressed in a thin toga and a breastplate, carrying a flaming sword in one hand and a shield in the other. Her angel's wings stretched out behind and above her head. She was Carl's vision of an *Avenging Angel.* "I'll get right on it, sir. Have it done in 48-hours. Color preferences?"

"Sure ... um, blonde hair, red toga, gold breastplate and shield."

Carl thanked the man and headed off for the operations building to meet his new radioman. Don Rushton had been sent out to a hospital ship via Navy PBY, and Carl needed to fill his position.

A young three-striped sergeant, dressed in his utility uniform, sat in a chair across from a clerk. His duffel bag lay on the floor beside him. Carl entered the personnel office and stopped in front of the clerk without paying any attention to the seated man behind him.

"Hello, sir, I see that you are Lt. Bridger," the corporal behind the desk greeted.

"You're correct, Corporal. I'm expecting a new Radioman for my crew. A C-47 landed about a half-hour ago, and I was hoping he might have been aboard."

"Your timing is perfect, sir. I was just beginning his in-processing. Meet S/Sgt. Wendell Price." The corporal motioned to the man sitting patiently, albeit wide-eyed, behind Carl.

Carl turned to face the non-com, who in turn jumped to his feet and threw Carl a salute worthy of a West Point upper classman. His fingers quivered a bit at his right eyebrow. "Sir!" he squeaked ... cleared his throat and repeated ... "Sir! S/Sgt. Wendell Price reporting for duty, sir."

Carl returned the salute, and the new Radioman lowered his hand.

"Welcome to the 501st Black Panthers, Sgt. Price. Get yourself settled in and meet the rest of the crew over at *The Pub* in one hour."

"The Pub, sir?"

"Yes. It's the enlisted club. I'm sure the corporal here can direct you." Carl received an affirmative nod from the clerk.

Carl walked through the swinging bar doors of *The Pub*. The doors were attached to the wooden frame of the tented structure. Above them hung a sign, painted in white letters on a three-foot-by-five-foot slab of plywood, announcing the name of the enlisted men's watering hole. He found Harry Osborne and Zed Carthage engaged in a two-handed game of penny-ante blackjack at the back of the room.

"Howdy, fellas. Mind if I join you?"

Neither Harry nor Zed jumped to attention. *The Pub* was the one place where salutes and other formal military protocol were set aside.

"Sure, take a seat, Skipper. What brings you to our little hide-a-way?" Zed Carthage inhaled a drag from a Lucky Strike and returned it to the ashtray where it lay smoldering next to Harry's cigarette. "Hit me, Harry."

Harry handed Zed another card face down on the table. Zed lifted the edge and took a peek. He was holding a solid 16 points. "Busted!" he said as he turned over a six of diamonds.

Harry raked in the pot, a whopping sum of 75 cents, gathered the cards together and turned toward Carl.

"Good news, boys. *Avenging Angel* is ready to go, and we have a new Radioman. He'll be here in about 15 minutes. I'd like for you guys to make him welcome. Have a couple of beers and get to know him. Then, meet the rest of us over at the hangar at, say, 1500 hrs."

"Roger that, sir. We'll take good care of him." Harry dealt another hand of blackjack as Carl exited the enlisted men's club.

At 1500 hrs, Carl, Lt. Phil Ortiz, and Lt. Alex Chekov stood chatting beneath the Plexiglas nose-gunner's enclosure.

"Here they come." Alex nodded over Carl's shoulder toward the three NCOs approaching them.

The three men stopped and held a salute. Carl, Phil, and Alex returned the salutes and the noncoms dropped their hands.

"Gentlemen, I want to introduce S/Sgt. Wendell Price. Sgt. Price, say hello to Lt. Alexandre Chekov, our copilot, and Lt. Phil Ortiz ... bombardier and gunner. This lady here is *Avenging Angel*. What do you say we all climb aboard and introduce Sgt. Price to *Angel's* inner workings?

Wendell eased himself into the Radioman's chair and examined the dials and switches of the BC-458 and BC-459 Command Radio System. The radio, mounted on a shock-absorbing platform to minimize vibration which could throw off the tuning of the plane-to-plane transmitter, was secured by six screws. His eye caught a subtle anomaly.

"Ah! I need a small Philips-head screwdriver." He unsnapped a canvas bag mounted next to the radio transceiver and found what he was looking for. "Two of the mounting screws on the shock plate are too tight. I'll just give them about a half-turn, and ... there. That should do it. These babies are sensitive. The shock plate needs to be just so." Carl scrutinized his new radioman who seemed clearly in his element. Sgt. Price carefully inspected the separate Command and Liaison radio-set components.

"I'm familiar with the 30-100 system, so I'm good to go" The new radioman wiped his hands on the rag he had brought with him.

Carl smiled. "I get the impression you know your way around a radio beyond what the Air Corps taught you."

"Well, sir, you might say I was weaned on vacuum tubes and copper wire. My father is a radio engineer for KFIZ in Fond du lac, Wisconsin. He even built his own amateur station at home. I loved to watch him tinker around with his equipment. I guess I caught the radio bug from him." Wendell smiled.

"Sounds like you were made for this job," Zed Carthage said.

"Actually I was a semester short of getting my degree in electrical engineering when I decided to join the Army Air Corps. I ... I lost a brother last June at the battle of Saipan in the Marianas ... Marine." His eyes glistened as he described walking into the house for a weekend visit after three weeks of classes at the University of Wisconsin in Madison ... of how he enjoyed his monthly 71-mile bus ride and seeing his parents and two younger siblings. On this particular visit, however, his parents and brother and sister were all sitting in the living room ... huddled together. A week later he was on a bus headed for boot camp. He never returned to Madison. Carl was shaken by the similarity of his own loss with that of Sgt. Price. He realized he hadn't quite pushed back in his mind the memory of George's death.

Harry Osborne gently patted Wendell's back. "We're all sorry for your loss, Price."

"It's okay, Sergeant." Wendell quickly ran his sleeve over his eyes. "Anyway, I applied for Radioman's School, and here I am. Oh, yes ..." He pulled a sheaf of papers from his pocket.

"These are carbon copies of my performance reports from Truax Field." He offered them to Carl. "I'm sure personnel will have the official file."

Carl took the file from his new radioman and pulled the men back to the task at hand. "Price, if you have any concerns, these fellas will answer your questions. They've been through everything that you're going to experience. Trust them. Men, I need you to get Sergeant Price situated and get a good night's rest, we have a mission briefing in the morning. You're dismissed."

Chapter VIII

January 26, 1945

–First Command (cont.)–

"Lieutenant, wake up … wake up." A voice called from the fog of anesthesia.

Carl opened his eyes, and his surroundings swam into focus. He was in a bed with an I.V. in his arm. Two bottles hung from a chromed stand. One was a unit of blood and the other was a clear liquid of some sort. He was positioned on his right side with a pillow tucked up against his back to prevent him from rolling onto his injured left side. He started to lift his arm, but someone held it down.

"Don't try to move, Carl. We'll let the fluids run out and then remove the needle. You've been wounded."

"Yes ... yes, I remember. We were ambushed by four Jap fighters. Was I hit by shrapnel? With awareness came an urgent concern. "My crew! Are they alright?"

"Yes. Your co-pilot got you all back safely. You need to rest. We'll talk later."

"You're Nurse Franklin. I remember you from the typhoon. Thanks ... for your kindness."

"You're welcome, Lt. Bridger. By the way, since we're going to be seeing quite a bit of each other over the next several days, how about you call me Samantha, Carl."

"Sounds right, Samantha. Again, thank you."

"I'm here to serve. I'll get the doctor for you, now that

you're awake." Samantha Franklin left Carl to his thoughts. He tried moving his left leg a little and was rewarded with a twinge of pain. *Not too bad. Maybe I can sit up.* Carl eased his legs over the edge of the bed and pulled himself to a sitting position by holding on to a triangle-shaped grab bar suspended by an overhead frame. He was content to sit without trying to stand.

"Stop, right there, Lieutenant!" A white-jacketed doctor approached from behind Carl. "What are you trying to do, rip out all of my fine embroidery work? Your wound took 26 stitches, mostly down deep. You're going to be fine, ... barely a flesh wound by comparison. Here, let me help you lie back down." The Army Captain lifted Carl's legs gently back to the bed. "Now then, here's what you need to know. We took out a piece of shrapnel a little over an inch long. It probably came from the armor plating in your seat ... lucky for you. The fragment nicked an artery which is why you bled so much. We got that all stitched up and fed you three units of blood. The fourth is still flowing into your arm."

Carl didn't think the wound sounded that bad, but he needed one question answered before he could relax. "So, when can I get back to my crew, sir?"

"In a few days. No bones were broken, and the fragment missed your vital organs. We'll look at you in 10 days. If everything is healed up okay, I'll clear you for flight status." The doctor stood up to leave. "Don't push yourself to be a hero, Lieutenant. If you rip those stitches holding your artery together, you'll be going home ... in a box."

A flood of thoughts filled Carl's mind. He relived every moment of the mission, and the ones before it. He thought about the Marine amputee he had met and the other patients in the open hospital ward with him. His mind turned to his crew, and he thanked God for their safety. He needed to write to Annie and his family. *What should I tell them?* He spotted the corpsman/would-be flight engineer, Sgt. "Doc" Henreid and called him over.

"Hi, Lieutenant, I'm glad you're feeling better. You were in pretty bad shape when they brought you in. How are you feeling?" The corpsman picked up Carl's chart which hung from the foot of his bed.

"I'm going to be fine. The doctor says I'll be good to go in a few days. Say, could I ask a favor of you, Sergeant?"

"Of course. What do you need, sir?"

"Could you get me some writing material? I'd like to catch up with my letter writing as long as I'm stuck in this bed." Carl scooted himself up into a semi-reclined position, and the corpsman put an extra pillow behind his head.

"Sure thing, sir. Anything else?"

"Yes, as a matter of fact. Have any of my crew been here to check up on me? I'd like to see them if it's okay." Carl needed to reassure his crew that he would be back with them soon.

"Are you kidding? They've been over here every hour asking about you." He turned at the sound of a door opening and closing. The crew of *Avenging Angel* trooped into the ward. "I guess I need to leave you alone for a few minutes, sir. I'll get that writing material you asked for."

Alex Chekov and Harry Osborne pulled up the only two chairs near Carl's bed, and the rest of the men remained standing.

Harry was the first to speak. "You had us scared, Skipper. When they lowered you out of the *Angel* I thought you were a goner. So, how bad is it?"

"Not bad at all, Harry. The doc said I should be back with you guys in a few days. Shrapnel nicked an artery, but they got it fixed up pretty well. How are you guys? Nobody else got hurt ... right?"

"We're all fine, Lieutenant. I'll tell you one thing: When those fighters came at us, and I got a look at them through my turret sights, I thought *those guys are really trying to kill us ...* and then I just started firing at them. I have no idea if I hit anything. Is it

175

like that every time?" Wendell Price's eyes were wide with excitement and fear.

"In my limited experience, I'd say that you should expect it to be like that, and then be grateful when it isn't. I'm really glad we all made it back. How's the *Angel*?"

S/Sgt. Zed Carthage fielded the question. "A few holes, but she's fine. I did an engine run-up and checked the hydraulic and electrical systems including the flight instruments. Everything checks out in good shape. The ground crew is busy fixing the holes including two in the cockpit."

They chatted on for another 20 minutes until Carl felt a need to sleep. Nurse Franklin asked them all to leave. "He's only been out of surgery four hours, boys. Now scoot. Come back tomorrow. Let him get some rest."

"I know just what you need, Carl; a nice alcohol rubdown."

She pulled down his bed sheet to his waist, poured some isopropyl alcohol onto her hands and began working it into his shoulders. The evaporation of the alcohol cooled and dried his hot, perspiring body. She worked her way down his left arm, kneading and gently rubbing his skin until he began to feel sleepy. His eyes became heavy, and he allowed them to close. By the time she was finished, Carl was in that happy twilight just before sleep overtook him. As Samantha pulled the sheet up over his chest, Carl's hand reached for hers and he pulled her to him. "Annie," he said. Samantha kissed his lips. Carl drifted into a deep sleep.

On the morning of his ninth day in the hospital, after Carl finished his meal of reconstituted eggs, canned bacon, toast, and coffee, the door to the patient ward opened and half-dozen men entered. One man carried an expensive looking 16 mm motion picture camera ... the kind a news reporter might carry. He wore a "PRESS" card pinned to his chest. Accompanying the group was Carl's doctor. With him were Col. Coltharp and Lt. Gen. Ennis Whitehead, Commanding General of the 5th Air Force.

Upon recognizing Gen. Whitehead from his photo on the wall of Col. Coltharp's office, Carl sat up straighter in his bed and brushed his hands through his hair.

As the men worked their way up the patient ward, meeting first one patient and then another, the final man, whom Carl didn't recognize at first, glanced at him, smiled ... and nodded. Gen. Douglas McArthur turned back to the patient who was the center of attention for the moment.

The visitors finally stepped up to the foot of Carl's bed. Gen. McArthur stepped around to the side closer to Carl's head.

"General, I would like you to meet one of our finest pilots, 1st Lt. Carl Bridger. He received a severe shrapnel wound in a daring bombing raid when the flight of B-25s he was commanding ran afoul of four enemy fighters. It was Bridger's heroism and skill that resulted in the destruction of three of the enemy aircraft and, although severely wounded himself, provided cover for a damaged aircraft in his flight until they arrived safely back at base.

"I am honored to shake your hand, Lt. Bridger." The Commanding General of the Allied armies of the Pacific took Carl's hand in a firm handshake.

"The honor is entirely mine, sir," Carl squeaked out. "The truth is, though, my co-pilot and crew had as much to do with getting us back to base as I did."

Gen. McArthur withdrew his trademark corn-cob pipe from his shirt pocket, stuck it between his teeth and received a light from Col. Coltharp.

"Thank you, Colonel. Now, I would like very much to have a photo taken with this young man if he has no objection." He pulled his hat over his thinning pate, took Carl's hand, and they both smiled into the camera lens. The reporter ran the movie camera for about 30 seconds while Carl and the General continued their conversation.

"I wish you a speedy recovery, Lieutenant. We need men

like you up there and on the ground. Where do you call home, if I may ask?" The General drew on his pipe and puffed a cloud of smoke. The sweet scent of House of Windsor Harkness-D blended pipe tobacco permeated the air around Carl's hospital bed.

"Cascade, Montana, sir."

"Big Sky country! I believe I recall passing through your town in '38 on a road trip to Glacier and Yellowstone National Parks. Somewhere close to Helena on the Missouri River as I recall."

Carl's eyes brightened. "You're exactly right, sir. It's about half-way between Helena and Great Falls."

"Ha! I knew it. The memory is still solid as ever! Well, young man. Good fortune to you." Gen. McArthur and Gen. White-head shook Carl's hand and the entourage left.

Carl gingerly eased himself back into a reclining position. "Wow! Wait 'til I tell everybody back home about this!" he said to no one in particular.

Carl lay in the hospital for 12 days recovering from his wound while the Black Panthers continued to take the war to the enemy. On January 23rd, with Alex Chekov as pilot and a new man flying right seat, *Avenging Angel* and her crew hit targets on the Bataan Peninsula and the Mariveles Harbor. They bombed and strafed Japanese facilities before moving on to the Verde Island Passage and more enemy emplacements including motorized transportation. Several barracks and storage buildings were destroyed along the route.

On January 28th, three '25s from the 501st attacked enemy coastal defenses and troop concentrations up and down the west coast of Bataan from Olongapo to Mariveles. Every time Alex told him about another mission, Carl was left feeling angry and frustrated. He needed to get out of the hospital bed and get back into the cockpit.

He finished writing another letter home, the sixth since his injury, and was sealing the envelope when his crew entered the patient ward. The officers were attired in their dress service uniforms, or "pinks", and the enlisted men were dressed in their khaki service uniforms with their ties neatly tucked between the second and third buttons of their shirts. Alex carried Carl's uniform on a wire hanger. Harry Osborne held his freshly polished dress shoes. His surgeon, Capt. Gene Ralston, joined them. He held a manila envelope.

"Lt. Bridger, Nurse Franklin states that your physical therapy is progressing as we had hoped, and your wounds have healed nicely. Would you like to get out of here?"

"Yes! I mean … Yes, sir, I would."

"Good. I want to try one more balance and strength test on you. Using your left leg only, I want you to hop up and down with your eyes closed. Thirty repetitions ... ready? ... go."

Carl got to his feet and hopped in place as instructed. After the prescribed number of repetitions, he stopped and opened his eyes.

"Well done. These are your orders clearing you for active flight status. You'll want to get dressed. I understand there's a little ceremony going on at the HQ building." Doctor Ralston walked to the door and exited the patient ward.

"Hurry up and get changed, Skipper. We need to get over there." Alex wore a telling smile that suggested to Carl that his co-pilot knew more than he was saying.

The Headquarters, 5th Air Force, was equipped with a theater-sized room for briefings, gatherings of dignitaries and award ceremonies. It was for the latter purpose that some 200 people were gathered on the afternoon of February 8th. The two front rows were roped off for the honored recipients. Also present were the crews of the rest of Bravo Flight who participated in the raid on Campanario and Diliman in the Central Luzon Valley.

Seated at the dais were the Commanding Officers of the 501st, 500th, 499th, and 498th Bombardment Squadrons. With them sat Lt. Col. Chester Coltharp. The CO of the 345th Bomb

Group stood and walked up to the podium. He tapped the microphone and was rewarded with two loud thumps from the speakers. He cleared his throat.

"Good afternoon, Air Apaches! As many of you are well aware, on occasion we gather in this room, not for a briefing of the next mission, but for a much happier reason: to honor those among you who have distinguished yourselves in our fight against the enemy. By so doing you have brought honor to yourselves, the 345th Air Apaches, to your families and to a grateful nation. Twelve days ago, I was privileged to lead a group of 24 Mitchells on a raid into the heart of the Japanese rail and road network in the Central Luzon Valley. One of several such actions yet to be undertaken, we successfully destroyed four locomotives, 22 rail cars, a large supply depot, three anti-aircraft gun emplacements, and three enemy Ki-43 *Oscars*. Will Capt. Bergman please step forward and assist me with honoring the men of the 501st Bombardment Squadron. We will do this by aircrew beginning with the crew of A/P173. Step up on the stage as I call your names: 1st Lt. Carl Bridger, 1st Lt. Alexandre Chekov, 2nd Lt. Phillipe Ortiz, S/Sgt. Harold Osborne, Sgt. Zedediah Carthage, and Sgt. Wendell Price. The crew of *Avenging Angel* stood shoulder to shoulder facing Col. Coltharp.

"While participating in the raid on Campanario, Diliman, and surrounding villages in the Central Luzon Valley on January 24, 1945, Lt. Bridger and his men demonstrated extraordinary courage in the face of heavy anti-aircraft fire. A/P173 and two other aircraft in the flight destroyed both gun emplacements, a locomotive, eight boxcars, a number of buildings and enemy motorized transports. While returning to formation, A/P173, A/P178, and A/P002 were attacked by four Ki-43 fighters.

"Lt. Bridger maneuvered his flight of three aircraft in such a manner as to obtain optimal firing position, whereupon they successfully shot down three of the enemy planes. A/P002, under the command of Lt. Edward Lamar, received damage to his fuel line and one engine, inhibiting his ability to form-up with the main body. Rather than leaving the crippled aircraft alone, Lt. Bridger ordered all three planes to remain in close formation in order to protect Lt. Lamar's aircraft, despite the fact that Lt. Bridger himself sustained a life threatening injury from the enemy attack. Lt. Bridger is hereby awarded the Distinguished Flying Cross. The citation reads as follows:

"One, for extraordinary demonstration of superior flying skills, and for gallantly protecting his wingmen by placing his own life in jeopardy while engaged in a combat mission.

"Two, for risking his own life from wounds received during a mission and remaining with his disabled wingman to provide defensive air cover.

"Three, for successfully directing fire at four enemy aircraft resulting in the destruction of three Ki-43 planes.

"Congratulations, son." Col. Coltharp pinned the four-bladed gold medallion with its white, blue, and red ribbon on Carl's chest. He stepped back, saluted Carl and returned to the podium.

"We're not done with Bravo Flight just yet. Lt. Bridger is awarded the Order of the Purple Heart for his wounds as well." Coltharp pinned the Purple Heart over Carl's right pocket. The two exchanged salutes.

"Finally, by order of the Commanding General of the 5th Air Force, each crewmember of A/P002, A/P173, and A/P178, is individually awarded the Air Medal for gallantry in action, and demonstration of superior flying skills in the successful destruction of three enemy fighter planes before returning safely to Tacloban Air Base.

Every man in turn received the gold sunburst under gold and blue ribbon Air Medal from Col. Coltharp. They were dismissed to return to their seats.

"Sadly, the mess hall is unable to serve up cake and ice-cream for everyone ... there's a war to fight. Briefing tomorrow morning for the following crews ... Coltharp read off the names of the crews assigned to the next day's mission. Carl felt a rush of excitement when he heard his name called.

The morning of February 9th greeted the men with overcast skies and rain; a double threat for any mission. At 0700 hrs, Carl and his men joined crews from all four squadrons in the briefing room. Behind the dais, where medals were handed out the day before, a battle map of Luzon Island hung from a cork-backed wooden frame mounted on wheels.

Col. Coltharp stood before the assembled group.

"Today, we are going to strike again at the aerodromes near the towns of Aparri and Tuguegarao in the northern part of Luzon. Our objective is to harass the enemy's rear areas in the Cagayan Valley and deny him any possible use of the air bases surrounding those two towns. Secondary targets will be any large structures suggestive of industry in the area. Your load-outs will be standard explosive .50 caliber rounds plus eight 100-pound demolition bombs each. As you can see, the weather is problematic. You will be flying low and with poor visibility. Because of the overcast, no air cover will be provided. We anticipate that the enemy's planes will be grounded for the same reason, so we'll have an opportunity to cause considerable damage to his ability to launch any meaningful attacks on our land forces. Capt. Green will give you your route and latest weather report over the target. Wheels up at 0830, gentlemen. Good luck."

Capt. Benjamin Green stepped to the podium. "Our path to the objective will take us up the west coast of Samar thru the Ticao Pass to the port at Pasacao where we will cross over and up the east coast of Luzon. At 17.61 degrees north latitude, the group will turn inland to the targets. Total distance to target will be 500 miles. The latest meteorological report shows basically what you see outside.

Hopefully the ceiling will rise a bit by the time we're over the target. Keep a sharp eye on the tree tops. Good luck, guys."

"Turning one!" Carl called out the side wind screen. The right engine caught hold with a puff of white smoke and settled into a smooth 1200 rpm idle.

"Turning two!" The left engine kicked over with no problem, and Carl allowed both engines to warm-up. When the needles on the oil temperature gauges worked their way into the green normal operating range, he scanned the other engine gauges. Satisfied, Carl gave the order to follow Lt. Marshall in A/P172. His gut and his heart began a quiet fight. His heart pounded joyfully, and he felt elated to be back with his crew. His gut sent forth a different message. *I am fear and caution*, was received by his grumbling stomach, and the familiar sour taste in his mouth acknowledged receipt of the memo.

"Taxi out behind Marshall, Alex. Let's get this show on the road."

Carl keyed the inter-plane switch and called for a crew check. "Radio check, boys. Call it back."

"Navigator, ready to go. Welcome home, Lieutenant," Phil Ortiz responded.

"Engineer. Good to go, Skipper."

"Comm radios are tuned and ready, Lieutenant."

"Tail turret. Ready in the rumble seat, Skipper," Harry Osborne replied in his trademark jubilant voice.

Alex looked at Carl. "How's the wound feeling, Carl?"

"It actually feels pretty good. Nurse Franklin wrapped my waist to help stabilize and support the surgery site. I'm fine." He took note of his co-pilot's concerned expression. "Don't worry, Alex, really. I 'm fine … er … *Ya zdorof, tovarishch*." He smiled at his friend and occasional Russian tutor.

"Your Russian is improving. Pretty soon, you'll be speaking it fluently." Alex gave Carl a friendly nudge with his elbow."

Just over two hours later, the group of 16 bombers, four each from the four squadrons of the 345th, reached their Intercept Point and turned inland to the coastal town of Aparri at the headwaters of the Cagayan River.

Flight Leader to Black Panthers, separate into line-abreast formation. Arm your bombs. We're following the Rough Raiders to the target.

Carl eased up off Alonso "Al" Marshall's left wing. Lt. Steve Denny in A/P175 assumed the right wing position and, Lt. Carey Hatcher fell in off Lt. Denny's right wing. Ahead, the four '25s of the 500th Rough Raiders descended into the cloud cover at 1,000 feet elevation. Flying in virtually zero visibility, the 501st Black Panthers kept just close enough to keep the lead planes in sight.

"Stay sharp, Phil. You may only get one quick look at the airfield! Arm one sleeve."

"Copy that. One sleeve of four, ready to go."

"Open bomb-bay doors," Carl ordered.

Phil Ortiz punched the button, and the bomb-bay doors sprung open with an audible thump as they locked in place.

At 500 feet elevation the formation came in too high on the first run over the target and had to circle back around. They dropped down to 200 feet and caught a break.

A small opening in the overcast revealed the airstrip at Aparri at their 2 o'clock position with several small structures between them and the runway. The ground raced by in a blur beneath *Avenging Angel.*

Bank right! Target at 2 o'clock! Al Marshall commanded from A/P172.

As if guided by the same hand, the four Black Panthers banked right. The flight of Rough Raiders was over the target and sixteen 100-pound bombs dropped. The group of fragile buildings blew apart amid a conflagration of billowing fire and smoke ...

splintered as if a child's pick-up sticks had been swatted by a giant's hand.

Take out the runway, Panthers! Marshall called out.

At 300 mph, and the runway speeding toward them, the lead pilot gave the order ... *Bombs away!*

A 1,000-foot section of runway erupted with the impact of the 16 high-explosive demolition bombs as the four Mitchells of the 501st Black Panthers roared by 100 feet above the surface.

On target! On target! Save the rest of your ordnance for Tuguegarao, Panthers. Banking left downwind of the runway. We're making another run along the flight line. There must be at least 20 Jap planes on the tarmac.

Marshall took point and led his flight on a course parallel to the paved landing strip.

Staggered-line formation. Let's strafe the hell outta them!

They made one pass strafing the planes while the other squadrons laid down more bombs on the runway rendering it unusable. One enemy pilot climbed into a Ki-43 Oscar and tried to takeoff. He rotated about 10 feet off the ground when he came into the sights of Carl's four .50 caliber nose guns and four side guns. The line of eight machine-gun tracers chewed up the tarmac and sped toward the Japanese fighter. The Oscar flew straight into the wall of armor-piercing bullets and disintegrated. Meanwhile the 499th Bats Outta Hell strafed the buildings including two barracks.

Form up! Form up! the Group Leader called.

The formation maintained 500 feet altitude. The sunlight had begun to burn off much of the fog, and the Cagayan River came into clear view. The 16 bombers flew down the course of the river which would take them south-south-west directly to their next target.

Tugueguarao was at higher elevation than Aparri and lay within a heavy blanket of the overcast. Visibility was very poor and the American planes had to content themselves with two light strafing runs. With the formation drawing close to the range of their available fuel for the return leg to Tacloban, they had no choice but to break off the attack and head for home.

Carl and Alex sat at a table in the Officers' Club with mugs of beer in their hands. The chatter of a group of Marine officers of VMB-611 could be heard above the usual hum of conversation in the "O" Club. Carl figured they were just blowing off steam due to the fact that they had yet to receive any missions since their arrival at Tacloban two weeks earlier. He understood their frustration, recalling the almost two weeks he had spent in the hospital. One Marine officer stumbled into a table of four Army Air Force officers spilling his beer on two of the pilots from the 498th Falcons. The Marine PBJ pilot recognized the 345th Air Apache patch and decided to take issue with the AAF taking missions from the Marines.

"Sorry, Apache. I know that injuns cain't hold their liquor," the man said referring to the spilled drink which had soaked the Air Corps pilot. Carl figured the Jarhead must have thought he said something funny because he released a loud stream of *har-dee-har-hars*. "Here! Have another one ..." he bellowed and poured the rest of his beer on the head of another of the Army pilots sitting at the table. What happened then could only be described as a head-banging slug-fest. Carl and Alex quietly moved their chairs out of reach.

The two beer-soaked Air Corps pilots leapt to their feet. One of them, Capt. Gerard Phillips, hit the Marine with a round-house right cross which spun the Jarhead around toward his table mate who added a left cross to the man's jaw.

The Air Corps officer who got in the second swing had just enough time to laugh in the Marine's face and yell, "You Jarheads can't fly your way off the runway on a clear day. What is 'PBJ' anyway ... a Peanut Butter and Jam sandwich? We eat that for

186

lunch!" At that precise moment the three remaining Marine pilots charged in, as did four other 345th officers. Chairs and bottles flew every which way, bodies tumbled over tables, men swung at anything within fist distance. One Air Corps guy smacked another Army man on the snoot.

"Oops. Sorry, Pete," he said when saw he had struck man from his own unit.

Carl got off a roundhouse punch when a Marine came at him with a beer bottle. He had no problem side-stepping the drunk Marine who went down with a crash, turning over a table in the process

"C'mon, Carl, let's get out of here. You don't want to take a fist in the gut. You're still healing." The two of them left the Officers' Club just as the MPs rounded the HQ building heading toward the "O" Club. They walked arm over shoulder laughing at the ruckus they left behind. "Man, that's the most fun I've had since we've been in this muddy arm-pit of the war. I really thought that big PBJ pilot was going to clock you on the noggin with his beer bottle ... fancy foot work on your part, by the way." Alex laughed again.

"It wasn't hard to side-step the Jarhead. He was so drunk he could barely stand as it was," Carl laughed. They walked past the hospital compound when they spotted someone wearing a rain poncho walking toward them.

"Carl ... er, Lt. Bridger, is that you?" Samantha Franklin approached the two men.

"Oh, hi, Lt. Franklin. You weren't headed over to the 'O' club were you?"

"Yes, I was, as a matter of fact. Why do you ask?" Samantha drew the poncho tighter around her.

"We just came from there. A bunch of Marines decided to start a fight with a few of us from the 345th. I'm afraid it turned out to be quite a scuffle. We got out of there just as the MPs showed up. You might want to steer clear of the place for tonight."

"I think that's a good idea." Samantha thought about Carl's wound, and her expression revealed her concern. "What about you ... you didn't get involved in the fight, did you?"

"I'm fine, really ... nothing to be worried about."

"The infirmary is right here. Let me check you out, anyway." The nurse insisted.

Alex cleared his throat. Sensing that there was more going on than a simple nurse-patient relationship, he excused himself.

"You go ahead, Skipper, I'll see you back at quarters." Alex walked on before Carl could object.

Inside the infirmary, Samantha had Carl remove his shirt. "Please lie back on the exam table."

Carl did as directed, and she gently probed the surgery site, applying pressure along the incision and abdomen.

"How does that feel? Any discomfort?"

"No, none. Look, Samantha, I'm glad I caught you alone. There's something I've been meaning to tell you." He sat up and put his shirt back on.

"Me, too. Let me speak first, though, alright?" She pulled up a chair next to Carl and held her hands in her lap, clasping her fingers tightly. "I think I know what it is you need to tell me, so I want to make it easier on both of us.

"When I first came here from Hawaii, I had just lost my fiancé. His plane was shot down over Burma." Samantha lowered her head, and her chin began to tremble. She brushed the back of her hand over her eyes. "I'm sorry. I ... I miss him so much. Anyway, when I met you the first time you came to visit your crewman, something drew me to you. I don't know if it was the compassion I saw in your eyes for your friend, or that you reminded me of Ste ... my fiancé. I was drawn to you, Carl. And then, when you were wounded, and I saw you lying unconscious on this very exam table, my heart suddenly sank. I wanted so very much for you to live! I

188

think I was falling in love, but ..."

Carl interrupted. "Samantha, we can't ..."

"Please, let me finish. When you were in recovery, I made the mistake of kissing you. I realized immediately what was happening. I saw Steven lying there. I couldn't save him, but I had a hand in saving you. Carl, I do feel love for you, but I know it's not healthy. I think I'm trying to mend my own wound by filling the void in my heart with you." She reached for Carl's hand. "I'm sorry. I hope you understand."

Carl squeezed her hand. "Of course I do. You know, when I woke up in recovery, your face was the first thing I saw. I thought for a moment that Annie, my fiancé, was there. I have to admit, I felt an immediate attraction to you even before that. The night of the typhoon, when we fought to keep the tent from blowing away, your courage and strength reminded me so much of her." Carl paused for a few seconds and shook his head.

"Sam, it would be easy to let my feelings for you get out of control. This ... war we're in is not part of the world that's waiting for us back home. When we leave here, we'll go back to our families ... to our *real* lives. So, you're right. We care about each other, but for all the wrong reasons."

Samantha nodded her head in agreement. "So, there's nothing else but to say good-bye?"

"Yes. I think we both know it's the only thing that makes sense." Carl released Samantha's hand and stood.

"Good-bye, then, Carl. Thank you for being, well ... *you*. You take care of yourself, now. No more barroom fights."

"I promise, Sam."

She walked out of the infirmary and into the drizzling rain.

Chapter IX

February 14, 1945

–Cascade, Montana–

Gifford stomped the snow off his boots and hung his coat on the hook to the right of the back door. He sat down on the bench, removed his worn-out Justins ™ and, in stocking feet, padded into the kitchen.

"Mmm ... smells good in here. Whatcha got cookin' good lookin'?" He stepped behind his wife and wrapped his arms around her waist.

"Chicken dumplings for dinner. Did you pick up the mail in town?" Letters from Carl over in the Philippines had come almost daily for the last ten days, and they all hoped for another one with each day's delivery.

"Well now, let me see here." Gifford thumbed through the thin stack of envelopes and came across the one he figured Carl's mother was hoping for. Then, he found another one, addressed to Annie.

"Maybe we should go through the bills first and save the rest for later," he teased.

"Oh, you! ...Give me that." Millie's eyes lit up. "Oh, there's one for Annie, too."

Millie walked to the foot of the stairs leading up to the bedrooms of the two-story brick main house. "Annie, come down here, honey. There's a letter from Carl waiting for you."

Annie came bounding downstairs in a flurry of hair and

skirt, followed by Penny like a puppy headed for his food bowl. "Gimmie. Gimmie!" she cried, grinning like a five-year-old on Christmas morning.

"We got one, too. Come in the kitchen, and we'll read it together."

Millie ran a knife along the edge of the envelope being careful not to tear the thin paper.

She sat down, removed the letter and began reading.

Dear Mom, Dad, Penny and Annie –

I'm sitting here listening to the unceasing patter of rain on the roof of the tent. It seldom rains this time of year, but a couple of weeks ago we had a freak typhoon of all things. Anyway, I've been grounded for a few days because of a minor injury. Nothing to worry about. I should be back in the air by the time you get this letter. The fight is going well. Our missions are mostly uneventful reconnaissance sorties. We get to sink some barges now and then. Pretty boring for the most part. I can't comment on certain things, but I believe my safety is assured ... at least for the time being.

I miss you all so much. At times I feel as though this is the only real world I've ever known, and the Double-B is just a fantasy world ... sort of like Dorothy felt about her Kansas farm in The Wizard of Oz.

I think things will wrap up before the end of the year. Maybe I'll even be home by Christmas. That'd be swell!

How are things at the ranch? I hope you're able to make ends meet what with the war and all. Alex Chekov, my co-pilot, says his folks told him the rationing of some things is relaxing a little. That may be a sign of happier days ahead, eh?

Well, I'll close for now. I'll write again soon.
All my love,
— Carl

"I wonder how he got hurt. Do you think he got shot? Oh, my goodness!" Millie stood up from the table and put the letter in the pocket of her apron. "I love to hear from our boy, but I worry so!" She pulled a handkerchief from her pocket and dabbed at her eyes.

Gifford approached his wife, turned her face toward him and kissed her cheek. "The important thing is, he's well. He said he'll be back in his plane before you know it. He'll be fine, Millie."

Annie rose from her chair and walked toward the stairs leading to the bedrooms. "If you don't mind, I'd like to read my letter upstairs, and then I'll come back down and help with dinner, Mother Bridger."

She closed her bedroom door behind her and sat down on the bed. Her heart raced with anticipation as she opened the envelope and withdrew the letter.

Annie, my love –
  I wish I could send a Valentine's Day card. If I were home, I would drive to Kress' five-and-dime in Great Falls and buy the biggest and swellest card in the store. Oh well, this will have to do until next Valentine's Day.
  Annie, I love you, baby. You are up there with me on every mission. I had the ground crew paint a picture of a winged woman carrying a sword and shield on the fuselage beneath the windscreen on my B-25. She's surrounded with the name "Avenging Angel." I made her to look like you, with your golden hair streaming out behind you, because you are my angel. In my mind, you're up there with

193

us ... protecting us. I guess that might seem silly to you. Anyway, the guys did a swell job. If I can find a camera someplace I'll take a picture for you.

As for my injury, I picked up a tiny sliver of metal in my side. It took a few stitches, but I'll be fine. I'll be back in the pilot's seat before you can blink an eye.

The crew and I are bonded like family now. We've flown enough missions that we've all become good friends. My co-pilot, Alex Chekov, is teaching me Russian. Say, do you remember old Mister Pinsky's Russian class back in high school? I liked that class ... mostly because I got to sit across from you. Alex says I'm getting pretty good at it. And then there's S/Sgt. Harry Osborne. What a character! He's always ready with a joke to keep us all laughing during even the most stressful times. He's become a close friend.

How about you? I imagine you're all still knee-high in snow. With spring around the corner, it'll soon be calving and branding time. Mom will be planting her garden as soon as the snow melts off. I picture you helping her with the victory garden you two plant every year. How about your parents? How is your dad doing with his breathing problems?

Well, I'd better quit for now, baby girl.

I love you, Annie – only forever, if you care to know,
– Carl

She opened the bottom drawer of her bureau and pulled out a shoe box with the lid tied securely by a red ribbon. She placed Carl's letter on top of the growing stack of letters he began writing less than a week after he left home the previous September.

"Until next time, my darling." Annie kissed her fingers and pressed them against the lid of the box.

Dinner that night was filled with cheerful talk about Carl

and the prospect of his coming home in time for Christmas. Annie was ecstatic about the idea.

"I remember last Christmas when we all came downstairs and found him sound asleep on the sofa. And the early Christmas dinner with my parents here ... what a wonderful time that was!" She laughed. "It was the best time ever. It's hard to believe that was only three months ago. It seems sometimes like it's been forever."

Gifford dabbed at his mouth with his napkin and smiled. "I have a thought. Since we're all in such a festive mood, what do you say we all jump in the truck tomorrow and drive into the Falls and grab a movie. I haven't been to see a film in over a year. What do you say?"

"Oh, Daddy, can we? That would be so much fun!" Penny beamed. Movies were a rare treat for the Bridgers. The Cascade Theater in town had closed down, making the Liberty Theater in Great Falls the show house of choice.

"Penny, get the paper from the living room will you? Let's see what's playing at the Liberty."

Gifford handed two dollars to the girl behind the ticket booth. She passed back four admission tickets and 60 cents. He pocketed the change, and the family entered the theatre.

"Oh, I had forgotten how beautiful it is in here!" Penny's eyes scanned the ornate sculptured crown molding and the crystal chandelier hanging from the coffered ceiling. A grand red carpeted staircase led to a balcony.

They found seats approximately in the middle of the half-filled theater.

"I'm going to get some goodies. Popcorn and soda, anyone?" Gifford was enjoying taking his family on a rare outing. He eased his way between the seats to the isle. Penny followed her father to lend a hand.

When they returned, Gifford and Penny handed out a small bag of popcorn and a soda each to Millie and Annie and settled into their own seats.

The red velvet curtain, with its gold scalloped fringe and tassels, pulled back on both sides revealing the big 25-foot tall square screen. The lights in the theatre dimmed, and the screen lit up with the Movietone News. The picture showed a movie camera with three lenses turned toward the audience, and the narrator began to announce the latest war news as the screen filled with scenes of the fighting in Europe and the Pacific. The scene moved to the inside of a field hospital's patient ward.

General Douglas McArthur and Lt. General Ennis Whitehead visit a hospital on Leyte Island to say hello to a few of the brave soldiers and airmen wounded in action ...

The narrator's voice droned on, but the Bridger family never heard a word. Penny froze with a handful of popcorn about to enter her opened mouth. Millie and Gifford gaped wide-eyed at each other in astonishment. Annie squeaked out a barely audible yelp. She quickly covered her mouth to stifle another one, while spilling her popcorn and drink on her lap.

There, on the screen, were Generals Whitehead and McArthur shaking hands and chatting with a young man lying in a bed. It was Carl!

When the newsreel ended, Annie grabbed Millie's hand, and Millie took hold of Gifford's hand letting go of her soda in the process. Gifford spilled his popcorn reaching for Penny's hand. The four of them sat open-mouthed, unable to speak.

Finally, Millie broke the silence. "What should we do?"

"Do? Well ... I guess ... uh ... Stay here. I'm going to get more popcorn." Gifford, always the practical one in a crisis, did just that. He worked his way past a few confused, staring patrons and out to the lobby.

By the time he returned, a Looney Tunes cartoon with Bugs

Bunny as "Buckaroo Bugs" was nearly finished. Gifford sat back down, relieved that the newsreel had ended.

He turned to Millie and whispered, "We're going to watch this movie and put our worries to rest. Carl's fine. His letter was written after he got wounded, and he's fine. Let's try to enjoy ourselves." *Anchors Aweigh* starring Gene Kelley, Frank Sinatra, and Kathryn Grayson filled the screen, and the family settled in for the feature. Their hearts and minds, however, were thousands of miles away.

Chapter X

February 14, 1945

–Relocation to San Marcelino–

Valentine's Day at Tacloban was just another day other than the fact that the Group Commander had called a briefing for every flight crew member of the entire 345th Air Apaches plus all ground crew personnel. Some 800 men gathered in the main hall in the Headquarters Building.

Alex leaned over to Carl as they awaited the appearance of Col. Coltharp. "What do you think ... is this about the big move guys have been talking about?" Rumors of a transfer of the 345th north to San Marcelino had been working its way through the grapevine for the past week.

"I don't know, Alex, but something's cookin' for sure."

Coltharp's Adjutant, Capt. Leonard Bills, entered the hall thru the door to the right of the stage. "Group, ah-ten-hut!" he called. Every man in the room rose to their feet and stood at attention.

Lt. Col. Chester Coltharp stepped up to the podium. "At ease ... take your seats."

As soon as the room was quiet, Coltharp started in.

"As you know, on the 3rd of this month, 11 days ago, elements of the 8th Cavalry Division entered the city of Manila following two weeks of fighting in the mountains east of the capitol. Since that time, the Japanese stranglehold from the Bicol Peninsula on the southern tip of Luzon to the northern beaches at the foot of the Sierra Madre Mountains has been weakening rapidly. Gen. Ya-mashita's three-pronged hold on Luzon is now nothing more than a retreating battle for them. Our intelligence people tell us that the Japanese high-command has ordered the evacuation of high rank-ing military and Japanese government officials from the island.

"The combined efforts of the 101st Airborne, 6th Army and 14th Corp continue to root out strongholds of the enemy from Manila to Baguio city. A benefit of that operation is their securing of the airbase at San Marcelino. That is the topic of today's briefing.

"The 345th is going to relocate to San Marcelino over the next several days starting tomorrow. One-half of the planes and crews of each squadron will be fueled and flown north to San Marcelino. C-54s and C-47s will be arriving from the Southeast Air Transport Command beginning today to load up everything not directly mission related. Minimum infrastructure needed to support missions will remain, but everything else is being packed up, loaded onto aircraft and transport ships, and sent north to San Marcelino. Capt. Bills will read-out the aircraft and crews who will be part of the first move tomorrow. Those crews will attend a brief-ing immediately following this meeting, so if your aircraft desig-nator is called, your crews will remain in your seats. The rest of you will be dismissed."

Two minutes later, the crew of *Avenging Angel* left the building.

"I guess we'll be flying a few more sorties out of Tacloban while the other guys set up housekeeping up north, eh, Alex?"

"Roger that, Skipper."

Acting Squadron Commander of the 501st Black Panthers, Maj. Benjamin Green knocked on Col. Coltharp's door.

"Enter!" The voice on the other side of the door announced.

"Good morning, sir." Maj. Green smiled and closed the door behind him.

"Come in, Ben. Sit down ... coffee?" Coltharp offered. Without waiting for an answer, he poured two strong steaming cups from the large carafe his clerk brought to him every morning. He handed a cup to Green and walked over to a battle map of Luzon Island showing the most recent battle lines, troop emplacements and enemy forces in and around the central Luzon valley.

"Reconnaissance photos show the presence of several luggers and barges approaching the areas near Polillo Island, Cabugao Bay, San Miguel Bay and Barceloneta. The enemy has approximately 80,000 infantry in the area of the Bicol Peninsula. Their hope is that this concentration of troops can hold out long enough for the evacuation of their key military and civilian personnel to take place. Your job, Major, is to thwart the enemy's plan to evacuate any personnel from the Central Luzon battle area by hitting enemy shipping in the bays and coves along the coast of the peninsula and coastal islands"

"I understand, sir, the 501st will do whatever is needed." Green sipped his coffee and placed the cup on Coltharp's desk.

"Other squadrons of the Air Apaches have been briefed on their part of the mission. Their job will be to hit troop emplacements, ammo dumps and supply depots up the peninsula to San Miguel Bay including the islands of Catanduanes, Barceloneta, and Polillo. I want you to send two flights of three planes each manned by your best crews and hit everything that floats. Leave the rest to the other squadrons."

"We'll get it done, sir" The Major stood and saluted the Group Commander.

Maj. Green met with 1st Lt. Carl Bridger, 1st Lt. Al Marshall, 1st Lt. Jack Hayes, 1st Lt. Horacio Ohnamus, 1st Lt. Zeke Bell, and 1st Lt. Leon Stone.

"Gentlemen, you and your crews have been chosen for tomorrow's mission. Zeke Bell will lead the Black Panthers in Alpha Flight. Lt. Bridger will lead Bravo Flight. You will strike at shipping

201

along the east coast of the Bicol Peninsula, north to San Miguel Bay, and along the coasts of any islands between here and there including Catanduanes, Barceloneta, and Polillo Islands." Maj. Green related in detail the rest of the mission as described to him by the Group Commander.

"The latest weather report shows clearing to the north starting at about 0800 hrs. Your load-out will be six 500-pound demolition bombs and standard explosive .50 caliber rounds for your guns. The 498th will depart at 0730. The 499th will launch one hour later at 0830 hrs followed at 0930 by the 500th Bomb Squadron. Wheels up for the Black Panthers at 1030 hrs. Questions?"

"Can we expect enemy fighters, Maj. Green?" Al Marshall asked.

"Negative. Most of the enemy's air power has been moved too far north to reach our target area without any fuel resources. Ack-ack is likely, however."

"What is our bombing altitude going to be, sir?" The question came from Leon Stone.

"You'll go in at mast height. You'll be hitting ships, the ports and the coves, so set your bombs with four second time delays and get as low as you can for optimum effect. I shouldn't have to teach you the fundamentals of low-level bombing. You all know the drill, guys. Let's do this!"

The next morning three trucks pulled up in front of the crew tents and took aboard the crews of the six Mitchells of the 501st Black Panthers. The men crowded shoulder-to-shoulder onto the benches lining the sides of the canvas-covered truck beds. They rode in silence, heads down ... each deep into his own private thoughts about what lay ahead, about family, and, of course, making it safely back to base. Carl sat across from Horatio Ohnamus, a devout Catholic who pulled a gold crucifix from inside his shirt and kissed it followed by making the sign of the cross.

"Half a league, half a league, half a league onward rode the 600, eh, Skipper?" Phil Ortiz' paraphrase of the Charge of the Light Brigade was an apt observation, Carl thought.

"Indeed, Phil. Only we're better armed than the Light Brigade, and we're flying above the Valley of Death. Try not to be so morose, pal," he laughed. His upbeat retort brought chuckles from all. He cast a wink at Horatio who nodded and smiled back. Although not of the same faith, they both placed their trust in Christ.

The trucks stopped in front of first one aircraft and then the next, unloading the crews. Carl climbed out of the truck, followed by Alex and then Phil. Another truck pulled up immediately afterword and unloaded the rest of *Avenging Angel*'s crew. Carl began his walk around and ran his hand along a couple of the patched holes, noting the slightly raised surface of the patches. The rudder that was damaged on his first mission, although in excellent condition, showed an almost imperceptibly brighter paint job. *Angel* was showing her battle scars, but she was still a beautiful lady. He kissed his hand and patted the winged lady before he climbed up the crew ladder.

When the last of the three '25s of Alpha Flight was airborne, Carl turned *Angel* onto the active runway and lined up the bomber's nose on the centerline.

"One-half flaps, please, Alex."

"Flaps set at 50 percent, Skipper.

Carl eased the throttles firmly forward, and the plane began her takeoff roll. At 100 mph, the nose wheel lifted off the runway. He pulled back slightly on the control yoke, and the mains rotated into the air.

"Gear up."

"Gear's up and locked," Alex responded.

"Flaps up."

"Flaps up."

The 501st Black Panthers initiated their sweep of Poliqui Bay and the coastal town of Legazpi about 250 miles north from Tacloban.

Alpha Flight Leader to all planes, Alpha Flight will initiate the first run on the target. Bravo Flight will follow in line-abreast formation. Acknowledge.

Bravo Flight Leader. Copy that.

Alpha Flight went in fast and low. Behind them, Carl formed Bravo Flight for their run on the target.

Alpha Papa One Seven Eight to Flight Lead, I see a barge in port at Legazpi. Permission to attack? The request came from Carl's left wingman, Jack Hayes.

Affirmative, Jack. You take the barge, Marshall and I will hit the two luggers in the jetty.

Bravo Flight Leader to Alpha Flight Leader, we're starting our run on the harbor.

As soon as Bravo Flight got into attack formation and dived on the target, anti-aircraft rounds began to explode around them. One burst followed by another buffeted the plane. The luggers were moored close together in the jetty, beyond the wall of flying shrapnel.

Guns only on the first pass. Save your bombs, Carl commanded.

The two bombers came in low, 50 feet off the deck, and opened fire on the two luggers. The small wooden vessels, used for ferrying food, supplies and ammunition to the Japanese soldiers, were decimated by the assault. A second run by the two Black Panthers was rewarded with fires and billowing smoke.

Jack Hayes approached the steel-hulled barge from 100 feet above the surface and released a single 500-pound bomb. The explosion sent a geyser of water skyward behind the bomber.

Damn! Overshot him. He pulled up and went in for two more strafing runs, raking the bridge of the barge.

Two bombs, one each from Lt. Marshall and Carl, scored near misses on the luggers and the second barge in the jetty.

Alpha Flight Leader to all planes, form up! Form up! Zeke Bell announced.

Bravo Flight Leader to flight, you heard the man. Form-up. I don't think anything will be moving out from that port for a while, boys. I wish our bombs had been more effective, though, Carl said.

The six planes proceeded northeast on the 85-mile leg to the islands of Catanduanes and Cabugao Bay.

Alpha Leader to all planes, our next sweep is coming up dead ahead, boys. Bombardiers, arm one bomb. We'll go in low, staggered-line formation, and strafe all vessels. On our second run, we'll light them up with bombs from a line-abreast formation. Copy?

Bravo Flight, copy. We're right behind you, Zeke, Carl announced. *Ready, Bravo Flight?*

Marshall, copy.

Hayes, copy.

Descending to 200 feet now.

Carl dropped to 200 feet above the water as they approached Cabugao Bay behind Lt. Bell and Alpha Flight. One lugger and one barge were sighted. Bravo Flight strafed them and climbed out to re-form for their bomb run.

Marshall and Hayes, take them out with your bombs. I'll drop in behind you and clean up.

Carl throttled back, and *Avenging Angel* fell into position behind the other two '25s of Bravo Flight.

Marshall and Hayes increased their speed to 270 mph and came at the two vessels with their combined sixteen .50 caliber guns laying down a devastating blanket of fire. When the bombers were in position, they each released a single 500-pound high explosive bomb. The first bomb from Jack Hayes' A/P178 overshot the target and exploded harmlessly 100 feet beyond the lugger sending up a towering spout of sea water. Al Marshall's bomb made a direct hit on the barge between the bow and the bridge. The explosion rocked the vessel, and a fire immediately ensued raising a column of black smoke. The flames spread out on the surface of the water in a quantity that suggested a store of oil and fuel below deck.

"Okay, boys, it's our turn. Lower the bomb-bay doors." Carl banked *Angel* around and came at the two vessels on a line parallel to and between the targets. He opened up with his eight fixed AN/M2 .50 caliber guns.

"Bombs away!" he called. One high explosive demolition bomb hit between the lugger and barge finishing the job begun by the other two Mitchells. The lugger was a floating undefined mass of wood, and the barge was listing badly to the port side engulfed by the fire. Somewhat surprising was the absence of anti-aircraft bursts.

Form up, Bravo Flight. Next stop is San Miguel Bay. Watch for ack-ack.

On the southwest shoreline of San Miguel Bay, at the coastal village of Barceloneta, three large 100-foot long barges were docked close together in the process of unloading various supplies and war materials for the Japanese forces scattered up and down the Bicol Peninsula. The arms and supplies were taken ashore and driven thru the jungle along the Cabasuao Road west and south to pre-arranged pickup points where the road met the encampments of the Japanese forces.

Approximately 80,000 enemy troops of General Yamashita's *Shimbu Group*, were assigned to draw out the battle for Luzon as long as possible. Yamashita needed time to organize the evacuation of critical military and Japanese government officials before the Americans could occupy the city. The *Shimbu Group* would attempt to slow the American advance toward Manila from the south up the Bicol Peninsula.

Alpha Flight completed their run and was forming for their

next target. Bravo Flight arrowed down for their first run.

There! Three barges! Marshall, you take lead. Hayes you're next. I'll follow up.

A/P178 was spot on target. His bomb hit the middle of the three vessels and caused a surprisingly large secondary explosion. A ball of yellow-orange flames roiled upward 200 feet amidst thick black smoke.

Al Marshall in A/P172 scored a direct hit on the docks, blocking any opportunity for the enemy to finish the off-loading of the shipment.

Carl and his crew nailed the coffin shut by scoring another direct hit on the barges. Again, the enemy offered nothing more serious than small arms fire from the ground.

"Wow! We caught them with their pants down on this sortie, Skipper." Harry Osborne said from his tail turret.

"Roger that, Harry. Is everyone okay, back there?" Carl asked.

The crew reported back that they were "A-Okay" and combat ready.

Form up, Bravo Flight. Damage report. Hayes?

Alpha Papa One Seven Eight is undamaged.

Alpha Papa One Seven Two is combat ready, Flight Leader.

Bravo Flight Leader to flight, turning toward Polillo Island.

The two flights split up. Alpha Flight would circle the island to the west. Carl led Bravo Flight to the east.

Avenging Angel and the other two '25s of Bravo Flight flew up the coast toward the village of Polillo. More of a town than a village, Polillo was a prosperous fishing and shipping port off the east coast of Luzon before the war. The town enjoyed a reputation for its craftsmanship in building fishing vessels. When the Japanese pressed the locals into service building luggers, the island became a central distribution point for the transport of supplies, arms, and troops for the entire Bicol Peninsula.

Let's make one pass at 500 feet, Bravo Flight. I want to get a good look before we start our run, Carl announced.

The serene Pacific blue sky exploded with black eruptions of ack-ack from two anti-aircraft batteries. Carl spotted the emplacements from the first burst, and a plan formed in his mind.

Hayes, Marshall ... hit those guns. Take them out! Starting my run on the boat sheds.

Carl zeroed-in on three luggers under construction in the boat sheds and a fourth completed and docked adjacent to the sheds. "Arm two bombs, Phil. I'll set you up on the boat sheds."

Angel over-flew the sheds and then banked around to attack.

"Bombardier to pilot, two bombs, armed and ready, Skipper."

"Copy. Starting our run now. I'll strafe them, and you hit 'em with the bombs. That should do it."

Avenging Angel dived on the boat sheds, and Carl opened up with the .50 cals laying down a blanket of fire. When he reached the desired altitude, he pulled back sharply on the yoke.

"Bombs away!" Phil called out. A single explosion erupted from the middle of the boat sheds.

Harry Osborne called in from the tail. "I only saw one explosion, Skipper. The second bomb must have been a dud."

"What about it Phil ... you forget to arm the second bomb?" Carl asked.

"No. It's armed and hanging half-way out the bomb bay. We've got ourselves a live bomb on board, Skipper." The tension in Phil Ortiz' voice came through Carl's headset.

"Alright. Things just got a whole lot more interesting. Stand by, Phil. Let me get Alpha Flight on the horn."

Carl keyed the plane-to-plane transmitter.

Bravo Flight Leader to flight, you boys finish taking

out the boat sheds and the dock. We have a live bomb hung up in the bomb bay. I'll orbit while you finish the attack. Call in when you're ready to form up.

Roger, Flight Leader. Starting our run now, Jack Hayes called back.

Carl watched as his two wingmen dived their planes on the target. The absence of ack-ack told him that they had been successful in destroying the gun emplacements.

"Navigator to pilot, Carl, the tail-fin of the bomb somehow got tangled up in a cable that came loose from the bomb-release mechanism. Sgt. Carthage is working on it now. Can you hold us steady, Skipper? And don't try to close the doors."

"Roger that, Phil. I'll keep *Angel* in a shallow bank." Carl looked over at Alex ... whose fear was etched on his face. He could only shrug his shoulders.

A/P172 and A/P178 completed their run on the boat sheds and the fourth lugger. They also expended the rest of their bombs on three camouflaged barges and strafed about thirty or so Japanese soldiers returning small arms fire from the dock.

Flight Leader, we're forming up with you now. We destroyed three more barges and finished up on the boat sheds, Jack Hayes announced.

Al Marshall formed up off Carl's left wing, and Hayes pulled up off his right wing.

Hold straight and level, Carl. I'm dropping under you to get a look at your bomb bay, announced Hayes.

He dropped underneath *Avenging Angel* and adjusted his throttles to match speeds.

Yep, I see the problem, Carl. It's hanging about half-way below the fuselage. I have an idea. Slow down and drop your landing gear. I want to see if the bomb is hanging below your mains.

Good idea. Slowing to 120," replied Carl.

"Give me two notches of flaps, Alex. I want to hold her level."

Alex lowered the flap levers two notches. "Flaps one-half, Skipper."

"Lower the gear." Carl's heart accelerated as he felt the plane shake when the landing gear went down.

Two green lights appeared in the cockpit. "Gear down and locked." Alex reported.

Jack Hayes dropped A/P178 slightly behind and level with A/P173.

"It looks to me like you have a few inches of space between your mains and the bomb, Carl. If that bomb doesn't slip any more, you may have a chance."

"A chance at what, Carl? Is he saying what I think he's saying?" Alex's eyes grew wide with fear.

A plan was forming in Carl's mind … one that would at least give his crew a chance at survival.

"Sgt. Price put me on the comm to Tacloban."

"You're on the air, Skipper." Wendell Price confirmed.

Carl pressed the talk button.

Tacloban, this is Bravo Flight Leader, Alpha Papa One Seven Three. Do you read? Over."

Roger, Alpha Papa One Seven Three. You are five-by-five. Over.

Tacloban, we are approximately three-five-miles out. We have live ordinance hung up in the bomb bay, protruding below the fuselage. Request emergency approach. I believe we have enough clearance to land safely if the bomb remains in position. I will circle south of the field and order my crew to bail out before landing. Over.

Roger, Alpha Papa One Seven Three. You are cleared for straight-in approach. Emergency vehicles are standing by.

Maj. Ben Green made a point of being in the tower when his boys came back from a mission. He had been the acting CO of the 501st Black Panthers for the past three months. His predecessor was downed by anti-aircraft fire during a bombing mission over Mindoro.

"Get Col. Coltharp on the horn. He's going to want to know about this." Green watched the last of the current flight of bombers from the 500th Bomb Squadron land.

"Are there any other planes in the air besides Bravo Flight?"

"Yes, sir. We have an inbound C-47 from Guam about 10 minutes out." The lieutenant manning the tower turned to one of the tower controllers, a three-striped sergeant.

"Radio the '47. Get a position, and tell him to get here A.S.A.P. Put him on a short final. I want him on the ground and clear of the runway in eight minutes." He turned back to Maj. Green.

"Excuse me sir, but are you saying your pilot is going to attempt to land with a 500-pound demolition bomb dangling from his belly?"

"He's the best we've got, Lieutenant. If he says he can do it, I'm going to trust his judgment and pray to God he's right ... and that I'm not killing him by letting him try."

The C-47 came in hot. It touched down and raced to the end of the runway, turning toward the hangars at a dangerously high speed.

"Wow! That guy should've been a fighter pilot ... seven minutes and 42 seconds!" the controller said.

–Riding A Bomb–

"Pilot to crew, prepare to bail out! Repeat ... prepare to bail out. Lt. Ortiz, check every man's gear. You're jumping over water,

211

so make sure your Mae Wests are in order, and your chute harnesses are tight. I'm climbing to 6,000. Jump on my command. Bridger, out."

"Take us to 6,000, Alex, and then put your chute on. When we're at altitude, I'll take the controls."

Alex threw Carl a questioning glance, unsure that he was hearing correctly. "You're bailing out with us, right? You're not going to try to land this plane ..." he let the sentence trail off.

"When we're at 6,000 I want you to see to it that every man is out, and then you follow them, Alex. I'll see you when you come ashore."

"Carl, if you're going to attempt this stunt, I'm not leaving. I'll ride *Angel* down with you."

"Negative, Lieutenant. I'm ordering you to bail out. Your 180 pounds is extra weight that I don't need."

Avenging Angel climbed to 6,000 feet. Carl began to circle over the coast of the island when he gave the order: "Pop the emergency hatches and bail out, now!"

First, Zed Carthage dropped through the forward hatch, followed by Wendell Price. Harry Osborne left through the hatch behind the bomb bay followed by Phil Ortiz. Finally, Alex Chekov, casting a final glance at Carl sitting alone in the cockpit, pushed himself through the escape hatch across from the radio operator's seat. Carl glanced back, caught his look and nodded at Alex. *Good luck, boys.*

Carl circled until he could count all five chutes deployed and drifting safely to the water below. A Navy launch had already cast off from the dock to rescue the flight crew.

The late afternoon air flowed from the island to the ocean producing a pleasant seven-knot coastal breeze, or, as in Carl's case, a head wind that meant he'd have to come in low over the water on his final approach. He began his descent for landing, ever aware that every bump jarred the bomb that threatened to snuff out his life ... and with it his future with Annie.

Carl recalled his mother's advice when he put Bristlecone down after the horse broke his leg. "When you're going through hard times, and you don't think you can bear the burden any longer, turn to the Lord, son." He remembered his heartache and how they all grieved following George's death. The whole family had prayed together. It helped him then ... *maybe it'll help now.*

"Father in Heaven, if you're up there looking down on us, please hear my prayer. Lord, have mercy on these your children and protect them. Amen."

Carl keyed his mic.

Tacloben, Alpha Papa One Seven Three is descending to pattern altitude. Request extended final. I want plenty of time to take it slow and easy.

At 700 feet, he began talking himself through his pre-landing check. "Speed 120, flaps at one-quarter." He heard the flap servos whine and then stop. "Good. Gear down." He pushed the landing gear lever down and secured the handle by pulling the wire locking loop over it. The wheels-down light flashed green, and he started a slow turn onto his base leg. He set the rpm at 2400. The aircraft began to buffet in the turbulence caused by cool air rushing out from the jungle to replace the warmer air rising from the water. Each time the plane shook, Carl's heart skipped a beat. "Set flaps to half," he said to himself and moved the flaps to 50-percent. "Hold your speed at 120 ... that's right. Okay, turning on final."

Carl keyed his mic.

"Tacloban tower, Alpha Papa One Seven Three is turning on final approach"

"Roger Alpha Papa One Seven Three. Emergency vehicles are standing by."

What for? he thought. "I'll either not need them, or there'll just be a big hole in the runway. Are you listening, *Angel*? Please get me safely down." There was no one to hear his plea.

213

Carl descended to 100 feet over the water's surface. Ahead and to his left, he could see his crew ... all five men floating close together about to climb aboard the launch. When he passed over and to the right of them, he glanced out the side wind-screen.

"You're all waving at me! Thank you!" With gratitude and love in his heart he saluted down to them.

"Set flaps to full, Carl. Charlie, where are you when I need you, man?" He hadn't thought of Charlie Temple much since he left the states. Then, he recognized the feeling that caused the memory of his mentor and friend to pop into his head: *fear. I'm scared, Charlie, like I was when I made my first landing in the Tiger Moth, but this time I have one huge delivery to make, and it's a real blast of a package.* "Ha-ha-ha, Carl. Very funny." He laughed out loud at his own macabre joke. "Get a grip on yourself, Carl. Shut-up and concentrate!" he said as his eyes scanned the instruments, and his right hand worked the throttle, mixture, and rpm settings.

At full flaps and a scant 100 yards from the runway, he began pulling back on the throttles with his right hand while maintaining slight back pressure on the yoke to keep the nose from dropping too fast. The airspeed indicator dropped to 110 ... 105 ... 100. When the needle read a hair below 100 mph, *Angel's* nose passed over the apron of the runway. He added the slightest bit of power. The main gear hung suspended three feet above the surface and then the rubber tires lowered gently to the pavement with a faint bump and an almost inaudible squeak. Pillow-soft, the nose gear eased onto the runway, and Carl pulled back on the throttle immediately. Using rudders only to stay centered on the narrow concrete strip, he didn't dare use his brakes for fear of jarring the bomb loose. He let the natural incline of the runway slow him down. *Angel* came to a full stop with 100 feet of pavement remaining.

Shaken and weak in the knees, he climbed down the crew ladder within arm's length of the bomb that threatened to end his life in a single violent blast of high-explosive death. He looked down at the warhead of the olive-green painted bomb with its characteristic yellow stripes around the fins and nose ... its warhead scarcely six inches above the ground. He shuddered as a cold chill shot down his spine.

A Jeep pulled up by him and stopped. Carl climbed into the back without uttering a word.

"Sir? ... Sir?" The driver put the Jeep in gear and started off toward Base Operations.

"Yes. What is it, Corporal?" Carl choked out, his voice so weak it was almost inaudible.

"Sir, Maj. Green and Col. Coltharp are waiting for you at Base Ops. When Carl didn't respond right away, the corporal cleared his throat and repeated, "sir?"

"Yes, Corporal. That's fine. Take me to the dock first.

"But sir, the Col ..."

"TAKE ME TO THE DAMNED DOCK, CORPORAL!" Carl was trembling. The sight of the unexploded bomb hanging ... waiting ... malevolent ... wanting to kill, flashed clear in his mind ... replaying like a series of film slides, but it was the only slide ... repeating over and over and over. He raised both hands to his head, wanting to scream, to shake himself from the fear that threatened to smother him. Instead of screaming, he reached over to the brake pedal with his left foot and stomped on it. He leapt from the Jeep and broke into a run toward the boat launch. *Run, Carl, run!* Every deliberate foot-fall was a defiant act against the insanity that pounded at the door of what was left of his reason.

Out of breath and spent, he reached the small pier where his crew was climbing out of the launch onto the dock.

"You're all safe! Thank God, you're all safe! Harry ... you got out of the tail okay. You're all safe!" Tears streamed down his cheeks. He embraced Alex Chekov and held tight ... trembling uncontrollably.

"Carl ... hey, pal. You're safe, too. It's okay ... you're okay.

Everybody's fine. It's over, partner." Alex whispered.

The rest of *Angel's* crew joined in. Their Skipper was in shock and needed them ... his brothers. They surrounded Carl, patting his back and ruffling his hair, and repeating Alex's words, "We're all fine ... you're fine."

"Hey, Skipper. Let's all go over to The Pub and get bombed!" When Harry said bombed, everyone broke out laughing except Carl.

He turned and looked at Harry. The wide-eyed thousand-yard stare left his face, and his eyes finally focused on his surroundings ... the light was coming back into them. *"Bombed,* Harry? Really?"* The corners of his mouth turned upward in a grin, and he began laughing. Harry's quip was the soothing balm Carl needed. The six of them started walking toward the "tent city," as the main housing, dining and entertainment center of Tacloban Aerodrome was descriptively named. A certain befuddled corporal was left behind, sitting in his Jeep.

Ten minutes later, they were all downing depth charges at the "O" Club ... shots of whiskey dropped into mugs of beer. After two of the high-octane drinks each, the crew of A/P173 felt no pain whatsoever. Songs filled The Pub and everyone joined in with "Danny Boy," "I'll Be Seeing You," "Bless em' All," and many other familiar songs sung by GI's everywhere from the Ardennes Forest to Okinawa. After two hours of merry making, Carl thought his self-control had returned. As a matter of fact, he was in such a good mood that he decided to make a late visit to Base Operations and apologize to Col. Coltharp for missing his earlier appointment.

"Shkooz me boys ... I ... I-gotta-go-shee ... go see Col. Crawthorn ... no, that'shnot it ... Col. Caltroooo ... oh crap. The boss! ... gotta' see the boss," he slurred. Carl stumbled out of The Pub, stepped off the porch (a wooden cargo palate) and fell flat on his face.

He woke up at daybreak. The early morning sun silhouetted

the taller palm trees to the east. In 10 more minutes it would rise above the ocean horizon.

He pulled his feet off the side of the bunk and lowered them to the floor. He was still wearing his uniform from the day before. After stripping down and tossing his wrinkled beer-stained garments into the laundry bag hanging from the foot of his rack, Carl retrieved his shaving kit from his locker and headed for the shower. The cool water pelting against his skin perked him up considerably. He lathered up, and as he showered, let the image of the bomb play through his mind in vivid detail. One thing was missing, though ... his reaction. He knew he was back in control.

Back at the tent, he dressed in a spare clean uniform and was about to walk over to Base Operations when a PFC from the headquarters mail office popped his head into the tent.

"Mail call, sirs!" He stepped inside and began to thumb through a two-inch thick stack of letters from the states. The mail clerk called out the names of three officers, and then Carl's name was called:

"Bridger! Bridger again!" Carl collected both letters, thanked the private and returned to his locker. He was excited to hold the letters, one in his mother's writing, and the other from Annie. He decided to read them later, not wanting to rush through them. "Business first, Bridger," he told himself. He unlocked the padlock, opened the door and put the letters on a shelf. He secured his locker door and headed for the HQ building.

"Maj. Green and Col. Coltharp are waiting for you, Lieutenant," the Staff Sergeant sitting outside the Group Commander's office said.

Carl rapped on the door. *Well, Bridger, get ready to take your lumps. Sure hope I don't get grounded.* His thoughts were interrupted with a loud "Enter!" from inside. He stepped in and closed the door behind him. He stood at attention in front of Coltharp's desk and saluted.

"Lt. Bridger reporting as ordered, sir." He held the salute until Coltharp returned it.

"Bridger, Maj. Green and I were in the tower yesterday when you landed with that bomb hanging out the bomb bay. I'm going to say two things: One, that landing was the smoothest piece of piloting I've ever seen ... textbook perfect. Second, whatever made you think you could pull off a stunt like that? By all rights, that bomb could have detonated at any point ... should have, actually."

"Well sir, my wingman, Jack Hayes, did an eye-ball assessment of the clearance between the main gear and the height of the warhead above the wheels. I figured if I lightened the aircraft by having the crew bail out, I'd have a good chance of landing safely. We tried to free the bomb from the tangled cable, but it held fast. Short of a pretty firm jolt, I felt that it was secure enough to risk it."

Coltharp opened Carl's personnel file. "Your performance all the way through pilot training up to this point has been exemplary, Lieutenant. From your first encounter with the enemy sub when you were ferrying the '25 to Australia, to your mission performance while here with the 345th, you have demonstrated superior piloting skills and outstanding leadership and military bearing. Your tactical acuteness under combat conditions is top notch. You have repeatedly demonstrated an uncanny ability to measure mission objectives and form strategies while at the same time minimizing the risk of injuring yourself or your crew ... even to the extent of risking your own life twice in the last few weeks to preserve the lives of your own crew and the crews of other planes under your command."

"Thank you, sir, but I was ..."

"I'm not done, Bridger," Coltharp interrupted. "Maj. Green here has spent the morning talking to Lt. Hayes and Lt. Marshall and to members of your crew. To a number, they have all supported, by factual account, that your mission yesterday warrants the award of an oak leaf cluster for the DFC you were awarded two days ago.

The citation is being written up as we speak. The actual award won't be presented until the next formal ceremony in March at San Marcelino, but I wanted to personally congratulate you. On a more personal note, I need to ask; how are you holding up, son? I hear there was quite a party at The Pub last night, and your crew was more than a little concerned when you met them down at the dock after you landed. So, I'll ask again; how are you doing? Are you mission-ready?"

"I have to admit; I was a bit shaken for a while there. Today, though ... I'm fit for duty, sir."

"That's good to know, Lieutenant. We're going to need every available plane and crew in the next few months. Again, congratulations, Bridger. That will be all." Carl saluted, did an about face and left the Group Commander's office.

Back at his quarters, he sat down on his bunk and opened the letter from his family.

> *Dearest Carl,*
>
> *It has been wonderful reading your letters. I can't tell you how much joy they bring to the family each time we get one in the mail. We're all doing well here. Your father is working extra hard because of the lack of good help. The older men help each other whenever they can though it's hard. But, all is well. You'll be happy to hear that Penny has a brand new driver's license. She runs a lot of chores for her father and me. We almost never get to drive anymore, (laugh here).*

Carl read on. Every sentence his mother wrote was a sweet song to his heart. He loved to read how things were going at the ranch, about Penny getting her driver's license and about Annie and the rest of the family keeping the Double-B thriving.

We all miss you, son. It is my constant prayer that you will return home to us. What a celebration we'll have on that day.

I'll say bye-bye for now, sweetheart. Stay safe, son. Love – Mom and family.

She ended every letter with that same phrase, stay safe, son.

Carl folded the letter and placed it back inside the envelope. "I will Mom," he whispered. He held Annie's letter to his nose and inhaled deeply. A faint aroma of lavender wafted into his nostrils. He closed his eyes and immediately his mind painted images of walking with Annie along sun-struck roads and through meadow grass on many a summer's afternoon ... of holding her close to him in the porch swing in front of the family's house on the day he proposed to her. His mind recalled the brush of her lips on his cheek as she told him she loved him ... only forever. His hand brushed his cheek in reflex of the image, and he smiled. "Thank God for you, Annie," he said.

He slid the single sheet of paper from the envelope.

My Darling,

You will be happy to know that all is well at the Double-B. Your father is getting the hands ready for calving and branding. He has some new, older men that have to be taught everything because the experienced hands are all off to war. The next month or so will be spent teaching them the ropes, so they'll be ready for spring when the real work starts. My parents are doing well. Dad's breathing hasn't gotten too much worse since you last saw him, and he manages to walk to work every day. As for me, I'm working with Dad Bridger quite a bit. One day he caught me showing one of the men how to tie a proper loop in a lasso. He says I'd make a foreman as good as you (tee-hee). I think he was just trying to make me feel good. Penny is doing her share, but school takes up most of her time. She's a straight "A" student this year. I help Mother Bridger in the house as much as I can, too. I have to say, though, that these last six months without you have been very lonely. I love the hard work because it keeps my mind off of thinking about how far away you are. Your letters are a godsend! I love the days when I get a new one from you. Sometimes, on days when nothing comes, I like to read all of your old letters. Oh, how I wish I could pick up the telephone and hear your voice! Maybe someday people will talk to their loved ones halfway around the world at the touch of a button.

When you come home, can we cut down the Christmas tree and cuddle in the sleigh like we did last year? Well, I'd better close for now. No more space on the paper. I love you, my darling – only forever.

Annie

Carl carefully slid the letter back in the envelope and put it with the rest of the letters from home.

February 18, 1945
–Bagac–

By the middle of February, the entire 345th Bomb Group had established themselves at the San Marcelino aerodrome. Carl and his crew arrived at the new base two days earlier, and were settled in. All of their belongings had been boxed and shipped via C-47 and were waiting for them at the quartermaster depot on their arrival.

The battle for Bataan Peninsula and Manila were drawing to an end. Gen. Yamashita's home guard in Manila had evacuated to Baguio City. The enemy supply lines from Manila Bay were reduced to a trickle, and Japanese forces were being squeezed into a strategic withdrawal. Gen. McArthur had already announced, almost two weeks earlier, the re-taking of Manila, but the fighting continued.

The morning of February 18th brought clear skies and warm weather. Carl walked over to the briefing room, which was built out of two 16-man tents stretched over wooden frames set atop a raised wooden floor. The several buildings left standing when the enemy evacuated were being hastily reconstructed. For the time being, another tent city had been erected.

Six crews from both the 500th Rough Raiders and 501st Black Panthers were being briefed by the CO of the 501st, Maj. Green.

"Yesterday, February 17th, elements of the 1st Cavalry Division, under command of Maj. Gen. Vernon Mudge together with Filipino guerillas, captured Fort William McKinley on the outskirts of Manila. Gen. Yamashita no longer controls the city. However, there are pockets of strong resistance from Manila eastward to Baguio City where Yamashita is believed to be hiding out. Japanese forces are trying to reorganize for a counter attack on Manila and are still receiving some supplies along the route from here at the port town of Bagac north of Manila, along the Bagac Road leading inland." He traced the supply route on the map with his pointer.

"The road loops over the top of Manila Bay and winds its way down to Manila, a distance of about 142 kilometers. The enemy is scattered all along that route grabbing whatever supplies they can. Your mission is this stretch of the road here, just outside the town of Bagac, at 120 degrees 27 minutes east longitude to the town of Bagac itself." Maj. Green pointed to a five-mile stretch of road leading from the town to a point where the road began its loop north over the top of the mountains skirting Manila Bay.

"Lt. Bridger will lead the two flights of the 501st Black Panthers in A/P173, designation 'Panther Leader'. Capt. Frasier will lead the 500th Rough Raiders in A/P098, designation 'Raider Leader.'

"The objective of the 501st is to strafe and bomb enemy bivouac areas along one side of the road and to destroy or scatter concentrations of supplies and troops along your assigned section of the road. The 500th will repeat the attack plan on the opposite side of the road."

Avenging Angel sat on the tarmac fueled and loaded with four 500-pound bombs and 8,000 rounds of 50-caliber ammunition.

Carl was the last to climb the crew ladder. He wriggled into his seat and secured his harness. His heart rate always quickened with the flood of adrenaline that began when the crew ladder was raised and the hatch slammed closed. He knew they were on their way.

"Mic check, boys. Call it in," Carl announced.

"Navigator. All set."

"Engineer. Ready to fire 'em up, Skipper."

"Radio is good to go."

"Osborne in the tail, Skipper. My babies are locked and loaded."

"Let's wake up the *Angel*, Alex. CLEAR!" Carl called out the opened side wind-screen.

"Ignition ON."

"Booster ON."

"Energizer ... prime two seconds."

Alex read back each step of the engine start sequence.

"Engage." Alex held down the energizer, primer, and engaging switches while Carl worked the throttle and mixture for the starboard engine. The R2600-29 Wright Cyclone 14-cylinder engine began to turn the 12-foot diameter three-bladed Hamilton propeller. A belch of white smoke coughed from the manifold, and the engine caught hold. Carl settled the engine into a smooth idle, and he and Alex repeated the engine-start sequence with the left engine. When the oil temperature gauge settled in the green

normal operating range, and a quick scan of the instruments revealed that all of the engine instruments were running inside the
green as well, Carl eased the throttles forward. The sound of the
engines increased in both pitch and volume, and A/P173 began to
roll. Carl turned the bomber and taxied to the beginning of the runway. The 501st Bomb Squadron would lead the mission, and Carl
was given command of the six planes of the Black Panthers making
Avenging Angel the lead plane.

"One-half flaps, Alex." Carl called out.

Alex pushed down the flaps lever. "Flaps set at one-half."

The engines roared as Alex throttled up. Carl held the nose
on the center-line with the rudders. As *Angel* increased speed, Carl
called for full throttles. The engines screamed, and the nose wheel
lifted off the runway, followed by the main gear.

"Gear up."

"Gear up and locked, Skipper."

"Flaps up."

"Flaps are up."

Carl held the '25 in a steady climb at 170 mph and began
circling the field waiting for all of the planes to form-up. At 1,000
feet, the two squadrons of Air Apaches flying in echelon-up formation, turned north toward Bagac.

"Skipper, I see an enemy bivouac at 3 o'clock low ... trucks,
crates, and at least a dozen tents," Phil Ortiz said from the Navigator position in the nose.

"Roger that."

*Panther Leader to Alpha Flight, form up in line-
abreast formation. Alpha Papa One Seven Three will drop
ordinance. You two follow up with strafing. Bravo Flight,
strafe the camp ... line-abreast formation.*

*Roger, Panther Leader. Bravo Flight has the
cleanup.*

Carl took *Avenging Angel* down to 200 feet above the surface and held steady toward the center of the enemy encampment at 270 mph.

"It's all yours, Phil. Opening bomb-bay doors."

With his eye on the Norden bombsight, Phil waited for the target to flash in front of him. He would have only a split second to release his bombs; his concentration was essential. There was an open strip of space in the jungle about 100 feet long and 75 feet wide just before the Jap encampment. He decided to release the 1,000-pound demo-frag bomb when the clearing came into view. Speed and altitude were keyed into the bombsight, and acting much like the windage and elevation knobs on a rifle scope, would allow Phil to release the bomb at precisely the right moment. The ballistic flight of the bomb would do the rest.

"Bomb away!" he called.

From the tail of the plane, Harry Osborne had a ringside seat. The bomb exploded exactly on target. The shock wave leveled most of the camp as well as blanketing the entire area with thousands of fragments of shrapnel. The strafing gunfire from Carl's wingmen significantly reduced the return fire from the ground sending the few surviving enemy gunners scrambling for cover. The three bombers of Bravo Flight came in low at tree-top level and started laying down a .50-caliber barrage of gun fire from a combined total of 24 AN/M2 machine guns. The camp was decimated.

"We nailed 'em, Skipper. Right on target!"

"Roger that, Harry. More Zombies dead ahead." Carl's reference to the walking dead was coined by GIs who had personal knowledge of the Japanese Banzai charges: the blind suicide charge into sure death by large concentrations of Japanese soldiers who found honor in dying for their emperor.

An even larger concentration of enemy troops was spotted a half-mile farther up Bagac Road. It seemed to be an established bivouac encampment complete with anti-aircraft guns in sandbagged emplacements.

All planes, drop your bombs for effect on the first run, line-abreast formation. Alpha Flight Leader will go in low and strafe the A-A emplacements.

When the enemy caught sight of the incoming Mitchells, the A-A guns were manned. As Alpha Flight Leader closed on the target to within 1200 meters, the Japanese opened fire with two emplacements of twin-barreled, Type 96, 25 mm weapons.

Carl dropped to tree-top level and opened up with *Avenging Angel*'s eight .50 cals. The enemy guns were only capable of firing 15-round magazines, and by the time they could be reloaded, Carl had strafed them quite thoroughly. *Angel* was holed, but to no effect. The enemy gunners dived for cover, and when A/P173 passed overhead it was too late for the gunners to load, re-aim and target the next plane. Lt. Marshall's A/P172 released its 1,000-pound bomb, and it exploded a scant 10 feet from the A-A guns that were shooting at Carl. The enemy gun emplacement became a part of the crater. A/P009, piloted by Eddy Lamar, dropped its bomb near the second A-A bunker. The bomb hit wide and left but was close enough to kill their gunners and knock the weapon off its mounts.

Black Panthers, re-form. We'll let the Rough Raiders drop their ordinance, and then we'll make two strafing runs.

Panther Leader to Raider Leader, Panther Group is forming up to strafe the east side of the road. We'll hang back until you've dropped your ordinance. Over.

Raider Leader. Roger, Panther Leader. We'll make a strafing run on the west side following the bomb run. Raider Leader, out.

All six 500th Bomb Squadron B-25s dropped their remaining bombs from a line-abreast formation blanketing the enemy bivouac area on the west side of the road. The entire target was obscured by smoke and dirt from the bombs. The planes had to re-form and wait for enough visibility to make their strafing runs.

Panther Group, Alpha Flight will go in first in staggered-line formation.

Panther Leader to Bravo Flight, you're the second wave. Choose your targets. Alpha Flight is starting our run now.

Carl winged over and dropped to the deck increasing his speed to 300 mph.

"Tail gunner, when I climb out, I'll drop the tail in line with the target. You'll have about three seconds," Carl directed.

Harry cocked his twin .50s and squeezed off a burst of fire. "Finally! I was nodding off back here. I'm locked and loaded, Skipper."

A/P173 came in no more than 15 feet above the tallest trees followed by his wingmen in A/P172 and A/P009. Bravo Flight dropped down to about 1200 meters behind Alpha Flight.

Panther Leader to Alpha Flight, see those trucks to our left? They're starting to roll. Let's hit 'em!

Carl kicked in a little left rudder and aileron. *Angel's* nose lined up on the four trucks and what looked like an armored personnel carrier with a machine gun mounted next to the driver. The '25s engines screamed as the rpm needles on both of them reached the yellow caution zone on the instrument panel. Carl opened-up on the vehicles attempting to escape the destruction. At a combined rate of 6,400 rounds per minute from all eight forward-firing guns, Carl held the trucks in his sight for a full four seconds. Concentrating on the target, he temporarily lost his situational awareness; directly ahead loomed a stand of palm trees. He had dropped the bomber dangerously low. He pulled back the throttles while at the same time pulling back hard on the control yoke. *Angel's* nose rose above the tops of the trees but her forward momentum tried to force her down into the trees. Threatening to go into a high speed stall, the belly of the aircraft brushed the upper leaves of the palms.

Carl's sudden maneuver dropped Harry's gun sight directly

onto the target, and he was ready. Laying down a three-second burst, the machine gun on the front of the enemy APC flew off the vehicle. Harry's twin .50s tore into the truck behind blowing off the hood of the two-and-a-half-ton vehicle and tearing the radiator and engine to shreds. The other two planes of Alpha Flight and the three planes of Bravo Flight spread their fire in a 100-yard wide path through the compound. A second pass left the compound empty of any sign of life. Half-dozen fires were all that remained as the Black Panthers climbed to altitude and turned toward San Marcelino ... and home.

By February 20th, the base at San Marcelino had become fully operational. All four squadrons, their aircraft, flight crews and ground crews were settled in. Officers' quarters were located in a "tent city" as were the enlisted quarters. Those hangars that had been damaged by the Japanese before they abandoned the facility, were either repaired or replaced with new structures. Fuel storage facilities were set up, and the infrastructure of motor pool, medical services, and quartermaster facilities were operational. The 345th Bombardment Headquarters operated from a compound of tents. Permanent structures were under construction. A few buildings that were left mostly undamaged were either repaired or in various stages of repair. Equally important were The Pub and Officers' Club, which were stocked and open for business.

Chapter XI

February 22, 1945

–SNAFU and Old Friends–

"Gentlemen, the Air Apaches are joining with the 38th Bombardment Group to form an attack force of 36 B-25s for a strike at Formosa … specifically here," Col. Coltharp aimed his pointer at a map of the island of Formosa, "at the industrial complex in the town of Kagi, and here … industrial and defensive installations in Choshu. Secondary targets are enemy troop encampments near Lal-Lo in Northern Luzon.

"The 500th Rough Raiders will lead the 345th contingent with Maj. Ericksen in command of the Group, followed by the 501st Black Panthers, the 498th Falcons, and the Bats Outta Hell of the 499th. Each squadron will fly in echelon-up formation. For this mission, radio communications will be opened between all squadrons for the purpose of coordinating the attack. Air cover will be provided by the 348th Fighter Group. Weather over the target is predicted to be broken clouds. Ceiling is at 6,000 ft. This will be a medium-altitude bombing mission with a load-out of ten 100-pound bombs and 8,000 rounds of ammunition for each plane."

Eight B-25s of the Black Panthers, in two flights of four, joined the formation at 1,000 feet above San Marcelino at 0930 hrs. Call named Red Two, the two flights of the 501st were designated Alpha and Bravo. Alpha Flight Leader, Capt. Lee Jones, led the 501st contingent. Lt. Zeke Bell led Bravo Flight. The remaining flights of

Red Group were the 500th Rough Raiders (Red One), 499th Bats Outta Hell (Red Three), and the 498th's Falcon (Red Four).

Carl flew right wing for Zeke Bell with Lt. Lincoln Wands flying left wing. Bringing up the rear was Lt. Hank Terwilliger to complete the diamond formation of Bravo Flight.

Group Leader to Flight Leaders, turn to heading three-four-zero degrees.

The Air Apaches turned to the assigned heading and proceeded toward the west coast of Formosa.

"Carl, I don't like the looks of those clouds building up along our flight path."

"Me neither, Alex ... hold on."

Carl switched to the group frequency.

Flight Leader, that weather ahead is closing in. What do you want us to do, Zeke?

Stand by, One Seven Three.

Silence ensued for about twenty seconds, then Zeke Bell came back on the com.

Bravo Flight, Alpha Flight Leader reports engine trouble and is turning back to base. I will be assuming command of the 501st. Lt. Bridger is now Alpha Flight Leader. Acknowledge.

Acknowledged. What about the weather, Zeke? Carl asked again.

Maintain formation for now, Red Two. Red Two Leader, out.

"I don't like this, Alex. If the visibility gets any worse we're going to have trouble maintaining visual separation from the rest of the group." Carl could see other bombers appearing and disappearing again as they passed through the thickening cloud layer.

Red Two, turn to heading one-three-zero. We're abandoning the primary target and going after the secondary target at Lal-Lo, Zeke Bell ordered.

The two flights of Black Panthers veered away from the main body hoping that Red Three and Red Four would follow suit. The 501st found themselves alone in the sky, and the heading change took them directly over Choshu Aerodrome. Almost immediately, heavy ack-ack poured into the formation.

All planes, arm bombs! Hit the flight line and airstrip! Lt. Bell ordered.

All seven Mitchells dropped one sleeve each of 100-pound demolition/incendiary bombs in a single run. There was plenty of smoke and flames but no time to assess damage.

Red Two Leader is hit! Repeat ... I'm hit!

Carl glanced over at Zeke Bell's '25. It was trailing smoke from one engine.

Red Two, form on Zeke's plane, and let's get out of here, Carl announced. *Turn to heading one-six-zero degrees. Bravo Flight Leader is assuming command of Red Two. All planes in Red Two acknowledge. Lt. Wands, take command of Bravo Flight.*

One by one, the five remaining planes acknowledged the change in leadership.

"This is a SNAFU if there ever was one, Alex. Price, call up Air Sea Rescue."

As soon as Wendell Price had the radio tuned, Carl made the call for a pick-up off North Island by a PBY Catalina "Dumbo" (nicknamed after Walt Disney's "Dumbo" for its ungainly appearance)

Alpha Flight Leader to Bravo Flight, Alpha Papa One Seven Two and Zero Zero Three, stay with Alpha Papa Three Seven Four to the Catalina pick-up point. From there, proceed back to base.

Zeke Bell's wingmen, Lt. Wands and Lt. Terwilliger, acknowledged the order.

Carl, leading the remaining Mitchells of the Black Panthers, needed to redirect the 501st contingent to a secondary target. Their numbers were cut in half by the absence of Zeke Bell with his two wingmen and the loss of Capt. Lee Jones' Mitchell due to engine failure.

Alpha Flight Leader to all planes, turn to heading one-eight-five. We're going to hit Lal-Lo before we head for home. Air cover from the 348th is with the main body, so we're going to do this the hard way. Assume diamond formation. From this point on we are one flight, designation Alpha Flight. Acknowledge.

The remaining three pilots of the 501st acknowledged Carl's order.

An unfamiliar voice abruptly came over the plane-to-plane communications frequency:

Bravo Two Five flight of four aircraft, this is Razor Flight Leader. Do you copy? Over.

"What the ..." Carl keyed his mic.

This is Alpha Flight Leader. We are on an active mission. Identify yourself! he ordered.

Alpha Flight Leader, we are a flight of four Papa Five-Ones from the 348th Fighter Group, and we're here to provide your air cover. We heard your distress call, and we broke away to cover your six. The rest of our guys are with your main group of Mitchells up north. We're at your 6 o'clock high.

"He's right, Skipper. I can see them ... a flight of four P-51s," Harry Osborne said from the tail.

Roger that, Razor Flight. You guys are a welcome sight. We're headed for Lal-Lo to drop our ordinance before heading back to base. We sure could use your cover.

Glad to do it. Beats delivering airmail back home.

Carl smiled at the coincidence.

Oh, I don't know, Razor Leader. The first time I ever flew a Tiggy it was plenty exciting. Over.

The P-51 pilot responded with an edge of excitement in his voice.

Now, I'm curious, Alpha Flight Leader. Just one question, and then we need to get back to business. Where do you call home?

Cascade, Montana ... you?

Well I'll be damned! You're Carl Bridger. So, you're flying something a bit bigger than that old Tiggy, eh, Carl?

Carl would have jumped to his feet if not for the fact he was strapped in the seat of a B-25.

Charlie Temple! It's you! Dear Lord, I ...

Carl calmed back down and got his head back in the game.

Charlie, I'll see you at the Officers' Club back at base. Carl returned his attention to the task at hand.

Flight Leader to flight, we're going to do an over-flight first to locate our target. They'll be close to the town proper. I don't want to kill a bunch of civilians, so be sure of your targets. Maintain 1,000 feet. Arm all bombs. We'll hit them with our bombs first and follow with a second strafing run.

Alpha Flight came in over the Babuyan Channel toward the coast of Cagayan Province as ack-ack started with a wall of black puffs of smoke. Suddenly all four planes were being rocked by the explosions. The town of Lal-lo, which intelligence reported held a large concentration of General Yamashita's 152,000 "Shobu" soldiers, was a significant target. The enemy camp's proximity to the town made an east-west attack necessary.

Flight Lead to flight, I see a double line of barracks-like buildings, vehicles and a fuel storage area north of the town center. That's where we'll hit them. Anti-aircraft emplacements appear to be coming from four bunkers on the borders of the camp to the east and the west. Move into line-abreast formation and descend to 200 feet.

235

Carl entered a deep descending bank and lined up on the enemy target. Explosions of 120 mm cannon fire rocked the planes.

Flight Leader to Razor Leader, I need you to plow the road for us. Can you keep the anti-aircraft busy? Over.

Thought you'd never ask. Rolling in now.

Charlie Temple's four P-51 Ds arrowed down like Zeus's spear at 400 mph. Each plane targeted a gun emplacement. Suddenly the ack-ack explosions in the sky around the B-25s became more dispersed and less intense.

"Approaching target. It's all yours, Phil." Carl held *Avenging Angel* level as Phil Ortiz focused his eyes on the bombsight.

"Bombs away. One sleeve!" Five 100-pound bombs dropped and arched downward at the cluster of buildings. The scenario was repeated by the other three bombers. Twenty explosions and smoke columns rose into the air. The Mitchells roared overhead and banked around for their second run.

The fuel dump remained unscathed from the first assault. Carl decided to assign it to Lt. Kyle Fisher.

Flight Leader to Alpha Papa Five Eight Zero, Fisher, get into position to take out that fuel dump off your left wing. The rest of us will strafe the buildings.

Roger, Lead. Got it in my cross-hairs.

Fisher's bomber banked slightly away from the formation.

As the Mitchells passed overhead they were rewarded with a few minor explosions, and then an enormous, boiling column of orange and yellow flames rose into the sky. Fisher's .50 cals were right on target. The armor-piercing rounds tore into the storage tanks and ignited the fuel.

Flight Leader to flight, form on me, staggered-line formation. A number of vehicles are making a run for the jungle. Take them out!

Several trucks and two armored personnel carriers were convoying out of the encampment on a road leading west from the town of Lal-Lo.

Avenging Angel

Avenging Angel dropped to 150 feet. The other three planes followed behind spaced 30 yards apart.

"C'mon *Angel*, hold steady. When the rear vehicle drifted into the top of his ring sight, Carl's left thumb depressed the "Guns" button. All eight of *Angel's* .50 calibers erupted, spewing 3,200 armor-piercing explosive rounds per minute into the convoy, ripping into the vehicles in a single four-second burst. As Carl pulled up, the targets rose into Harry Osborn's sights. He opened up his twin "babies" and raked the lead two vehicles as a good-bye gesture.

By the time all four '25s were done, not a single vehicle was road-worthy, and at least three dozen enemy bodies lay scattered on the ground or hanging out of burning trucks.

Flight Leader to flight, form up, boys. Let's go home ... and thanks, Razor Flight. Your air cover was excellent. You fighter jockeys saved our bacon today.

We're here to serve, Carl. Catch you back at base.

Charlie and his flight of fighters climbed and disappeared into the clouds.

Alex Chekov shook his head and looked at Carl with an intensity that echoed Carl's feelings about the mission. "I am not looking forward to being debriefed by Col. Coltharp after this SNAFU, Skipper."

Coltharp sat at his desk as Carl stood at attention in front of him. A clerk stenographer, a sergeant, sat at a small table recording a transcript of the debriefing.

"Have a seat, Bridger. I'll get straight to the point. Intelligence wants to know why a squadron of seven B-25s aborted an important primary target and diverted to the secondary target. Now, I know you were not in command when the decision was made, but you are the only pilot who was in a position to assess what went wrong up there."

"Sir, in the first place, I wouldn't characterize the situation as something that went wrong. When Capt. Jones turned back to base with engine trouble, he assigned Lt. Bell command of the squadron. We flew into heavy cloud cover and lost visible sight of the rest of the formation. Lt. Bell decided to divert the 501st to the secondary target. Unfortunately, we ran into enemy fire quite unexpectedly over Choshu Aerodrome. We seized the opportunity to drop one sleeve of bombs each on the flight line. There was no time to assess the damage to the enemy, but a look back showed several fires in the area where planes were parked. Lt. Bell lost an engine, and he diverted to the Catalina pick-up point off North Island. The other two Mitchells of Bravo Flight, Lt. Terwilliger and Lt. Wands went with Bell to provide cover, leaving my flight on our own to head back home. We didn't have enough fuel to attempt to reform with the main group and decided to harass the enemy at Lal-Lo on our return to base. That's about it, sir."

"At any time, Lt., did you think that Bell's order to divert was premature?"

Carl weighed the question. To answer in the affirmative could result in his appearing to be disloyal to Zeke Bell. To answer in the negative could cast a dim light on his decision making ability in combat.

"Sir, in my opinion Lt. Bell made the decision that he felt would best get us back into the fight. My job was to follow his orders at a crucial point in the mission, not to cause confusion and doubt by challenging them. As it turned out, the secondary target at Lal-Lo proved to be a significant one. A sizeable encampment of well equipped ... what I would estimate to be from 300 to 400 hundred soldiers ... was crippled by the 501st." Carl hoped his oblique response to Coltharp's question would suffice.

"Lieutenant, you are going to hear about this sooner or later. Bell had to ditch in heavy seas. His aircraft broke apart and sank. Air-Sea rescue reports two crewmen were recovered. Lt. Bell, his

238

co-pilot Lt. Alvin and two other men perished. I know that Zeke was a friend of yours. I'm sorry for your loss. That will be all."

Carl felt sick over the news of Zeke's death. He found himself standing outside Coltharp's office not knowing if he had saluted his commanding officer. He left the Headquarters offices of the 345th and started toward his billet, but then he remembered his promise to Charlie Temple. He changed directions heading toward the Officers' Club.

"Hey, Carl, over here!" Al Marshall and Jack Hayes were sitting at a table below a logo of the 501st Black Panthers painted on plywood. Similar plaques of the other three squadrons hung on the walls along with squadron logos of the 348th Fighter Group.

"Hi ya, boys. I missed you guys on today's mission." Carl pulled up a chair and ordered a beer. He scanned the room for Charlie

"I wish we had been there. It sounds like you got into quite a SNAFU on this one.

"Yeah? ... where'd you hear that?"

"Couple of guys in your flight. They came straight here after they landed. According to them, you stepped up, took command and turned a debacle into a minor victory."

"Well, it was a bitter victory at best. Zeke Bell lost an engine and had to ditch off North Island. He didn't make it. Two of his crew survived ... I guess we can be thankful for that, at least."

Al Marshall shook his head. "Zeke Bell dead? Man, that's tough."

"Airmail for Carl Bridger!" A voice called from the bar.

Carl turned to see a bottle flying at him. He deftly reached up and caught it. "Hey, Charlie, c'mon over here. I want you to meet a couple of pals of mine."

Capt. Charles Temple, P-51 jockey for the 348th Fighter Group, 340th Razor Backs, pulled up a seat and stuck out a hand.

"Charlie Temple. Hi ya, boys." They all shook hands. Al

Marshall and Jack Hayes instantly made a new friend of Carl's former pilot instructor from before the war.

"Okay, Captain, we want to hear all the embarrassing details about Carl, so give," Jack Hayes laughed.

"Well, I'll tell you, boys, there isn't much that's embarrassing about Carl. Oh, yeah ... this might make him blush a little. He has the for sure most gorgeous girlfriend I've ever seen. Annie ... something, I don't remember. I tell you, she could stop traffic just walking down the street. Say, Carl, are you and Annie still together?"

"As a matter of fact we are ... got engaged just before I shipped out, back in December. Man, Christmas seems like forever ago. She's living at the Double-B with my folks until I get back. Her parents fell on some hard times when the war broke out. Mister Petersen ran the newspaper in Cascade. You remember, don't you Charlie?"

Charlie thought a moment. "Oh, yeah, *The Courier*. You delivered papers for him before you came to work for me, as I recall."

Carl was smiling. Talking to someone who actually shared his history in Cascade was almost like having a family member there. He enjoyed this conversation immensely.

"Yep, that's right. Well, he had to close down *The Courier*, and they all moved to Great Falls. Her dad ended up having to rent a small apartment and sell his car. Annie moved in with us so she could graduate with our class at the high school."

"What about you, Charlie, do you have a girl back home?" Al Marshall asked.

Charlie shook his head. "Nope, never had the time. Airmail service kept me so busy, that I never settled in one place long enough to have a steady girlfriend. I met a gal from Helena back in '41. We hit it off pretty well ... probably would have turned into something if the war hadn't come along. Anyway, that's all water under the bridge, I guess. I'll tell you what though ... and you gotta' promise you won't start in on me, Carl ..."

"What? Okay, I promise I won't say anything ... so tell, me, Charlie."

"I met a girl right here in San Marcelino. I got her a job here in the "O" Club. She's waiting on that table over there."

Carl looked across the room and immediately noticed the stunning woman serving four officers.

"Her name's Alyanna."

They talked over beers for another hour. Jack Hayes and Al Marshall were good sports. Charlie talked about his confirmed five kills and achieving ace status in one breath and about Alyanna in the next breath. Charlie checked the time on his chronometer. The fighter Ace stood, clicked his tongue, and winked at Carl and his friends.

"Gotta go, boys. I have a date on the beach with my gal after she quits for the night." Grinning, he turned and left.

It was getting late, and Carl wanted to get back to his bunk and write home. He swung by the mail room first. Nothing new had arrived from the States for him. It was like that; letters tended to come as many as two or even three times in one delivery. Routing of civilian mail to APOs in the Pacific and FPOs in Europe was irregular at best.

–Alyanna–

Twenty-two-year-old Alyanna Santos lived a peaceful life in San Narciso on the coast of Luzon Island before the war. She was called Alyanna Deschales, after her father, Phillipe Deschales. He was an affluent French chemist who had worked for the American Rubber Company on the island.

When the Japanese invaded the island, the Deschales moved out of the city and Alyanna assumed her mother's more common Tagalog surname of Santos. Their intent was to live in obscurity as peasant villagers thus avoiding the sharp blade of the samurai sword. Alyanna, her Filipino mother, Bianca, and two brothers, Basilio and Raanan, hid in a small village while her father joined the resistance in their fight against the invading Japanese. Eventually he was captured in Bataan and was not heard from again.

The Santos family subsisted on what little the Japanese provided in return for working 14 hours per day washing the clothes of the soldiers, or working in the rice fields and banana groves as was the case for Basilio and Raanan. Laboring under near-starvation circumstances, many women were taken as concubines by the Japanese and brutalized. Alyanna was more fortunate. She was taken in by an infantry captain and was well treated ... for a slave. Capt. Toshiro Fujiwara, Alyanna learned, was educated in America, of noble ancestry and a wealthy family. He demonstrated to her, in sometimes cruel fashion, that he was accustomed to taking what he wanted ... and he wanted her ... the uncommonly beautiful, Alyanna.

Alyanna feigned a liking for the captain, knowing that her family would be treated better because of her acquiescence. She rarely saw her mother and brothers during that time. On those occasions when the opportunity presented itself, she smuggled food to them.

When the American invasion of Luzon began in January, 1945, the Santos family awakened one morning to the clamor of men and trucks leaving the small village to fight the Americans in the northeast quadrant of the island. It happened during one of Alyanna's overnight visits with her family.

On January 27th, the word came to them that Filipino guerrillas had captured the airbase at San Marcelino, only seven miles to the south. Alyanna, her mother and brothers decided to go to the new American Air Base seeking security and, perhaps, work as well. Packing their meager belongings, they struck off toward San Marcelino.

Arriving at the village nearest the airbase, they found the Americans hard at work building a base of operations for fighters and bombers. The first such group of aircraft to arrive was the 348th Fighter Group of the 5th Air Force.

Capt. Charles Temple was among the first pilots to settle in at the base. Many villagers clambered around the Americans offering themselves as "number one houseboy," or "number one laundry ... I take good care, Joe." Everything was "number one."

The second day Charlie was at San Marcelino, he was walking from the officers' tents to the Base Operations building when he spotted a woman walking toward him. A young boy in what looked like his early teens was walking alongside her. He stopped and watched them for a minute. They stopped at three tents. Each time the woman waited outside the tent while the boy went inside. The boy would always exit carrying three laundry bags. With their arms full they started back in the direction of the village. *That's exactly what I need,* Charlie thought, and trotted across the street.

"Excuse me, Miss!" he called out and walked over to Alyanna and Basilio.

"I'm sorry to stop you, but I see that you are washing the clothes of the Americans. Am I right?" Charlie asked.

Alyanna turned and faced the American pilot, and when her face came into full view, Charlie drew in an audible gasp of air. For a moment he was at a loss for words.

"Yes. My mother and I wash and fold the clothing. My brothers clean, make beds and collect the laundry. When the clothes are ready to be returned, my brothers place them on the beds of the Americans. Do you want to hire my family, Captain? We do excellent work." Alyanna held Charlie's gaze with her aquamarine blue-green eyes. Her complexion, while darker than his own, was much lighter than the other natives he had seen. She was taller, too, at about five-feet seven-inches. Her light brown hair was tied back and hidden beneath a bandana which was knotted at the nape of her long aristocratic-looking neck. Her nose was straight with a prominent bridge, decidedly European.

Charlie had never seen any woman who even approached such beauty. He was curious about her command of English. "Your English is perfect. Do I hear a slight French accent?"

"I'm sorry. We really must return to our work." She turned to walk away.

"Wait! ... Wait, ... please." Charlie didn't want her to leave. "How much do you charge, uh, ...for laundry?"

"Two hundred piasters each month for laundry. Another 200 piasters for cleaning and making beds."

"That's about nine dollars per month. Miss, you're hired. My name is Charles Temple." He offered the hand of friendship. Alyanna hesitated returning the greeting, but when Basilio reached out and shook Charlie's hand, she relaxed.

"My name is Alyanna Santos. I am pleased to meet you, Captain."

One morning, about a week later, Charlie spotted her leaving one of the tents after dropping off some clean laundry. He had been working on a plan to help Alyanna and her family and to create an opportunity for seeing her more often as well. He spoke to Sedro Aquino, who managed the bar at the Officers' Club, and talked him into hiring her to wait tables. She would be able to make four times the money she was making doing laundry.

"Alyanna!" Charlie called to her. She stopped and put down her empty basket.

He jogged over to her. "Alyanna, I need to ask you something."

"Yes, Captain? What is it?"

"First ... will you call me Charlie ... please?" He found himself wanting to be proper and removed his hat. "After all, you've been doing my laundry for a week now."

Alyanna smiled. She liked Charlie. He was kind and respectful toward her. "I will call you Charles." She pronounced his name *Sharles*.

"The way you say it makes it sound so ... French. I like that, very much. Will you meet me on the beach at 22 hun... I mean 10 o'clock? I have something to tell you that I think will make your family very happy."

"Why can you not tell me now, Charles?" She suspected she knew the answer, but enjoyed playing coy with him.

"To be honest, Alyanna, I want to see you ... um ... privately, if that's okay."

"Oui ... yes, that is very okay. I will be there. And Charles, I must tell you something. Santos is my mother's last name before she married my father. My last name is Deschales."

"Alyanna Deschales; a name as beautiful as the woman who bears it." Charlie felt he needed to be more formal in his language toward Alyanna.

Alyanna took the bar job. She was paid 4,000 piasters per month which was about $88.00. That amounted to roughly half what she made in tips. Her mother and brothers continued taking in laundry and houseboy work. The Deschales, aka Santos, family was prospering.

In the next six weeks, Charlie and Alyanna saw each other frequently. They walked along the beach in the setting sun every evening, sometimes later, depending on her work schedule and Charlie's mission assignments. During the days when he wasn't flying missions, he could occasionally be found at the family hut dining on chopped pig's snout or fried milkfish over rice.

One night, Alyanna was sitting on the beach crying, when Charlie walked up to her. He sat down and took her in his arms.

"Alyanna, what's wrong ... has something happened?"

"My uncle. He is in the mountains hiding from the Japanese.

They are hunting him." Alyanna lifted her head and looked up at Charlie. "They're looking for us, too, Charles."

"You? Why do they want you? Who is your uncle?"

"My mother is the sister of Alejo Santos. Do you know of him?"

Charlie thought for a moment. "Yes. Yes, I've heard of him. He's a leader of the Filipino resistance, isn't he?"

"Yes. He has been watching over us since my father left to fight against the Japanese. We received a message saying the Japanese are hunting down the families of the resistance leaders. If they cannot find Uncle Alejo, they will find us and ... and."

Charlie held Alyanna close and whispered, "Shhh ... it's alright, Alyanna. I won't let anything happen to you or your family. I promise you." He turned her face up and looked deeply into her eyes. "I ... I love you, Alyanna."

"Oh, Charles ... Charlie. How can I dare to love you? It is dangerous. Still, I cannot deny my heart. I love you, too, mon cher." She parted her lips slightly and pulled Charlie's head down to her. The kiss was tender, warm ... and frightening.

What happens now? He thought.

February 23rd, 1945
–"Nicks" over Indo-China–

Of the 117 B-25s assigned to the 345th Bombardment Group, fewer than half that number were in combat-ready condition at any given time. Aircraft were flown under such stressful flight conditions that maintaining them was a constant battle for the ground crews. Parts were often not available and had to be scavenged from more seriously damaged aircraft in a sort of "triage" operation to keep the most possible planes in the air. One such Mitchell that had received the benefit of this prioritizing was A/P184, nicknamed *The Crab Lady*. She was so named because her aerodynamics had been changed due to repeated rebuilding of her airframe and skin, causing the bomber to crab to the right in order to maintain straight and level flight. A pilot would have to trim the rudders a couple of degrees to the left to keep her on course. It was *The Crab Lady* to which Carl's crew was assigned while *Avenging Angel* underwent an engine overhaul and general airworthiness once-over.

Six crews each from the 501st and 498th squadrons were chosen to sweep the Japanese sea lanes along the Indo-Chinese coast from 14 degrees to 15 degrees north latitude. Al Marshall was assigned to A/P571, Lt. Wands to A/P009, Lt. Jack Hayes was assigned A/P175, Lt. Denny Hoffman to A/P102, and Carl got A/P184.

The two squadrons were designated Red Group (501st), and Blue Group (498th). The two three-plane flights were call-named Red One and Two and Blue One and Two, respectively.

The 501st Black Panthers led the formation of 12 Mitchells with Al Marshall leading the group in Red One. Carl led Red Two of the squadron with Jack Hayes and Denny Hoffman as his wingmen.

When the formation assembled over San Marcelino at 2,000 feet, Al Marshall turned the group on a heading of 320 degrees to a rendezvous point. There they were to meet an XB-24 Liberator, a specially equipped flying radar station, that was supposed to provide target vectoring for the bomb group. Her designation was *Hawkeye Two Four*.

When the group was in position, Al Marshall radioed the B-24:

Hawkeye Two Four, this is Red Leader. Over.

He waited a few seconds, and then tried again:

Hawkeye Two Four, calling on one-one-niner point two-five. Do you copy? Over.

Again, there was no response. Then, a voice ... very faint and scratchy thru a blanket of static came over Marshall's headset:

Come in ... oger ... ed Leader ...this is ... Hawk ... do you ...

The voice disappeared behind the static. Marshall tried a few more times. His radioman switched to other frequencies commonly used for air-to-air combat communications, but to no avail.

Group Leader to all flights, negative contact with our eye-in-the-sky. We're going to drop to 500 feet and fly up the coast to look for targets. Maintain formation. Watch for our air cover. They should be showing up soon. If they are above the cloud cover, we may miss them. Over.

Blue Group. Copy that, Group Leader.

The formation flew up the coast along the shipping lanes for almost 20 minutes when a voice came over Al Marshall's head set again. This time it was from one of the P-51s assigned to provide air cover.

Razor Leader to Red Leader. Over.

This is Red Leader. Read you loud and clear, Razor Leader.

Roger, Red Leader. We have a downed P-51. My right wingman blew an engine and turned back south toward North Island. I lost him in the clouds. Initiating track-line search. Can you assist? Over?

Roger that, Razor Leader. We'll spread out in line-abreast formation and fly down the coast. Turning to course one-four-zero and starting track-line search.

Red Group to Blue Group, you continue up the coast and look for targets of opportunity.

Red Group to Razor, I need you to send four of your fighters to provide air cover for Blue Group. We'll stay down here and help with the search for your missing pilot. Over.

Roger, that, Red Group. They're on their way.

The six bombers of the 501st spread out and began their

first sweep down the coast in search of the ditched P-51. They flew south for 20 minutes and then turned left on the reciprocal heading of three-two-zero degrees. Their air cover had flown south in the direction of North Island taking them well away from the bomber group. Blue Group and their fighter escort proceeded north in search of targets. Carl noticed the absence of air cover and called in his concern.

> *Red Two to Red Leader, Al, I'm feeling a bit edgy about not having any air cover. Over.*
> *Roger, Red Two. We should be fine. We haven't seen ... BOGEYS, THREE O'CLOCK HIGH!*

Al Marshall and his right wingman, Lt. Wands were jumped by enemy fighters arrowing into them in trailing formation.

Four Ki-45 "Nick" twin-engine pursuit/fighters, each armed with one fixed 37 mm cannon, one fixed 20 mm cannon and one flexible 7.92 mm machine gun, had dropped down out of the cloud cover taking all six Black Panthers by surprise. In an instant, all thoughts of the downed fighter pilot had vanished. They were in a fight for their lives.

The Nicks stayed together thinking to down three of the bombers before taking on the other flight. Red One was above and behind the attack, vectoring into position for an attack of their own. The much larger and heavier bomb-laden Mitchells were in no position to get into a dog-fight with the more agile Japanese fighters.

> *Red Two Leader to flight, turn toward the Nicks. Let them come to us. When they start to fire, drop your nose, and bring them into range of your turret and tail gunners. We'll fly under them where they can't hit us. Lock and load, boys. Splash those Nicks.*

The enemy fighters spread out so they could hit more bombers. When they had closed to within 200 yards, they opened fire. At almost the same instant, Red Two dipped sharply down, bringing the Nicks up into the turret gunners' sights. The three turret gunners opened up simultaneously, raking the Nicks which sped past them no more than 100 feet away. The bombers' tail gunners opened fire when the enemy planes sped past the formation.

"We got them good, Skipper. Why didn't they break-up?" Harry Osborne called from the tail gunner's position.

Red Two to flight, here they come again, boys. Same as before. They're consistent, I'll give 'em that.

The Nicks came at them again. This time, they dropped their noses in anticipation of the American maneuver, and their cannon rounds tore into the bombers. Jack Hayes' right wing caught fire. The flames reached a fuel tank, and the explosion ripped off his wing. A/P175 spiraled into the ocean.

"Jack!" Carl screamed involuntarily.

Twenty mm cannon rounds ripped into Carl's aircraft from the engineer's compartment to the tail. The noise was as though someone had put a trash can over Carl's head and beat on it with a hammer. *The Crab Lady*, slipped hard left when the port vertical stabilizer was partially torn off by the attacker; Carl applied right rudder and aileron to compensate.

The enemy maneuver did not come without cost, however. They were raked thoroughly by the Mitchells' turret and tail gunners. One Nick, trailing fire and smoke, climbed into the clouds and exploded in a bright orange burst. The other three decided they had enough and abandoned the attack.

Red Two to wing, damage report, Denny! Carl yelled into the mic.

We're good, Flight Leader. Took a few holes, but we're combat ready.

"Skipper, Carthage is hit!" Sgt. Price called over the comm. "He's bleeding badly!"

"You and Phil do what you can for him. We're an hour from base." He turned off his transmitter. "Damn!" he uttered. "Alex, go back there, and see if you can help with Zed."

Red Two Leader to Red Group Leader, we have one badly wounded man. What are your orders, sir? Over.

Red Group, form up. Let's go home, Al Marshall ordered.

The remaining five Black Panthers turned toward San Marcelino ... and home.

Carl flew in silence. He was positioned behind Red Leader who had only his left wingman remaining. The vacant right wing position didn't go unnoticed by Carl.

Alex reached over and patted Carl's knee as he unbuckled his harness. "He was a good friend."

"My God! Why does this have to keep happening, Alex? ... So many friends ... so much heartbreak."

All Alex could do was to leave Carl to himself as he climbed back toward the engineering compartment. Carl remained stoically silent; his expression set in steel ... cold, determined ... but betrayed by a single tear carving a muddy path down one cheek.

San Marcelino, Red Group is returning to base. Request priority landing for Alpha Papa One Eight Four with one wounded aboard. Over.

Roger, Red Group. An ambulance is standing by. Wind is one-seven knots at two-zero degrees. You are cleared for straight-in approach.

Carl lined up with the runway. He applied right rudder and aileron to counteract the crabbing tendency of the bomber now made worse by the damage from the "Nick" fighter. As *The Crab Lady* was about to touch down, Carl straightened out the plane, and the main wheels squeaked onto the tarmac.

Outside the door to the surgery room, Carl had been sitting in the same chair for over an hour. Alex, Harry Osborne, Wendell

Price, and Phil Ortiz paced the floor and were quietly talking among themselves when a doctor opened the door from the surgical unit and approached them. The physician's surgical mask hung down below his chin, and his white gown was opened in the back. As he approached Carl, he removed his blood-streaked gown and tossed it into a linen hamper.

Carl stood up and extended his hand. The other men gathered around, "Doctor, my crewman, the one the ambulance brought in from our plane, is he ... is he going to be alright?"

"Lieutenant." The doctor shook Carl's hand.

"Bridger, Carl Bridger."

"Lt. Bridger. We worked hard to stop the bleeding. There was just too much organ damage. I'm sorry." The surgeon said.

Carl's heart dropped. He sat back down. Harry Osborne stood next to his skipper and placed a gentle hand on the young pilot's shoulder. After a moment Carl looked up at the surgeon. "Thank you, Doctor." Carl stood up and walked back to his tent.

He lay in his bunk for the next hour, his mind filled with thoughts of Zed Carthage. He decided to pay a visit to Harry Osborne, who bunked in the same tent as Zed.

"Sgt. Osborne, may I speak with you privately?" Carl's use of Harry's rank was for the benefit of the half-dozen other enlisted men inside the tent.

"Of course, sir, sit down." Harry sat on the end of his bunk, and Carl sat down next to him.

"I would appreciate it very much if you would put Zed's belongings in his duffel bag. I'll need to see that his family gets them. I'd like to stay and help if it's okay with you."

"Of course, sir. I'd like that." Harry removed a set of dog tags from around his neck. A single key belonging to a padlock accompanied the chain. Osborne slid the key into the padlock on Zed's locker and the hasp snapped open.

"The doctor gave me these after you left the hospital tent. I guess they're yours, now." Harry handed the key and tags to Carl.

Harry found a small cardboard box among Zed's belongings and began thumbing through a bunch of photos. "Hey, Skipper, do you remember this?"

Carl took the two-and-a-half- inch by three-an-a-half-inch black and white photo and smiled. The picture was the one Zed had asked a flight mechanic to take in front of *Avenging Angel* back in Inglewood, California, before they boarded for their long journey to Townsville, Australia. He dropped the photo back into the box which he would send to Zed's family with the rest of his personal effects.

"I wish Zed was still with us and the *Angel*, Harry." Carl shook his head sadly.

"We'll all miss him, Skipper," Harry lamented.

Carl took Zed's personal possessions back to his tent, where he spent the next hour going over anything that would give him more information about his family back in San Antonio. He read letters from Zed's parents and sisters. They always included phrases of praise to God and words of prayer for his safety and eventual safe return home. There were photographs of them as well ... smiles of innocence from a land that had never known a war on the scale of the one their son had fought in so bravely.

Finally, he was ready to write the letter, that as Zed's commanding officer and friend, he knew he must write ... dreaded as the task was.

The next day, Carl took Zed's belongings to the Graves Registration Service, who would send Zed's body and effects to a central clearing depot in Kansas City. From there, they would be delivered to the family.

Three days later, Carl received a letter from Annie. He opened it with his usual excitement.

My Darling Carl,

Yesterday, your parents, Penny, and I enjoyed a rare and pleasurable drive to Great Falls where we decided to see a motion picture. As usual, the Movietone News came on first, telling about the latest war news around the world. One particular scene caused us all quite a stir. It showed General Douglas McArthur shaking hands with a wounded pilot lying in a hospital bed somewhere on Leyte Island. Do I need to say more? Pop-corn and soda went flying everywhere!

Your most recent letter tells me that you are fine and that your injury was minor. I trust that you are telling me the truth.

Carl, I worry about you. There are thousands of men dying around you all of the time. How many of them do you perhaps know? Oh, my darling, how I pray that the Lord will protect you and bring you home to me. You have no idea what's waiting for you when we are together again. Or, perhaps you do (I know what an active imagination you have ... tee-hee).

I need to tell you that Daddy is getting worse. His doctor tells us that his condition is causing his heart to overwork. He's still at the Tribune, but I don't know for how much longer. Mother says it's nothing to worry about, but I know better.

Your parents and Penny are doing great. Work at the ranch is hard, as you can imagine, but we're getting by. The money you send each month is helping a lot. I love you for taking care of us while you're fighting in this horrific war. More later, my darling.

I love you, Carl... only forever – Annie

Avenging Angel

Carl and the rest of *Avenging Angel*'s crew held a memorial service at The Pub the day after Zed Carthage died, meaning they all got drunk as an Irish longshoreman on St. Paddy's Day, and toasted Zed at least 20 times. After The Pub they all weaved their way over to the mess tent for coffee. Many cupfuls later, followed by repeated trips to the urinal, sobriety ensued. Five days later Carl got a call to meet a Flight Engineer candidate over at the Personnel Office.

He approached the same clerk who had introduced him to Wendell Price. "Hello again, Corporal. I understand I'm supposed to meet my new Flight Engineer here."

"Yes, sir. Here's his file." The clerk handed the personnel file to Carl. "He's brand new, sir ... former medic."

Carl's interest peaked when the corporal mentioned the man's background as a corpsman. He looked at the tab on the folder: Henreid, Alan A. SN:89706621, Rank: E-5. He carried the file with him to a room adjacent to the clerk pool with their clattering typewriters. He entered the room and sat down across from Henreid.

Carl and Doc Henreid had met two months earlier at Tacloban Air Base when the two men tried to keep a hospital tent from blowing away during a typhoon. The man's intellect, quick decision making ability, and natural affability impressed Carl at the time. It was at Tacloban that Carl learned of Doc's desire to become a Flight Engineer and be a member of a bomber crew.

"So, Doc, you finally made it. You're my new engineer-gunner."

"Yes, sir. I passed my certification test with a near perfect score, and after two months of waiting for a slot to open up, my name came up to join the crew of *Avenging Angel*. You didn't have anything to do with that did you, Lieutenant?"

Carl offered a knowing grin, but said not a word. He and the rest of *Angel's* crew welcomed Doc into the fold.

Spencer Anderson

February 25, 1945
–Wingman Down–

At 6:00 a.m., the pilots of the dozen B-25Js of the 501st Bomb Squadron gathered in the briefing room with other pilots of the 499th Bomb Squadron. The 24 men sat on benches and whatever folding wooden or metal chairs as availed them. A map of the southeast Pacific featuring the island of Formosa and the Indo-Chinese coast down to the northernmost tip of Luzon Island filled the map board behind the podium.

Outside the Quonset hut, a constant drizzle fell. The moisture did little to lessen the suffocating blanket of humidity. At 92 percent the sweat couldn't evaporate from one's body which made the 90-degree Fahrenheit temperature seem more like a 110 degrees. Several fans kept the air moving but provided minimal relief. Geckos skittered about on the rounded steel walls of the structure. The tiny lizards chirped sounding much like birds.

First Lt. Carl Bridger sat next to 2nd Lt. Michael O'Hanlon as they awaited their next mission briefing. By comparison, after the intensity of the Iwo Jima battle two months ago, these constant cleanup sorties on Luzon Island seemed almost routine. Occasionally, they would be called on to strike at important shipping in the many harbors the Japanese controlled throughout the region of northern Luzon.

"This is your 14th mission, isn't it, Carl?" Carl's eyes dropped down to Mike's trembling hand as he lit up a cigarette. Mike had been assigned to Carl's unit only two weeks earlier. This would be his second mission.

He saw a lot of himself in Mike and it took Carl back to his own early missions at Tacloban. He had experienced a few life-threatening challenges growing up on the Double-B ranch back in Cascade, Montana. Being thrown from a bucking horse, charged by an angry breeding bull, even fighting off a marauding pack of

256

wolves had not prepared him for the bone-jarring, mind-numbing violence of flying into enemy gunfire. The concussive force of being hit by shrapnel and watching one's friends die as ack-ack bursts threatened to tear your plane apart were experiences that invaded his dreams and drove him to the edge of insanity. His heart ached for Mike. The violence of war is an insult to the soul. Fortunately for Carl he had an anchor that kept him centered on something greater than the ravages of battle ... Annie. Their love for each other was Carl's beacon of hope in a dark and dangerous land of despair. He shook off the memories of the last few weeks and got his head back into the present.

Carl had come to know O'Hanlon when he was assigned as Carl's wingman on his first mission. An attack on a group of Japanese ships which included two oil tankers and two Akizuki class destroyers equipped with 100 mm anti-aircraft guns, was a pressure cooker for the rookie pilot. Anti-aircraft fire pock-marked Mike's B-25 with bullet holes and shrapnel, but that didn't stop him from dropping two 500 lb. bombs skipping them into the side of a tanker. The battle ended almost as soon as it began, but had left O'Hanlon badly shaken. After landing back at San Marcelino aerodrome, Carl saw the poor lad run behind a tent and puke his guts out.

"Counting missions will drive you nuts, Mike. If you concentrate on the mission today and not think about what's ahead, you'll be better off." He smiled at the new pilot. "Anyway, I don't think this war is going to last much longer. You'll be back home in Boston watching the Red Sox play before you know it."

Maj. Gerald "Butch" Henry, adjutant to the 345th Bomb Group Commander, entered through the side door, stepped in front of the assembled officers and called the men to attention. Col. Chester Coltharp, commanding the 345th Air Apaches, entered the room through the rear door and walked up to the front in loud, clomping strides. He carried a thirty-inch pointer under his arm like a riding crop. If he wanted to establish who the cock-rooster of this particular henhouse was, he accomplished it with style.

"As you were, gentlemen. Take your seats." Lt. Col. Coltharp grinned and then added a hearty, "Good morning, Air Apaches!"

"Good morning, sir!" 24 voices answered in unison.

"I hope you men enjoyed a relaxing three-day R & R. Did you all get over to Subic Bay to enjoy the beaches? That's about as close to the white sands of Honolulu that there is over here."

Laughter rippled through the audience. The room full of Army Air Force pilots understood the reference to Subic Bay to be a jibe at the Navy. The roads between San Marcelino and the growing Navy base at Subic Bay were still too dangerous to drive for recreational purposes. Pockets of Japanese resistance still remained scattered throughout Luzon Island. The beaches of white sand could only be enjoyed by the Navy and a handful of Marines.

Carl compared the privileges of the Navy to those of the AAF crews who were restricted to the confines of San Marcelino, spending their R&R time writing home, drinking beer, playing cards and throwing darts. Oh, yeah, sitting at the bar in the "O" Club telling war stories always presented a favorite pastime. He smiled at the thought. Every flight crew on the base understood that joking about their experiences was a way of keeping the true terrors of air combat at bay. If you could joke about the missions, at least for the moment a man could distance himself from the fear that always pushed at his mind and drove sanity to the edge.

The rotation of aircrews in and out of combat helped to ward off battle fatigue and maintain a combat-ready edge. Four weeks of being on constant alert status followed by three days of rest and relaxation was a local decision made by the 345th, and seemed to mitigate at least some of the stress and fatigue of maintaining a constant state of alertness. Of course the ultimate goal for every B-25 crew was to accrue 40 missions. That accomplishment assured a stateside reassignment for some, and a minimum 30 days of leave for others. Meanwhile, R&R on the white sands of Subic Bay continued to be a source of conjecture in the rumor mill at San Marcelino.

The Group Commander aimed his pointer at Tourane Bay in Indo-China. "The harbor at Tourane Bay, gentlemen. Three enemy freighters, believed to be SDs, and at least one SCL tanker are in port. Six Mitchells of the 501st Squadron will participate in the attack on Tourane Bay in two waves. Capt. Bingham will lead in A/P572 in the first wave. Other pilots are Lt. Hatcher, Lt. Wilkinson, Lt. Bridger, Lt. O'Hanlon, and Lt. McKewen. Your assignment is to hit Tourane and destroy the ships.

"The second wave will be led by Capt. James in A/P118 with Lt. Hayes, Lt. Gavins, Lt. Bell, Lt. Coppotelli, and Lt. Hasket. Capt. Bingham's two flights will finish up with any remaining shipping. At that time the 501st will attack secondary targets of opportunity: the airbase at Tourane, fuel storage, maintenance facilities, and enemy shipping from Tourane Bay down to Cape Batangan." Coltharp punctuated every target location with a firm rap of his pointer.

"The 499th will hit Cape Batangan in two waves. Both squadrons will fly in close formation, approaching from the east to this point in the Pescadores Channel midway between our two targets. The 499th will turn south to Batangan, and the 501st will turn north to Tourane. Coordinates, and mission details are in your mission packets. Wheels up at 0800."

Col. Coltharp fielded a few questions and left the briefing with his adjutant in lock-step behind him.

Pilots and crews of both squadrons sat in the ready room in small groups. Carl hunched over a table with his crew and briefed them on the mission.

The only new crew member, the Engineer/Gunner, came in the person of S/Sgt. "Doc" Henreid. This would be his first mission

259

since certifying as a B-25 Flight Engineer. He replaced Zed Carthage who died from severe wounds following an attack on the squadron by four Japanese Ki-45 "Nicks". One, in a head-on attack, managed to rake Carl's aircraft from behind the cockpit to the tail. Carl and his wingmen managed to splash one of the Nicks and holed the other three, but not before one of their rounds found its mark. Carl found writing the letter of condolence to Zed's family, on behalf of himself, the Black Panthers' CO and the 345th Bombardment Group Commander, to be the hardest part of his responsibility ... one that would haunt him for many years. He sometimes wondered ... *Who will write to Dad and Mom and Annie about me? What words could ever soothe the loss of two sons?*

Following the briefing, Carl took Sgt. Henried aside. "Doc, this is your first mission. I want you to get to know every man on that plane. We're brothers. We fight together to get us all back home to our families. You're not alone up there, even though it may seem at times that you are. Is there anything you need to ask me?"

"No, sir. I just need to do this ... get my feet wet, Lieutenant." Doc fidgeted, nervously shifting his weight from one foot to the other.

The blaring squawk of the claxon filled the room followed by the command, "Pilots, man your airplanes!"

Carl and the five members of his crew, each wearing their inflatable "Mae West" life preserver in the event of a water landing, ran to one of the jeeps parked in front of the operations shack and jumped in. Twenty seconds later they stood in front of the crew ladder and climbed into the belly of A/P173 *Avenging Angel*. The last man in, Flight Engineer/Gunner Doc Henreid, pulled the ladder up behind him and secured the crew hatch.

"Radio check, boys. Everyone secure back there?" Carl buckled himself into his harness.

"Check your gear."

"Tail gunner, check," Harry Osborne replied

"Engineer, check."

"Comm is ready, Skipper."

"Navigator, check."

"Co-pilot, check."

"Engine start sequence, Alex," Carl directed his co-pilot. He could feel his body and mind gearing up for combat. His senses ran like a check-list: *Heart rate? ... up. Fear level? ... rising. Run or fight response? ... Run, but under control. Shakes? ...* like a leaf. He clenched his right fist to stop the trembling in his fingers.

"Clear prop!" Alex called out the opened side screen.

"Ignition on."

"Booster pump on."

"Energizing ... priming."

Holding down both the energizer and primer switches, the propeller began to turn with a whine while Alex toggled the "Engage" switch. The 14-cylinder R-2600-29 engine coughed a puff of white smoke and fired up. He repeated the sequence with the port engine, and soon both engines purred along at a steady 1,200 rpm.

"Gauges are all in the green, Skipper. Hydraulics look good as well." Doc's eyes scrutinized every instrument checking for any anomalous readings.

Carl eased the throttles forward, and *Avenging Angel* began her taxi roll. He followed the aircraft in front of him, far enough behind to avoid prop wash and flying debris.

"Give me one-quarter flaps, Alex." Carl scanned the engine instruments and checked the crowded taxiway. Mission 15 was about to begin.

A/P173 turned onto the runway, and Carl eased the throttles forward to 25 percent using the rudder pedals to keep the nose of the bomber on the center line. Satisfied, he pushed the throttles all the way forward with a single, smooth motion and pulled back on the yoke until the weight of the plane eased off the nose wheel. At full throttles, *Angel* roared off the runway.

"Wheels up," Carl watched Alex's hand pull the gear lever upward.

"Flaps up."

"Flaps up, Skipper," Alex responded.

Carl leveled off until his airspeed climbed to 170 mph. He put the bomber into a 1,200 feet-per-minute climb and maintained his speed while banking left toward the formation of '25s above him.

Flying in diamond formation in flights of three planes, the Mitchells reached their intercept point.

Blue Group, turning south. Good luck, Red Group.

The 499th Bomb Squadron separated from the formation and turned south down the coast of Indo-China toward their assigned target at Cape Batangan.

Roger that, Blue Group. Catch you back at base.

The dozen Pappy Gunn modified B-25Js of the 501st banked right and flew north toward Tourane Bay.

Capt. Bingham ordered:

Keep an eye out for Zekes, boys. We should pick up our escorts from the 348th Fighter Group shortly. All planes, charge your guns.

Carl keyed his intercom. "Arm the bombs, Phil. Harry, time to wake up the tail guns."

Harry squeezed life into the two .50 caliber AN/M2 tail guns, sending twin lines of tracers behind them. "Locked and loaded, Skipper."

Carl pushed the red firing button on his yoke, and all eight forward-firing .50 caliber guns roared into life at 800 rounds per minute each.

"Doc, how are the engines looking?"

"Gauges are all green, Skipper," S/Sgt. Henreid affirmed.

"Dead ahead below us, Skipper, here they come!" Alex yelled as a flight of at least a dozen A6M Mitsubishi Zeros came at them.

"Hold formation! Hold formation!" Capt. Fletcher ordered.

Carl restrained himself against the urge to drop his nose to put the zeroes in his gun-sights. He maintained level flight.

"Skipper, I've got '51s at 12 o'clock high. The cavalry has arrived." Alex Chekov pointed up at the formation from his right seat.

Nine P-51Ds from the 348th Fighter Wing spotted the enemy at the same time and winged over in line-formation dropping from the sky at over 400 mph. They arrowed into the Zeroes, scattering them asunder. The enemy found themselves in an air battle with the American Mustangs and abandoned their attack on the formation of Air Apaches.

"Thank you, you beautiful fighters!" Alex Chekov yelled.

Carl glanced at his left wingman; Mike O'Hanlon was too far out.

"Mike, ease in ... no more than 15 feet off my wing."

O'Hanlon moved A/P018 into a tighter formation position. Lt. Dan Calvin remained tucked in close off Carl's right wing.

"Coming up on target. Move into line-abreast formation," Fletcher ordered.

The first two flights of three B-25s, led by Carl, fell into attack formation to give them the widest span of bomb disbursement.

Dropping to 200 feet above the surface of the water, the first six '25s sped toward Tourane Bay, close enough to identify four vessels in the harbor. Every nerve in Carl's body tightened like an over-stretched violin string.

Alex pointed at the harbor. "I see one destroyer…looks like Akizuki class, and three other ships; two SD freighters and one tanker."

"Lower bomb-bay doors and arm bombs!" Carl commanded. The whine of the servos when the doors opened, told him all was ready.

"Bombs armed and doors down, Skipper," Navigator/Bombardier 2nd Lt. Phil Ortiz confirmed.

Carl dropped *Avenging Angel* to the deck and set her nose on the destroyer. Black smoke from her stacks told him she was under way…turning toward the mouth of the bay.

He keyed his mic to his wingmen,

I've got the destroyer. Mike, Dan, you two take out the tanker. Leave the rest to the next flight.

The destroyer's profile grew smaller as she turned toward the inbound bombers. The ship's deck guns started blinking fire at them, and shell bursts dotted the sky in front of the wind screen. The plane bucked upward each time an anti-aircraft round burst beneath them. Carl brought the '25s nose in line with the approaching ship's bow. He was wound so tight that his lungs froze, momentarily unable to expel the air trapped in them.

"This isn't going to be easy … a head-on bow shot. Bomb release on my command, Ortiz … Now! Bombs away!"

A pair of 500 lb. bombs dropped from the plane, and Carl pulled the yoke sharply back putting the bomber into a steep climb.

Avenging Angel screamed over the enemy destroyer at 270 mph. The rat-tat-tat of machine gun fire from the ship raked the belly of the plane.

Harry Osborne enjoyed a ring-side seat from the tail gunner's position. "Skipper, we got one miss and one hit. The bow of the destroyer took the second bomb. The other bomb went wide and took out the dock. She's still underway."

"Acknowledged. The destroyer is nearing the mouth of the Bay. If she gets up a full head of steam, she'll be much harder to kill. We have one more bomb. Coming around for a broadside attack!"

Avenging Angel

He banked the bomber to the right and came at the ship from over the tops of the palm trees. Clearing the trees by only a few feet, he dropped down to the deck and throttled up to 300 mph. *C'mon, Angel, make it count.* This time the full length of the ship presented a broadside view in front of him. He lined up the gunsight mid-way between the bow and amid-ship and forced his breathing to slow.

"Bombs away!"

The last bomb dropped into the water. The rounded nose of the bomb allowed it to skip much like a stone on a pond. One skip and the bomb struck the hull of the ship just above the water line. She rocked from the explosion, but the blast lacked the drama Carl wanted … until the ship's ammunition magazine ignited. The destroyer's hull lifted from the water, bending in the middle in an inverted "V" shape from the force of the blast, sending a visible shockwave in a 360-degree arc. In less than a minute she sank at the mouth of the bay.

Five minutes later, the Japanese supply depot at Tourane Bay was a smoking ruin.

Form up! Form up! The command came from Capt. Bingham.

Well done, Black Panthers. Flight Leaders, I need a damage report.

Carl keyed his mic. O'Hanlon, report damage, he called out.

Took a few holes. No serious damage, Lt., Mike responded.

Calvin, here, Flight Leader. No damage.

Flight Leader to Group Leader. Bravo Flight is good, sir, Carl reported.

All four flights of the 501st Bombardment Squadron reported in. No planes reported severe damaged, and all reported combat ready. Four bombers held a total of eight bombs remaining in their racks. Those planes and five others attacked the secondary target, the airbase at Tourane, which was the source of most of the ack-ack, and strafed hangars and enemy aircraft on the ground. Carl's flight of three bombers attacked enemy anti-aircraft emplacements imbedded in the village of Tourane itself.

I don't want to shoot up any native hootches, boys, so identify your targets before you strafe 'em. We'll go in at tree-top level in line-abreast formation to draw their fire, then give 'em hell!

Tracers rose up from four locations on the edge of the village to greet Carl's flight of three planes. The Jap emplacements stood no more than 50 yards apart from each other.

Choose your targets, boys. Let 'em have it.

All 24 of their .50 caliber machine guns breathed fire down on the enemy positions at a combined rate of fire of over 38,000 armor piercing/incendiary rounds per minute. As the three Black Panthers of the 501st Bomb Squadron screamed overhead, enemy fire continued, albeit at a much lighter concentration of fire.

At times like this, Carl almost wished he could trade places with any infantryman on the ground. At least those guys could see the enemy before pulling the trigger. He worried about killing civilians with his bombs. He knew it was unavoidable, but the image of innocent families dying at his hands tortured his mind and ran contrary to his Christian upbringing.

One more pass, boys.

Carl banked *Avenging Angel* around and lined up for another pass. The three bombers laid down a concentrated pattern of fire. No enemy tracers tracked them after the second pass. Carl ordered his flight to join the rest of the 501st who destroyed a large portion of the airfield.

Form up, Flight Leaders. We're heading down country to check for enemy troop movement, announced Capt. Bingham.

He led the squadron inland until they spotted a well-used

road weaving south through the jungle.

> *Ahead ... two miles ... a convoy of five vehicles. They're all yours Bravo Flight. The rest of you maintain formation.*

Carl's three planes dropped back while the rest of the planes veered away, leaving the attack path clear for Bravo Flight.

> *I'm going in first. Mike, you follow me. Clean up the left-overs, Dan.*

> *Roger, Lieutenant. I'm the caboose,* Dan Calvin confirmed.

Carl centered the nose of the plane on the road below him and dropped his gun sight to a point just behind the trailing vehicle. *Here we go again. God protect us all.* His heart pounded and tension sent painful spasms across his shoulders. He mentally ticked off the closing distance between them and the convoy. He pressed the fire button and all eight forward-firing .50s tore into the line of vehicles. Enemy soldiers jumped from three canvas-covered trucks onto the ground. Carl was satisfied that none of the vehicles would be reaching their destination.

Mike O'Hanlon strafed the convoy, and at least two dozen enemy soldiers tried to take aim on the screaming terror of the bombers approaching them. Their meager fire failed to strike a single '25. Bravo Flight headed out to the coast to join up with the rest of the squadron which lay about two miles ahead at 3,000 feet above sea level.

> *Well done, Bravo Flight. Let's join up and head for home.*

A/P018 and A/P003 drew up to his right and left wing. Carl released a pent-up breath and started to relax a little as he rotated his neck to relieve the spasms.

> *Zero One Eight to Flight Leader, I've got trouble on my port engine. Oil temp is rising ... so is the cylinder head temp. Oil pressure is dropping. I need to reduce rpm*

and slow my speed. Dropping out of formation now.

Mike O'Hanlon's voice had an edge of tension in it, but Carl judged him to be in control of his aircraft.

Roger, Zero One Eight. I'll stay with you, Mike. Zero Zero Three, join-up with the rest of the squadron. We'll be along shortly.

Lt. Dan Calvin continued on toward the squadron formation as they flew down the Indo-China coast over the Pescadores Channel toward their base on Luzon Island.

At the southern tip of Formosa, Carl and Mike O'Hanlon turned their planes east toward Bashee Channel.

The left engine of A/P018 began streaming black smoke from its nacelles.

Flight Lead, I'm feathering my port engine. Experiencing engine roughness in the starboard engine. I don't think we're going to make Luzon, Carl. We can't maintain altitude. Mike began a shallow descent.

Carl's mind raced for an answer.

Mike, turn left to one-three-zero degrees toward the Bashee Channel. I'll radio our location to Group Leader.

Turning east, continuing to descend. Zero One Eight.

"Sgt. Rushton, bring up Group Lead on the radio."

Sgt. Donald Rushton dialed up the assigned mission frequency for the Group Leader.

"You're on the air, Skipper."

Red Leader, this is Bravo Leader. Do you copy?

Carl released the talk button on his mic.

Capt. Bingham's voice sounded through Carl's ear phones.

Red Leader reads you Bravo Leader. Over.

Alpha Papa Zero One Eight is declaring an engine-out mayday. Ditching at coordinates one-five-point-five-

seven degrees north and one-zero-niner-point-one-five de-
grees east. Request Cat. Bravo Leader will remain to pro-
vide air cover. Over.

Roger. Carl, you get your crew back to base. We
don't need to lose two planes today.

I'll be right along, sir. Carl switched to the intercom
frequency.

"Pilot to crew, our wingman is going to try to make for one
of the atolls in the Bashee Channel where he will ditch. He's lost
one engine and is losing power in the other one. I intend to stay
with him to provide air cover until a Cat can reach him. With any
luck, we won't run into any hostiles, but we need to hang around
just in case."

Zero One Eight to Flight Lead. We're going in!
Mike O'Hanlon radioed in.

Copy. You can do this Mike ... by the book.

Carl dipped his wing and reduced his airspeed to 140 mph
and applied one-quarter flaps as he began to circle the downed
bomber. Mentally, Carl coached ... *Ease back on the yoke a bit,*
Mike ... wings level. Looking good... don't stall. His stress level
steadily rose as he watched Lt. O'Hanlon raise the nose of his '25,
timing it perfectly so the tail would strike a trough between swells
first. The plane settled into the water and stopped about 40 yards
from the beach of one of the larger atolls in the Bashee group north
of Luzon Island.

Three minutes later, all six men, wearing their life vests,
paddled their way toward shore. The plane sat on a reef only about
two-thirds submerged.

"Good job, Mike. You got them all out," Carl whispered to
himself and released a sigh of relief.

"Skipper, we have company down there. A small vessel
behind us headed toward the atoll. I can't be sure, but she looks
like a converted barge used for coastal patrol."

"Roger that, Harry." Carl banked hard right until the enemy boat appeared at his 2 o'clock position. A little more bank, and the small craft came into his gun sight. Dropping low, Carl hoped to scare off the enemy craft. He knew it would be suicide for the enemy vessel to try to engage the crew of the downed B-25. Instead of coming about as he expected, the patrol boat opened up on *Avenging Angel* with its single 7 mm A-A machine gun.

"What the ...! Those idiots are shooting at us!" He veered away and banked around for another run. This time *Avenging Angel* stitched a line of .50 caliber bullets in the water fewer than 50 ft. off the bow of the converted barge. The enemy anticipated the move and fired ahead of the bomber, allowing A/P173 to pass through the line of tracers. A loud staccato metallic sound akin to that of a jack-hammer on metal sheeting reverberated through the interior of the bomber.

"I gave you a chance, you bastards!" Turning and approaching the target at mast height, Carl flew head-on at the enemy vessel. He opened up all eight .50 caliber guns firing 800 rounds per minute each. The front of the barge disintegrated. On the next pass, Carl put the bridge of the ship in his gun sights. The structure exploded with the onslaught. The vessel lay dead in the water, listing to starboard and no longer posing a threat. The few surviving enemy sailors in the water would be picked up by the Navy.

"Damage report! Are you guys okay back there?"

"Navigator is aces, Skipper."

"Engineer is good."

"Radio, here. Good to go, Skipper."

"Osborne in the tail, Skipper. Me and my babies are good."

–Flying on Fumes–

Despite a few holes in *Angel's* fuselage, both crew and aircraft seemed combat ready.

Avenging Angel returned to circle the crashed B-25. All of

O'Hanlon's crew stood safe on dry land on the atoll.

Army Bravo Two Five, this is Navy PBY Four Zero One Niner. We are four miles from your reported location. Drop smoke to confirm. Over.

The Navy P-BY Catalina arrived right on time.

Roger, Navy. Dropping green now.

Ortiz dropped a green smoke flare from the bomb bay directly above the downed crew.

"Skipper, our fuel reserve is dropping. I think one of those Jap rounds hit a fuel line. We need to head for home," Doc Henreid called from behind Carl.

"Roger that, Doc. I need you to calculate how much fuel we need to make it back to base. Turning for home now." The yo-yo that was his anxiety level was on the rise again. He swallowed the bile rising in his throat and he began to sweat heavily as his heart-rate shot up.

San Marcelino remained 100 miles distant. The extra time spent to protect O'Hanlon's crew used up most of their fuel reserve. Five minutes later, Carl asked for another update from Doc.

"Give me some good news, Doc."

"Skipper, we have about 20 minutes, maybe a little more if we trim this lady for best performance. The good news is, I found the leak and patched it," Doc responded.

Damn, we.ve lost too much fuel! I hope I haven't killed us all, Carl thought. He hated that he had placed his crew ... his friends ... at risk for their lives.

"We're a good half-hour from home. Okay, this is what we're going to do. We're going to start throwing everything we can out the bomb bay including the bomb racks ... rip out everything that's bolted down. You need to give me 10 more minutes, Doc. How much do we need to dump?"

Doc Henreid crunched some numbers, calculating fuel consumption against weight and moment.

271

"Skipper, we need to jettison at least 1200 pounds to give us any chance."

"Alright, get to work, Doc. I don't care if we land this aircraft in our skivvies. Get it done."

While Wendell Price, Harry Osborne, Alex Chekov, and Phil Ortiz piled every loose item they could find on top of the bomb-bay doors, Doc set to the task of dismantling the four .50 caliber side guns and removing them from their blisters. All of the ammunition that could be accessed, all of the flotation and survival gear; even the radioman and navigator's seats were unbolted and removed.

"Ready, Skipper," Doc called out.

"Open the doors and drop it all," Carl ordered.

The sudden loss of ballast pushed *Avenging Angel*'s nose up. Carl throttled back to 140 mph and trimmed the plane for level flight. "Okay, men, spread out back there. Distribute your weight as evenly as you can and sit still."

At only 3000 feet above ground level and flying over dense jungle, the thought of landing the plane if they ran out of fuel was a pipe dream.

Alex double-checked the throttle and mixture settings. "I wonder if this is how those fellas in the Doolittle raid felt ... no place to go but straight ahead. Most ended up in the Sea of Japan."

"All we can do is fly on, Alex ...," *and pray*, Carl thought. He had done everything he could. He appeared calm to his co-pilot, but he was clenching his teeth so hard his jaws ached.

Alex chuckled. "If *Avenging Angel* should lose power before reaching safety ... and she probably will ... we won't survive the crash. So, at least we won't have to worry about being captured and tortured." He grinned over at Carl.

"That's what I like about you, Alex ... always looking for the pony in the pile of manure." Alex's sense of humor reduced Carl's anxiety a bit and his jaw relaxed.

Carl's thoughts turned to home and the Double-B ranch in Montana, and to Annie ... *my love, my life. I promised to return and that we'd be together ... only forever, if you care to know.* The Bing Crosby song, played at their high school graduation dance, echoed in his mind as if mocking him for his decision to join the fight for his country.

His Flight Engineer shook him from his thoughts. "Skipper, the port engine is trailing smoke. If that fuel leak catches a spark, we'll light up like a roman candle."

"Copy that. Feathering the port engine." Carl closed the fuel line and feathered the engines. When the remaining fuel in the lines ran out, he pulled the mixture back to idle-cutoff. As the propeller wound down, so did Carl's hopes. He watched as the propeller came to a stop. He increased power to the right engine and trimmed the '25 to compensate for the increased drag on the left side. The loss of an engine gave him no choice but to begin a gradual shallow descent in an effort to conserve fuel. He flew the '25 "clean" ... no flaps and gear up. He gripped the yoke with both hands and glanced over at his co-pilot. Alex Chekov returned the look and shrugged his shoulders in a gesture that echoed the thought in Carl's mind, *we're not going to make it.*

Crippled, *Avenging Angel* continued her slow descent, dropping ever closer toward the top of the trees.

Carl called the base.

Alpha Papa One Seven Three to base, declaring engine out emergency. We are niner miles north at 1,000. Do you copy? Over?

Roger, Alpha Papa One Seven Three. You are cleared for straight in approach. Emergency vehicles standing by.

Two miles from the base, at only 300 feet altitude, Carl had to measure risking the additional drag of lowering the flaps and gear against the resulting loss of airspeed.

"Alex, I'm going to call for flaps and gear when we're about a half mile out. I'll call for full power just before and hope the engine won't die. The fuel gauge is already reading empty."

"Roger, Skipper. On your command."

The engine coughed once. Carl called for full flaps.

"Full flaps now!"

The sound of the servos lowering the flaps and the lifting of *Angel's* tail confirmed the flaps were down even before Alex's verbal confirmation.

"Gear down!" Carl ordered.

Alex pressed the gear lever down. A green light flashed on. "Gear down and locked, Skipper."

A clearing opened up ahead, and the tops of buildings and tents popped into view alongside a beautiful strip of concrete.

"I think we might make it! C'mon, *Angel*, just a little way to go!"

"Flaps full, Carl."

At 50 feet above and 100 yards short of the runway, the remaining engine sputtered, smoothed out for a moment ... and quit.

"Oh crap!" Carl immediately pulled back on the yoke just enough to pull the '25's nose up slightly. Threatening to stall, the main gear touched down with a jarring thump on the compacted dirt 20 yards short of the runway. *Angel* rolled up onto the pavement just in time for the nose wheel to settle onto the surface. Carl let her roll as far as she could and stopped. He unplugged his headset from the radio jack and unbuckled his harness.

He sat back and released a sigh of relief.

"She truly is an angel, Alex. I was dead certain we were going to join the bananas in those trees back there."

Alex slapped Carl's shoulder.

"Roger that. If you hadn't laid in a quarter flaps to bring *Angel's* tail up when you did, that last bit of fuel wouldn't have found its way to the engine. Let's get outta here. I want to feel the ground underneath my boots."

"Pilot to crew. You all did outstanding work getting us back home."

"We're going to need to requisition new ... well, everything, Skipper. It'll be like Townsville all over again. Poor *Angel* just had all of her teeth pulled up there." Harry quipped from his unarmed turret position.

"Roger that, Sergeant, I'll get the Crew Chief on it right away."

That evening at the Officers' Club, Carl, Alex, and Phil joined some of the other pilots already there, and the beer and whiskey flowed. An attractive Filipino girl in traditional island attire, a dress with butterfly puff-sleeves and close-fitting skirt, took their orders.

Phil whistled loudly. "Wow! Get a load of that dame. She's gorgeous!"

"She's pretty, alright. I saw her the last time we were here. She looks to be about half-Filipino and half ... something else." Alex Chekov observed.

"Go easy guys, the lady is taken." Charlie Temple pulled up a chair next to Carl.

They talked and drank for a few minutes, until Carl decided to excuse himself.

"Time to head over to The Pub, boys. There's an initiation going on that we don't want to miss. Why don't you come along, Charlie?"

"Hell yes. I'm always up for a party."

The four officers adjourned to The Pub.

"Form-up and prepare to ditch!" Harry Osborne announced. Wendell Price, Harry and a few enlisted guys from the 499th gathered around Doc Henreid who sat in a chair in The Pub. "Raise 'em up, boys!" Six bottles of beer were raised over Doc's head. "Bombs away," Harry called as bottles were upended, and Doc Henreid was initiated into the brotherhood.

"It's a lot more fun doing the pouring than it was getting drenched." Wendell Price laughed.

Everyone sang a round of "He's a Jolly Good Fellow," and someone from the 499th ordered another round of beers. They talked together of the mission to Tourane Bay, the "Zero" attack and the skin-of-their-teeth landing.

"*Angel's* being re-armed as we speak. She'll be ready to go in a couple of days." Harry Osborne said. "You know, Doc, you kept your head on pretty straight for your first mission. You spotted that fuel leak fast. If not for you, we may not have gotten everything jettisoned as soon as we did; and, if you hadn't told the skipper in time, we'd be sleeping in the jungle tonight. You're okay in my book, Doc."

Carl knew that Doc was living his dream. He remembered his conversation with him back at Tacloban.

"Well, Doc, you're not just listening from the sidelines anymore. You're one of us. Is it what you imagined it would be like?"

"More, sir ... much more. Man, that was intense up there!"

Two Days Later
–Map Room, 345th Bombardment Group, 0800 hrs–

Lt. Col. Coltharp, Intelligence Officer Capt. Ben Green, and Maj. John Bentley of the 71st Reconnaissance Group based in Mindoro, Leyte, were looking at recent recon photos taken by a specially equipped B-25 overflying the Indo-China Coast from 11 degrees north to between 16 and 17 degrees North Latitude and inland from approximately 108.20 degrees east to 109.07 degrees East Longitude.

"What's this group of vessels here, Major?" Chester Coltharp pointed at a group of at least 20 small shapes just off the coast inside a small inlet.

"You're looking at Bong Son. There's a recently constructed portage there which suggests movement of goods and materials into the area. Until now, we did not consider it much of a threat ... just normal merchant travel into and out of the villages and towns up and down the coast ... that is until recently. Fleets of sampans and junks have been moving just off the coastline carrying materials believed headed for Japanese encampments in the area. We know this to be true because reconnaissance flights have caught Japanese cargo vessels, SCLs and SBSs, off-loading materials onto these smaller vessels that you see here; they deliver the supplies to the same towns and villages you see scattered all along the Indo-China coast."

"Thank you, Major." Col. Coltharp paused to consider the latest aerial reconnaissance intelligence. He looked at the colored push-pins denoting the location of the French forces and continued.

"Our French and British friends are concerned that a possible fifth column of Japanese loyalists may be massing for some sort of major push east into Burma and India or possibly across to Formosa. Command is concerned the Japs will attempt to establish a new offensive on Luzon Island. The General Staff wants to keep Indo-China isolated ... even to the extent of pushing the Japs north to their home islands. Right now, the French and the forces of Ho-Chi-Minh's Viet-Minh Army are barely maintaining control of the region. What Washington doesn't want is to get embroiled in a regional war between the Japs and the French for control of what is, in reality, a French colony. It is in the best interest of the United States to keep the enemy isolated and confined to the area of the South Indo-China coast. To maintain the current equilibrium of the political balance in the region, 5th and 13th Air Forces have been ordered to harass shipping up and down the coast of Indo China in addition to the work we're doing in Formosa."

Coltharp moved his pointer to two larger vessels anchored farther out to sea. "And these? They look like warships."

Maj. Bentley nodded. "You're right. You're looking at a

mine layer and a destroyer. These others, the ones nearest the coast line, are patrol boats. They're big and slow. Unlike the smaller and faster American PT boats, these are converted older Minekaze and Momi-class destroyers. They're slow movers ... no more than 15 knots, but they're big. Each patrol vessel is 900 to 940 tons of displacement with crew compliments of 100 to 110 men. Farther up the coast, here ..." Bentley tapped two images even farther north, hugging the coast line, "are two enemy freighters: SCL or SBS class; and a pair of warships: a destroyer and a destroyer escort."

Coltharp paused ... nodding his understanding. "We'll put together a series of missions and begin launching at first light. I'll need your most recent aerial photos with coordinates, Major. What about interception by Jap fighters? It looks like there'll be plenty from the Jap- controlled aerodromes. We'll need air cover."

"I'll look into that, Colonel. I know the fighter escort from the 348th is spread thin with assignments to cover the heavies and providing fighter cover for our ground troops. If there are no further questions, sir, I need to get busy on those updated maps you need."

"Of course. Thank you, Major."

Maj. Bentley left the room.

Col. Coltharp turned to Capt. Green. "Ben, I figure a dozen '25s should do the job. Which squadrons are the freshest?"

"The 500th for sure. They've had a couple days' rest. The 501st is on the ground. The 499th and 498th are on a mission as we speak."

"Very well. Capt. Green, I want six bombers each from the Rough Raiders and the Black Panthers. Tell the Squadron Commanders to have their crews ready for the mission briefing at 1600 hrs for a strike on the Indo-China coast. I want you to call the 348th Fighter Group and tell them we need all of the air cover they can provide."

"And if they can't, sir?"

"Then we'll do it the hard way ... by ourselves."

Avenging Angel

–South China Sea–

Lt. Carl. Bridger flew *Avenging Angel*, designation Bravo Leader, to the left and behind Capt. Al Marshall in A/P571, designation Alpha Leader. Capt. Marshall was also the Group Leader for the Air Apaches.

Carl glanced to his right wing to make certain Lt. Denny Hoffman was maintaining good position. Hoffman caught his look and threw him a salute. Carl smiled and returned the gesture. The third flight of two Mitchells, led by Lt. Claude Lamar in A/P580, designation Charlie Leader, and his wingman Lt. Boris "Bo" Kuta in A/P500 were positioned behind and to the left of Carl's Bravo Flight.

Alpha Leader to all flights, we're coming up on our Intercept Point. Watch for bogeys.

Carl keyed his intercom. "Gunners, charge your guns. Bombardier, arm bombs."

The dorsal turret guns fired a one-second burst of .30-caliber ammo, followed by Harry Osborne and his .50-caliber AN/M2s.

"Bombs are armed, Skipper," 2nd Lt. Phil Ortiz reported.

"Roger that. Price, I need you to stay in the turret. Keep an eye out for bogeys. Call out at the first sign." Carl needed his crew in position and ready for what he knew was coming: *We're in for one helluva fight,* he thought.

The group approached the coast at precisely 12 degrees north latitude. Immediately, they spotted a convoy of two enemy freighters, an SBS of about 1,600 tons and a larger SCL at about 2,300 tons of displacement. The 500th Rough Raiders were the lead squadron and immediately fell into line-abreast formation and dived on the two freighters. Whether by design or they just didn't notice, the lead squadron bypassed five warships.

Alpha Leader to all planes, a destroyer and a

minelayer at 3 o'clock low with four patrol craft. Line-abreast formation. Charlie Flight you're with me on the destroyer. Bravo Flight, hit the mine layer.

Copy, Lead. We have the minelayer.

Carl banked left and descended to 200 feet with Lt. Hoffman in A/P009 tucked in close off his right wing. The minelayer was positioned about 150 yards astern of the destroyer.

Al Marshall and his wingman were first to drop their bombs. He dropped three 100-pounders at mast height, flying into the face of anti-aircraft fire from the deck guns. Two of them hit short and exploded harmlessly, but his third hit the destroyer amidships and detonated. His wingman went for the bow and released two bombs scoring near misses. Both planes banked sharply to the left to position themselves for another pass when a secondary explosion rocked the destroyer. The ammunition magazine had ignited and sent up a massive fireball, and more explosions followed that tore the destroyer in half. The two planes banked away from the destruction and joined Charlie Flight in the attack on the four patrol craft.

Carl and Lt. Hoffman approached the minelayer at mast height.

They flew into a barrage of 13 mm machine gun fire from the four barrels of the Type 93 guns on the deck of the minelayer.

Phil, drop two. Hoffman, you too, Carl ordered over the plane-to-plane frequency.

"Bombs away!" Phil Ortiz dropped one bomb then another spaced a fraction of a second apart. The first bomb hit halfway between the bow and amidships forward of the bridge, obliterating a forward A-A gun and blasting a hole in the deck. His second scored a near miss, striking the water off the starboard side.

Lt. Hoffman's two bombs were aimed aft of the bridge scoring a direct hit on the stern. The second bomb missed, sending up a 50-foot water spout. Three simultaneous explosions occurred.

The ship might have survived had it not been for his follow-up stern hit. The ship had mines lined up aft of the bridge ready to be dropped into the water. They blew it apart in a chain of at least a half dozen blasts ripping it to shreds.

Carl and Denny Hoffman banked hard left toward the patrol boats. As Carl got into position to attack, Wendell Price caught sight of a flight of three enemy fighters.

"Bogeys, 12 o'clock high, flight of three! Where's our air cover, Skipper?"

"Looks like we're all alone. All guns, fire at will!"

"Two more coming in from our 5 o'clock! They're swarming on the formation, Skipper!" Harry sighted his guns on the nearest inbound bogey.

One of the Nakajima Ki-43 Oscars came at *Angel* blinking death from his 20 mm cannon. Carl never saw him until Wendell Price hollered, "I've got him!" At about 400 yards, the fighter and Wendell's turret guns opened up at the same time. The fighter's fixed wing guns were slightly off, shooting above the bomber. Sgt. Price's flexible twin 50-caliber guns had the advantage. Wendell led his target perfectly. Smoke erupted from the fighter's engine, and the pilot broke off his attack.

Carl pressed his attack on the patrol boats. He and Denny Hoffman each had one bomb left. At mast height and closing to less than 200 feet from two boats, he pressed the bomb-release button on his yoke. The 500-pound demolition bomb dropped from the bomb bay and nosed into the water, emerging again climbing five feet into the air and nosing downward, striking one of the Japanese PT boats at the water line amidships. The direct hit ripped open the hull of the 900-ton converted destroyer turned patrol boat.

Hoffman's remaining bomb missed wide astern, exploding harmlessly. As Carl banked *Angel* up and away from the burning rubble looking for other targets, another Oscar dived at him from his 5 o'clock position. It was a difficult oblique approach. The

Oscar tried to turn into the bomber's flight path, but before he could fire, Harry Osborne had him pinned in his sights.

"Gotcha!" He grinned and squeezed the firing levers on his twin .50s. His arms and hands vibrated as though he were operating a jack-hammer. The smell of cordite filled his nostrils as he watched his tracers enter the fighter's engine. Harry maintained a five-second burst of gun fire until the enemy plane suddenly exploded in flames. It veered away and spun into a flaming death spiral toward the ocean.

"Splash one Oscar! This is our day, Wendell!" Harry called over the intercom.

"Knock off the chatter!" Carl commanded over the intercom. "If you're talkin' you're not watching! We're not out of this yet."

As Carl banked around to line up for a strafing run on one of the patrol boats, they were ambushed by another Oscar; this one coming in from 6 o'clock high again ... just like the first one.

"Bogey, 6 o'clock high. Hold us steady, Skipper. I've got this."

The Oscar pressed his attack to within 100 yards before running into Wendell's hail of gunfire. Trailing smoke and flames, the enemy plane still came at them, firing ... *Rap! Rap! Rap! Rap! Rap!* The sound of five rounds penetrating the fuselage of the Mitchell a mere foot below Price's turret reverberated through the interior of the bomber. Wendell felt a sudden forceful tug at his left leg.

"I'm hit! I'm hit!" He looked down at his leg. The 20 mm round had torn a hole in his flight coveralls. It didn't even break the skin.

"Never mind, I'm not hit! I'm not hit!"

"Damage report, Doc. Did those rounds hit anything critical?"

"Checking ..." Doc scanned his instruments: engines, fuel system, hydraulic and electrical. "Negative, Skipper. All systems are in the green."

Carl's wingman wasn't faring as well. Lt. Hoffman was turning onto his second pass at a patrol boat at about 200 feet above the ocean's surface when he, too, was targeted by an Oscar. The enemy dived on Hoffman's plane from 6 o'clock high, opening fire and sending a round into the fuselage where it exploded behind the radioman's position wounding two men: his radioman and turret gunner. Despite his serious wound, the gunner continued to fire on the Oscar until the enemy plane burst into flames and turned away.

Bravo Wing to Lead, we've been hit! Two wounded. We're still operational! Lt. Hoffman reported, as he re-formed off Carl's right wing.

Charlie Flight to Group Lead, starting my run against a second patrol boat.

Carl caught a glimpse of Charlie Flight Leader diving for the kill, strafing the vessel on his first run and then banking sharply 180 degrees to set the ship up for his wingman.

Charlie Flight Leader to Group Leader, my wingman is down hard! I'm going to do a fly-over to check for survivors.

Al Marshall's voice came over the plane-to-plane com, Alpha Lead to Black Panthers, form up! Charlie Flight Leader, join up when you can.

The 11 remaining B-25s of the Air Apaches formed up and turned toward San Marcelino. From the time they arrived over their target, the fight had lasted only 15 minutes.

Avenging Angel was second to land following Lt. Hoffman's plane with its two wounded crewmen.

Carl taxied up to the flight line and stopped. He and Alex shut down the avionics and engines, and his ground crew chalked the wheels. Doc Henreid lowered the access ladder, and the crew climbed down to the tarmac.

Chapter XII

March 28, 1945

–Hainan Island Raid–

The sky was still dark, however every light bathed the 345th Bombardment Group HQ briefing room in an incandescent glow. Carl and two other pilots met with Col. Coltharp in his office a half-hour prior to the mission briefing scheduled for 0500.

"I've called you men in to assign you as leaders for today's mission. You are all 0-2s and in line for promotions to Captain which will come with the next officer allotment in May. You all need the command responsibility in your personnel files. You are three of my finest junior officers, and I know you will perform to the highest level of the Air Apaches. Lt. Mckelvey will lead the 498th Falcons. Lt. Drudd, you will lead the Bats Outta Hell of the 499th. Lt. Bridger will command the group from his lead position with the 501st. I'll see all of the crews in the briefing room in 30 minutes. You're dismissed."

Carl took in a deep breath and released it as he joined his crew in the briefing room. He felt the weight of command heavy on his shoulders. He was apprehensive and at the same time excited by the challenge of his first group command of a mission. *Okay, Carl, command responsibility is to be expected. Suck it up!*

Eighteen crews, six from each of the 498th, 499th, and 501st squadrons were gathering in the briefing room and finding seats. The target map behind the podium showed a tactical overlay of the southern quarter of Hainan Island and Yulin Bay.

285

Three colored lines approached the island from the east. A miniature B-25 on a stick-pin anchored the end of each string. Each of those had a tag in black letters above the miniature planes; one for each numbered squadron.

"Gentlemen, our target is the inner harbor of Yulin Bay. You will hit the shipping there in three waves. "Lt. Bridger will lead the group in A/P173 with the 501st Black Panthers. Lt. Drudd will follow with the 499th, and Lt. Mckelvey's 498th will cleanup with the third wave. Fuel will be an issue. You're looking at about 900 miles round trip. Air cover will be provided by twelve P-51s with drop tanks from the 348th Fighter Group led by Capt. Charles Temple, call name 'Razor Leader.'

"Your approach will follow this path ..." Col. Coltharp indicated the colored strings. "... approaching Yulin Bay from the west shore of Leong Soi Bay just east of your target.

"These markers in the target area show the shipping in Yulin Bay as of three hours ago. They are as follows: three freighters ... here, here, and here. Four Patrol boats and two destroyers are anchored at the mouth of the bay. Expect A-A fire and probable air interception. Your load-out will be four-each 500-pound demolition bombs with four-second time delay fuses and 8,000 round of ammunition. The weather over the target is low overcast as of one hour ago. Figure on no more than a 500-foot ceiling with two miles of visibility at best. Because of the poor visibility, your approach will need to be spot on. Keep your eyes open for the mountains west and north of the target. We don't want any of you landing in the trees. Wheels up at 0715, gentlemen."

Carl and his crew gathered outside the Operations Building following the briefing. "We have an hour before we need to be on the flight-line, boys. What do you say we hit the mess tent for a bite? Go easy on the coffee, though. There won't be any potty stops after we're airborne." Carl led the way.

The mess tent was abuzz with activity. In anticipation of

early morning missions, the mess hall crew always had the stoves fired up and coffee urns filled with hot dark Java. Most of the crews had the same idea as Carl, because in a matter of minutes the tables and chairs were alive with men and the clinking of glass and silverware. They all sat in groups talking about their strategy for hitting the targets. The pilots could always be identified by their hand-gestures miming the banks and turns of their planes as they talked.

Carl spotted Charlie and several other P-51 jockeys entering the mess tent and looking around for a place to sit.

He raised his hand and called out. "Hey, Charlie! Over here!"

Charlie turned toward the voice and saw Carl waving. He said something to the men he was with and headed over to Carl's table.

"Hey, Carl. I guess we'll be covering your butts upstairs on this one, eh?"

"Reckon so. You remember Alex and Phil don't you? These other guys are my Flight Engineer Doc Henreid, Radioman Wendell Price, and the best darned tail gunner in the business Harry Osborne. Harry and Wendell were credited with three kills a few days ago ... all of them were Oscars."

"I'm happy to meet all of you." Charlie pulled up a seat. "So what do you think about the weather over the target, Carl. Can your bombers get in and out of Yulin Bay with that cloud cover?"

"It'll be tough. We'll be forced to go in at mast height and skip our bombs. Medium altitude bombing won't be possible. A-A will likely be pretty intense, and we won't have a lot of maneuvering room because of the low ceiling, but ..." Carl shrugged his shoulders, "what else is new, right?"

"True that." Charlie chuckled. "Fear not, though, my friend. We'll make sure no Zekes are going to bother you. You hear from Annie lately?"

"No, not in a few days. You know how the mail is ... like

grapes. Letters come in bunches." Carl grinned. He hoped there would be mail waiting for him when he got back from the mission.

"How about you and Alyanna? Things still working out for you two?"

"Yep. Fine as frog's hair. She's worried about the Japs, though. Her uncle is a leader in the Filipino resistance, and she says the Japs are looking for her uncle's family to use against him and the guerrilla movement."

Carl shook his head and whistled. "Like what? ... reprisals? ... kidnappings?"

Charlie shrugged. "Any and all of the above, I guess. At least Alyanna is safe as long as she's at the 'O' club. I think her family is being watched over by some of the young boys and women in the village. I wish I could get them to move into the town. I think it's more secure there."

They chatted while finishing their chow and then headed for the flight line.

At 0715 *Avenging Angel* was lined up and ready to go.

"Let's get this show on the road, Alex. Take us up."

Alex throttled-up, and the Mitchell began her takeoff roll. At 80 mph he eased back on the yoke taking the pressure off the nose wheel to let the air pass beneath the airfoil and lift the bomber into the sky. At 100 mph the main wheels released their grip on the earth, and Alex nosed the bomber into a gentle climb. At 170 mph, he increased the climb angle and banked around to the rally point. Twelve minutes later, all 18 B-25s, led by Carl, formed up over San Marcelino and set their course for Hainan Island.

Ten minutes out from the target, Charlie and his P-51s took position ahead and above the bombers. He keyed his plane-to plane com.

Razor Leader to Alpha Leader, do you copy. Over?

Alpha Leader. How does it look up there, Charlie?

We're at 6,000 about five miles ahead of you, Carl, and no sign of bogeys. We're orbiting now.

Copy, Razor Leader. We're coming up on the IP now.

Alpha Leader to Red Group, arm bombs and charge your guns. I'm dropping to the deck. We need to get under this cloud layer. Tuck-in close, wings. Bravo and Charlie Flights, I want you to stay close on the tail of the flight in front of you. Dropping to two-zero-zero feet on heading two-niner-five degrees.

Carl throttled back a bit and started his descent of 1,200 feet per minute. As *Avenging Angel* dropped into the clouds, wisps of mist flashed past his windscreen.

"Sgt. Osborne. I want you to keep an eye out for Bravo Flight. I don't want them to lose sight of us."

"Copy. They're riding our tail, Skipper."

"Good. Let me know if you lose track of them. Pilot, out."

At 200 feet, they still hadn't broken through the cloud cover.

"Alex, read off the altitude. I'm dropping to the deck."

Alpha Leader to all planes, dropping to 100 feet.

The temperature in the cockpit was cool, but a trickle of sweat running down his back reminded Carl that his stress level was at its peak. He watched the altimeter drop to 190 feet ... 180 ... 150 ... 125. *C'mon, show me some daylight!* He keyed his mic to the other planes to abort the mission, but before he could speak they broke through the clouds. Instead of coming at the bay head-on over water, Carl had drifted to the right of their desired flight path and saw nothing but the tops of palm trees coming at him. He banked hard left toward the water and Leong Soi Bay. Their target lay just four miles west of their present position.

Carl led the group farther out to sea until Yulin Bay opened up to his right. He immediately spotted the destroyers ... two

Yugumo-class. Capable of speeds of 33 knots, they had a heavy A-A defensive capability with sixteen 20 mm anti-aircraft guns.

Alpha Flight, line-abreast formation. We'll hit the destroyers. Bravo and Charlie Flight, hit the Freighters with two bombs each. Save the other two for our second pass. Acknowledge.

Bravo Flight, roger. Lt. Blount confirmed.

Charlie Flight, roger. Lt. Gavins reported in.

We don't have to do this all by ourselves, boys. Red One and Red Two are right behind us. We'll wait until all squadrons have made a pass before we start our second run.

Carl was beginning to understand that the burden of command was lessened by the support of competent pilots and crews. *These guys are the best*, he thought.

O'Hanlon, line up on the starboard destroyer ... I'll take the port side.

Roger, Lead.

Mike O'Hanlon angled away from Carl's wing and dropped A/P008 toward his target at mast height.

Carl brought his speed up to 280 mph and centered his nose amidships of the lead war ship. They caught the destroyers by surprise. They were not showing any smoke, and were lying still in the water. Sailors swarmed on deck and manned the anti-aircraft guns. Bursts of ack-ack pocked the sky ahead, and Carl began to zig-zag, forcing the enemy gunners to adjust angle and elevation. At 200 feet from the destroyer, Carl pressed the red "bomb" button twice. One 500-pound demolition bomb dropped into the water followed an instant later by a second. The first bomb skipped high and flew over the bow of the ship, exploding harmlessly in the water. The second bomb missed as well, passing just in front of the bow of the destroyer. One of Mike O'Hanlon's bombs struck the second destroyer astern. The explosion tore into the engine room. His second bomb skipped high and hit between the stern and amidships four feet above the water line. That explosion was much more spectacular. The torpedo tubes on the deck were loaded. The shock from the bomb blast caused one of the torpedoes to discharge. The ensuing fireball rendered the ship critically damaged.

Nice shooting, Mike! That's one less Jap destroyer to worry about.

Carl smiled as he held *Angel* in a 60-degree bank to position his squadron for a second pass.

Red Leader to Red Two, Red One has plowed the field. A-A from the destroyers is minimal.

Roger, Lead. Red Two is starting our run now.

Alpha Leader to all planes. Form up! Carl ordered the 501st Black Panthers.

He could see several fires burning where other Black Panthers had found their targets. As his planes were leaving the target area, the 498th Falcons roared in and hit the patrol boats and the freighters. Finally, the 499th Bats Outta Hell finished its run. Both destroyers were in flames, but the one Carl missed was under steam and heading out to sea.

Alpha Leader to Black Panthers, start your second run now. Bravo and Charlie flights, hit the patrol boats. Mike, let's sink the big guy.

Roger Lead. I'm right on your wing.

Fly ahead of me and strafe his deck guns, Mike. Draw off that ack-ack! Carl ordered.

A/P008 banked away, climbed and took position for a shallow-diving strafing run from stern to bow. Carl waited for Mike to line up on the ship's stern, then dropped to mast height and accelerated to 300 mph.

Again, Carl lined up on the destroyer. She was smoking still, but there were no visible flames.

The deck guns began firing at the in-bound Mitchells. Ack-ack was much lighter, thanks to Mike O'Hanlon's diversion, and Carl held *Angel's* nose steady at the bow. He timed the release of the high-explosive bombs perfectly. The first bomb struck the starboard side behind the bow. Carl pulled the 25's nose sharply up. He put his ring sight just above the ship forward of the bridge and released his final bomb. The bomb arched down just as the bridge passed in front of its trajectory. It struck the ship just above the deck and below the bridge, lifting the bridge tower off the super structure and shredding it. The destroyer began to list and her bow, heavy with water, dropped downward, bringing her still turning screws above the ocean surface. Several Japanese crewmen were seen diving overboard, and a few life rafts had been deployed.

Alpha Leader to Red Group, form up!

All 18 B-25s grabbed some altitude forthwith and headed for home.

"Hey, Skipper. There's our air cover! Three o'clock high!" Alex pointed at the two flights of P-51s. Carl counted them. All 12 were in diamond formations of four fighters each, orbiting at 7,000 feet altitude.

Razor Lead to Alpha Leader, welcome back to friendly airspace. Carl, how was your vacation on the isle of Hainan?

Too many ships in the harbor to enjoy the beach, and they weren't friendly. We decided to take our beach balls and go home.

Roger that. I'm counting your planes. All 18 are present and accounted for. That's a win in my book.

Roger that, Razor Lead. That harbor is out of commission for quite a while and the Emperor's fleet is quite a bit smaller in the bargain.

As is the case with every mission, the mission leader must submit a full report to the group Intelligence Office. This would be

Carl's first experience with the paperwork that accompanies the responsibility of command.

In the 35 minutes that the 345th had been over the target, they had expended thirty-six 500-pound bombs, and 37,800 rounds of .50 caliber ammunition. One destroyer was sunk and the second crippled beyond repair. Both SCL class freighters were sunk, and five patrol boats received damage. Three A-A shore batteries were strafed and silenced. Four buildings appearing to be storage facilities were heavily strafed. Five planes were holed by anti-aircraft gunnery, and one crew member of the 499th Squadron suffered a shrapnel wound to his left thigh. No awards were recommended for the mission.

At 1300 hrs, Carl met Charlie for drinks at the "O" Club. Together with officers of the 348th Fighter Group and the 345th Bombardment Group who participated in the day's mission, the revelry began.

"I can't believe our first two bombs missed." Carl explained to Charlie. "We zig-zagged to avoid the anti-aircraft fire, and I misjudged my approach to the destroyer. I should have aborted the pass and gone around for another try."

"Yeah, but we nailed him on the second run, Skipper." Phil chimed in. "That ship opened up like a tin can. Boom! What a fireball!"

Charlie nodded and smiled in appreciation. "The whole mission was a damned gutsy call on your part, Carl. I'm surprised you found your target at all. When your entire group disappeared into that low blanket of clouds, I was afraid the jungle was going to reach up and grab you out of the sky."

Alex laughed. "It darned near did. We came into the clear over the jungle instead of the water and had to make a sharp turn back out over the bay to avoid the terrain."

Charlie had been looking around the room for some sign of Alyanna. He checked his wristwatch.

"I don't see Alyanna. She should have started her shift over an hour ago." He stood up from the table. "Excuse me, fellas. I'll be right back."

Charlie started walking toward the bar to ask Sedro Aquino if he had seen Alyanna when Basilio and Raanan Deschales charged into the "O" Club.

"Hey, kid! No natives allowed. Go back to your hooch!" one officer yelled.

"Yeah, kid ... scram!" said another.

Charlie walked up to the boys, concern etched on his brow. "Basilio ... Raanan. What are you doing here? Come outside, you're really not supposed to be here."

Carl had been watching the exchange between Charlie and the two Filipino boys. From the expression on their faces something serious had happened ... something requiring Charlie's help. He put his beer down and followed them out of the club.

–Taken–

Alyanna arose at 10 a.m. after six hours of sleep. Her mother and brothers were working in the enlisted and officer's quarters cleaning, delivering clean folded laundry, and picking up soiled laundry.

Her shift wouldn't begin at the Officers' Club for another two hours. She dressed in faded khaki pants and an army T-shirt frayed at the collar. A much-worn traditional wide-brimmed conical-shaped peasant hat called a *saklat* hung by the entrance to the family's gita. Alyanna pulled it over her head and walked outside to build a fire for the laundry tub. Her mother and brothers would be returning with bags of soiled clothing soon.

Behind the row of gitas, six laundry tubs stood on strong steel legs. The two nearest the Santos' family gita, one for washing and one for rinsing, were reserved for Bianca and Alyanna. The cut-in-half 60-gallon barrels had to be filled twice each day. She picked up two pails and started out on the path to the stream which passed by the village about 30 yards into the jungle. Once there, she lowered the pails into the water, filled them and suspended them from a curved wooden yoke which she balanced on her shoulders for the return trip. It would take 10 trips to the stream to fill their tubs with enough water for the laundry.

Her shoulders ached as she returned to the stream and lowered the pails to the ground for the eighth time. She smiled at two older women who walked into the clearing and approached the water's edge.

Pagbati. Isang magandan gumaga ito ay hindi ito? (Greetings. It is a beautiful day, is it not?)

One of the women smiled. *Oo ito ay. Isang magandang araw para sa trabano.* (Yes. It is a good day for work.)

The women chatted while they performed their chores. Alyanna lifted the yoke onto her shoulders and started back to her gita when two men, dressed in Japanese infantry uniforms leapt from behind the dense foliage and pushed her to the ground. Alyanna screamed once before she was gagged, and a burlap sack was pulled over her head. The two older women crouched low in the tall grasses bordering the stream and watched. After the soldiers dragged Alyanna into the jungle the women scurried back to the village.

Raanan, Basilio, and their mother returned to the gita and found Alyanna gone. The fire for the laundry tubs had burned down to coals.

Bianca Deschales called out her daughter's name, "Alyanna! Alyanna!"

The women who witnessed the abduction, heard Bianca yelling for her daughter and rushed to her side. They described the details of what they witnessed. Bianca almost fainted, and the women helped her up the steps to her gita.

"Mama, what is it?" Basilio knelt by his mother and was joined by Raanan.

Upon hearing the story of their sister's abduction, the brothers didn't hesitate.

"We will find mister Charlie." They dashed from the gita in a dead run for the Officers' Club.

"What's the problem, Charlie? Who are these boys?" Carl asked.

"Alyanna's brothers." Charlie answered curtly. He put his hands on Basilio's shoulder.

"Calm down, Basilio. This is my friend, Carl. Tell us what happened."

"She is gone! Alyanna is gone! The Japanese soldiers came and took her away!" Basilio repeated the story that the two women told his mother.

"How long ago did this happen, Basilio?" Charlie asked.

"One hour ... perhaps less."

"Alright. Return to your mother. Wait at your gita. I will meet you there in 15 minutes. Go!" Charlie turned to Carl. "I'm going after her, Carl. Cover for me, will you? I'll try to bring her back sometime tonight."

"No, Charlie. You can't do this by yourself. There's no telling how many Japs are out there. I'm going with you. I know somebody who might help. Give me 10 minutes to check it out. I'll meet you back here, and we'll go to Alyanna's gita together."

Carl ran to the tent next to his. He knew a pilot name of Ed Storch who flew an L5 spotter plane ... one of three of the Stinson-made tail-draggers stationed at San Marcelino. Slow flying and maneuverable, the American ground forces used them for spotting enemy encampments and helping with targeting artillery.

Carl found Lt. Storch in his quarters. He paused to catch his breath. "... Ed, I ..."

"Oh, hey, Carl. What's up with you, pal? You in a hurry about something?"

"I am. An emergency situation came up, and I need your help. Are you on stand-down right now?"

"Yes. Why?"

"I need you and your plane for a couple of hours, ... off the books. Can you fake a check-flight, and do some spotting for some Japs that kidnapped one of the villagers?"

"What? Carl, what the ... are you nuts?"

"I'll explain on the way. Come with me. Please, trust me Ed. I wouldn't ask if it wasn't a matter of extreme urgency. It involves the sister of an important resistance leader."

"Okay, I'll come, but no promises until I get the whole story, and it had better be good." The two headed for the Officers' Club. They found Charlie waiting there with two .30 caliber M-1 semi-automatic carbines, ammo belts and jungle machetes. He purloined the machete from one of his tent mates. The other one was his.

Carl introduced Charlie to Ed Storch. "Charlie you have one minute to tell Ed here everything. Don't ask questions. I'll explain later."

Charlie gave Ed the gist of the story, about his involvement with Alyanna, and her relationship to Alejo Santos."

"Cripes, you guys. This is a fine mess you're pulling me into. Why don't you just report this to HQ? They could ..."

"They could do what, Ed? ... Convince the army to put together a sweep with a squad of infantry? How long do you think that would take? Maybe they could put a platoon in the field by tomorrow at best. By then, Alyanna could be on a boat to Japan. No! We need to go after her now. We need to take care of the Japs now!"

"Okay, okay. First, you'll need to grab yourself a field radio. Keep it set to channel two. I'll carry one with me. They're only good for short line-of-sight communications, but it'll do the job. The battery pack and transceiver unit is in a shoulder pack ... pretty heavy. There's an L5 over at the hangar in need of a check ride. I'd better head over to the flight line." With a wink and a nod,

Ed Storch broke into a loping run for the L5 spotter plane.

Carl and Charlie were walking past the Base Operations building on their way to the quartermaster to requisition a radio, when they spotted a Jeep idling unattended by the main entrance.

"Hey, Carl. There's a field radio sitting on the floor." Charlie grabbed the radio. "Let's scram!"

They ran to Alyanna's gita carrying the field radio.

"Col. Coltharp's driver will be scratching his head when he finds his radio missing. It saved time from trying to requisition one, though." Carl said, out of breath. "I feel like a school boy who stole his first candy bar from the corner grocery store."

"True that, old sport. We'll just haveta try and bring it back before he realizes it's gone." Charlie clapped a hand on Carl's shoulder as they walked. "I'm going to owe you big time for this."

"You sure as hell are. I think free beer until the end of the war sounds about right." Carl laughed. His humor lightened Charlie's mood and brought a grin.

"Done and done."

Basilio and Raanan hurried down the steps from the gita when they saw Charlie and Carl. An old man stood beside the boys.

"Mister Charlie, this is Diego Ocampo. He is an elder of the village ... most wise. He will guide us on our journey." Basilio waved the old man forward. The elder stepped alongside the boy and kept his hands clasped in front of him with his head bowed beneath his saklat.

Charlie looked at the old man and then at Basilio. "This is too dangerous for you boys. I want you to stay with your mother."

"Mister Charlie, you need a translator for Diego. He speaks only Tagalog. He knows the land. My brother and I are strong. We carry radio, yes? You will see. We know jungle ... all of the trails."

Charlie scrutinized the thin, frail looking elder and was afraid that he would only slow them down. Basilio read Charlie's expression and whispered something in the old man's ear. The elder raised his eyes and held Charlie's gaze while his right hand dropped to the handle of the machete at his side. Basilio took two coconuts from a basket which sat at the bottom of the stairs to the gita. He moved next to Charlie and tossed both coconuts high into the air.

Diego spun full circle on the ball of one foot. The blade of the machete flashed in the sunlight, and then he froze with the machete held vertically in front of his face ... eyes fixed again on Charlie. A trickle of coconut milk ran down the glistening razor-sharp blade and onto his hand. Four half-shells of coconuts lay on the ground.

Charlie met Carl's eyes, then Basilio and Diego's. "Alright, let's move out." He said with a conceding shrug.

Diego led at a blistering pace; dancing between rattan vines and through dense undergrowth that threatened to tangle the feet of the two American flyers. They moved quietly as they could, pausing every few minutes while Diego discerned the direction of the fleeing Japanese soldiers.

The engine of the L5 spotter plane droned overhead. Carl removed the bag carrying the radio from Basilio's back and sat it on the ground. He flipped a couple of switches and checked the channel setting.

Ground to spotter, do you copy? Over.

Roger, Ground. I read you. I'm flying a grid pattern west of the San Tomas River about six klicks west of the village. Can you see me? Over.

Negative, but I can hear you, Ed. You flew over us about 30 seconds ago. Over.

Roger. I see a dirt road about one klick north. I'll check it for vehicles. Spotter, out.

Diego kept them moving west toward the sound of the spotter plane. He quickened the pace through the jungle until they came to the San Tomas River. He knelt at the banks and pressed his hand to the earth, moving the soil between his fingers, and smiled. He uttered a short phrase in Tagalog.

"Diego says they crossed the river here one hour ago. We go."

The Japanese soldiers pushed Alyanna deep into the jungle. She stumbled and fell several times. After about an hour of arduous and slow progress, the leader ordered the sack and gag removed.

She squinted her eyes against the glare of the sun and took in her surroundings. They were standing in a small clearing.

Her vision cleared and she counted the men. *Four of them. All armed.* Her mind began collecting information. She recognized Mount Negron. She turned around to check the road behind her. The blue edge of the ocean showed through a clearing in the distance.

"Do not think you can escape, Alyanna Santos ... or should I say Deschales? You would be shot before you could run 10 meters."

Alyanna turned toward the voice. "You! What right ...?"

"I have *every* right to claim what is mine." Capt. Toshiro Fujiwara said in an even tone. "Did you think that I would not return to claim my property?"

"I am not your property!" She spat in his face. The gesture of contempt bought her a sharp backhand slap that sent her to the ground.

"You will learn to appreciate what I offer. In time, you will become more Japanese than either Filipino or French. Of course, if you were to continue to resist my generosity, I would have no choice but to turn you over to the *Kempeitai*. I am certain that the Imperial Army Intelligence Department would be happy to have the niece of Alejo Santos in their custody." Fujiwara removed a handkerchief from his trousers pocket and wiped Alyanna's spittle from his face.

They marched on through the jungle, waded across the Santo Tomas River and worked their way north toward Mount Negron.

Finally, they exited the jungle onto a road where a vehicle awaited them. A soldier prodded her in the back with the barrel of his rifle, and she climbed into the half-track.

Alyanna heard the engine of the plane before it appeared

coming in low over the tree tops. A flood of anticipation pushed up her heart rate. When the red smoke appeared she was certain ... *Charlie is coming!* Despair turned to hope, and Alyanna began to search for some way to slow the enemy soldiers.

Lt. Storch banked the L5 and came toward them again. The half-track came to a stop and the Japanese soldiers leapt from the vehicle and began firing at the small plane. When the American spotter plane left them, Capt. Fujiwara ordered his men forward with a heightened sense of urgency ... "Faster! We are being followed! Drive faster!"

The driver pressed the accelerator to the floor, and the vehicle's speedometer rose to 60 kilometers per hour, the maximum speed of the half-track. The dirt road was full of deep ruts which made steering all the more difficult. Just as the heavy armored personnel carrier rounded a curve, a dark figure dashed onto the road from the jungle. The creature startled the driver who swerved to miss it; causing a front tire to hit a water-filled rut. The front end jumped out of the rut as the driver cranked the steering wheel hard toward the downward incline. They lost traction and plunged into a shallow ravine. The axles became hopelessly entangled in vines. The wild hog dashed into the dense foliage on the other side of the road and disappeared with a series of squeals and grunts.

Capt. Fujiwara jumped from the vehicle. "Get us back on the road! You men, free the wheels. We must not waste any more time!"

Not wanting to argue with their angry and obsessed commander, the men started hacking away at the thick tendrils. After 20 minutes, it became obvious to even the educated Toshiro Fujiwara that their transportation had been claimed by the jungle.

"Up to the road! ... move! We will find other transportation! We must keep moving!"

Alyanna grinned. *Good. He is afraid of who might be coming for us. How can I slow their progress?* In a flash of inspiration, she released a yelp of pain and fell to the ground. She sat holding

301

her ankle. "I've twisted my ankle! Ooow!"

"Stand up! Do it now, or I'll shoot you myself!" Fujiwara drew his pistol from its holster.

"Oui! Alright. Can one of your men help me?" Alyanna balanced herself on one foot, and with the help of a young private, was able to limp forward. She would play out the injured ankle ruse as long as she could. *Charlie must be close ... I must go slower.*

She allowed her pretended limp to worsen. After a few more minutes, she stopped. "Please, I must rest. I need water. Please!"

"No! Keep moving!" He beckoned the private, "You, give her some water!"

The private, who was half-carrying Alyanna, handed his canteen to her, and she drank thirstily.

Diego rubbed his body with mud, as did Basilio and Raanan.

"Mud will help keep leeches away." Raanan said as he applied mud to his neck and shoulders. Charlie and Carl followed suit and began covering themselves with the odious goo.

After 10 minutes of negotiating submerged vines, dead animals, slippery rocks and poisonous snakes, they ascended the bank of the river on the opposite side.

"Remove your shirts. Check for leeches. They make you sick." Raanan and Basilio checked each other. They found a few of the black slimy blood-suckers and pulled them off.

The two American pilots removed at least a dozen leeches from various parts of their bodies. Charlie even found one clinging to his inner thigh; *close call*, he thought. They pulled up their trousers and re-buttoned their shirts.

Panting and soaked with perspiration, Charlie stopped and checked his chronometer, 1700 hrs. The unlikely team of trackers had been marching steadily for over three-and-a-half grueling hours. Diego stopped, squatted on the ground and motioned to the boys. They chattered back and forth, and then Basilio walked up to Charlie.

"Mister Charlie, Diego says they turned north. There is a road there, one kilometer."

"Damn! If they beat us to the road, we're done for." Charlie grabbed for the radio, but Carl beat him to it.

Ground to Spotter. Over.

Roger, Carl. I read you. Give me some news. Over.

Our guide says the Japs headed for the road that leads to the base of the mountain. Follow it a ways and see what you can find. Over.

Roger. Keep your radio on. If there's anyone there, I'll spot 'em. Hold on ... dead ahead, just around the bend about one klick ahead of me there's a half-track. I count five people. One is a civilian wearing a coolie hat. I'm going to try to slow them down a little.

Ed flew in front of the enemy half-track, banked around and came at them head on. The vehicle stopped, and all four soldiers jumped out, aimed their rifles at the plane and started firing. Ed flew a zig-zag course and passed over their heads.

Spotter to Ground, I'm taking fire. Dropping smoke one klick up the road from their position and returning to base. Get a move on! Good luck, fellas. Spotter, out.

Roger that. Thanks, Ed. Happy landing. Ground, out.

"There! Red smoke!" Charlie exclaimed as they broke out of the jungle onto the road. "No more than one klick. Let's move!"

As they rounded a bend, Diego suddenly stopped and squatted low. He pointed toward the blockade.

Stooping low with his carbine at the ready, Charlie moved quietly forward until he stood next to Diego. The old man pointed toward the road. Charlie's eyes followed the direction of the gnarled finger and spotted the half-track. He exchanged grins with the toothless Diego, and hurried back to Carl and the boys. "Up ahead. Off to the left. I think it's the half-track Ed spotted. It's off the road and tangled in the brush."

"Good. That means we're getting close. With Alyanna in tow, they won't move very fast," Carl said.

Charlie added, "If I don't miss my guess, they know they're being followed. Alyanna is probably doing everything she can to slow them down."

Hugging the mountain slope, they moved quickly along. The sun lowered toward the western horizon.

"Another hour and it'll start getting dark. We need to hurry," Charlie said between gasping breaths. He and Carl were near exhaustion.

Diego stopped, reversed his direction and motioned for Basilio. He whispered something to the boy, and Basilio trotted over to the men.

"The Japanese and Alyanna are ahead no more than 200 meters. Diego knows how we can cut them off by going back into the forest."

"Alright. How many are there?" Charlie asked.

"Diego says four Japanese soldiers. One of them is an officer. They all have guns."

Charlie and Carl huddled together with Diego and Alyanna's brothers. Charlie began to draw a plan of attack into the dirt beginning with the road they were on.

"Ask Diego to draw his path through the forest."

Diego extended the line of the road to a point where it cut back on itself.

"Ask him if he can lead us to where the road turns here." Charlie pointed to the switch back.

Basilio chattered in Tagalog and Diego nodded.

"Good. Let's go." Charlie stood and followed the old man

as he led the way back into the jungle.

They dropped down to the bottom of a shallow ravine with a narrow stream wind through it, and stepped across onto a trail cut through the jungle.

The well-travelled path in such a remote area surprised Charlie. "What is this trail, Basilio? It looks like it's been used many times."

Basilio asked Diego about it, and the old man rattled off a couple of sentences. Basilio moved alongside Charlie and explained, "Diego says it is a hunting trail used by the Negrito people."

"I've heard of them," Charlie said to Carl. "They're a tribe of natives who live in small villages throughout much of the Philippine Islands. They hate the Japanese and are friendly to the Americans."

Ten minutes later, Diego raised his hand and stopped.

"Why are we stopping?" Before Diego could answer Carl's question, the foliage in front and to the left of the trail moved."

Three tiny, black-skinned, potbellied little people, attired only in loin-cloths and carrying long rods and spears, stepped onto the path in front of Diego. The tallest of the group, standing not quite five feet tall, spoke to Diego in some language other than Tagalog. Diego seemed to understand the language and motioned for the two Americans.

Carl and Charlie knelt alongside Diego who explained their situation to the natives. One of the Negritos motioned to another man who darted into the jungle. He returned a moment later with an older man. He wore several braided necklaces made from some indiscernible animal hair interlaced with carved bone ornaments. Carl judged them to be a symbol of rank.

"I am called Hepe. Americans go away for many seasons. Negrito see only Hapon. You hunt *Hapon*?" the old man asked.

"We hunt the Japanese soldiers."

"Yes, Japanese ... *Hapon*."

Diego explained their mission quickly. He told Hepe about

Alyanna and about the kidnapping. He introduced Basilio and Raanan as Alyanna's brothers.

"You come!" Hepe said. He and the other Negritos trotted up the path in an easy lope. Diego matched their stride. Carl and Charlie tried to keep up, but found themselves pausing to catch their breath every couple of hundred yards. An hour later, they reached their destination.

"Americans stay in jungle. Hepe bring girl."

–Closing In–

Carl, Charlie, Basilio, and Raanan, hid among the dense foliage just off the road.

The Japanese soldiers appeared from around a bend less than a 100 yards away. Alyanna limped along with the help of one of the enemy soldiers.

An armed soldier led the procession followed by Toshiro Fujiwara. Behind him was the soldier helping Alyanna. The final soldier brought up the rear about 20 paces back. He was the first to be felled by the stealthy Negrito's deadly blow gun. The soldier clapped his hand over his neck as if stung by a bee. He released a yelp of pain and dropped to the ground, convulsed twice and lay motionless. He was still breathing but paralyzed by the potent toxin from the dart.

Capt. Fujiwara, upon hearing the cry behind him, spun around. His man lay on the ground. There was no enemy in sight. Before he could turn toward the front of the column, the man on point suddenly collapsed to the ground. Alyanna's escort did likewise, twitching momentarily as he lay in the dirt ... a dart protruding from his eye.

The moment that the soldier released his grip on her, Alyanna wasted no time picking up the man's rifle from the ground. She aimed the gun at her kidnapper and pulled the trigger.

Nothing happened. Before she could figure out that there was no bullet in the chamber, Capt. Fujiwara withdrew his sidearm.

"Hey!" Charlie yelled from behind the Japanese officer. Fujiwara turned to face the American P-51 pilot-turned-jungle fighter. "Drop your weapon!" Charlie ordered.

Capt. Fujiwara released a scream of rage and raised his pistol. Charlie wasted no time hitting him in the chest with three .30 caliber slugs from his carbine.

"Charlie!" Alyanna yelled as she ran into his arms. "Charlie! Oh, Charlie!" She clung to him and wept.

He held her close. "Thank God you're alright."

Diego, Raanan, and Basilio emerged onto the road, and Alyanna's tears of relief became tears of joy. "Raanan! Basilio! What are you doing here? Oh, my dear brothers!" She wrapped them both in her arms. "And Diego, my friend. Thank you for bringing them here."

"Come, we must return to the village," Diego said in Tagalog. They all started back down the road toward San Marcelino. The sun had dropped to the horizon, and nightfall soon cast the landscape in a blanket of darkness.

An hour later, finding their way only by the light of a three-quarter moon, they heard the sound of motors behind them. Headlights appeared, and then disappeared ... and appeared again as three trucks came into view.

"Quick, into the jungle!" Charlie ordered them, and then stood in the glare of the approaching headlights.

A man stepped out of the truck's cab and onto the running board. "You bloody fool! Get out of the road!"

Charlie lowered his carbine to the ground and raised his hands. "I'm an American. I have four refugees in need of a ride to San Marcelino. Can you help us?"

"Oh, sure thing, mate. There's plenty of room in the back. The other lorry's chockers with equipment. Why don't you sit up here with me, and tell me about these refugees of yours. I rather suspect you've got quite a ripper of a tale to tell ... judging from the Japanese bodies lying back there a ways."

"I'll be happy to tell you all about it." Charlie whistled for the others. Carl and the rest of the group stepped out onto the road. "If you don't mind, though, my friend, Carl, can ride up front with you. I need to sit in back with the others. He'll explain everything."

Carl climbed into the cab of the truck after making certain the others were secure in back.

"You're Australian. What brings you out here this time of night?" Carl asked.

"We're repairing roads and bridges, so you Yanks will enjoy a cushy surface for your butts to ride on when you push further north."

Carl told the Aussie Sgt./Maj. the entire story of Alyanna and her family, of his involvement with Charlie, and of the Japanese abduction.

"Well, mate. That is one fair dinkum tale, for sure. You just sit tight, and you and your mates will be back at San Marcelino in a jiff."

They pulled into the base at 2330 hrs. Carl climbed out of the cab and walked to the rear of the truck.

"Charlie, I'm heading for the shower and then some sleep. I hope you can work things out okay with your CO."

"It shouldn't be a problem. Technically I was A.W.O.L for a few hours, but no harm done as far as missions go. Don't worry about me, Carl. What about you, though? You're not going to run into any problems, are you?"

"No. Like I said, we're on a two-day stand down. I don't think anyone missed me."

Carl sneaked into his tent to the sound of men snoring. All he could think about was washing away the stench of the jungle and the sweat from his body. He stripped off his clothes, stuffed them into his laundry bag tied to the head of his bunk, and headed for the showers. Twenty minutes later he returned to his tent, washed the mud from his feet with water he carried in his helmet from the showers, and then toweled them off.

Carl fell asleep almost before his head hit the pillow. At 0500 hrs a firm shake of his shoulder abruptly awakened him.

"Hey, Carl, rise and shine!" Lt. Mike O'Hanlon stood over him. "Briefing in one hour."

"Huh? ... what? I thought we were on stand-down." Carl rubbed the sleep from his eyes and scooted his feet off the bed onto the floor.

"Not anymore. C'mon. I'll treat you to breakfast: S.O.S, eggs, and coffee."

Carl dressed in his one-piece heavy cotton flight suit and headed to the mess tent with Mike.

"So, what's this all about? When did you hear about the briefing, Mike?"

"Last night. By the way, Capt. Marshall needed to see you last night. You were nowhere to be found. Where did you go?"

"Oh ... uh ... I was helping a friend of mine over at the 348th with something. I hope Marshall wasn't too upset."

"No, I don't think so. I guess you'll find out soon enough if he is." The two pilots entered the mess tent to be greeted by the aroma of coffee, bacon and the mystery concoction referred to as S.O.S.

After his second cup of coffee, Carl felt more awake. He pushed his chair away from the table, and he and Mike O'Hanlon headed to the operations building for the briefing.

Chapter XIII

April 2, 1945

–Plane Down–

Carl was flying A/P175 off the right wing of Squadron Leader, Capt. Al Marshall. Lt. Dan Blount flew left wing. Their mission was to locate, intercept and destroy an enemy shipping convoy moving north off the coast of Indo China.

Marshall dropped the group down to 2,000 feet above the surface. They arrived at their primary target. There were no ships in sight.

Group Leader to all planes, we're going to proceed up the coast for 10 more minutes. If we still don't see the ships, we will rally at the coordinates for Ny Thanh town and hit our secondary target. Looks like Intelligence doesn't know their left hand from their right ... again! Group Leader, out.

"Hey, Skipper! Our air cover is right on time. Three o'clock high." Harry Osborne announced from the tail.

"Roger that, Harry. You all set back there? Gunners, check your weapons. The last crew to fly this bucket may not have checked them out as well as you did on the *Angel*."

Carl and his crew drew A/P175 while *Avenging Angel* sat on the tarmac back at San Marcelino waiting for a thorough going over by the ground crew. Their assigned bomber sported a newly overhauled left engine. With over two years of service, her airframe chocked up more hours than any active B-25 in the Air Apache inventory earning her the apt nickname of Grandma. This was Grandma's first mission since the overhaul.

Group Leader to all planes, turning to course one-seven-two degrees. Bombardiers, arm your bombs.

At 1,000 feet altitude the group separated into four line-abreast attack formations and swept over the rail yards and surrounding buildings. The 501st hit the town of Ny Thane. A busy rail yard sat on the outskirts of town. Two locomotives and at least 20 rail cars were positioned in the yards and appeared to be transferring supplies onto a number of trucks.

Ack-ack began to dot the sky around them. It was thick, but ineffective. The enemy ground artillery batteries sending up the A-A appeared to be in at least three installations located near a pink pagoda-like structure sitting atop a hill.

Left wing to Flight Leader, requesting permission to take out those guns.

Lead to left wing, go get 'em, Carl.

Carl banked 15 degrees to the right of the group's flight path and climbed to 1,500 feet.

"Phil, drop two on them. We'll strafe the rest."

"Roger that, Skipper."

A/P175 came at the gun emplacements at 280 mph.

"Bombs away!" Phil called.

One 500-pound bomb ripped into the pink building. Four seconds later the pink shrine erupted in an explosion that tore the building apart. The second bomb took out one of the twin-barreled anti-aircraft artillery guns.

"Going around for another pass. I changed my mind, Phil. We'll drop the rest of our load on them."

"Copy. Say the word, Skipper"

Grandma came at the enemy gun emplacements again. Phil

dropped the remaining two demolition bombs right into the lap of a second bunker. The last of the two bombs hit close enough to damage the third and final pair of anti-aircraft cannons. One enemy 20 mm Type 96 gun was still functional, and when Carl banked around for a strafing run, two Japanese gunners opened up on the incoming B-25. The tell-tale staccato-hammering of bullets piercing the fuselage stopped as Carl pressed the "Guns" button on all eight forward-firing .50 caliber guns, spewing forth 800 rounds per minute of armor piercing rounds from each barrel. The remaining A-A gun was silenced. He pulled up sharply and turned toward the rail yards.

Alpha Papa One Seven Five to Flight Leader, the A-A is out of business, Captain. Re-joining the attack on the rail yards.

Roger, One Seven Five. Good work.

"Pilot to Engineer, damage report."

"Checking ... uh oh. Manifold pressure is dropping on number one ... oil pressure, too. Cylinder-head temp is rising fast. Skipper, we're going to lose the right engine."

"Copy that. Reducing rpm and throttling back on the starboard engine. We're going to stay in the fight, boys. Keep an eye on that engine, Doc.

Carl spotted a building at the far end of the rail yard that appeared large enough be some sort of storage facility. He banked the plane toward the building and held his speed at 250 mph while applying left rudder to compensate for the drag induced by the damaged right engine. He pressed the firing button again raking the building with a sustained burst. Windows disintegrated, but there were no explosions. He climbed out and banked *Grandma* around for another run when he spotted a series of a half-dozen generators with large fuel supply tanks.

"Something is going on in that building that requires an awful lot of power, Alex. I don't know what it might be, but they're

313

building something in there. Let's hit those fuel tanks and see if we can start a fire."

"Roger that, Carl. By the way, we're starting to throw smoke from the starboard nacelles."

"One more pass, and then we'll grab some altitude and turn back to base." Carl put the fuel storage and generators in his sights.

A/P175 screamed in over the tree tops. He dropped her nose and pressed the red "Guns" button on the yoke. Hundreds of rounds tore into the 2,000-gallon fuel tanks. At first nothing happened, but then the whole place turned into the roiling fire and brimstone of Hades itself. A giant column of black smoke and orange-yellow-red flames erupted into the sky in front of them. Carl pulled hard back, and A/P175 pointed her nose to the sky. She flew through the conflagration and out the other side ... her propellers spinning vortices of smoke behind her.

"Yee-haw! Skipper! You nailed them to the barn door!" Harry yelled over the radio from the tail.

"Well done, boys. Let's go home." Carl ran his sleeve over his brow. His hands trembled noticeably.

"You okay, Carl? How about I take us home? You rest easy for a minute." Alex offered.

"Yeah. You're right. That was intense!" Carl released a size-able sigh of pent-up air. "You've got the controls. I'll call it in."

Alpha Papa One Seven Five to Flight Leader, we have one engine out. Returning to base.

Roger, One Seven Five. You need an escort, Carl?

Negative, Lead. Port engine is in the green. Our air cover is still over us. Catch you back at base. One Seven Five, out.

Twenty minutes later, the rpm on the remaining good engine began to drop.

"Crap! What now?" Carl blurted as he keyed the intercom. "Doc, the port engine is acting up, and the rpm is dropping off. I'm opening the cowl flaps to full. What's going on?"

"Skipper, we're getting oil spray around the nacelles. An oil line must have worked its way lose. Oil pressure is dropping off. We're good for another 10 ... maybe 12 minutes in the air. We need to get this piece of junk on the ground.

Alpha Papa One Seven Five to Alpha Flight Leader, declaring an emergency. We are at one-zero-point-four degrees north, one-zero-niner degrees east on a heading for the Paracel Islands. Do you copy? Over.

Carl heard only static in his ear phone. "Sgt. Price, I'm not getting anything on the com. What's happening with the radio?"

"Lieutenant, we lost our antennae ... must have gotten shot off. The air group is too far away to hear us, sir. We can't hear anything from more than five miles out."

"Damn! What's next? Alex, we need to prepare to ditch." Carl pressed the alarm and the claxon sounded. He switched to the crew intercom again.

"Pilot to crew. Prepare to ditch. Phil, unbolt the Norden and jettison it out the bomb bay. Gather your gear together and stand by for a water landing. I'll try to set down by one of the larger islands in the Spratlys. Price, start sending the SOS now. There's a chance that someone may pick up the Morse code. Secure the portable field radio and life raft. Keep the radio dry. Jettison all guns and ammo and any other loose items. Pop the emergency hatches as soon as the plane stops. It may be a rough landing, so hang on tight. Buckle in and assume ditching position. Pilot, out."

"There, Skipper, at our 10 o'clock ... land!" Alex pointed at the top of an island, barely visible above the horizon.

"Got it." Carl toggled the intercom. "Pilot to crew, take your positions and report!"

"Navigator. In position."

"Engineer is ready."

"Radio is buckled in."

"Tail gunner is strapped in, Skipper."

"Set flaps 20 degrees, Alex. I'll throttle back to 140."

Carl calculated the direction of the flow of the swells relative to his flight path. He banked A/P175 to a course parallel to the island and dropped to 100 feet above the surface. He flew on until the island was behind them at about their 7 o'clock position and then turned back in the opposite direction into the wind.

"Set flaps to 30 degrees, please, Alex."

"Flaps at 30, Skipper."

"I'm going to try to settle in between the swells."

Carl dropped the plane to 50 feet over the water. "Brace for impact!" he called over the intercom.

"Full flaps, now!"

"Alex pushed the flaps lever all the way down as Carl gradually pulled the power back. The B-25 flared and the tail smacked the surface. The jar was no more severe than that of a hard short field landing, but the impact forced the nose down. Carl hauled back on the yoke and lifted the nose slightly before it plowed into the water at 100 mph. The impact threw Carl's chest hard against his harness.

"Pop the forward hatch, Alex! Phil, you're first, go!" Carl pushed Phil's butt as the Navigator crawled up and out of the hatch above the cockpit.

"You're next, Alex. Hurry! We're taking on water." Carl checked behind him. The crawl space to the crew compartment was filling with water. He saw Wendell Price climb through the rear hatch to the top of the fuselage. Doc and Harry pushed the raft through the side escape hatch. Good. *They're all making it out.*

"C'mon, Skipper! Take my hand!" Alex Chekov's hand appeared, and Carl took it. Alex lifted him through the hatch to the top of the fuselage. The aircraft appeared to be intact and bobbed lazily, half submerged in the water.

"I'm going back for the flare gun and a parachute." Doc

Henreid called out. He disappeared beneath the surface of the water.

Carl climbed down to the wing just as Harry began inflating the raft.

"Wendell, secure the field radio in the raft with all of the first-aid gear."

The water rose nearly to the top of the fuselage. Worried that Doc might be trapped inside, Carl decided to go in after him, but the Engineer broke through the surface of the water and tossed a parachute and a satchel containing the M-8 flare pistol into the raft.

"Everyone into the raft!" Carl called. He stood on the wing while his crew climbed aboard the tiny raft. Carl tossed in his sidearm and then jumped into the water.

"Welcome aboard the *U.S.S. Grandma*, shipmates!" Harry quipped.

"Do you ever stop with the jokes, Harry?" Doc chided.

"Nope. I figure if I ever stop making wisecracks, I'll be dead." Harry laughed.

"Humor is always the best medicine, Harry. Keep it up." Carl laughed. "This raft is designed for four men. I need a man to join me in the water to kick. Two of you will row. Alex, how are your swimming skills, partner?"

"You're looking at the 100-meter State High School Free-Style champion, Carl. Mind if I join you?"

"Phil, you and Sgt. Price man the oars." Alex stripped down to his skivvies and dove into the water. Hanging onto the ropes that tied the raft into a neat bundle for storage, the pair began kicking.

"Grab an oar, Wendell. I'll take this one." Lt. Ortiz said.

Phil Ortiz and Wendell Price started paddling toward the thin strip of beach on one of many islands and reefs in the Spratlys.

"Listen up, men. There may or may not be Japs on that island. There are more than 700 islands, reefs, and atolls, mostly uninhabited. Japs like to use some of the bigger atolls for forward reconnaissance. We only have three side arms ... mine, Lt. Chekov's and Lt. Ortiz'. Did any of you men secure a weapon before you climbed out?"

"I did, sir." Wendell Price pulled a Government APC semi-automatic .45 caliber pistol from his pocket.

"I tossed one in the raft along with the chute and flare gun, Skipper." Doc Henreid said.

"Hang on to them. If there are no Japs we'll head into the brush and get ourselves organized. Sgt. Price and Sgt. Henreid, you men will hide the raft in the jungle ASAP. Lt. Chekov and I will take point as soon as we hit the beach."

Fifteen minutes later, the crew landed on a 100-yard stretch of white beach. Pulling the raft ashore, they dragged it under cover of the trees and foliage.

Alex dressed, and Carl began issuing orders.

"Okay. We need to take inventory of our supplies. Then, we need to find some high ground and see if we can get a sense of what we're up against. I thought I got a glimpse of a gray tower and the roof of a smaller building before we ditched ... in that direction." Carl pointed to the northeast. "I think we should head there. Load up everything you can carry, especially the water bags and thermos bottles. Everybody, grab some palm leaves. I want to lay out a big arrow on the beach showing our direction of march."

The crew collected a bundle of coconut palm leafs and laid them out in a 20-foot arrow pointing to the top of the peak and Carl's gray tower.

Five minutes later the men of the good ship, *U.S.S. Grandma*, began chopping their way through the underbrush in the direction of the highest point on the island.

Capt. Al Marshall radioed in the loss of A/P175 after Carl reported the engine out problem. He assumed that the bomber made it safely back to San Marcelino, having heard nothing further to indicate a worsening of the situation. The first thing he did after climbing down the crew ladder of A/P578 was to check for A/P175's tail number on the flight line. The plane was nowhere to be seen. He walked over to one of the big repair hangars. *What the ...?* He flagged down a Jeep and jumped in.

"Sergeant, take me to Base Ops."

"Yes sir." The driver cranked the wheel and sped toward the Base Operations building which stood next to the control tower.

Al Marshall leapt from the Jeep and slammed open the door of the Quonset hut. He walked over to the door marked Air Operations, 345th Bombardment Group and entered. The room was abuzz with radio operators sitting in front of radio consoles, clerks at desks typing up mission reports to be signed later by whatever intelligence officers happened to be on duty. A map room stood at the back of the Communications Center. A Master Sergeant standing over one of the radio operators caught Al's eye.

"Sergeant." He called out as he approached the senior NCO.

"Yes, sir. How can I help you?"

"I'm Capt. Al Marshall with the 501st. We just returned from a mission. One of my planes had to abort early and head back ... engine knocked out by ground fire. Call name is A/P175, 1st Lt. Carl Bridger commanding. Did he radio in, by chance?"

"No, sir. Any inbound in-flight emergencies cause quite a stir around here. A lot of things need to happen on our end before the plane gets here. We've had no such contact." The Sergeant stood patiently waiting for a response. "Well, if there's nothing else, sir ..." he turned back to his business at hand, and Capt. Marshall headed over to the 345th Group Headquarters Building. He approached the Executive Officer's door, knocked twice and waited.

"In!" Maj. Bernard "Buzz" Giese called from the other side

of the door. Al Marshall stepped into the room. Col. Chester Coltharp sat in a side chair with his legs crossed, and Maj. Giese sat behind his desk.

"Al! Welcome back, my friend. How goes things over at the Black Panthers?"

"Well, sir. Up until about 20 minutes ago, I would have said '*Dandy*'. One of my planes never made it back from the mission." That got the Group Commander's attention.

Col. Coltharp turned to face his subordinate and stood up. "What do you mean you only found out 20 minutes ago, Captain?"

Al explained the whole situation from the first and only radio call from A/P175 until the squadron landed at the base. "I figured he'd be waiting for us, but when I never saw hide nor hair of him after we returned to base, I headed to Base Ops thinking he might have radioed in ... no luck there, so I came here."

"Let's check the mission map in my office. I want his last reported position, Capt. Marshall. Major, call the 2nd Emergency Rescue Squadron. I want a Cat to start a search." He reconsidered his command. "No ... make it two Cats."

The three men bent over a map of the South China Sea and the coast line of Indo-China.

"We were finishing our sweep of Phan Rang ... here ... when Lt. Bridger reported an engine-out emergency. He affirmed he had a good port engine and declined an escort, stating he could make it back to base. We never heard from him after that. Following our second run on the rail yards, we formed up and headed home."

Coltharp drew a red pencil line from Phan Rang to the Spratly Island archipelago. "Alright, if he flew a direct heading to San Marcelino, his course would have taken him over the Spratly Islands. We need to start our search there with one Catalina. The other PBY should back- track his flight path between the Spratlys and Phan Rang."

After the rescue of Alyanna from her Japanese captors, Charlie remained with her and her family for a while following their tearful reunion. He described to Bianca the bravery of her two sons and the contribution they and Diego made that led to Alyanna's recovery. Finally, at 0115 hrs, he returned to his quarters. At 7 a.m. the next morning, he knocked on the door of the Group Executive Officer, Lt. Col. W.D. Dunham at the Headquarters building of the 348th Fighter Group. Charlie didn't wait for an answer, deciding to open the door and stick his head in.

"Charlie! Come on in, Captain. Where 'ya been keeping yourself since your initiation as an Ace? It's been, what ... three weeks ago?"

"Yes sir." Charlie approached the XO's desk. "Truth is, sir, I wanted to ask if I could still take you up on the three days of R&R you offered me."

"I think that can be arranged, Captain. Frankly, I'm a little surprised that you didn't take the three days off at the time." Col. Dunham reached into his drawer and withdrew a form. "All I need is your Squadron Commander's okay. Take this to Maj. Bryant for his signature, and you're good to go."

"Thank you, sir. I really appreciate this."

"Well, you earned it. How many missions have you logged, Charlie? It seems to me you're up there every time one comes along. You're probably overdue for two weeks in Australia aren't you?"

"Thirty-seven since my last break, sir. Frankly ... I'd rather be flying than sitting on the beach." He held out the form. "Thanks for this, sir."

Col. Dunham smiled. "Welcome, now get out of here," he chuckled.

Charlie got Maj. Bryant's okay and returned the signed form to Sgt. Kershaw. He made a bee-line for Alyanna's gita to tell her the good news. Three days of uninterrupted time with her would go a long way toward cementing the strong bond that he wanted to forge before taking the next step in their relationship. With his 26th birthday coming up in a few days, he figured on spending his R&R with Alyanna. He couldn't imagine a better present.

Later, they walked hand in hand along a secluded beach in a small cove. They stopped and sat in the fine white sand beneath the shade of three coconut palms, while the gentle surf lapped against the beach in concert with their racing hearts.

Charlie turned to Alyanna and brushed the hair from her eyes. "You've never talked much about your father. The only thing I know is that he is a Frenchman and that you lost him at Bataan. When did he meet your mother? Where did you learn to speak French and English so well?"

"Alright, I will tell you. I warn, though, that it is a boring story." She smiled and kissed Charlie's cheek.

"My father took my mother to France after they married. They lived in Nogent-sur-Marne for two years so my mother could receive her French citizenship. I was born there in 1923. After my mother became a citizen in 1924, they returned to Manila where my father took an assignment as a special envoy to the French Consulate. I attended school in there until my father decided to send me to visit Paris and finish my schooling at the *Lycée Janson de Sailly*. In 1938, I returned to Manila because of the talk of war with the Germans. My parents wanted us all to be together. The consulate released my papa from his duties, and he went to work for the United States Rubber Company. He held a university degree in chemical engineering, and earned a good salary.

"The war came, and my father could not find a way for us to leave the country." Alyanna's voice became forced and her eyes welled up with tears. She brushed a hand over her eyes and continued:

"My Papa and Mama decided to hide us in the village

where we would live as peasants. He went to fight with the Filipino resistance. We knew that he was somewhere near Bataan when we lost contact with him. That is all there is to tell."

"I'm so sorry, Alyanna. I wish I could do something to find your father."

"It is well with us, Charlie. Three years have passed. If he were alive, I am certain he would have contacted us by now."

They talked for a while longer and lay back in the sand at the edge of the water. Alyanna dozed off. Charlie felt her body relax and her breathing slow. He drew her closer to him and kissed her gently. He remembered the *premonition* he told his mother, and repeated to Charlie back in Cascade. *Is this the sign that I will go on living? Will Alyanna be the answer?*

"I love you, *Sharles*," she said sleepily.

"I love you, Alyanna." They slept in each other's arms as the water licked gently at their feet in rhythmic waves.

After spending the morning on the beach with Alyanna, Charlie dressed in his civvies wearing khaki shorts, sandals and an "Aloha" shirt, and headed for the Officers' Club in search of Carl. He wanted to tell his old Montana pal the intentions of his heart toward Alyanna and to ask his advice on how to proceed. Charlie's expertise did not extend to matters of the heart, and he figured that Carl's experience with Annie qualified him as an expert in the subjects of love and women. Charlie could fly a Mustang as well as Beethoven wrote symphonies, but he possessed 10 thumbs when it came to navigating a relationship with the opposite sex.

He scanned the smoke-fogged room for Carl. *Not here*, he thought. He sat at the bar, ordered a San Miguel in a bottle and drew in a mouthful of the cold pale lager. Behind him, three pilots wearing the unit patch of the 501st Black Panthers caught Charlie's attention. Their conversation centered on a Mitchell the squadron lost on the day's mission.

"It's strange. He was fine one minute, then radioed an engine-

323

out emergency and turned back to base," one of the men said.

Lt. Ned Lathrop nodded and added, "You'd think that if he couldn't make it back, he'd radio in his location and ditch somewhere. None of us heard a thing from him."

"Too bad ... I liked Bridger a lot. I figure he went in fast and hard if he didn't even have time to call in his position."

At the mention of Carl's last name, Charlie spun around on his bar stool. "Excuse me, fellas. Did you say Carl Bridger's plane is down?"

Ned Lathrop caught Charlie's concerned expression. "Yea, that's right. He flew with us on this morning's mission. He never made it back. Why ... do you know him?"

"He's my best friend from back in the states." Charlie sat in the empty chair next to the three Black Panthers. "I need you to tell me everything you know about what happened."

The two pilots repeated the story including the plan to send two PBY Catalinas from the 2nd ERS to search the Spratlys for signs of the downed bomber.

"Thanks guys." Charlie headed for the door just as Alyanna came into the club to start her shift.

Charlie took her arm and led her outside. "Carl is down. He never made it back from a mission."

Alyanna's eyes flashed wide opened. "Lt. Bridger? How can that be? We were all together only last night."

"I know. He got called up for a mission before sunup. Alyanna, I need to do something ... search for him. I may not see you for a day or two."

Alyanna squeezed his arm. "Of course, you must go." She stood on her toes and kissed Charlie. "May God go with you, my love."

Charlie's first stop ... the Operations Building of the 2nd Emergency Rescue Squadron. He entered the building and approached the first man he spotted.

"Excuse me, Lieutenant, who do I see about a Search and Rescue mission for a lost Mitchell that went down this morning off the Spratlys?"

"Me, sir. I'm Lt. Miles ... Duty Officer for today. If you don't mind me asking, what's your interest in this, Captain?"

"The pilot of that plane is my best friend. Before you say anything, I know that your missions are not open to anyone outside the 345th, but I'd be much obliged if you would answer one question: When did the Cats take off, and is air cover being provided?"

"That's two questions, sir." Lt. Miles grinned. "The Cats go wheels up ASAP." He looked at the unit patch on Charlie's uniform shirt. "I believe the 348th is providing air cover."

Charlie ran out of the building, and sprinted toward the 348th Fighter Group. He spotted a Jeep coming in the opposite direction and flagged it down.

"Corporal, get me to the 348th ASAP!"

The Jeep pulled up in front of the fighter group's Operations Building on the edge of the tarmac behind a dozen P-51Ds and as many P-47 Thunderbolts.

Charlie entered the busy main outer office and nearly ran in to Col. Dunham.

"Whoa, slow down, Captain. What's the rush? I thought you'd be drinking margaritas on the beach by now," he laughed.

"Sir, my best friend is down over the Spratlys. He's a Mitchell jockey for the 501st Black Panthers. Sir, I need to be assigned to the air cover for the Cats from the 2nd ERS who are launching a SAR mission as we speak."

"Follow me to the briefing room right now, Captain. They're about to take off. I'll order one of the pilots to stand down." Dunham led the way.

Fifteen minutes later, Charlie, dressed in a khaki flight suit he pulled over his beach wear, climbed into the cockpit of *Dirty Old Man*, his P-51D with seven miniature rising-sun flags painted on the side of the fighter below the cockpit, denoting the number of "kills" credited to Charlie. Those downed enemy planes earned him Ace status.

He jacked-in to the radio, buckled his harness, and began the engine-start sequence. He knew the routine by heart and performed each step quickly and almost without having to think about it:

> *Flaps set to "Up."*
> *Carburetor Induction set to forward position.*
> *Coolant set to "Auto."*
> *Set rudder trim to five degrees left.*
> *Prime engine for four seconds.*
> *Hold starter switch to "Start" position.*

The four-bladed propeller began to turn. After two complete revolutions, Charlie turned the ignition switch to *both*, and the Rolls-Royce/Packard 12-cylinder 1,700 horsepower engine fired up. He held the rpm at 1200 until the oil temp rose to 40 degrees centigrade and reduced the rpm to 1,000. He reached up and pulled the bubble canopy forward and latched it.

Charlie lined up on the runway, found a cloud directly in front of and above the nose of the fighter and added power, working the rudder to stay lined up with the cloud. The tail of the Mustang lifted off the ground and *Dirty Old Man* rotated into the sky. He brought up the gear as soon as he felt the plane leave the runway.

He climbed out, joined the flight of three other Mustangs and keyed his mic:

> *Razor Four in position, Razor Lead.*
> *Roger, Razor Four. Maintain diamond formation until we reach the search area. Razor Lead and Razor Two will cover for Search One. Razor Three and Four, you fly west and cover Search Two. Acknowledge.*
> *Razor Two. Roger*
> *Razor Three. Roger*
> *Razor Four. Roger*

The four fighter escorts reached the Intercept Point and split off. Charlie and his wingman banked west on a heading of two-five-five degrees at an altitude of 5,000 feet. Search Two would be in front and below them at 3,000 thousand feet. The clear sky, with only a few scattered clouds, made for excellent visibility. They flew on for another 20 minutes until the coast of Indo-China appeared in the distance

Wing to Razor Four. Cat at 1 o'clock low.

Charlie spotted the PBY Catalina below them and set his radio frequency to the Cat's frequency.

Search Two, Razor Four is in position at your 7 o'-clock high. Do you copy? Over.

Roger, Razor Four. We are beginning our track-line search now.

Razor Four to wing, Spence, we'll orbit here. We need to stay above them as they work their way back to the east. Keep your eye out for bogeys. I don't expect any, but you never know. Keep your radio on the plane-to-plane frequency. I'll circle clockwise, and you circle counter-clockwise. Break now.

The two Mustangs banked away from each other and began to circle the search area.

Wendell Price walked ahead on point when he stopped and squatted low. He waved his hand at everyone else to do the same and worked his way back to Carl.

"Sir, the tower is up ahead. How do you want to approach it?" he asked.

Carl whispered to the crew. "Show me, Wendell. The rest of you stay close. No talking. If you're carrying a sidearm, lock and load."

Carl peered through the ferns and low plants at the gray tower, and formed a clear picture in his mind, noting the undergrowth grew closer to the building to the left of their current position

"Okay, this is how we're going to do it. We'll work our way to the left until we're about 10 feet from the building. Wendell, do you think you can stay under cover until you reach that broken window and take a peek inside?"

"Yes, sir ... like when I used to sneak up on my sister and her boyfriend."

"Good. Listen for any noise before you poke your head in front of the window. Be careful, Sergeant." Carl patted Wendell on the shoulder.

Once they were in position, Wendell drew his weapon and ran in a low crouch at an oblique angle to the window. He paused there for a full minute. Finally, he peeked through the broken panes and quickly withdrew his head.

"Careful, Price," Phil Ortiz whispered as they all waited anxiously for Wendell to take another, longer look into the room. He reappeared and waved everyone forward.

Carl worked his way along the wall to the door, which stood ajar. Standing to the side, he nudged it open a crack, then a little more, but only far enough to squeeze into the room. He closed his eyes for a moment to let them dilate and then opened them again. He carefully worked his way around the room, looking for trip wires, loose boards, anything that would suggest a booby-trap. Nothing suspicious caught his eye, and he motioned for the others to enter.

Carl pointed his finger and moved his hand in a sweeping motion. "Watch for trip wires. Don't move anything unless it's necessary. Let's see if there's anything we can use."

"Here's something, Lieutenant." Wendell lifted a rag covering a large rectangular-shape object on a table. "Well, hello, sweetheart." His face lit up in a grin. "I found us a radio, Skipper. It's been pretty badly beat up. We need to find a power source."

Doc Henreid called out from one of the two adjoining

rooms. "Lieutenant, there's a power line coming through the wall in here. I'm betting there's a generator somewhere outside. I'll check it out. Harry, back me up?" Harry and Doc walked out the door and circled around to a smaller white building ... the one Carl saw before they ditched.

Inside, they found a single room full of tools and several cans with spouts screwed onto the tops. Harry twisted a filler cap off one of the cans and sniffed the contents. He shook the can and sat it on the ground.

"There was gasoline in it, but it's empty. Let's check the others." They both lifted up another can each.

Doc dropped an empty can on the floor and reached to pick up another one. He felt the weight of it and removed the cap. "We're in luck, Harry. This one's mostly full."

Harry moved a table, several stacked up chairs and a large, dusty canvas tarpaulin from in front of a wall. Behind the pile of junk sat a generator.

Doc found the pull starter and gave the rope a pull. The cylinder moved freely. "It's not frozen. We might be able to fire it up, Harry. Check the room for a switch box.

While Harry searched for the switch, Doc removed the filler cap from the generator's fuel tank and smelled the pungent odor of gasoline. He began to tap the side and heard the hollow echo of an empty tank until he got to about three inches from the bottom. The noise changed to a higher pitch and less hollow sound.

"I found the switch, Doc," Harry said.

"Good. Make sure it's off. Put in the rest of the gas, and let's see if we can start up this old thing."

Doc wound the rope around the wheel of the starting crank and gave it a pull. Nothing happened. He tried several more times and still got not so much as a pop or a wheeze from the motor.

He banged his fist on the uncooperative machine. "We need to find some tools ... pliers, wrench, screwdriver ... anything."

"Will this do, Doc?" Harry handed him an old sparkplug puller from a table next to the generator.

"Harry, I could kiss you!" Doc managed to work loose the sparkplug and examine it. He soaked a dirty rag in the dregs of the gasoline can and wiped the plug clean. He checked the gap and found it mostly blocked with carbon deposits which he carefully chipped away. He inserted the plug back in its place before removing the rubber fuel line which he examined for blockage. He removed the air cleaner, blew as much dirt out of it as he could and banged it against the wall a few times to knock off some more dust before reinstalling it.

"Okay, Harry. Cross your fingers." Doc found what he assumed to be the "off-run" switch and put it in what he hoped was the "off" position. He pulled the rope three times to prime the fuel line. Satisfied, he toggled the switch up and pulled the rope through again. With a chug-chug, the engine acted like it wanted to start. He primed the fuel line again and tried one more time. The motor chugged ... almost died ... and then came to life, blowing out white smoke before settling into a sweet purr.

"Throw the switch, Harry."

Harry threw the switch and a dangling, dusty light bulb lit up above their heads.

Doc shut down the generator, and the two men walked back to the other building to join the rest of the crew.

"We have power, Skipper. Doc brought the old 'genny' to life," Harry announced.

"Yea, we noticed, Harry. The lights came on in here for a minute. Good work." Carl turned to Wendell Price. "What about it, Sergeant ... can you make any use of the radio?"

"Maybe, sir. If the insides are still operational, I think I can jury-rig the field radio to send out a strong enough signal to reach any search planes in the area. All that's needed is to hook up the antenna to the radio mast outside and rout the power line from the ruined radio to the field radio. When that's done, we'll fire up the generator and send out a distress call."

"Why not just use the battery in the field radio?" Harry asked.

"That battery isn't powerful enough to handle the power drain caused by the big antenna. We need the extra power to put out a strong enough signal," Wendell replied.

Wendell Price removed the outer shell from the transmitter of the smashed Japanese radio. He carefully examined the guts of the radio, removing each vacuum tube and inspecting them before reinserting them and smiled. "All of the tubes are still good. I think this might work. The Japs managed to smash up the dials pretty good, but the inside is still functional for the most part. I can splice-in the frequency modulator from the field radio to allow us to tune the set to the distress frequency."

"That's great news, Sergeant. That's our number-one priority, then. We're all here to help."

"Thank you, sir. All I need is some needle-nosed pliers and a small screw driver. A soldering iron and some solder would be nice, but I'm not going to wish for Christmas ... yet." That brought a laugh from the crew. "I'll need to check the lead from the antenna to the transmitter ... make sure it's still attached."

"I can do that, Wendell. Tell me where the antenna goes, and I'll track it down." Doc offered.

Five minutes later, Doc dangled precariously from a broken out second-story window. The antenna mast, attached to the window frame, extended an additional 20 feet into the air. He called down to Sgt. Price:

"The antenna lead's still hooked up to the mast, Wendell!"

"Good. C'mon down and follow the line to the wall. Check for breaks along the way ... I think we're almost in business!" Wendell said as he busily spliced wires from the frequency tuner of the damaged radio to the field radio.

He turned to Carl with a pleased expression. "Lieutenant, I think I'm ready to power up this thing."

"Great. Harry, Doc ... bring the generator on-line and let's get someone's attention ... maybe." Carl ordered. He held up both hands showing crossed fingers.

Carl sat next to Sgt. Price who carefully checked his work. He made certain no bare wires were touching any metal and that the field radio was set to the correct channel. The room suddenly brightened as the unshielded overhead light bathed the room in an incandescent glow.

"Okay, here we go." Wendell toggled the power switch on the Japanese transmitter and then the field radio. The sound of static came from the simple box speaker next to the transceiver. He pulled the handset from the army field radio.

Mayday! Mayday! Mayday! This is Alpha Papa One Seven Five. We are down. Over.

Wendell paused, but only the sound of static could be heard. He repeated the distress message twice more.

"I'll try tuning the frequency modulator on the Jap radio. I won't be able to read the numbers, but we might hear some chatter. If everything is working okay, we should pick up any active chatter within a hundred miles." Wendell began slowly turning the knob. Suddenly, a voice broke through the static.

...urning to heading...ive two...grees, Search Two.

The signal was broken and faint, but readable.

Search Two, this is Alpha Papa One Seven Five. Do you read? Over!

Charlie and Spence Reed had been orbiting above Rescue Two for nearly an hour. The Catalina flew 10 mile legs north and south as they worked their way gradually east toward the first dots of the 700 plus islets and atolls that made up the Spratly Island group.

Razor Four, Search Two. Turning to heading three-five-two degrees.

Before Charlie could respond another voice broke in over the plane-to-plane channel:

Search Two. This is Alpha Papa One Seven Five, Mayday! Mayday! Mayday. We are a crashed Bravo Two-Five out of San Marcelino. Position one-five degrees three-two minutes north and one-zero-eight degrees, five minutes east. Do you copy? Over.

Roger, Alpha Papa One Seven Five. We read you. Search Two is turning to your location now.

Razor Four to Alpha Papa One Seven Five, state condition of crew. Is Lt. Bridger with you?

The crew of six is well ... no injuries. Is that you up there, Charlie?

It sure is, Carl. Stay put. The Cat is on the way.

Charlie closed his mic and yelled into the cockpit of his P-51, "Yes!"

Alpha Papa One Seven Five, can you make smoke? There are a lot of islands below us and a vector point would be much appreciated.

"Doc, get outside and fire off a flare."

"Yes, sir." Doc grabbed the flare gun stepped out the door and fired one into the air. He waited for 30 seconds and sent up another one.

We have you, Alpha Papa One Seven Five. Make your way to the beach on the west side of the island. We'll do a fly-over before landing. Rescue Two, out.

"Grab your gear, boys. We're going home!" Carl slapped Alex Chekov on the shoulder. "Let's get out of here."

"Roger, that, Skipper." For once Harry didn't offer a joke. His cheerful grin spoke volumes.

They made it most of the way to the beach when the

Catalina flew over the tiny island. Then, as Carl led the crew into the open, a fighter approached, angling down and arrowing toward them. At first Carl thought it was Charlie setting up for a low pass, but the plane's approach was too fast and deliberate.

"Head for the trees. Jap!" Carl ran for the trees, pushing a stunned Wendell Price ahead of him. "Run, Sergeant! Move!"

Wendell's legs finally moved, and he ran like Satan's minions were on his tail. A line of 13.5 mm gun fire sent fingers of sand exploding upward from the beach.

Razor Four to wing, bogeys at 11 o'clock low. I'm going in!

I'm right behind you, Lead.

Charlie winged over and went into a power dive. Lt. Spence Reed followed close behind him. One enemy A6M5b Zero banked around toward the PBY. The "Zeke" came at the Cat just as Charlie dropped down behind him. He put the enemy fighter in his ring sight and squeezed the "Guns" button on his control stick. Six lines of .50 caliber gunfire issued from the Mustang's wings, and immediately the zero went vertical and banked sharply in a well-executed chandelle maneuver. He reduced power and pulled the control stick back to put the Mustang into a tight turn toward the enemy. He strained to force blood into his brain as the high-G turn threatened a blackout. The '51's nose came into lead position to the "Zeke's" line of light. Charlie fired off a snap shot and raked the enemy fighter the length of the fuselage. The Jap plane's engine sent a trail of black smoke behind it, and the pilot pulled the plane into a climb. Charlie followed him up, bringing the enemy into his gun sight for a perfect rear assault. He squeezed off a burst, sending the "Zeke" into a slow spiral toward the ocean.

Razor Four! Bogey on your 6'clock! I'm on him!

Lt. Reed's warning wasn't a second too soon. Charlie added military power and pulled the Mustang into a nearly vertical climb. The enemy behind Charlie piloted a J2M "Raiden." The plane's vertical speed couldn't match the '51 and lacked a turbo-booster. Charlie extended the distance between him and the enemy plane. Finally, the J2M faltered and, losing momentum, abandoned the pursuit. The pilot rolled the fighter over and went into a dive toward the Catalina. Spence anticipated the maneuver and put his Mustang in a head-on frontal assault with his six .50 caliber wing guns zeroed in on the target. The enemy plane took several rounds into the engine which exploded and ignited the fuel tank. The pilot died instantly as flaming debris fell toward the ocean.

The PBY Catalina landed and taxied to within a hundred feet of the beach. The crew of A/P175 waded out to the plane and climbed aboard. As the pilot of Search Two angled the nose of the plane toward the open sea, the final enemy J2M came at them with Charlie closing rapidly on his tail. The enemy had no choice but to open fire at a greater than optimal distance because *Dirty Old Man* had him set up for a rear assault.

Spouts of water shot into the sky as 20 mm cannon rounds erupted around Rescue Two. One of the large caliber projectiles tore into the fuselage but passed through harmlessly. The Jap fighter roared overhead with Charlie on his tail ... guns blazing and Lt. Reed following close behind.

Carl watched as the enemy plane shot skyward. Charlie climbed after the enemy in close pursuit.

Charlie heard a loud "Whang!" from the engine. Immediately smoke filled the cockpit. The engine rpm needle fell back, and the Mustang lost sustainable airspeed.

Reed. Get that bogey. Splash him!

335

Charlie managed to choke out the words through the smoke filling his lungs.

He banked the crippled plane to make room for Spence Reed to take up the pursuit.

His eyes burned as he tried to level the plane, but he couldn't read his instruments. He tried to peer through the thick smoke for a place to ditch or do a wheels-up landing, but he lost his visual reference to the ground. Charlie reached for the canopy lever and slid the Plexiglas bubble back on its tracks. *I don't think I'm high enough to bail out*, he thought. His vision blurred and his ears buzzed. His oxygen-starved, smoke-filled lungs burned. He released his harness and tried to climb out but was overcome by the smoke. He sunk back into his seat in a fit of coughing. He felt his life draining away. *Alyanna, my love ...*

Charlie's Mustang nosed toward the gray tower. At 300 mph, the plane plowed into the building and exploded, sending a column of black smoke skyward.

Lt. Spencer Reed finished the job on the last enemy fighter, splashing the Raiden into the South China Sea. He turned his plane toward San Marcelino.

Carl stared out the Plexiglas waist bubble of the PBY, unable to take his eyes off the fight. When Charlie's Mustang faltered and burst into a trail of thick black smoke, his heart leapt in his chest.

"No! No! No! Charlie! Bail out! Bail out!" Helpless to do anything, Carl's eyes followed the fighter as it nosed into the gray building exploding on impact.

"Noooooo!" he cried. Doc Henreid and Alex Chekov pulled Carl back into his seat.

Numbed by the tragedy, Carl allowed himself to be strapped into the metal-framed canvas-netting seat. Inside, his mind raged. His heart raced from the flood of adrenaline assaulting every nerve and muscle. He lowered his head into his hands, wanting to scream and never stop screaming. He lifted his head again, silently. His friends saw only their skipper, sitting resolute and without expression. The only sign of any emotion at all was evidenced by a single tear that sat drying on Carl's left cheek.

Chapter XIV

–Cascade, Montana–

The Spring of 1945 brought both the promise of a new season of life and renewed hope ... and tragedy.

"Dinner's on the table, everyone," Millie announced.

The usual day-to-day meals were consumed at the kitchen table, but dinner this night would be shared in the dining room. Millie ironed and laid out her best linens and china. She and Annie polished the silver flatware for the celebration of a joyous event, Penny's birthday.

"Everything smells so delicious." Annie drew in the aromas of roast beef, garlic mashed potatoes and fresh-baked rolls. She and Penny pulled out their chairs and sat down.

"I've been looking forward to this all day. The table is beautiful, Mom." Penny reached for the potatoes.

"Uh, uh, uh, young lady. Wait for your father."

"Oh, Mom ... I'm starved!" She mimicked a pout and laughed. "Oh, guess what? Jimmy Bozeman asked me to the Sophomore Dance in two weeks He's the most!"

"Hello, everybody. My oh my. Who do we have here? I think Lauren Bacall must be coming to dinner." Gifford sat himself at the head of the table. "Now who's this beautiful young lady sitting next to you, Annie?" He winked at Penny and chuckled.

"Oh, Daddy, you know very well it's me."

"Penny, my darling, how on earth did you get so grown up and pretty?"

"Alright, everybody. Let's say grace and dig in." Millie placed a dozen rolls, hot from the oven, on the table and sat down.

As Gifford was about to offer a blessing on the food, a loud knock sounded from the front door.

"Are you expecting someone?" Millie asked.

"No ... no one." He stood and walked to the door.

Penny's eyes grew wide with fear. "You don't suppose it's about ... Carl?" More of a statement than a question, it was enough to bring everyone to their feet.

"Sit down, ladies. Let's not borrow trouble." Gifford went to the door.

Returning to the dining room, Gifford smiled.

"It was Fred Wickerman. He drove over from town to drop off some mail ... figured he didn't want us to wait until tomorrow. I invited him to share dinner with us, but he said he had to make a couple more deliveries." He held a small stack of envelopes and separated out two bearing the "V"-Mail stamp reserved for letters sent to the states from service personnel overseas.

"I think we should wait to read these after dinner?" Gifford joked.

Penny gave her father a reproving expression. "Oh, sure, Daddy, as if the only thing any of us can think about right now is food. Can we read them now, Mom ... please?"

Millie covered the roast. "Go ahead dear, read the one, but give Annie hers. She can share later." Millie winked at Annie, who smiled her thanks at her future mother-in-law.

"Alright, then." Gifford removed the two censored pages from the envelope and began reading:

Dearest Family,

First, I apologize for not having written sooner. We've all been busy what with flying so many missions. I've been struggling with the loss of my very best friend as well.

340

I'm sad to tell you that Charlie Temple was killed two weeks ago. He died while saving my life and the lives of my crew. We had to ditch our plane and wait for rescue. He kept the enemy at bay while Air-Sea Rescue picked us up. I'm sorry to alarm you with the news of my landing in the water, but I am unharmed, and we are continuing to fight to bring the war in the Pacific to an end.

Mom, Dad, and baby sister Penny, (no longer "baby" sister, though), the recent past has been a real wakeup call for me. I've come to learn two things. First, life is fragile; as delicate and tentative as a butterfly perched on your shoulder. Second, I have learned never to put off reaching toward our best hopes and desires for the future. Now, more than ever, I want to come home and begin to live the dreams of our hearts, Annie's and mine ... for all of us. Happy Birthday, Pen. I hope you get this before the 12th. Today is March 30th. I promise I will write more often.

All my love – Carl

Gifford paused then folded the letter and inserted it into the envelope which he gave to Millie. "Our boy is doing fine. That gives us two things to celebrate today."

"What a wonderful birthday present!" Penny wiped tears of joy from her face.

Annie reached over and took her hand. "It's a wonderful present for all of us."

"Alright, everybody. Let's eat." Gifford carved generous slabs of roast beef, and the family dug in.

After dinner, Millie nodded at Annie, and the two of them walked into the kitchen. The decorated cake with 16 candles had been sitting out on a table in the screened-in back porch. While Millie lit the candles, Annie scooped home-made, freshly churned

341

ice cream into small bowls. She placed them on a platter and carried them into the dining room while beginning a chorus of *Happy Birthday to you, Happy Birthday to you ...*

Anxious to read Carl's letter, Annie whispered to Millie:

"Do you mind if I run up to my room and read Carl's letter?"

"That's fine, sweetheart. You go right ahead. Penny can help with the cleanup."

"Thank you." After hugging Millie, Annie went upstairs. She closed the bedroom door behind her and lay back on the bed, propping herself up with a pair of plump, down-filled pillows.

She opened the flap on the envelope and withdrew the letter.

My Darling Annie,

    Never have the words "Only forever, if you care to know ..." meant more to me than they do now. My best friend Charlie Temple is gone. I wrote the details in my letter to the family. What I want most to share with you, though, is of a much happier vein. I love you, Annie. I want to come home. I want to come home NOW! If I could fly my plane all the way to the Double-B, I would take-off this instant! How I miss you! I can close my eyes and picture us dancing at the graduation dance as if it were yesterday.

    By the way, I need to thank you for continuing to write to me even though my mood has kept me from the right frame of mind to write back. To be honest, I didn't want to bring the darkness I've been feeling into our families' lives. Charlie's death worked its toll on me. I'm doing much better today, though.

    I can picture you all bringing the ranch to life after a long winter. Calving must be starting up, I'm sure, and the alfalfa fields are sprouting, and the sorghum is planted. Before you know it the lofts and barns will be full of hay. I guess you and Mom are hard at work in the garden. Gosh,

I miss the Double-B!

    You and I never had a chance to talk about where we want to live, Annie. I love the ranch, but I'm thinking we might want to make our own way ... maybe even live somewhere else. I've been thinking I might want a career in the aviation business. What do you think, Annie? It's something I want us both to think about. Oh, and I don't want to forget to ask about your family. Is everything about the same? I hope the spring weather will make your dad more comfortable.

    I'll sign off for now, my love.

    I am yours ... only forever, if you care to know.

    — Carl

Annie folded the letter. She felt much more at peace now knowing her fiancé was safe and well. She thought of Charlie Temple, the Airmail pilot who taught Carl to fly. She remembered his care-free spirit and effervescent personality. She liked Charlie, and her heart ached for Carl.

"Annie, come downstairs, please. The radio news is making a special announcement," Millie called from the foot of the stairs. Annie joined the rest of the family in the living room.

    ... announcement came from the President's personal secretary, Grace Tulley. The President had just finished sitting for his official presidential portrait with Madame Shoumatoff when he suddenly took to his bed. He slipped into a coma from what his physicians later called a cerebral hemorrhage. President Roosevelt passed peacefully at his retreat in Warm Springs, Georgia shortly after 3 o'clock p.m. Within the hour, Vice-President Harry Truman was sworn in as the 33rd President of the United States of America.

Gifford turned the radio off. "He was the greatest President of the 20th century. I doubt there'll be another like him."

"What do you think will happen to the country, Daddy? What about the war and everything?" Penny asked.

"Business as usual, Pen. The war will continue. The wheels of industry will continue to turn as the nation mourns. That's the beauty of our system of government. President Truman is probably being briefed on the war situation as we speak ..." Gifford shook his head, "What a shame."

May 8, 1945
–San Marcelino–

Carl and a handful of other O-1 and O-2 grade Mitchell jockeys, all seasoned pilots with over 25 missions each and who had otherwise distinguished themselves, were invited to a promotion ceremony. Their crews were in attendance as well. The unusual thing about this particular event was that all 257 officers of the Air Apaches were in attendance; not the usual procedure for a simple junior-grade officer promotion ceremony. Carl was the first to step up to the dais. Col. Chester Coltharp did the honors.

"Lt. Bridger, it is my honor to officially announce your promotion to the rank of Captain in the United States Army Air Corps." Coltharp removed the silver bar from each of Carl's epaulettes and pinned the double silver bars of a Captain in their place. "Congratulations, *Capt.* Bridger." They exchanged salutes, and Carl moved across the stage to join his crew.

The Commander of the Air Apaches called the next candidate. "2nd Lt. Alexandre Checkov."

Alex approached Col. Coltharp. His promotion to First Lieutenant put a smile on his face. Alex had proven himself an invaluable asset to Carl and the entire crew of *Avenging Angel*.

Carl shook Alex' hand when he returned to his seat. "Congratulations, Alex. It's long past due in my opinion." Each candidate received his new bars in turn and, when the promotions were all handed out, Col. Coltharp stepped up to the microphone one last time.

"In case you men are curious about why the entire officer compliment of the 345th is in attendance at this little soiree, it's because we are being reassigned to Clark Air Base. Other 5th Air Force units and several operational units from other commands are already there. They're working on repairing older buildings and constructing new ones, so our billets should be more comfortable than what you're used to here. We'll leave in two stages. First out will be the 501st and 500th Bomb Squadrons. In three days, the 499th and 498th will follow. Get your gear together, gentlemen. The first two squadrons will depart at 0700 hrs."

In January, 1945, the 6th Army occupied Clark Air base on Luzon Island. Fighting continued as the airbase was being repaired and made ready for 5th Air Force and other operational units to move on to the massive facility. Other 5th Air Force groups had already moved onto the base as early as March, but as the geography of the war changed, the mission of the 345th changed as well. The Japanese were attempting to establish an independent puppet empire in Vietnam in order to hold control over Southeast Asia. To accomplish their goal, they would need to oust the French Vichy government. The new mission of the 345th was to attack enemy strongholds, both in Formosa and in Vietnam, which meant a temporary relocation to Clark Air Base.

Carl had flown 36 missions since joining the 345th at Tacloban in January. He had led missions, performed the duties of assistant intelligence officer and earned the respect of his fellow pilots and the Group Commander as well. Capt. Carl Bridger's exemplary performance placed him at the top of the list to command his own squadron of B-25s. His achievements included a Distinguished Flying Cross with one oak leaf cluster, two Air Medals and a Purple Heart.

Since the death of his friend and mentor, Charlie Temple, Carl had immersed himself in his work. He swore no member of his crew would die at the hands of the enemy as a result of piloting insufficiencies. He had made it his mission to learn everything about the B-25's performance capabilities beyond what he read in the manuals. He spent countless hours with his chief mechanic going over do's and don'ts of what the '25 could do ... pushing the envelope to the edge. He learned from the finest of the Air Apache pilots who, in Carl's opinion, were master strategists and tacticians. Sometimes he became the tutor, sharing his experiences with *them*. Carl became, arguably, the best B-25 Mitchell pilot in the Air Apaches.

The evening before the scheduled departure of the Black Panthers for Clark Field, the need to close the door on the San Marcelino Chapter of his personal war pressed hard on his mind. It was not the war with the Japanese that vexed him, but the war of his own conscience. He had been reunited with his best friend here. He had seen Charlie happier than he had ever seen him, and for a while it seemed like he and Alyanna were going to share a rare storybook ending. Added joy came in the person of Doc Henreid's addition to the crew. Carl had forged a strong friendship with his new Flight Engineer. But, war was never the definition of enduring happiness as he had learned firsthand: war took Charlie from him and ripped the joy from Alyanna's heart. She quit her job at the Officers' Club and withdrew into herself. Carl had not seen her since that dreadful day after Charlie's death ... the day he had broken the news to her. She never wept ... never asked the inevitable *why?* She bore the news with little sign of emotion at all. Alyanna Deschales disappeared, he was told, not to be seen again for three days when her body was discovered by a local fisherman, washed up on the beach six miles from the air base. Carl's greatest joy of flying and his deepest grief were here at San Marcelino along with the nag-

ging questions: *Was it my fault? Could I have done something more
... something different?* Carl struggled to make sense of the irra-
tionality of war that toys with the minds of those who would tempt
fate and hope to see a better life ahead.

Carl welcomed the move. He had demons chasing him here
at San Marcelino, and so it was that the following morning,
A/P173, *Avenging Angel*, lifted into the sky at 0715 hrs.

**May 13, 1945
–Clark Field–**

Harry Osborne looked down at Clark from the tail gunner's
position. "There she is, boys, 52 miles in circumference, two concrete runways, permanent housing structures, and home to 5th Air
Force. She's a pretty picture compared to the *Tac* and San
Marcelino. Hey, Skipper, do you suppose there'll be hot running
water at Clark? I'd die a happy man for a hot shower."

"Could be, Harry. Let's cut the chatter now." Carl turned to
the task of lining up the 501st for landing.

The designation for the 501st Black Panthers was "Blue
Group." Carl flew the lead plane in Avenging Angel, call sign: Blue
Leader. The four flights of four B-25s each were designated Blue
1, Blue 2, Blue 3 and Blue 4 respectively. The four flights of the
500th Rough Raiders were designated "Red Group."

*Blue Leader to Red Group, you're first on the
ground, Gary. Take the Rough Riders down.*

Roger, Blue Leader.

Capt. Gary Westcott ordered his 18 Rough Raiders to descend for landing. Each flight flew a left traffic pattern in line-formation to runway two-zero left.

After the last of the Rough Raiders cleared the runway, the
first of 16 Black Panthers turned onto final approach. *Avenging
Angel* was the last Mitchell to taxi to the parking area.

Carl stepped down to the tarmac and gazed up and down

347

the rows of aircraft. Stretching the full length of the flight-line were groups of planes of every description: B-24s of the 43rd Bomb Group, B-25s from the 38th and 345th Bomb Groups, sleek P-61 Black Widow Night Fighters of the 421st Fighter Squadron, and P-51s of the 35th Fighter Group to name a few. It was the biggest gathering of war planes Carl or his crew had ever seen in one place.

Alex whistled his amazement. "Get a load of this. The entire Pacific Air Force must be here. This place is huge!"

"Okay, we're here. What now, Skipper?" Doc Henreid asked.

"We check in at Base Ops for billeting assignments and debriefing, get settled in, and go from there, Doc. Let's hop into one of those six-bys. Grab your gear, boys." Carl whistled at one of the two-and-a-half-ton transports moving in a constant stream up and down the flight line. The big 10-wheeled GMC truck with its canvas-covered bed pulled up to the crew, and the men climbed aboard. When they were seated on the two benches, the driver secured the tail gate, and they rolled toward the new Base Operations center.

Carl and his crew spotted the 345th Air Apaches logo over a set of double doors and walked into an open office buzzing with the sound of clattering typewriters and people walking busily about. A big Master Sergeant sat at a desk on the opposite side of a railing with a swinging gate. Carl stepped into the NCOs personal work space.

"Excuse me, Sergeant, I'm Capt. Bridger of the 501st, in from San Marcelino. We're checking in for billeting and debriefing."

The tank of a man held out one hand. "Orders, please, sir."

Carl dropped the manila document-sized envelope into the sergeant's hand. The non-com opened it and withdrew the papers. He separated out the enlisted crew members' orders from those of the officers.

"Enlisted over there." He pointed to a row of desks over which hung a sign reading "Enlisted Processing" in neat black letters. He gave each man his individual orders, and they walked over to the waiting area and sat down.

Harry shook his head and grinned. "Here we go again, the famous 'hurry up and wait' of bureaucracy."

"You officers will be assigned to the Officers' Barracks. Here's a map." He spread it out on his desk. "You're here at Base Ops." He pointed at the map and traced his finger along the only road leading into the heart of the base. "As you pass Base Supply, to the right is Officers' Housing. These four buildings are assigned to the 345th Bomb Group." The sergeant circled the buildings with a red pencil. "Welcome to Clark Air Base, sir." He handed the map to Carl showing the locations of all of the pertinent buildings and roads on the base. "Oh, by the way, I also circled the enlisted barracks where your men are assigned."

Carl noted the location on the map, folded it neatly and smiled at the man. "Thank you, Sergeant." Carl, Alex, and Phil left the building. It was a short walk to the housing compound, and they decided to stretch their legs after the cramped flight. Ten minutes later they stood at the entrance to the collection of two-story barracks. They found the one marked "501st Bombardment Sqdn."

"Home sweet home, fellas. Let's find our nest and settle in." Carl led the way.

A double-door Army-green steel locker was arranged to the side of each bunk bed. A writing table with a small lamp sat between each pair of beds. Folded linens were neatly stacked on the mattresses.

Carl and Alex took adjacent bunks and stowed their gear in the lockers. They put padlocks on the doors and were about to head back to the Officers' Mess for some chow when two young Filipino boys approached them.

"You are American pilots? I am Rafael. He is my brother

Eduardo. You want number one houseboy? We clean clothes, change bed linen ... number one job. Two American dollars every month. We take number one care."

At the sight of the two young Filipino brothers, Carl experienced a déjà vu flash back to San Marcelino and Alyanna. His heart pounded in his chest, but he was able to shake it off.

He glanced at Alex who was waiting for him to make a decision. He signaled to his co-pilot with an affirmative nod. "You and your brother are hired, Rafael. You can start by cleaning everything in this bag." Carl handed him his laundry bag full of underwear, socks, and soiled utility shirts and slacks. Alex did the same, and the two men walked to the Officers' Mess for some chow.

Later, the officers and men of the Black Panthers and Rough Raiders seated themselves in a small auditorium. Battle maps hung on the wall behind the dais. Col. Coltharp stepped up to the microphone.

"Good afternoon, Air Apaches. As we speak, your planes are being fitted with extended-range fuel tanks. For the next several weeks we will strike enemy supply depots, ground and sea transportation and military installations in and around the island of Formosa. As you well know, the range of the Mitchell is a hair over 1,300 miles. Loaded, we can figure 1,200. We'll be hitting targets between 700 and 800 miles away, necessitating the added fuel tanks. Because of the reduced space for bombs and added weight, ordinance load-outs will be 250 pound demos, free-falling frags, and para-frags depending on the mission. No 500 or 1,000 bombs. Targeting will be low-level in most instances. Needless to say, we are entering the East-Asian monsoon season. For the next three months you can expect low visibility and a lot of rain. This added complication will make demands on your navigation and low-level flying skills. Most missions will not receive the benefit of air cover because of the low altitudes you'll be flying and poor weather. These next weeks will test your abilities to the nth degree.

"As to the local civilian population, we are ordering all personnel restricted to base. The town of Angeles is off limits, so we are building facilities here at Clark to make things as comfortable as possible. If there are no questions, gentlemen, enjoy your next three days off. They will be your last for a while."

The Officers' Club was only 100 yards up a paved walk from their quarters, so Carl, Alex, and Phil decided to check out the quality of beer at the club. They turned a corner, and there in front of them was a single-level building of framed construction with a gabled roof. Painted white, a covered walkway invited guests to enter. Inside, tables filled every space from wall to wall with men and women seated at most of them. Phil spotted an empty one, and the men hurried over to it. They were immediately approached by a white-shirted Filipino waiter dressed in black slacks and polished shoes. His white opened-collar *Barong* with its brocaded front added a comfortable yet formal appearance to the young man's attire.

"How may I serve you, gentlemen?" The waiter asked in impeccable English.

"How about a pitcher of your cold San Miguel and three glasses?" Alex ordered.

"Of course." The man disappeared.

"Got your hopes up a little high there don't you, Alex?" Phil Ortiz chuckled. "When was the last time you had anything but a warm beer in a bottle?"

"Look around you, Phil. This place is like The Brown Derby compared to the 'O' Club at San Marcelino. I could get used to this really fast."

The waiter returned with three sparkling clean mugs and a half-gallon-sized pitcher of San Miguel beer. The pitcher was dripping streamlets of condensation down its frosted side. He filled the three mugs and left the pitcher on the table.

Carl lifted his mug to his lips. "Oh, Sweet Molly Maguire!

351

This is the best brew to pass over my lips since we left California." The chilled beer slid down his throat like heavenly nectar.

The sound of a live band filled the room, and a uniformed man stepped up to a microphone.

"Ladies and gentlemen, officers and friends." A captain in class-A dress announced over the microphone, "As you know, the USO is proud to sponsor the very best entertainment and entertainers from the states. Tomorrow, the king of USO entertainers, Bob Hope, himself, will entertain every soldier, airman, and sailor here at Clark with an hour-and-a-half of comedy and music. Well, we have a very special preview of tomorrow's show. Please welcome to our stage Mister Bob Hope!"

Bob Hope stepped out on the small stage and paused, smiling, as he waited for the applause to settle down.

"Thank you ... thank you. We're happy to be with you. Miss Francis Langford is with me. Francis, come on out here." Miss Langford made her entrance dressed in white summer shorts, red high heels, and a red polka-dot blouse tied above her naval. "Beautiful, isn't she?" Bob growled lustily, eliciting laughter from the crowd.

"Anyway, as I was saying, we're happy to be here. We were afraid we might get lost because of the overcast coming in to Clark Air Base. I told the pilot not to worry and asked him to open a window, which he did. I took one sniff of air with my gifted and beautiful shnozz ..." He turned his classic profile to the audience and grinned. "Beautiful, isn't it? It's a toss-up between the nose and Francis." The crowd roared with laughter. "So, I said to the pilot, 'drop down right here, I'd recognize the smell of Angeles anywhere.'" Again the audience erupted with laughter and applause.

Francis Langford closed the short program with a special song that transported Carl back to a time when war was only a distant thought.

"To all of you fellas with wives and girlfriends waiting for you back home, this is for you."

The small combo began the lead-in to *Only Forever*, the song of Carl and Annie's love. Carl closed his eyes and was at his Junior Prom at Cascade High School when Bing Crosby's voice spoke to the enduring love growing in their hearts and declared anew in every letter: *Will I want to be with you, as the years come and go? Only forever, if you care to know.* The words fed joy to his heart and lifted his spirit. *Annie, my love, I wish you were here right now.* He smiled at the thought.

"Only forever, if you care to know" Carl whispered.

"Did you say something, Skipper?" Alex asked.

Carl turned to his friend. "What? Oh, nothing ... just thinking of someone back home."

2345 hrs, May 17th
Mission Briefing

Maj. Bingham stepped up in front of the map of the island of Formosa. "Good evening, men. Col. Coltharp has asked that I brief you on tomorrow's mission ... or this morning's, however you choose to look at it. Two flights each from the 501st and 500th will participate. The 500th Rough Raiders, call name Blue Group, will hit rolling targets between Shinachiku and Toroku along the rail lines and the rail yards at either end of the line. Coordinates are in your mission packets. The 501stBlack Panthers, call name Red Group, will strike the rail yards at Chikunan and Bydritsu. Visibility will be limited. Load-out will be six 250-pound bombs each. Other targets of opportunity: watch for any rolling stock on the roads and any buildings of industry ... factories, warehouses and the like. Wheels up at 0200 hrs. Get some chow, men, but go easy on the coffee. You'll be in the air for the better part of 11 hours."

After having a light breakfast of chipped beef and gravy over toast topped with eggs and ketchup, Carl, Alex, and Phil left the mess hall and returned to their barracks to await the ride to the flight line.

One of the trucks assigned to shuttle the crews to their planes, picked the officers up in front of their barracks and drove to the enlisted men's housing compound. Carl stuck his head out the back of the truck and whistled at Harry, Doc, and Willard who were standing beneath the yellow glow of an incandescent light bulb. At 0115 in the morning, it was black as pitch beneath the cloud cover of the starless night.

Five minutes later, they were off-loaded at *Avenging Angel*.

"Drop the crew ladder down and climb aboard, men. Lt. Chekov and I will do a walk-around."

Carl and Alex, with flashlights in hand, performed their outside pre-flight check. Satisfied, they climbed up the ladder and into the cockpit. Carl began calling out the engine start sequence. Alex read each step back as they were completed.

Both engines started up, and Carl adjusted their rpm to a smooth idle. As soon as the oil temperature gauges were reading in the green "normal" range and all other engine gauges on the instrument panel were firmly in the green, Carl waited his turn to taxi to the runway.

"Radio check, men. Call it in." He announced over the plane's crew frequency. Each man called in from his station.

Avenging Angel led the six Mitchells of the Black Panthers to the end of the runway.

"Set flaps at 25 percent, Alex," Carl ordered. He heard the sound of the servos as the flaps lowered.

"Flaps at one-quarter," Alex confirmed.

Alex throttled up for the takeoff run, and the pitch of the engines rose. The tires kicked up spray from the wet runway. Carl applied slight backpressure on the control yoke and brought the nose wheel off the pavement. He let *Avenging Angel* rotate into the air and allowed the airspeed to climb to 140 mph. Alex raised the gear and flaps and Carl increased the climb rate, climbing at 1,200 feet per minute at 170 mph.

Carl ordered over the plane-to-plane frequency:

Group Leader to Red Group, radio in when in position.

Red Two is right behind you, Red Leader, Lt. Casey, commanding the second flight, reported back.

Roger, Red Two. Stay close behind us. I don't want you to lose sight of us in these clouds. I'm taking us up to 6,000 to get out of the soup.

The formation turned toward Formosa, which lay 740 miles to the northwest.

"Sgt. Henreid, I want you to keep an eye on the fuel situation. If you notice anything out of whack, call it out. I'm concerned about leaks from the extra tank. They installed them in a hurry, and I don't want to take chances flying over open ocean."

"Copy, sir. It's looking fine so far."

"Osborne and Price, keep an eye out for bogeys. There's no cover on this mission, so be sharp."

Carl's Black Panthers flew on toward Formosa staying above the thick cloud cover. Red Group approached Formosa and began their descent hoping for a break in the overcast. He could barely see his wingmen.

"Harry, do you see Red Two behind us?"

"Barely, Skipper, they pop into sight every few seconds."

"Copy that."

Carl didn't want to risk a mid-air collision.

"Alex, I think we can do the job with our three planes. I'm going to send Red Two back to base. This overcast is likely to take a plane or two into the trees. What do you think?"

"I think it's risky, but doable, Skipper ... your choice."

"Red Two has two green pilots. I'm ordering them to abort."

Red Leader to Red Two, this cloud cover is too thick. I don't want to risk a mid-air collision with too many of us in the target area. Return to base. Wingmen, tuck in close. I don't want to lose you in this stuff. I'm dropping down to the deck now.

Red Two is RTB, Captain.

The three bombers of Red Two veered away from the formation and turned back toward Luzon Island.

Carl dropped *Avenging Angel* into the thick cloud cover and made a shallow descent of 500 feet per minute. He was about ready to abort the mission all together because of the overcast when they broke into the open.

"Arm the bombs, Phil, and open the bomb-bay doors." Carl ordered over the intercom.

Coming up on a bridge. Take it out, Lt. Harrah.

Carl directed the last plane in his flight of three to hit the rail bridge south of Banshiden.

Stay with me, Blount. We'll vector on the town. There's supposed to be a Butanol plant and a rail yard there.

"Phil, give me a heading."

Phil Ortiz checked his chart and calculated the course change. "We're too far east of the town. Turn to heading three-zero-five. The town should be on the other side of the mountain off to your left."

Carl banked *Avenging Angel* to Phil's assigned course and headed toward a low-lying densely forested mountain. He angled toward the left slope of the mountain. Lt. Del Blount stayed close off Carl's wing in A/P199.

Red Lead to wing, we'll strafe anything we see on our first run. Once we locate our targets visually, we'll hit them with our 250s on our second pass.

The pair of Mitchells roared from the cover of the mountain, banking toward the town of Banshiden. Directly in front of them stood a large structure suggesting a warehouse or manufacturing plant of some sort. Train tracks paralleled the building. One locomotive was stopped with several cars positioned alongside the loading docks.

Hit the building with your guns, Blount, Carl directed.

Carl pressed the red "Guns" button on his yoke as he centered the locomotive in his ring sight. Blount went for the building. Flying debris told them they were on target, but no substantial damage resulted from their first run.

Put your bombs on the building, Del. We'll hit the train.

Carl positioned the plane on a head-on approach at the locomotive. Del Blount separated slightly away from Carl and angled toward the building. Both planes throttled up and raced toward their targets at 280 mph. The two bombers released their bombs simultaneously. Blount's bombs tore into the flimsy structure and exploded causing a spectacular explosion and fire as stores of what was probably Butanol ignited adding to the blast.

Carl's first bomb smacked into the locomotive. His second went wide and struck a transport truck parked next to one of the train cars. The boiler of the locomotive ruptured sending up a billowing bloom of smoke, fire, and steam into the sky. Men ran in all direction as the two '25s banked away from the destruction below them.

Red Leader to wing, form up and let's grab some altitude. Red Leader to Alpha Papa Five Seven One, do you read? Over.

Lt. Harrah, do you read? Over.

Carl waited for a response from his other wingman, but got only silence. He tried twice more with the same results.

"Don't worry, Carl. He probably got lost in the fog and decided to head for home."

"Yea, maybe." Alex' reassuring words were not convincing. Carl busied himself with getting them all above the cloud layer and

357

back into clear skies.

"Bogey at our 6 o'clock high, Skipper. Looks like a DC-2," Harry Osborne called out from his position in the tail.

"Copy that. Do you see any fighter escort?"

"Negative, sir. He's all alone."

Red Leader to wing, we have a bogey at our 6 o'-clock high, type Delta-Charlie-Two. Do you want to pay him a visit, Del?

Roger, Red Leader ... leaving formation.

A/P199 climbed up and away from Carl's flight path. A couple of minutes later he was in position to engage the enemy transport. Approaching from above and behind the DC-2, he put the enemy in his gun sight and squeezed off four bursts of .50 caliber gunfire from his eight forward-firing AN/M-2 Browning machine guns. The transport never had a chance. A trail of smoke and flame marked its spiraling descent into the South China Sea.

Chapter XV

May, 19, 1945

–Change of Command–

Carl sat at the bar chatting with 1st Lt. Tad Warner and 1st Lt. Dean Marsden about the day's mission.

"I'm glad that Harrah finally made it back to the formation. I thought maybe he got too low in the fog and buried his plane in the palm trees. What happened to him up there, Bridger, did you ever get the straight scoop?"

"His radio antenna vibrated loose and he couldn't acknowledge my call. By the time he found us we were already too far ahead for him to catch up. He landed about five minutes after we did. I think he's over at the hangar making sure the radio is working and ready for the next mission."

The conversation switched from the mission details to the man who led the sortie, Lt. Col. Glenn A. Doolittle

Carl leaned forward and dropped his voice to a whisper. "So, Dean, you were his wingman. What do you think of our XO's skills up there?"

"I like him … cool under fire for sure. When we picked up heavy ack-ack outside of Canton City, he ordered me and Bo Flanders to follow him in and direct our fire on the gun emplacements along the edge of the river. We strafed the hell out of the nips, but Flanders took a few holes anyway. When one of the guys ditched his plane … Lt. Britton, I think … Col. Doolittle didn't hesitate to ask us all to refuel at Lingayen and return to Donsol Bay to search

361

for him. It's a good thing we did, because it allowed the Cat to arrive on station faster and pick up the crew."

Carl nodded. "I agree. He makes good decisions under pressure, and he's a good strategist. It'll be interesting to see how he does as Group Commander. My gut tells me that the logic behind the rumor lends a lot of truth to it. Coltharp has been a respected and competent CO. The way I figure, Doolittle will fill his shoes just fine." Carl raised his beer mug. "A toast, then, to the two best leaders in the Air Apaches!" Everyone at the table lifted their beers and clicked bottles.

Ted Warner wiped his mouth on his sleeve and continued the critique of their new CO in waiting. "I overheard a couple of guys saying he requested a transfer here to the 345th because the 42nd Bomb Group was top heavy at the command level. With Coltharp moving up to 5th Air Force, Doolittle is in a good position to replace him. I'm glad he's a hands-on commander instead of a pencil pusher. That's what I liked about Coltharp as well."

"Hear, hear." Carl raised his glass.

"Hear, hear!" Dean Marsden repeated as they all clinked glasses. again

Four days later, 2,500 officers and enlisted men of the 345th Air Apaches assembled at an empty hangar. Most crowded inside, out of the light rainfall, but many sat outside beneath tarpaulins hung on poles to shield themselves from the drizzle that fell almost constantly during the monsoon season in the South Pacific.

The 5th Air Force Band played the usual fare of Souza marches and other tunes of a military genre until the men were seated. The 345th's First Sergeant, dressed in his Class-A uniform, marched up onto the makeshift stage, snapped a right-flank turn and stopped with a click of the heels of his polished shoes, facing the microphone stand. Remaining at attention, the NCO bellowed:

"Group! Atten-hut!" The assembled men and women rose

to attention. A line of officers ascended to the stage and stood line-abreast in front of a row of seats behind the podium.

"Present arms!" the First Sergeant called out, followed by: "Present the colors!"

Three NCOs marched down the middle aisle between two armed soldiers. They stepped up onto the raised platform and placed the stars and stripes in the center standard. The Guidons, one for the 5th Air Force and one for the 345th Bombardment Group, were placed on either side of the nation's flag. The flag bearers stepped back and held a salute.

The First Sergeant called out in his best drill-sergeant voice, "Order arms!" whereupon those assembled lowered their hands smartly.

Brigadier General Ken Walker, commanding the 5th Bomber Command of the 5th Air Force, approached the podium.

"Be seated. Men of the 345th Bombardment Group. Welcome, Air Apaches, to this Change of Command ceremony." The General spoke of honor and tradition, of Col. Coltharp's exemplary service and to that of his replacement Col. Glenn A. Doolittle. He applauded the contribution of the Air Apaches to the war in the Pacific Theatre of Operations. After 15 minutes, he got down to business.

"Will Col. Coltharp and Col. Doolittle please step forward."

Chester Coltharp stood and marched forward, positioning himself in front of and to the right of the podium. Glenn Doolittle did the same on the left side of the podium. The two men faced one another.

"Present the Guidon." The First Sergeant ordered. A soldier drew the 345th Guidon from its standard and presented it to Col. Coltharp. The two senior officers took two steps toward each other.

Holding the flag with the Air Apache logo emblazoned upon it in front of him in the port arms position, Chester Coltharp said simply, "Sir, I relinquish command," and stretched his arms forward to Doolittle, who accepted the Guidon and stated, "Sir, I assume command."

Col. Coltharp saluted and then returned to his seat. Col. Doolittle returned the Guidon to the soldier who placed it in the standard. The new Commanding Officer saluted the flag and returned to his seat. The ceremony concluded with welcoming comments from Col. Doolittle followed by a cheer of "Hip-hip, hurrah!" repeated three times. Then, it was off to the Officers' Club for Carl and a few friends for drinks and celebration.

The next few weeks were punctuated with a steady stream of low-profile "milk-run" missions. The Japanese were in full retreat. The 345th was continued to harass the enemy on Formosa, but was met with only light resistance. The remaining Japanese forces were forming for a defense of the Empire's hold on Taipei.

–Tan Sui River Mission Briefing–

The pre-dawn morning of July 10th greeted the day with a rare gift of partly cloudy skies and a full moon. Pilots always considered a blue sky a great day for flying. Good visibility made for precision approaches to targets, more accurate bombing, and observable results of damage. The recently added K-1 cameras both fore and aft in the bombers would prove valuable to the intelligence people when it came to damage assessment and planning future missions. This day seemed to be such a day.

At 0400 hrs, Carl stepped out of his quarters beneath a sky filled with stars. A wisp of cloud drifted across the face of the moon. He and other yawning men shuffled into the briefing room and seated themselves.

Col. Doolittle stepped in front of the mission map showing the northern half of the island of Formosa. A red line encircled the Tan Sui River and harbor.

"Good morning, Air Apaches!"

"Good morning, Sir!" The 72 assembled men responded in unison.

"This morning you are going to attack the enemy outpost

near the headwaters of the Tan Sui River ... here, four klicks down river from Taipei." Col. Doolittle set the tip of his pointer at a red dot on the river. "Intel reports a force of regimental size ... approximately 1,800 men, equipped with artillery, anti-aircraft weapons, armored personnel carriers, transports, and small arms ... everything they need to mobilize for a sweep of the northern half of the island. We don't know yet if this is a precursor to a larger scale operation, but we're not going to wait around to find out. Fifth Bomber Command has tasked the 345th to destroy the outpost and any shipping that may be in the harbor.

"There will be two groups consisting of four flights of three '25s each. The 500th Rough Raiders will be designated Blue Group and will lead the attack on the enemy encampment." He continued with Blue Group assignments for the three planes each of Blue One, Blue Two, Blue Three, and Blue Four.

"Red Group will be led by Capt. Hatcher of the 501st Black Panthers. Capt. Bridger will be Flight Leader of Red Two in A/P173. Other Flight Leaders will be as follows: Lt. Chealander in A/P571, and Lt. Kuda in A/P500." The remaining pilots of Red Group were called out.

"You will make your approach here, east of the Pescadore Island group along the west coast of Formosa. At precisely 25.03 degrees north latitude, you will turn inland toward Taipei.

"When you reach the intercept point at the coordinates contained in your mission packets, both groups will turn inland south of Taipei and attack in staggered-line formation south-to north in two waves. After the target is destroyed, you will re-form and proceed to Lingayen for refueling and return to Clark. Load-out will be 20-pound parafrags and two Mark-7 rockets each. Air cover will be provided by the 49th Fighter Group out of Lingayen. You can expect moderate to heavy anti-aircraft fire as well. Good luck, gentlemen."

Thirty minutes later, the last Mitchell off the ground joined the formation, and the 24 Air Apache bombers turned northwest toward the coast of Formosa.

> *Blue Leader to all planes, we are climbing to niner thousand. All planes arm and test your guns.*

An hour from their target, a formation of nine American P-47 Thunderbolts from the 49th Fighter Group appeared overhead. The radios of all of the planes, both bombers and fighters, were tuned to the same command frequency. Carl listened to the chatter as the lead P-47 pilot made himself known:

> *Thunder Lead to Blue Leader, do you copy. Over?*

> *Roger, Thunder Leader. We copy. You are a welcome sight, fellas.*

> *Blue Leader, we will provide air cover as far as your IP when we'll break off. Another flight will pick you up over the Pescadores and will escort you on your return leg to Lingayen. You'll be on your own until you pick up your air cover coming back.*

> *Copy that, Thunder Leader. Blue Leader, out.*

"Alex, keep your comm tuned to the command frequency and take the controls while I talk to the crew."

"Roger, Skipper. I have the controls."

Carl released the control yoke and withdrew his feet from the rudder pedals. He flipped the radio switch to intercom.

"Pilot to crew. Charge your weapons." A short burst of gunfire from the dorsal turret confirmed the readiness of the twin .30 caliber guns. Carl pushed the red "Guns" button on his control yoke and eight AN/M2 Browning .50 caliber guns came to life in a one-second burst.

"Tail gunner, I didn't hear your guns. Harry, what's happening back there?"

"Jammed, Skipper …working on it."

"Phil, check the parafrags for proper loading in the racks. I don't want any of them hanging up."

"Roger, Skipper." Thirty seconds later, Phil reported that the bombs were good to go.

"It should be business as usual today, fellas. A half-hour over the target and we'll head for home. Just do your jobs and we'll be fine. Harry, how are your guns?"

"Bad news Skipper. When the guns were serviced, some knucklehead left out a spring in the retracting slide assembly of one of them. They rushed the job and didn't test fire them. I have one good one, though."

"That's just dandy! ... Crap! Alright. Harry, I want you to man the dorsal turret. I just hope we don't get any Zekes on our six ... Damn!" *So much for business as usual,* he thought. He needed his best gunner on the twin .50 caliber dorsal guns. The decision left *Angel* with only minimal means of defending against an attack from the rear.

Blue Leader to all planes, descending to 3,000. The weather has built up a cloud cover, so tuck in close. I don't want to lose anyone in the soup.

Capt. Carey Hatcher led the Black Panthers of Red Group behind Blue Group into the thick line of clouds which enshrouded the planes. Carl could barely see Red One in front of him.

The formation flew north. The Pescadores lay off their left wing, and Mount Yu Shan stood to their right. Rising to 12,900 feet, the mountain forced them to turn inland toward Taipei. They used the town as a reckoning point to turn down river and begin their bomb run.

Red Leader to Red Group, we are at the IP. Turning on heading eight-five degrees now.

Carl followed Hatcher's flight of three planes as they banked east on the assigned heading.

Red Leader to all planes, I lost visual on Blue Group. I think they missed the IP.

Carl keyed his mic:

Red Two to Red Leader, are we going to continue the attack?

Affirmative, Red Two. Red Leader to Red Group, it looks like we'll have to do this by ourselves. Move into staggered-line formation. Approaching the target now.

Carl issued orders to his flight:

Red Two Leader to flight, open bomb-bay doors. Be sharp boys. We're coming up on target.

As the 12 bombers of Red Group turned toward the Tan Sui River from the protection of Mount Yu Shan, the Japanese encampment came into view about a kilometer dead ahead. They were met by blossoms of black anti-aircraft bursts erupting in front of them, buffeting the planes.

Hold your course, Red Group. I'm starting my first run on the A-A positions, Capt. Hatcher announced.

The enemy stronghold was located on the east side of the Tan Sui River. The larger structures suggested supply and fuel depots, motor pool and artillery compounds. The tented compound positioned further inland appeared to be living quarters and mess facilities. A narrow bridge stretched across the river where a small village stood, beyond which lay a checkerboard network of rice paddies being worked by villagers. Four watch towers posted at the corners of the compound dominated the encampment. A makeshift dock accommodated several sampans. Carl surmised that the small, shallow draft river boats were used to ferry supplies from the harbor in Tan Sui Bay.

Red Leader led Red One flight in staggered-line formation toward the cluster of buildings, while Carl led Red Two behind the Group Leader in follow-up position.

As if on cue, the bombers throttled up to the stops. Carl toggled the water injection switch designed to cool the engines during the use of military power. *Avenging Angel*'s speed climbed to 300 mph.

Hatcher's flight vectored on two of the A-A bunkers and dropped to tree-top height. All three planes opened-up with a combined total of 24 machine guns. The A-A emplacements were in sandbagged bunkers … virtually unprotected against the onslaught of Mitchells.

Carl immediately understood Hatcher's strategy. He adjusted his approach, nosing *Avenging Angel* toward the other two gun emplacements. His two wingmen stayed with him as Red Two descended on the anti-aircraft batteries.

One pass, Red Two. Take out those guns!

Carl put one of the bunkers in his ring sight and pressed the red "Guns" button. Tracers rifled ahead, showing that his aim was on target. The other two bombers followed him in. They roared 50 feet over the heads of the Japanese gunners and entered a tight climbing turn to position themselves for a bomb run on the enemy camp. The defensive ack-ack bursts continued, but much lighter. Fragments of shrapnel pierced the fuselage of *Avenging Angel* as she lined up the bomber with the motor pool and artillery compounds.

In the heat of every battle, the moment arrives when a man becomes attuned to every heartbeat. He is hyper-sensitive to every sound and every movement. His sense of time, place and event become so acute that it seems as though every second stretches outward, and the world around him slows down.

Every beat of Carl's heart pounded in his head … an endless cycle of explosions. Each breath he drew was as the rush of the ocean surf to his ears … slow and rhythmic. The target lay frozen in his sights. He noted the cool, smooth surface of the bomb release lever as he pulled it, releasing one sleeve of 23-pound parafrags. Each tiny bomb deployed a small parachute so it dropped back behind the path of the bomber. When it hit the ground it exploded into hundreds of tiny metal fragments. Together, the dozens of bombs saturated a half-mile long area with a carpet of high velocity shards that tore into structures, vehicles, and enemy soldiers. Fuel storage tanks exploded in bright yellow-orange billowing columns of fire. While the bombs fell, Carl fired a four-second burst of his eight guns. It seemed as though his heightened state of awareness made him conscious of the sound of every round exploding from the barrels of each of *Angel's* AN/M2 .50 cals. His mind raced to devise a strategy that would compensate for the absence of his tail guns against the agile enemy fighters.

Red Group roared down on their targets and released their bombs. Red Leader yelled over the com:

Incoming, dead ahead! Red One break right! Break right!

At the precise moment Red One broke right, Carl saw what was coming at them. The dozen B-25s of Blue Group were converging on a head-on collision course at a combined speed of over 600 mph.

Red Two, break left! he shouted.

Carl banked hard left to avoid the incoming bombers of Blue Group who, in two flights of three planes, strafed the enemy troops amassing in the streets as they roared by in the opposite direction.

We've got it from here, Red Group. We'll finish up and join you shortly.

Roger, Blue Group. Where the heck have you been? Carey Hatcher demanded.

We missed the IP and turned around. We decided to hit the encampment coming down from the north. Looks like you fellas started the party without us. Capt. Gene Fredericks of the Rough Raiders explained. I think we surprised those boys down there. Somebody ought to write-up this strategy in the manual.

Carl heard the entire conversation and shook his head. "Danged fools almost killed us all with that stunt, Alex."

"Roger that, Skipper. You gotta admit, though. It was a very effective strategy."

Red Leader led the Group as they climbed to 5,000 feet and turned toward Lingayen for refueling.

Sgt. Harry Osborne scanned the skies in a 360-degree sweep from the dorsal turret. A blink of sunlight reflected from between two clouds and caught his attention.

"Skipper, we have company. I count two … no, three flights of Zekes above and behind us at our nine o'clock high."

Stay close, Red Group. Move in tight. Red Leader directed. We should pick up our escorts any time now."

The first flight of four Jap A6M Zeroes dived on the American bombers, knifing through the formation. Carl heard the enemy's bullets strike the fuselage as all 12 Mitchells opened fire with their .50 caliber turret guns. In the turret of *Avenging Angel*, Harry waited for the next wave. He focused all of his attention on the lead plane and placed the center of his ring-sight in front of the enemy fighter to lead him just enough. Satisfied that he had the Zeke, he squeezed the firing grips of the twin dorsal turret guns and sent two lines of tracers flashing toward the bogey. His aim was spot on. The engine of the Zero exploded and the fighter spiraled down toward the ocean.

Harry spun around in time to see a flight of two enemy planes coming at Red Two's three Mitchells. The lead fighter's 20 mm cannon blinked its death fire. As before, Harry's aim was perfect. The Zero wobbled oddly and veered away from the formation, trailing black smoke. The second enemy plane opened up on *Avenging Angel*, and she bucked beneath the impact of the rounds tearing into the tail section.

Finally, the P-47s arrived. They didn't hesitate to join the fray. The enemy pilots found themselves in a dogfight for their lives and forgot all about the bombers. The '25s were safe … almost.

One lone Zeke had sneaked in behind the group of American planes. He raked Carl's right wingman with cannon fire. Flame and smoke erupted from Lt. Speagle's plane. Speagle entered a steep descent, falling out of formation. The Zero decided to follow the crippled bomber and vectored into position for the kill.

"Harry, let's splash that Zero!"

Carl dived on the enemy fighter with full military power. He worked the rudder pedals with his feet bringing the enemy fighter into the center of his sights. He fired his nose guns at the precise instant that Harry opened fire from the dorsal turret. The Japanese war plane waggled its wings as if the pilot was unsure of what to do. The brief uncertainty allowed *Angel* to shoot past the enemy's left side giving Harry a broadside opportunity. His turret guns came to life, and a row of .50 caliber bullets stitched the plane from the engine, thru the cockpit, and blew off the vertical stabilizer. As quickly as the dog fight began, the sky was clear of enemy planes.

Carl pulled the throttles all of the way back. He and Alex had to use their combined strength to pull the bomber out of its power dive as *Avenging Angel* raced toward the white-caps at 310 mph. She wasn't responding to the full-up elevator.

"That Zeke must have shot away some of the elevator, Alex. C'mon, baby, climb DAMMIT! ... CLIMB!" He yelled.

Angel began to lift slightly ... then more. The horizon came into view and dropped to a point where it stretched across the top of the bomber's nose. She screamed over the white-caps so low that ocean spray spattered the windshield. The altimeter needle crept above zero as A/P173 started to climb. Carl throttled-up and turned to rejoin the formation.

"Phew! That was too close. I thought we were done for, Alex." Carl's voice trembled.

"*Angel* pulled off another miracle for sure. Lordy, I can't stop shaking." Alex' eyes were still wide with fear. "Let's not do that again, okay?"

Carl counted the number of planes in the Red Group formation, expecting to see only 10 other than his own. There was an 11th Mitchell, flying with one prop feathered.

> *Speagle, you made it! It's great to see you, ya bum! Carl was genuinely thrilled. I thought we lost you back there.*

> *Copy that, Flight Leader. The power dive doused the engine fire. Oh, hey; thanks for splashing that Zeke. You saved our bacon.*

> *Any time. How's your fuel situation? Are you going to make it to Lingayen?*

> *Affirmative, Flight Leader. We'll see you on the ground. Beers are on you! Wing, out.*

Carl climbed down the crew ladder at Lingayen. It would require two hours for all of the planes to be refueled and ready to go for the short flight to Clark. He walked to the tail of the plane to look at the damage the Zeke had caused. Doc Henreid and Harry Osborne joined him and Alex.

Much of the Plexiglas enclosure was blown out. There was considerable damage to the guns themselves as well as the ammo cans that contained the belts which fed the twin Browning .50 caliber AN/M2s.

"Look at the elevator, Skipper." The Flight Engineer was examining what remained of the panel. Nearly half of the Alclad sheeting was torn away, leaving a jagged edge. One elevator trim tab was missing. The port-side rudder had been holed and a full, 25 percent of its surface had torn off.

Doc whistled and shook his head. "Harry, I'm glad you weren't back here when that Zeke hit. You'd be dead."

"Doc, if I *had* been back here, he'd be floating face down in the South China Sea, and the *Angel* would be fine and dandy. I can't wait to get my hands on that idiot that never tested the guns back at Clark."

Carl gathered his crew together. "Fellas, the good news is, we're safe and sound. The bad news is *Angel* needs a face lift. I'll let HQ know. I think we'll be stuck here for a few days. Sgt. Henreid, I need you to check with the maintenance guys in the hangar to see what they can do. The rest of you, stay close to Base Ops until we get a handle on what we're up against."

An hour later, Carl met with his men at the mess facility and chatted while dining on dehydrated mashed potatoes and some sort of goulash: a mixture of elbow macaroni, ground beef, tomato sauce, dehydrated carrots and peas.

"Here's the skinny, fellas," Carl began as he wiped his mouth on a paper napkin. "Command is moving the 345th to Ie Shima northwest of Okinawa in six days. We are to remain here until then. We'll coordinate forming up with the main body when they overfly Lingayen enroute to Ie Shima.

"Temporary housing has been set up over at the 309th Bomb Wing. We'll have to make do with the clothes on our back unless we can scrounge something. It won't be pleasant for the next few days, so make the best of it. Doc, I'm heading back to the hangar. I want you to come along."

M/Sgt. Wallace Adams, Chief mechanic for the 38th Bombardment Group, stood on the floor of one of three maintenance and repair hangars supervising the dismantling of *Avenging Angel*'s empennage.

Carl and Doc Henreid approached Sgt. Adams who was barking out orders to a pair of his subordinates.

"Excuse me, Sergeant, I ..." Before Carl could finish, the big NCO spun around and faced him.

"One moment, sir." He turned back to the men on the scaffolds. "Careful with that hoist! I want that elevator and vertical stabilizer in one piece!" Satisfied that his crew was practicing due diligence, Sgt. Adams turned back to Carl and saluted.

"Sorry, sir. Gotta watch those knuckleheads every minute.

374

What can I do ya for?"

"I'm the pilot of that '25 you're working on. This is my engineer, S/Sgt. Henreid. I hope you can use him. He's the best at what he does."

"Well, hell yes I can use him. Henreid, Wall Adams. Grab yourself some overalls, and I'll show you what we're up against." He turned back to Carl and grinned.

"Just one question, sir; how by all that's reasonable did you get that plane down without burying her nose in the ocean? Most of the control surfaces are either damaged or blown away."

"Not sure, Sergeant … just didn't feel like going swimming, I reckon." Carl chuckled.

"Well, all I can say is, if I was to ever get back in the air, I'd want you as my pilot-in-command. That was some piece of work. Guess I better get back to it, sir." The man saluted and turned his attention back to the task at hand.

"Doc, find me when you're done for the day here. Try to find out when we can have *Angel* ready to fly."

Five days later, a small stake-bed truck pulled up to the hangar. A corporal climbed out and called out to Sgt. Adams:

"Hey, Sarge! I got 'em!"

"Great. Let's have a looky see!" Adams, Henreid and the truck driver walked to the rear of the vehicle. Two more men sat in the back atop two six-foot long crates. "Hand me that crowbar."

One of the men handed a crowbar to the senior NCO who pried the top off of the crate. There, nestled in packing excelsior, lay a refurbished AN/M2 Browning .50 caliber aircraft machine gun. Its twin was in the second crate.

"Take them into the hangar, and let's get them mounted," Sgt. Adams said.

"We were able to repair the turret itself. The mounting plate is the same as in the '24. I scavenged a couple off a wrecked Liberator that belly landed and ripped off a wing a couple of months back. We should be able to install them right away with no problem. Henreid, you should let your crew know that she's ready for a test flight." Adams turned toward the hangar.

Doc Henreid found Carl and Alex at the Base Operations building. Carl was on the land-line to Clark.

"Yes sir ... yes, sir, just as soon as I ... hold on a second, please, sir." He looked at Doc with an inquiring expression. Doc gave him a thumbs up "A-Okay" sign. Carl returned to his phone call:

"Sir, my engineer just told me that A/P173 is ready to go. Yes, sir. We will be standing by on the flight-line at 0900 for your radio call." He placed the black receiver on its cradle.

The following morning, Carl and the crew of *Avenging Angel* waited in the Base Operations crew lounge at Lingayen for the call from Clark.

An Air Corps corporal opened the door to the crew lounge and poked his head in.

"Captain, I have Clark on the horn, sir."

"Thank you, Corporal." Carl quick-marched to the nerve-center of Flight Operations where he picked up the hand-held receiver.

"Capt. Bridger, here ... yes, sir. One hour out, copy that. What's their altitude and heading? ... Yes ... got it." He hung up and placed the paper he'd written on in his pocket.

"Let's go, men!" Carl announced, and the crew of A/P173 jogged to their B-25 waiting on the tarmac for them.

Carl and Alex walked around *Avenging Angel*. In addition to the normal check-list items, they performed a thorough inspection of the empennage right down to the pitch angle of the trim tabs. Sgt. Adams and his hangar rats had done a craftsman's job. The new Plexiglas enclosure of Harry's "Man Cave," as he liked to call it, was tight as could be. One might never suspect that five days ago, almost the entire tail assembly had been shot to pieces.

Alex released an appreciative whistle. "The only thing that's lacking is a new coat of paint, but we aren't in the new car business."

"Let's fire 'em up, Alex." Carl followed Alex up the crew ladder and squeezed forward into the cockpit. Sgt. Willard Price pulled the ladder up and secured the hatch.

Both engines started without any problems, and Carl held the Wright Cyclone 2600 power plants at a smooth 1,200 rpm idle until the needles of the oil temperature and cylinder head temperature gauges rose into the green range. He taxied *Angel* forward and turned toward the end of the runway.

"One-quarter flaps, please, Alex."

"Flaps one-quarter," Alex confirmed.

Carl keyed his mic.

Lingayen tower, Army Alpha Papa One Seven Three requesting permission to depart straight out.

Alpha Papa One Seven Three is cleared for take-off. No traffic in the pattern.

Carl eased the throttles forward a bit and the bomber's wheels began to roll. He used the rudders to keep the nose centered on the runway and then firmly pushed the throttle levers all of the way to the stops. At 80 mph, he pulled back on the yoke until he felt the nose wheel lift slightly and then held the yoke steady as he let *Angel* fly herself off the runway.

"Flaps up."

"Flaps up, Skipper."

"Wheels up."

Alex pulled up the gear lever and the mains rose into their respective bays. A green light flashed on. "Wheels up and locked."

Carl flew A/P173 north of Lingayen, climbing until he reached 8,000 feet. He began to circle at 240 mph while maintaining altitude. His radio headset came to life:

Apache Leader to Alpha Papa One Seven Three, do you copy? Over.

Copy you, Apache Leader. Orbiting at 8,000 one-zero miles north of Lingayen on heading of zero-zero-five degrees magnetic.

Roger, Alpha Papa One Seven Three. I have you at our one o'clock. Slow to 200. We are a group of 23 flying in echelon-up formation. Form up on the trailing flight. We're holding the final slot open for you, Captain.

Roger, Apache Leader. We have you at our seven o'-clock. Dropping back to join-up now.

Carl allowed the group of Air Apaches to pass below him.

"They're a beautiful sight, Skipper. I have a great view back here," Harry announced over the intercom.

"Roger that, Harry. What do you guys say to joining the parade?" He descended to the altitude of the trailing flight in group. Matching the speed of the formation, *Avenging Angel* moved in behind the final flight of four, completing the diamond formation.

Alpha Papa One Seven Three is in position, Apache Leader.

Roger, Captain. Your flight designation is Apache six. Your Flight Leader is Lt. O'Hanlon.

Roger that, Apache Leader. Alpha Papa One Seven Three, out.

Carl changed over to the frequency assigned to "Apache Six."

Apache Six Leader, this is Alpha Papa One Seven Three. Do you copy? Over.

I read you, Capt. Bridger. My tail gunner has you flying the number four position. It's nice to have you join us, Carl. I hear 'Avenging Angel' took quite a beating over Formosa.

Roger that. We are combat ready, though, and anx-

ious to settle-in at Ie Shima. Alpha Papa One Seven Three, out.

Five hours later, the first of two groups of Mitchells of the 345th Air Apaches landed at Ie Shima Air Base.

From the time the group arrived at Ie Shima on July 25th, the Black Panthers hoped to be a spear-head in the air war against the main islands of the Empire of Japan, but found themselves flying a series of what amounted to target practice sorties. The Japanese air forces didn't even show up to harass them. The Air Apaches were supposed to attack shipping and rail works on the islands of the Japanese Archipelago, but the weather had other plans. They were forced to divert to secondary, less significant targets such as lighthouses, towns, and bridges.

The 0500 mission briefing on August 1st involved a total of 24 crews from all four squadrons. Carl and his crew filed into the room expecting another uneventful assignment.

Col. Doolittle welcomed the selected crews and got down to business.

"Gentlemen, the break in the weather we have been hoping for is here. At last, our weather specialists have forecast clear to partly cloudy skies around Kyushu and Honshu islands. We're going to hit the harbors hard. The heavies will target the factories and industrial complexes inland. Your objective will be to destroy shipping in the harbors. Two squadrons, the 500th Rough Raiders and 501st Black Panthers will strike the main harbor at Kyushu. Your Group Leader will be Capt. Bridger, call name 'Apache Leader.' The 498th Falcons and 499th Bats Outta Hell will attack the southern port of the island of Honshu at Kudamatsu. Your Group Leader will be Maj. Benson, call name 'Falcon Leader.' Air cover will be provided by P-47 Thunderbolts of the 318th Fighter Group, but you can expect moderate to heavy anti-aircraft fire as well as aerial attacks. Because of fuel considerations, air cover will fall off 60 miles from the target. You will pick up air cover on your return leg at those same coordinates. Load-out will be four 500-pound demolition bombs each. Wheels up at 0700, gentlemen. God speed."

Carl led the attack on Kyushu in *Avenging Angel*. The two flights of three '25s of the 501st were Panther One and Panther Two respectively. The two flights of the 500th Bomb Squadron were Raider One and Raider Two. Capt. Albert Cummings led the Rough Raider contingent. His call sign was "Raider Leader."

The Thunderbolts arrived right on time. Flying above the formation of bombers, nine P-47s provided an umbrella of security. They flew on, unhindered, until they lost their air cover.

Eagle Lead to Apache Leader. It's time to bid you adieu, Apaches. Watch your six and good luck. We'll see you on the return. Over.

Copy, Eagle Leader. We've got it from here. Apache Leader, out.

Apache Leader to all planes. Our air cover is RTB. We're on our own. Charge your guns. I want someone on every turret. Look sharp.

Less than 20 minutes later, the harbor at Kyushu came into view. The sky around them began to be dotted with black bursts of deadly ack-ack. The high explosive 25 mm shells of the Type 96 anti-aircraft cannons were effective at ranges up to 7,000 yards. Each barrel had a firing rate of 110 rounds per minute. Most often they were set up in pairs or even three guns to each unit. The intensity of the A-A grew to a thick curtain of deadly air bursts.

"I see six vessels, Skipper: three in the harbor and three tied up at the docks. How do you want to do this?" Alex asked.

Apache Leader to all planes. The Panthers will hit the three ships at the docks. Raiders, hit the ones in the harbor, line-abreast formation ... mast height. Two bombs on the first run. Starting our run now.

380

Carl in A/P173, Lt. Raven in A/P062, and Lt. Jeans in A/P944 lined up on the left. Capt. Burg in A/P258, and Lt. Armistead in A/P014 and Lt. Mathews in A/P950, lined up on the right. With all six planes in line-abreast formation, they had the three merchant ships at the docks spread out in front of them.

Carl caught a glimpse of three of Al Cummings six Rough Raiders lining up on the Mogami-class cruiser at the mouth of the harbor. The other three Raiders knifed-in low toward a pair of Fubuki-class destroyers. Deck guns from all three war ships opened up on the bombers. With their bomb-bay doors open, the Mitchells streaked toward them 50 feet above the surface at nearly 300 mph.

Carl's Black Panthers vectored straight for the three merchant vessels.

"Bombs away!" Carl yelled. One sleeve of two 500-pound bombs dropped from beneath A/P173 and struck the water 75 yards abeam of the first ship, a Ukishina Maru-class armed merchant ship. The other Panthers dropped four more bombs. Carl's first bomb detonated in the water 10 yards shy of the ship's hull, but the second struck the ship's water line and exploded, rupturing the hull. Ordinance from the five other Panthers hit either ships or the docks. Multiple explosions boiled upward in red-orange plumes behind the bombers.

Carl banked left in a steep climbing turn to position the planes for a second pass. As they descended and lined up for their next run, the right wing of A/P258 burst into flame.

I'm hit! I'm hit! Panther Two Leader is on fire. Capt. Burg called out.

Continuing the attack, he shouted over the plane-to-plane frequency.

Carl watched Burg's plane as it released its two remaining bombs scoring direct hits on one vessel. The ammunition stored in the cargo hold ignited and an eye-popping blast encompassing most of the dock area erupted. With his plane burning, Burg angled toward one of the A-A emplacements and strafed the position with all eight of his .50 caliber forward-firing guns silencing the enemy fire. He began to bank right to head back out to the water when he got hit again by flak, and the left engine threw out a trail of flame and smoke. He was able to level the plane and tried to perform a controlled ditch. Carl knew the brave pilot never had a chance.

A single word came over the comm. ... *Damn!*

Panther Two Leader, this is Alpha Group Leader, do you copy?

There was no reply. Acting fast, Carl needed to assign a new Flight Leader for Panther Two.

Armistead, you're Flight Leader for Panther Two. You and Mathews choose your targets. We're taking out those A-A guns, Carl ordered.

The mission report would describe Burg's plane going into the water, skipping once, and then nosing in. The second impact broke the fuselage in two, and it filled with water trapping the men inside. Lt. Armistead, flying Burg's right wing, circled the crash site but saw no survivors.

The Black panthers went after the gun positions. A close air burst rocked *Avenging Angel* and a gaping hole appeared in the fuselage a foot behind Phil Ortiz' navigator position.

"Damage report!" Carl yelled. His eyes were wide with fear and intense determination. *Not us. Please, Lord, not us!*

"We're holed, Skipper. No other damage." Doc Henreid reported back.

Carl re-focused on the attack.

Apache Leader to all planes. One pass on those guns and we're done. Make it good, Panthers.

The anti-aircraft emplacements were in the hills behind the town. It wasn't difficult to spot their location; shell-bursts were all around and tracers arrowed toward them.

Whang! The wind screen next to Alex's head shattered. He

looked over at Carl and smiled.

"How the hell did that miss me?" Alex put his hand up to his head and then held it, dripping with blood and tissue, before his eyes.

"Oh, crap. I'm sorry, Skip ..." He slumped over, his unseeing eyes staring at the instrument panel.

Carl still had a job to do. The intensity of the battle demanded that his grief remain unanswered despite his torn heart.

Panther Two, break left. Hit that gun. Panther One, follow me. We'll take the other two in order.

Avenging Angel led A/P062 and A/P944 toward the two remaining gun emplacements. Working his rudder pedals, Carl zigzagged the bomber making it difficult for the enemy cannons to get a sight picture. All eight of *Angel's* nose guns rained down 6,400 rounds per minute of death and destruction on the first anti-aircraft installations, followed by another chorus each by Lt. Raven and Lt. Jeans. Carl banked hard right to bring the final pair of A-A cannons in front of him. His ring-sight held the Jap guns in the center and again, as before, the fiery spears of Zeus's revenge spewed forth death on the enemy below.

Form-up, Apaches. We are RTB.

Carl turned A/P173 onto a southwesterly heading away from the harbor. He took note of the three burning ships at the mouth of the inlet. He counted the Mitchells of the Rough Raiders forming up off his left wing ... five planes.

Apache Leader to Raider Leader, damage report! Carl called out.

Raider Leader to Apache Leader, we are down one plane. Three aircraft are holed. Two crewmen wounded aboard Alpha Papa Three-Zero Zero. Alpha Papa Zero Niner Niner collided with the bridge of the cruiser after being hit by deck fire.

Copy that, Raider Leader. The Panthers will lead

out in echelon-up formation. Tuck in close behind us. We should pick up our escort shortly.

Carl keyed the intercom.

"Pilot to crew. Stay alert for bogies. Our escort is on the way. Doc, I need you in the cockpit. Lt. Chekov has been hit."

Doc Henreid poked his head between the pilot and co-pilot's seat. The first thing he saw was the gaping hole in the wind screen in front of Chekov's head. The copilot was slumped over to the side ... motionless. His eyes took in the rest of the flight deck. Blood spatter covered the windscreen, instrument panel, and the right side of Carl's face, arm, and torso.

"Are you hurt, Skipper?"

"I'm uninjured, Doc. He's gone, isn't he?" Carl asked.

Doc put the tip of his finger to Alex's neck. He removed his hand and closed the co-pilot's eyes.

"Yes. I'll get Price to help me get the Lieutenant to the back of the plane, Skipper."

–August 2, 1945–

Carl sat on Alex's bunk looking through his friend's personal belongings: a few photos of his family and letters from them and his wife Charisse. Carl remembered that Charisse Chekov was pregnant with their first child. *You'll never get to see your child, Alex. I'm so very sorry, my friend.* The thought brought tears to his eyes which threatened to escape down his cheeks. He brushed them away with his sleeve.

"How do I tell them that they'll never see him again ... that he's dead?" Only the walls of the empty Quonset hut heard his plea. It was unanswerable by even those who had written many such letters to the families of the fallen heroes who died in the air and on the battlefields of nearly every continent on the planet. It would be a scar on his soul that would ever remind him of the unspeakably painful loss that the families of the fallen ... enemy and ally alike

... had to suffer, and which always left them with another unanswerable question; *what is the sense of it all?*

Two hours later, Carl carried a wrapped box containing Alex's most cherished mementoes from home, together with his personal letter to the family, to the base postal office in the Headquarters building. The rest of his belongings would be sent home by the Graves Registration unit.

Activity at Ie Shima slowed to a snail's pace. No bombing missions were flown after the raid on Kyushu that ended in the death of his friend. Carl was grateful for the three days of down time, but grew curious about the sudden inactivity. A few planes were sent out on search and recon missions over the Sea of Japan and the islands of the South China Sea, but that was all. The Officers' Club floated rumors including plans for an invasion of the main islands and Tokyo itself, and despite the relief at having a few days of R&R, there was a heavy air of anxious anticipation hanging over the base. Carl couldn't shake a sense of foreboding.

Chapter XVI

–Cascade, Montana–

At 5:30 p.m. on August 6, 1945, Annie was driving back to Cascade from Great Falls after visiting her parents for the weekend. The visit filled her heart with joy from good news on many fronts. Abe Petersen's promotion to Assistant Editor of the Great Falls area news bureau ended her parent's financial hardships. His new job of putting to bed every edition's news and events of the greater metropolitan Great Falls and surrounding areas brought with it a modest salary increase allowing Annie's parents to move in to a larger home and purchase a four-year-old Buick Roadmaster Sedan. An unexpected upturn in Abe's overall health brought an additional blessing to the Petersens. A third event, one that caused a mix of joy, uncertainty, and emotional conflict, came from their request to move Annie back home with them.

How can I be this happy and so conflicted at the same time? Whatever decision I make someone will be hurt. While the prospect of once again living with her parents warmed her heart, she had grown to love the Bridgers in the three years she lived at the Double-B. She knew that Carl's parents needed her help. She became an indispensable hand at every facet of ranch work as well as helping Gifford with managing the books. Annie proved herself a capable accountant.

She turned on the radio hoping that some music would take

her mind off the turmoil she was struggling with. Les Brown's "Sentimental Journey" filled the interior of the car. After a minute, the music abruptly stopped and the announcer came on the air.

> *We interrupt this program to join a special broadcast from the Whitehouse in Washington, D.C., where President Truman has spent the past several hours with his Secretaries of State and Defense as well as his Chiefs of Staff of the armed forces discussing the war in the Pacific. From the Oval Office, Ladies and Gentlemen, the President of the United States.*

A brief pause, during which muffled voices spoke in the background, peaked Annie's curiosity. She found her heart racing with a fear-edged anticipation. Finally, the President addressed the nation:

> *Sixteen hours ago an American airplane dropped one bomb on Hiroshima and destroyed its usefulness to the enemy. That bomb had more power than 20,000 tons of TNT. It had more than two thousand times the blast power of the British Grand Slam which is the largest bomb ever yet used in the history of warfare.*
>
> *The Japanese began the war from the air at Pearl Harbor. They have been repaid many fold. And the end is not yet. With this bomb we have now added a new and revolutionary increase in destruction to supplement the growing strength of our armed forces. In their present form these bombs are now in production and even more powerful forms are in development.*
>
> *It is an atomic bomb. It is a harnessing of the basic power of the universe. The force from which the sun draws its power has been loosed against those who brought war to the Far East.*

Avenging Angel

Annie pulled Gifford Bridger's '41 Ford pickup truck to the side of the road and set the emergency brake. Her heart was beating like a trip-hammer, and her breath came in rapid gasps as she listened to the rest of the President's speech.

> *We are now prepared to obliterate more rapidly and completely every productive enterprise the Japanese have above ground in any city. We shall destroy their docks, their factories, and their communications. Let there be no mistake; we shall completely destroy Japan's power to make war.*
>
> *It was to spare the Japanese people from utter destruction that the ultimatum of July 26 was issued at Potsdam. Their leaders promptly rejected that ultimatum. If they do not now accept our terms they may expect a rain of ruin from the air, the like of which has never been seen on this earth. Behind this air attack will follow sea and land forces in such numbers and power as they have not yet seen and with the fighting skill of which they are already well aware.*
>
> *The Secretary of War, who has kept in personal touch with all phases of the project, will immediately make public a statement giving further details.*

Annie's mind flooded with questions:

She shifted the pickup into first gear and sped onto the concrete surface of Highway 91 toward Cascade and the Double-B.

Twenty minutes later, Annie locked up the brakes and skidded to a stop in a cloud of dust at the back of the main house. She leapt from the truck and slammed open the screen door to the kitchen.

"Mom, Dad! Where are you?" she called.

Millie's voice, strained with excitement, called out, "We're in here, dear."

Annie entered the living room and found Gifford, Millie, and Penny sitting around the big Philco console radio.

She sat on the sofa next to Penny. "You heard the news. Does this mean an end to the war? Do you think Carl will be coming home soon?"

"I think we'll learn more in the next few days, Annie." Gifford spoke calmly. "The Japanese Empire hasn't surrendered yet, and Carl's unit is still likely to be flying missions. My guess is Japan isn't going to cave in to our demands after only one big bomb."

"We need to stay near the radio, honey. I'm sure there'll be more news soon. In the meantime, why don't you two come into the kitchen and help with dinner?" Annie had come to know Millie well enough to know her future mother-in-law always responded to important news, good or bad, with food. Cooking was her chief coping mechanism for dealing with the uncertainties of life. The Bridger women stood and went into the kitchen. She turned on the small table-top radio to KFBB and adjusted the volume. The station had returned to its regular program of music and commercial advertisements.

"I'll be out in the barn, Mother. Call me if you hear anything important." Gifford pushed open the screen door to the back porch, clomped down the three steps, and headed toward the barn.

Everyone resumed their work on the ranch, although the war never left their thoughts.

Two days passed. The radio news spoke of ultimatums being given to the Japanese and threats by the United States to drop more atomic bombs. The Emperor didn't budge from his stubborn and prideful position. Then, two things happened that forced the enemy to its knees: Russia formally declared war on Japan and invaded the Emperor's puppet nation of Manchukuo, and on August 9th a second atomic bomb was dropped on the city of Nagasaki. The announcements of those events were heard by Americans across the country. The war in the Pacific was at last grinding to a halt.

Avenging Angel

On the afternoon of August 15th, Gifford dropped a stack of mail on the kitchen table. A letter from Carl to the family was among the envelopes.

"Hey, everybody, we have mail from Carl. I'm in the kitchen." He called out.

Millie entered the kitchen from the living room. "Hurry and open it, Gifford. Don't keep us in suspense." Annie hurried downstairs from her bedroom. She looked around the room.

"Where's Penny?" She asked.

"Penny is at a church activity. She'll be home around seven o'clock," Millie explained. "She can read them later."

"Here goes …" Gifford removed the two sheets of writing and began to read. "It's dated August 2nd. The first bomb hadn't been dropped yet."

Dearest family and my beloved Annie,

How I pray this war will end soon. Yesterday, I lost my dear friend and co-pilot Alex Chekov. I have just finished writing a letter to his family, so forgive me if I am not in the most cheerful mood. We had a difficult mission, but we destroyed the target. However, we lost two crews and my own good friend and co-pilot. I pray that the killing will stop.

Writing to you and reading your letters are the two things that keep my sanity from fleeing my mind completely. I dream of happier days ahead for us all. I will say this: there is an air of anticipation in the Air Apaches that the intensity of the war is lessening. It's as though some event of a grand nature is about to happen ... that we are on the verge of seeing a sudden end to hostilities. I pray that such is the case.

Annie, I promise to come home to you soon, maybe

even before the end of the year. I love you, Annabeth Pe-
tersen ... with all of my heart and soul ... only forever, if you
care to know.
> *Until next time my dearest family. Pop, get my sad-*
dle ready, will you?
>> *Love,*
>> *Carl*

"That must have been a very difficult thing to do, writing to his friend's family." Gifford placed the letter back in the envelope and handed it to Millie.

"Our poor boy. He's gone through so much. The emotional scars ... the horrible memories he'll have to carry with him. I just pray he'll still be our Carl. Please, excuse me." Millie left the kitchen and retreated to her bedroom, weeping tears of sorrow and grief for her only living son.

–August 6, 1945–

Carl, Phil Ortiz, and a group of officers of the 501st Black Panthers were sitting in the Officers' Club discussing the four-day lull in missions. A few flights flew out on search and recon missions, but the Air Apaches remained unusually quiet. Other AAF units were more active; mostly the fighter units providing air cover for the heavies.

An enlisted man set up a microphone and placed a podium on the small raised platform used as a stage for the rare entertainment that the USO provided. He tapped the microphone and left. He was replaced by a Second Lieutenant, dressed in class "A"s who approached the raised stage against the far wall of the "O" Club. He wore no wings above his left breast pocket, and Carl correctly identified him as a command "gopher" ... a delivery boy for Col. Doolittle. The officer stepped up to the microphone.

"Officers of the 345th Bomb Group, listen up. A briefing

is scheduled for tomorrow morning at 0900 for all Air Apache personnel. Because of the large number expected, the briefing will be held in maintenance hangar number two. This briefing is for personnel of the 345th only. Other units can expect notification of similar briefings forthwith. That is all." The officer departed the club, ignoring the rumble of questions directed at him.

"So, what do you think that was all about, Skipper? I hope it's about more missions. I'd like to get back up there. Oh, and that begs the question ... we haven't talked about the replacement for Alex. We can't go anywhere without a co-pilot," Phil opined.

"You're right, Phil. I'll check with HQ tomorrow." Carl took a swallow of cold San Miguel and wiped his mouth on his sleeve. He nodded toward the stage. "Whatever that was, it's gotta be something big for the boss to call the whole group together. I think I'll head back to quarters." He drained his beer bottle and left.

The military relies on procedure and protocol for all decisions as well as for the dissemination of information, assignment of personnel and mission assignments. Generally, this structure facilitates rapid and accurate flow of information down through the ranks. For four days of relative inactivity to occur within a large organization such as the 345th Bombardment Group, without explanation, was highly unusual. At least for Carl, it gave reason for a flood of questions and speculation. He always did better in such circumstances when he chose a path of aggressive investigation and information gathering, but a sense of caution moved him to proceed with discretion.

Carl had become friends with Capt. Benjamin Green, a fellow pilot from North Dakota. Like Carl, Ben was a product of rural life in America ... hard working people of the land. Carl knew that Ben's family worked a large farm southeast of Fargo where they produced hearty winter wheat, barley, and sugar beets.

He needed to talk to Ben Green, but not about farming and

not about flying. Capt. Green filled dual roles for the Air Apaches ... those of pilot and Intelligence Officer. It was the latter of those two roles that caused Carl to seek him out. *If anyone below the rank of bird colonel knows what all of the secrecy is about, it'll be Ben.* He grabbed his service hat and walked to the HQ building. He checked his chronometer ... 1845 hrs. "Okay, Ben, if something's going on, you'll be here," he said under his breath.

He walked into an office abuzz with activity. The energy in the intelligence office was palpable. Every typewriter was clattering and spitting out reports of one kind or another. Clerks scurried about carrying memoranda from office to office. Voices chattered at a heightened level of excitement. Radio dispatches sent runners from the communications center to the War Room in a steady stream. The activity was on the level of organized frenzy.

"Excuse me, Sergeant." Carl smiled at an attractive WAF S/Sgt. sitting at a desk typing the text of a radio dispatch in plain language for later review by the intelligence people.

"Yes, sir. How can I help you?" the Sergeant said without breaking the pace of her typing while keeping her eyes glued to the dispatch. Her fingers flew over the keyboard at a feverish pace.

Carl lowered his voice to a conspiratorial level and whispered, "I need to speak to Capt. Ben Green on a matter of urgency."

"I'm sorry, but Capt. Green and the Intelligence staff are in a meeting." The Sergeant replied without making eye contact with Carl.

He took a chance and changed his tactic. "Sergeant, please look at me. I must see Capt. Green now! It is a matter of extreme importance concerning what those men in that room are discussing while you are filling that page with data that's probably going to be old news before it's ever read by the man to whom it's addressed. Now, if you prefer, I will walk into that room myself and stop whatever those officers are doing, or you can discreetly poke your head in there and get Capt. Green out here ... *now*." He glared at the woman with a fixed gaze that would freeze alcohol.

"Yes, sir." The noncom pushed herself away from her desk, stood up, smoothed her khaki uniform skirt and walked to the door marked *Operations, 345th Bombardment Group.* When the door opened, Carl caught a glimpse of a familiar face. He remembered Col. Marion Cooper from the awards ceremony at San Marcelino back in March when Carl was awarded the Distinguished Flying Cross. Col. Cooper was General Ennis Whitehead's Chief of Staff. What's he doing here? Carl wondered. *If the CO of 5th Bomber Command is in the loop, something big is being planned.*

Capt. Green approached Carl with his hand extended. "Hey there, Carl, what's got your skivvies in a knot that's so important?"

"C'mon outside. We need to talk." He didn't wait for his friend to ask *why* as he strode quickly toward the door.

"Ben, I'm sorry to pull you away from such an important meeting, but I need for you to tell me what's going on in there, and what the big briefing in the morning is all about. The guys are going nuts with speculation. We've been ordered to stand down from further missions, and it's driving us all crazy."

Ben laughed. "Whoa, there, pard'! Slow down." He paused, and his eyes scanned around as if checking for listening ears. "Okay. You're going to hear about this tomorrow after the fact anyway. What I'm going to tell you, you can't repeat to anyone."

Carl nodded. "Sure ... okay ... sealed lips, I promise."

"I'm not kidding, Carl. I could be court-martialed if anyone finds out I told you." Ben shifted from one foot to the other nervously.

"Wow. Okay, maybe I shouldn't have asked. I'm sorry. Keep it to yourself." Carl turned to walk away, but Ben stopped him.

"Wait! Okay, I will give you my best guess without spilling the beans. Something big is going to happen tomorrow that will stop the Japs in their tracks. Keep your mouth shut ... got it?" Ben

Green turned and walked back into the Headquarters building.

Ben's cryptic comment caused even more questions to press on Carl's mind … *What one thing could end the war so abruptly? … Invasion? What?* An all-out invasion would take weeks to bring the enemy to full surrender. It would take something of a cataclysmic nature to bring the machinery of the Japanese Empire's might to a sudden stop as his friend suggested. A bomb! That's got to be it. "Holy crap!" Carl yelped. He practically ran back to the Officers' Club.

"Skipper! You're back!" Phil Ortiz grinned. He looked more closely at Carl. "Hey, you look like you've seen a ghost. What gives?"

"Huh? … Oh, nothing. How about passing me that pitcher, I could use a cold one ... or three." Carl laughed nervously and filled a mug with foaming chilled beer. "A toast, gentlemen; to a rapid and decisive victory!"

Chapter XVII

–Change of Mission–

Col. Glenn Doolittle approached the microphone stand which was set up on a quickly constructed dais. A half-dozen chairs behind the podium were filled by the four squadron commanders of the 345th Bombardment Group, Col. Doolittle's XO, and the Deputy Commander of 5th Bomber Command, Col. Marion Cooper.

"Good morning, Air Apaches!" Col. Doolittle announced. He was immediately greeted by the voices of 2,000 men and women as they called out a hearty "Good morning, sir!"

He cleared his throat, and after shuffling a few papers, spoke in a subdued tone:

"This morning, about one hour ago, a weapon of unspeakable power was released upon the Empire of Japan on the island of Hiroshima. A bomb equaling an explosive force in excess of 20 kilotons of TNT was dropped from high altitude by a B-29. The bomb was a nuclear bomb or "Atom Bomb," the science of which employs the splitting of atoms in a process called nuclear fission. While assessment of the damage by the bomb is ongoing, it is estimated that the large military complex and surrounding area will suffer an initial loss of life in excess of 80,000 people. Many more, perhaps an equal number, are expected to die in coming days, weeks, and months.

"I am authorized to inform you that the mission of the Air Apaches has changed. Until further notice, squadrons will participate in search and patrol missions of the coastal areas around Japan's southern shores. Your planes will continue to be armed, but you will not be assigned specific bombing targets. In short, gentlemen, we are to show our presence, but refrain from engaging the enemy unless directly fired upon.

"Furthermore, we will be reducing the combat role of the 345th with an eye toward rotating some crews back to the States on extended leave. Those personnel who have flown the most missions and have been awarded commendations for gallantry, or wounds received in combat, will be given first priority. We anticipate this reduction in force will begin as soon as three weeks from now.

"We are still at war, men. You are all expected to remain ever vigilant and attend to your duties with complete professionalism reflecting honor in all that you do."

–August 9, 1945–

Three days later, Carl and his crew were getting antsy for some action. Even "Search and Patrol" was preferable to sitting around doing nothing. *Avenging Angel* still didn't have a co-pilot, which left Carl and his crew being assigned crew relief duty for other crews. He found himself in the less desirable position of flying occasional patrol missions to give other pilots some down time. He flew left seat on some, and on others as co-pilot. The majority of these milk-run missions were flown by crews junior to himself with less time in theatre and fewer missions under their belt.

At 1100 hrs, a coded dispatch was received by the Communications Center and delivered directly to Col. Glenn Doolittle. He thanked his aide and removed the classified message from its sealed envelope.

"Jack, I need to meet with all of the squadron commanders ASAP. Another bomb has been dropped; this time on Nagasaki. Also, the Russians have declared war on the Japs and are invading Manchukuo as we speak." Lt. Col. Jack Kinnion sent runners out to the essential personnel, and within 20 minutes they were all seated in Col. Doolittle's office.

News of the second bomb brought cheers in every building and hangar on Ie Shima.

Carl was in his quarters writing a letter to his family when he heard a commotion of shouts and celebration approaching from outside. He put down his pencil and ran to the door just as Mike O'Hanlon pushed it open.

"Hey, Carl, it looks like it may be all over. Another 'A' bomb has been dropped, this time on Nagasaki."

Carl joined in on the back slapping and allowed himself to be taken along by the growing crowd of revelers trooping toward the Officers' Club. It was a time for celebration, but it was also a time of conflicted loyalties: go home to the safety of family and an easy chair or look for another windmill to tilt ... another cause to fight or die for.

August 9, 1945
– Cascade, Montana –

Slowly, following the end of war in Europe and the armistice that brought about VE day on May 8, 1945, the American agricultural and industrial complex began to breathe a little easier. It wasn't a joyous all-out celebration of final victory, for the war continued in the Pacific. But, the winds of war ebbed, and a bright line of dawning victory rose which pushed back the dark night of war against Japan. It was not the sacred rising sun of Hirohito's empire that turned night to day, but the morning sun of a new day of peace. For many Americans it meant the return of some long-awaited commodities on the shelves of the corner grocery store. Sugar was staging a comeback ... and butter. Gasoline rationing, though still in effect, was relaxing as fuel and petroleum products gradually became more available.

Gene C. Bozeman, owner of the Rocking-C brand up in Teton County, pulled into the gravel driveway of the Double-B and shut off the engine to his 1940 Dodge half-ton green pickup. He and a handful of ranchers from Cascade, Teton, and Lewis and Clark counties were discussing setting up a cattlemen's association to co-op out services and equipment in order to reduce the rising costs of maintaining a large cattle ranch. On the agenda, too, was the need to build some influence over beef prices. Small ranchers wanted to remain competitive with larger beef producers. Government regulation of the industry took a stronger hold over such issues as disease control, regulation and standardization of food quality and market pricing. There arose a growing need for ranchers and farmers alike to band together in a move to gain some influence over the increasing burden of government regulation. Gene was in more of a hurry than the occasion called for, however, due to a radio announcement he had heard on the way to the Bridger place. He practically sprinted to the front door of the main house, no small feat for a man soon to turn 64 who, two years before, had broken his back in three places after being run up against the side of a loading chute by an upset breeding bull.

Millie heard loud banging on the screen door. Wiping her dishwater-wet hands on her apron, she greeted Gene and invited him in.

"Where's Gifford? Have you heard the news?" he gasped, trying to catch his breath.

"He's out in the barn. What's got you so fired up, Gene? Why, you're all out of breath. Now you just sit yourself down at the kitchen table, and let me pour you a nice glass of iced tea." Millie fetched three glasses from the cupboard as Gifford came in through the back door. Gene stood up.

Gifford took one look at Bozeman and noted his flushed complexion and rapid breathing.

"Well now, Gene, has this meeting got you so excited that you had to run all the way here?" He laughed. "You're early. The other boys won't be here for another 10 minutes."

"I always like to be early to these things, Gifford. I don't believe in making folks wait on me ... too much to do other than wastin' time sittin' around for some darned fool man that can't show up when he's supposed to. It's a good thing I'm here, though. Did you two hear the news?"

Giff looked at Millie who shrugged her shoulders. "No, what news, Gene?"

"Another atom bomb was dropped on a city called Nagasaki. At the same time, the Russians have declared war on Japan. Gifford, this has to mean that the Japs are going to surrender, doesn't it?"

Gifford looked at Millie, eyes wide with amazement. "It would seem so. Let's go in the living room and turn the radio on. I want to hear more about this."

Soon, three more ranchers had joined them, and the purpose of the meeting gave way to more news updates and a long discussion the main topic of which was centered on one question: When will our boys be coming home?

Aug. 15, 1945
–Ie Shima, Okinawa–

Six days after the Emperor of Japan ordered his Supreme Council for the Direction of the War to accept the Allied terms for surrender, Hirohito recorded an announcement to his people ordering the cessation of all hostilities in order to "pave the way for a grand peace." He directed the citizenry and the military to remain calm in order to prevent any complications during the transition to peace.

Carl felt certain the war was over, at least insofar as target-directed missions were concerned. Since Hirohito's announcement ordering the end of aggression, there were no more targets to attack.

The stress of flying into the face of death every day ... of preparing himself and his men to charge into the breach of battle, was lifted ... removed in a twinkling of the eye. The occasional Search and Patrol sorties produced no threat to his safety, nor were they fraught with the constant looming emotional conflict of making decisions that he knew would end many lives. The inevitable clash between the strong moral conviction that punctuated his upbringing and the turpitude of war that tore at the fabric of his soul after so many missions, and after so much loss of life, was gone. As if waking from a nightmare, he found his mind turning away from the night terrors of blood, ack-ack, and death to thoughts of Annie ... and home. Home ... *Yes, I'm going to go home. It's really over!*

He opened the drawer of the small table next to his bunk, sharpened a pencil with his pocket knife and began to write:

> *Dearest Annie, Mom and Dad, and Penny,*
>
> *It's over! No more bombing missions, no more death, no more fearing that I might never get back to my family.*
>
> *I assume you have been kept informed of Japan's announced surrender by their Emperor. Since the end of hostilities, we have been flying nothing but non-combat search and patrol sorties to make certain that the Japanese military are minding their Ps and Qs. I don't know when I'll be home, but it looks like we will be sharing Christmas as a family. I can't wait. I wish I could climb into "Avenging Angel" right now and come straight home.*
>
> *It's strange. It seems like I've been here forever. On one hand, I feel like I'm ten years older than when I left the ranch. But, then I remember that only last Christmas, Annie, you and I cut down the tree, and we all decorated it. Can we do that this year?*
>
> *I'll let you know more about when we'll all be com-*

ing home as soon as we hear from the powers that be.

*I thank God that we've made it through together, to
see the end of this terrible war.*

I love you all - Carl

*P.S. Annie, our love for each other has been the one
thing that has always given me hope. I love you and will
love you ... only forever, if you care to know.*

He addressed and sealed the envelope and was about to take
the letter over to the mail room when a knock came at his door. He
opened it and recognized a clerk from the Group HQ.

"Oh, hello, Corporal. What can I do for you.?" Carl asked.

"I'm sorry to disturb you, sir, but Col. Doolittle wants to
see you ASAP, in the briefing room. I have to notify several other
flight crews as well."

"Do you know what this is all about, Corporal?"

"No idea, sir. It's all very hush-hush. If you will excuse me,
sir, I need to get the word out." He didn't wait for Carl's response
and left to continue his rounds.

Twenty minutes later, Col. Glenn H. Doolittle stood before
the crews of five B-25s.

"Men, if you look around you, you will see that there are
five crews present. You are five of the best Mitchell crews in the
345th Air Apaches. There is not a single man among you that has
not been awarded at least one air medal for gallantry. You exemplify
the very best of this unit and the 5th Bomber Command. I say this
because you have been chosen to fly with me on one final mission.

"Tomorrow, two Japanese airplanes, Mitsubishi GM-4
"Betty" Bombers carrying the Japanese surrender envoy and other
dignitaries, will depart from a Japanese air base near China at 0715
hrs on a heading to Ie Shima. Thirty-six P-38 Lightnings from the
347th Fighter Group will provide high air cover and six of our
Mitchells will escort the Bettys into Ie Shima. When we intercept

403

them just off the southern coast of the island of Kyushu, two of the five flights, designated Apache Two and Apache Three, will break formation and fly point back to Ie Shima scouting for trouble along our flight path. Capt. Bridger of the 501st squadron will lead Apache Two, and Capt. Sam Ellsworth of the 500th Squadron will lead Apache Three. I will fly right seat with Maj. Jack McClure of the 498th squadron in Apache One as Flight Leader. Apache One wing will be Maj. Wendell Decker of the 499th Squadron.

Carl was given the opportunity to choose the co-pilot to fly with him in *Avenging Angel*. He immediately thought of Mike O'Hanlon and found his young friend at the "O" Club sitting with a group of officers at a table in the middle of the room. Music was blaring from a portable record player that was piping Glenn Miller's "Pennsylvania 6-5000" over the loud speakers. Carl walked over to O'Hanlon's table.

"Hi ya boys, mind if I pull up a chair?" Carl grabbed an empty chair from another table and slid it up next the Mike.

"Hey, Carl. Haven't seen you for a few days. You look like you're happy about something. Care to share?"

"Well, I have a favor to ask you, Mike. I'm in need of a co-pilot to help me out on an escort mission. It's kind of an important assignment ... interested?"

"Right seat? Huh. Gee, I don't know, Carl. What's so danged important about some escort mission? I like you Carl, but flying co-pilot's sort of a demotion to my way of thinking."

"We'll be escorting a pair of Jap Bettys to Ie Shima. They'll be carrying the Japanese surrender envoys. From here, they'll hop on a C-54 to Manila and then be taken out to the USS Missouri where they will meet with General McArthur to sign the formal surrender papers. You interested?"

"Well heck yes! Why didn't you say so to begin with? So, this is it, then ... the war is really over? Wow! Raise your drinks, boys. It looks like we'll all be going home!" Mike raised his own mug. Carl lifted a half-full pitcher of beer and joined in the cheer.

"Turning one." The starboard three-bladed Hamilton propeller began to turn, and the engine fired up. Mike O'Hanlon adjusted the throttle, set the mixture and watched as the rpm needle settled on the 1200 rpm mark.

"Turning two." Carl called out. The left engine came to life with a belch of smoke and settled into a matching idle. A minute or so later the needles of the oil and cylinder-head temperatures were pointed in the green normal operating range.

Carl keyed the transmit button and called in.

Apache Two Lead to wing, follow me to the runway. Apache One is airborne.

Apache Two left wing to Lead, I'm right behind you, Carl. Capt. Strauss, at the controls of Lucky Bat acknowledged.

Nose to tail, the two Mitchells taxied to the runway. Carl led the way as he throttled up, and *Avenging Angel* roared down the centerline.

Apache Leader to all flights, we'll intercept the Bettys off the southern coast of Kyushu, 700 miles north of Ie Shima. Apache Two and Apache Three will then proceed back to Ie Shima ahead of the main group to scout for anything suspicious. We're not sure there won't be a kamikaze attempt on the formation, so we need you boys to run interference. Acknowledge?

Apache Two. Roger.

Apache Three. Roger.

The six American bombers flew on for another two hours, when Col. Doolittle called in the sighting of two aircraft flying underneath heavy air cover.

Apache Leader to all planes, two Bettys sighted at our 12 o'clock. Right on schedule. Apache Two and Apache

Three, break off and return to base."
Apache Two. Roger. Breaking off now.

Carl banked *Avenging Angel* away from the main group. He checked off his right wing to make certain Capt. Straus was tucked in close. Apache Three, led by Capt. Ellsworth maintained position behind and to the right of Apache Two.

"Pilot to crew. I guess this is the last big hurrah, boys. Once we land back at base, I reckon we'll all be grounded. It's been an honor serving with you men. Harry, Doc, and Phil, we've been together since the beginning, and I am privileged to call you my friends. Wendell, you stepped in and filled some mighty big shoes. Mike, you've been there during some pretty dark times. You are a heck of a pilot. You men have all become … well … nothing short of 'family' to me. What do you say we scrounge up some beers and hit the beach after we land? I feel like celebrating."

"Roger that, Skipper. I'm in," Harry Osborne said from the tail.

"I'm there already," Doc Henreid affirmed.

About 60 miles from Ie Shima, Mike O'Hanlon nudged Carl and pointed toward their three o'clock position.

"What's that, Carl … are they ours?"

Carl looked in the direction Mike was pointing. A formation of seven airplanes was heading toward Ie Shima. They were green and bearing the red rising sun emblem.

Apache Two Leader to all planes, bogeys at 3 o'-clock low. Throttle up to intercept. Staggered-line formation!

"They're 'Judys', Carl. Two-man crews. Dive bombers. I don't see any armament, though. What are they doing way out here?" Mike O'Hanlon asked.

"I don't know," Mike, but I'm not going to wait around to find out.

Gunners, charge your guns. We're going to put the

sun behind us and then drop down on them. Apache Three, follow us in. I'm aiming for the lead plane.

Apache Three Leader to Apache Two. We're right behind you.

Avenging Angel dropped her nose and winged over into a steep dive. Three Mitchells followed suit. Before the Japanese pilots knew what hit them, the American bombers were on them, guns blazing. One Judy exploded in a disproportionately large and violent burst of flame. A second plane lost a wing and spiraled down after being raked by Capt. Ellsworth's eight .50 caliber machine guns.

Carl's target must have seen him coming, because just as Carl was about fire his nose guns, the plane executed a perfect Immelmann maneuver.

"Harry, he's going to get a firing resolution on me in a few seconds. When he does, I'll throttle all the way back and force him to close-in on our tail. That's when you nail him with your .50s."

"Copy, Skipper. I'm ready."

Carl didn't try to outrun or out maneuver the faster and more agile enemy fighter-bomber. Instead, he waited until the "Judy" dropped in behind him. He throttled all the way back and put the bomber into a steep climb as his airspeed quickly dropped off. He added full flaps as the enemy plane rocketed toward him. Harry had him in his sites and squeezed the levers of the twin ANM-2 .50 caliber machine guns. Both 3.3 mm guns of the enemy plane opened up, but the tracers were wide and right. The pilot immediately applied left rudder, but before the tracers found the target, his aircraft burst into flames. It nosed toward a remote beach two miles from the harbor that held three American ships: a destroyer and two destroyer escorts.

"Great shooting, Harry. Let's go home."

"Skipper, I think they were loaded with high explosives the way that one exploded back there. I'm thinking kamikaze."

"Roger that, Harry. Likely some die-hards trying to sabotage the official surrender ... nuts."

Apache Two Leader to all planes, form up. It looks like the other bogeys have had enough and are headed back to Japan. We are RTB.

The four B-25s of Apache Two and Apache Three flew on to Ie Shima without further incident.

Avenging Angel had prevented a devastating kamikaze attack. The charred body of Vice Admiral Matome Ugaki was found and identified several days later. It was learned after the war ended, that Ugaki had organized one last kamikaze attack, as his suicide letter stated, "… to sink the ships of the arrogant Americans."

Carl and his crew sat in the shade of *Avenging Angel's* wings. It was a clear and hot mid-August day. Above them, vectoring for a landing, two "Betty" Bombers flew over the field flanked by the two B-25s of Apache One. The Bettys were painted white with green crosses on the fuselage signifying surrender. The Japanese planes, similar in appearance to the American B-26, dropped out of formation and entered their downwind approach. First one and then the other landed and taxied to parking. The crew doors opened, and the Japanese dignitaries de-planed followed by the crews. As protected guests of the 5th Air Force, the crews would remain at Ie Shima where they would be well treated under the watchful eyes of an armed security detail until the dignitaries returned from the USS Missouri four days later for their flight back to Tokyo.

The morning of August 21st, Carl enjoyed a cold shower and dressed in his flight overalls in anticipation of another milk-run mission patrolling the South China Sea for die-hard Japanese shipping, particularly warships that might require closer scrutiny by those in command. Since Hirohito's radio announcement to his subjects on August 15th, the Japanese armed forces had shown no signs of renewing hostilities. The regular patrol missions, though necessary, were boring and routine. The emotional winding down and healing had begun after months of intense combat and fearing for one's life and the lives of one's "brothers".

Carl strode over to the Base Operations building to check the mission roster for his name and was surprised to find another crew had been assigned to fly the *Angel* on a patrol of the southern coast of Kyushu. He was about to leave the Operations building for the Officers' Club, when Lt. Horace Kingston called his name. Carl turned and looked in the direction of the voice. He recognized the young officer as the same one who had made the announcement at the "O" Club a few days earlier of the big briefing about the atom bomb drop on Hiroshima.

"What is it, Lieutenant, uh, Kingston," Carl asked, noting the name tag above the right pocket of the lieutenant's jacket.

"I have some orders for you and several other flight crews. If you don't mind, sir, I'll give yours to you."

Carl took the manila envelope back to his quarters and sat on the edge of his bunk. Anxious, he squeezed the tabs of the fastener together, lifted the flap, and withdrew the orders.

"Oh, dear Lord!" Carl yelped. He continued reading ... *furlough ... 45 days ... report to redistribution center, Santa Ana Army Air base ...*

"What's all the excitement, Carl? Lt. Alan Gross heard Carl's loud exclamation from four lockers down the row, and walked over to him.

"I'm going home, Al. I'm going home!"

"When, Carl? My gosh! You just won the lucky draw. I knew they were going to start rotating crews stateside. Man, you are a lucky dog!" Abe pounded his back. "I've only been in-country two months. I'll probably have to wait a couple of months before

I get to go home."

"Tomorrow … I leave tomorrow!" He stood and hugged the young pilot before running out of the Quonset hut toward the Officers' Club to find out if anyone he knew got their furlough orders.

Carl stood in front of the nose of *Avenging Angel*. He was dressed in his service flight overalls with his "crush" cap atop his head and stood next to his duffel bag which he had lowered to the ground. Harry Osborne, "Doc" Henreid, Phil Ortiz, and Wendell Price stood with him. This would be the last time they would stand together as a crew.

"I'll miss this old bird." Harry stroked one blade of the left propeller. "She's seen us through some rough times, eh, Skipper?"

"Indeed she has, Harry. I'll miss her, too. After leave, I'll be going to Tokyo for the occupation. I don't think any of us will see the *Angel* again."

"At least you, Lt. Ortiz, Harry, and I will be going home at the same time, Skipper." Sgt. Henreid checked his watch. "The plane leaves in an hour. We'd better load up."

"Hold on, guys." Harry reached into one of the large pockets of his coveralls and withdrew a Brownie camera. "This is Zed's old Brownie. What do say we get a group picture?"

"That's a swell idea, Harry. Hold on …" Harry whistled at a mechanic standing nearby. "Hey, Mac, c'mon over here, will ya?"

"Yeah, what do you want, Sarge?" the mechanic asked.

"I need for you to take a picture of all of us standing in front of *Avenging Angel*. Here's the camera. It's ready to go. Just point and shoot."

The mechanic returned the camera to Harry.

Carl shouldered his duffel bag. "Well, boys, it's been quite a ride. Wendell … keep in touch. One year from today, I want us to all get together for a reunion. You have to promise me that we won't lose track of each other … that's an order, and I want a copy of that photo, Harry." Carl chuckled. The laughter belied the emotion that welled in each other's hearts. "So long … 'till then."

"For sure, Skipper. We're brothers, after all." Phil Ortiz embraced Carl.

Forty-five minutes later, Carl, Phil Ortiz, Doc, and Harry, boarded the C-54 that would take them to Guam, then to Hickam Field on Oahu. From there, they would fly straight to Santa Ana, California. With any luck, Carl hoped to be in Annie's arms by August 27th.

Chapter XVIII

–The Journey Home–

Since leaving Ie Shima, Carl had been shuffled from plane to car, to plane again, until, on August 27th, he found himself stepping off another C-54 transport at the Great Falls Army Air Base. His duffel bag would be offloaded at the small passenger terminal adjacent to the Flight Operations Office. He walked into the familiar passenger lounge. The last time he had been in this building was in early December, 1944, a little more than eight months ago. He sat down on a smooth hardwood bench and waited for his bag. *Eight months ago?* It seems like it's been eight years, he reflected, looking around the room.

A cart full of duffel bags and suitcases was rolled into the terminal. Carl pulled his bag from the pile and headed for the men's room. He removed his shaving kit from the duffel and stood in front of a mirror over a wash basin and began cleaning himself up.

Ten minutes later, feeling … and smelling much fresher, Carl changed into his class-A dress uniform with the drab shade 54 "pink" pants. He knotted his tie, picked up his bag and headed for the Flight Operations office and a telephone. He had not had an opportunity to call his family since leaving Ie Shima and couldn't wait to hear their voices.

A burly Master Sergeant sat at a desk outside the Duty Officer's office. He was riding herd on a half-dozen clerk typists. They were busy at their desks typing up various dispatches, manifests and other documents needed for the efficient operation of the

Air Transport Command's C-54s that shuttled in and out of the large air base 24 hours per day.

The Master Sergeant looked up at Carl. "What can I do ya for, Cap ... he started to say before he froze in mid-sentence. "Well, I'll be roped and tied! Lt. Bridger!" The man snapped to attention and threw a salute worthy of a West Point cadet. Carl returned the salute with equal zeal.

"Captain, now, but who's counting?" Carl smiled. "It's good to see you again, Sgt. Blysdale. I wonder if I might use your phone. I'd like very much to call my family. I'm just in from the Pacific ... Ie Shima."

"You're welcome to use my phone, Captain, but ..." Blysdale checked his watch. "... the four o'clock Greyhound for Helena stops just down the road from the main gate. If we get a move on, we should be able to get you there in time to catch a ride."

"Excellent! I'm much obliged, Sergeant."

Sgt. Blysdale stepped around to the front of his desk. He turned to a corporal sitting two desks down from his own. "Cpl. Underwood, take charge. I'll be back in 15 minutes." The two men left the Ops Center and climbed into an olive green Chevy motor pool car.

Carl looked around the interior of the car. "This looks familiar."

"It should. I've been driving this same old bucket for going on two years now. Last time you sat in her it was a freezing night. This old girl has never failed to start up regardless of the weather."

Ten minutes later the Chevy ground to a stop with a spray of gravel in front of the bus station. The bus was in the process of loading up.

"Follow me, Captain. I'll get you on, don't you worry." Blysdale sauntered up to the Greyhound driver who was supervising the loading of luggage in the storage bins underneath the chassis.

"Hey there, partner. You got an extra seat for a bonafide

war hero? He needs to get to Cascade."

The driver looked at Sgt. Blysdale and then gave Carl the once over. "Well, hell yes, he can ride on my bus. Climb aboard, Captain. It's an honor to have you aboard. We're almost full, but I have a couple of extra seats."

"Thank you, sir. I really appreciate this." Carl released his grip on the duffel bag when the man took it from him and loaded it in with the rest of the bags. He turned to the portly cigar-smoking noncom.

"Sgt. Blysdale, it was good to see you again. You've been a great help."

The two men exchanged salutes. Carl climbed aboard content to leave the driving to Greyhound. As he worked his way toward an empty seat about half-way down the aisle, a young woman began to clap her hands. Soon, everyone on the bus was applauding and whistling. Carl stood still, looking at the men, woman, and children who applauded him. He was truly at a loss for words. He nodded his gratitude and sat down for the half-hour ride to Cascade.

He let his eyes drink in the familiar hills and distant snow-capped mountains as they drifted past the window. Many times over the past eight months he wondered if he would ever again see the fertile farm and ranch land of his youth. He lifted his head and focused on a cowhand sitting astride a roan quarter-horse, slapping his chaps with his lariat, as he herded a stray back toward the main herd of Angus beef cattle about a quarter-mile in the distance. Carl pictured his dad, Annie, and Penny doing the same thing up in the summer range northeast of the Double-B. The bus pulled into Cascade across the street from the Bailey Motel and Restaurant.

"This will do just fine. My family lives down the road a short piece." Carl stepped down onto the pavement ... at last his feet were on Cascade land.

He allowed his eyes to take in the small once-booming railroad town. In 1890, at its peak of activity, Cascade boasted

52 businesses including a grain elevator, tailor shops, General store and Mercantile, restaurants, saddler, newspaper, hotel, 11 saloons, and many more. In 1940, the last census counted only 417 residents within the .57 square-mile city limits and fewer than half the number of businesses of 1890. Of course, that number did not take into consideration the flourishing farm and cattle industries and the people who lived and worked beyond the town limits.

Carl slung his duffle bag over his shoulder and started walking toward the entry road which led a quarter-mile up a gravel drive to his family's ranch. The high gate straddling the road had a large three-foot by seven-foot plank of wood hanging from a pair of chains, with the words DOUBLE-B RANCH boldly burned into the wood.

Annie was sweeping and dusting the living room while Millie busied herself in the kitchen preparing the evening meal of roast chicken, mashed potatoes with cream gravy, garden green beans, homemade rolls and currant preserves. Fresh cold milk from the ice box would top off the repast.

Annie had the blinds up and the curtains pulled to the side to let the late afternoon sunlight into the room. She never grew tired of the view beyond the window. The neatly cared for white fence that led down the gravel drive to the main road and then extended for a good two hundred yards in either direction communicated order and proudly showed claim of the Double-B to the largest cattle ranch within 1,000 square miles. A lone figure walked along the fence toward the main entrance. *A soldier ... coming home ... probably lives up the road a ways*, she thought. A pang of loneliness hit her, then. *Oh, Carl, where are you my darling? When will you come home to me?* She wiped her tearing eyes and returned to her work. She couldn't resist looking at the lone traveler one more time. The man stopped in front of the gate and stood staring at the placard hanging above him. Annie's heart jumped. Then, the man started toward the main house.

"Oh, my dear God in Heaven!" Annie yelled at the top of her voice. She dropped the sweeper and threw open the front door. "It's Carl! He's home!" She yelled back over her shoulder as she flew down the steps and sprinted toward him.

"Annie!" Carl yelled. He dropped his duffel bag onto the drive and ran to his beloved fiancé. "Annie!" he called again. They flew into each other's arms.

Carl buried his face in Annie's shoulder. "Annie, my Annie! I'm here ... home at last."

Annie held him with all of her strength, her body trembling. "Oh, Carl. I can't believe this. How I have missed you!" She sobbed, nearly unable to speak, unable to loosen her grip on Carl. He swept her up in his arms and walked the rest of the way to the house. The front door flew open and Millie and Penny dashed onto the porch. Carl allowed himself to be hugged and fussed over. With Annie still in his arms, he nudged the door open with his toe and stepped into the living room where he lowered Annie to her feet.

"Your father had to drive up to Helena for some fencing and a few things. He should be home any minute. Take your jacket off and come into the kitchen, son. I'll cut you a nice big slice of my bread with butter and honey and pour you a big glass of milk. Just like when you were a boy." Millie grinned broadly, leading the way to the kitchen.

"Thanks, Mom. I can't think of any better treat than that. I've dreamed about this very moment every day for the past year." For a moment, the war, Charlie and Alex's death, the bombing and strafing ... the fear and nightmarish horror of war, were forgotten. Then, it all came screaming back into his mind ... vivid and terrifying. Carl covered his face with trembling hands, leaned against the wall for support, and began to sob. As if seeing and understanding the spinning cascade of gut-wrenching terror going on in his mind, Annie gently pulled his hands away from his face. Her heart nearly broke at the anguish and torture written there. She pulled Carl's head to her breast and rocked him. He wept in great trembling sobs, pouring out the agony, fear, and anger that had punctuated every day of the past eight months. Finally, after a couple minutes, he began to calm down. He took the dish towel that Penny offered him and wiped his face before blowing his nose into it.

"Well, I guess this is ready for the hamper," he said sheepishly and handed the towel back to Penny.

"Eeeuuuu! She said with a look of disgust as she carried the soiled towel between her thumb and forefinger to the hamper. She glanced back over her shoulder with an impish expression of delight. "Just kidding, big brother," she laughed.

Annie and Millie poured cups of coffee for everyone, and they all sipped the brew in silence. Finally, Carl spoke.

"It's okay you guys. *I'm* okay. The trembling started about three months after I landed at Tacloban. It only hits me when things get too stressful." Carl stood up from the table. "The war is over and there aren't any enemy fighters trying to knock me out of the sky. I expect I'll be fine after a few days of being home. For now, I'd better go outside and grab my duffel bag."

"Ya mean this duffel bag, son?" A beaming Gifford Bridger stood in the kitchen doorway with Carl's olive drab duffel bag sitting on the floor beside him. "Welcome home, son!" Gifford opened his arms and Carl stepped into his father's embrace.

"Hi, Pop. Gosh, it's so good to be home." Carl squeezed his father in a back-cracking hug.

"Whoa! Take it easy on an old man, boy." Gifford laughed.

Millie checked the chicken in the oven. "Annie, take Carl upstairs. Dinner will be on the table in 40 minutes."

While Carl took a long hot shower, Annie hung up Carl's uniform pants and jacket and put the rest of his clothing in a hamper.

Freshly showered and shaved, he wrapped himself in a towel and stepped into the bedroom where Annie sat on the edge of the bed waiting for him. She stood and enfolded her body into Carl's muscled arms. She drank in his essence with all of her senses. Her hands explored his body while he held her. She caressed his neck and shoulders while listening to his heartbeat with the side of her face pressed against his chest. Each inhalation of his breathing flowed through her and quickened her own heartbeat. Her right hand drifted down to his left side. Suddenly she became rigid and took in a gasp of air.

"What's this?" Her fingers traced a hard line of scar tissue eight inches long running laterally from his lower rib cage to within two inches of his spine.

"It's nothing, Annie … a bit of shrapnel is all." He pulled her hand away from the scar and kissed her palm. "I'm completely healed. I'm fine …really." He smiled reassuringly.

"Oh, Carl, I can't begin to imagine the horrors you've lived through. Promise me you'll never go back to that again."

Thirty-five minutes after leaving the kitchen, Carl and Annie joined the family at the table for dinner. Carl wore a plaid cotton chambray western-style shirt tucked into faded Levi-Strauss boot-cut jeans above his ranch-worn Justin boots. His tooled leather belt sported a large silver-plated buckle with the Double-B twin interlocking "Bs" crafted in the center of a horseshoe. The buckle was a present from his parents on his 16th birthday.

"Well now, look at you. You look like you're ready for some serious wrangling, son." Gifford grinned broadly.

"True that, Pop. My butt wants to feel saddle leather again … but, not tonight. Tomorrow soon enough? "

"Yep. For now, let's get some of your mother's home cookin' into you. You're as skinny as a rail. Pass me those potatoes, Penny, darlin'." She passed the large bowl of mashed potatoes, garnished with nutmeg and topped with a generous dollop of butter, to her father.

Penny brought up the elephant in the room; the question that nobody wanted to ask. "How long do we get to have you home, big brother? Where do you go from here?"

"Thirty days at least. Then, back to Japan with the occupation forces. I expect the 345th will be deactivated by the end of the year. Annie and I will probably decide by then what we want to do."

"What about the ranch, son? I was hoping you'd come home and help run things. Now that the war's over, the Double-B will be getting more business from the commercial beef industry than we can manage. I need you and Annie here."

Annie looked at Carl. Her eyes told him she shared Gifford's feelings on the subject.

"Annie and I will talk about it, Pop. There's going to be a lot of things happening between now and when I'm officially discharged … the wedding for one. The ranch is a definite possibility. I just don't want to rush into a decision right now."

"That's fair, I guess. Eat up, everybody. Hey, son, do you and Annie feel like doing some fence mending tomorrow? I brought a truck load of wire and posts from Helena," Gifford asked, glad to change the subject.

Carl smiled at the opportunity. "Is Butch still around, Pop? I missed that old roan. He's probably going on seven years-old now. I can't wait to climb into a saddle."

"Sure is. I ride him once in a while. He can still cut with the best of 'em."

The rest of the meal was punctuated with ranch talk, Penny's approaching junior year in high school, Annie's parents' health. Catching up on life at home was a balm to Carl's heart. He felt his spirits lifted by the conversation and laughter. Home never felt so good.

He gazed into blue eyes that, a week ago, he wondered if he'd ever see again. Annie's face was angelic. The sun caught her blond hair and turned it into sparkling flax. "I want us to get married, Annie. I want us to get married now … this week if we can."

She turned to face him and rose up on her elbow. "Yes! Yes-yes-yes! Shall we do it here at the ranch?"

"Absolutely. I wonder if Bishop Pierce is still around. We'll have to go into the 'Falls' to get the license. And your parents … we need to tell them. Let's do all of that tomorrow. Mom will want to have time to decorate." Carl was as excited as the day he proposed to Annie. She couldn't help but giggle at his effervescent enthusiasm.

"Oh, yes. Let's!" They wrapped themselves with arms and legs locked around each other … reveling in the moment.

–Only Forever–

On a perfect August Saturday afternoon, in the same grove of aspen trees where Carl and Annie had picnicked nine days earlier, the intimate site had been transformed with crepe-paper streamers, white papier-mâché bells and an eight-foot tall white arch with opened gates.

Twenty folding chairs were placed facing the open arch. Under it stood Carl dressed in his Army Air Corps dress uniform. His wings and Captains bars glistened in the sunlight. Standing with him was Bishop Jeffrey Pierce of the Great Falls LDS Stake, 2nd Ward, who officiated.

The chairs were occupied by Carl's family, Annie's parents, and a few friends from town and the surrounding ranches.

Annie was adorned in her mother's wedding dress, a floor-length silk gown with modest bodice, overlaid with lacey tulle that flowed in the meadow breeze. Her veil was a simple fingertip-length silk bordered in delicate lace and held close to the crown of Annie's head by a band of wild snowberry and globe flowers …

held together and formed by bailing wire which had been wrapped in crepe paper. Abe Petersen escorted Annie to the altar where Carl awaited.

Bishop Pierce cleared his throat. "I understand you have both written your own vows. We'll begin with Annie. Please take each other by the hands. You may begin."

"Carl, I have loved you forever, it seems. I realized it one day in high school and discovered that I was in the middle of it before I knew it had begun. I can't say in words where the beginning or the end lies, because my love for you is as eternal as the days of our souls which are without end."

"Annie, in the entire universe there is no heart for me but yours ... and no love for you like mine. The battles of my body have strengthened my heart's resolve that my love for you cannot be ended, but rather has forged a stronger bond that will endure ... only forever, if you care to know."

The End

Spencer Anderson

Spencer Anderson, Author

Spencer Anderson is a former pilot and retired Air Force Vietnam War veteran whose passion for aviation is clearly portrayed in his writing. He is an outspoken advocate of the WWII Warbird legacy and is a contributing Colonel in the Commemorative Air Force. He lives in St George, Utah with his wife Carole. The couple enjoys travelling the air show circuit, writing, and viewing the scenic wonders of southern Utah. He is the author of the popular *The Last*

Spencer & Carole

Raider, which is the first novel in the series featuring Carl Bridger. *Avenging Angel*, the second in the series, is a prequel that takes us back to Carl's WWII adventures in the South Pacific.